THE Multima Scheme

Gary D. McGugan

For Tom,

Enjoy the story.

08·10·19

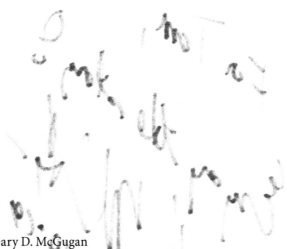

Tellwell Talent
www.tellwell.ca

ISBN
978-0-2288-0004-0 (Hardcover)
978-1-77370-645-0 (Paperback)

*For Tracy, Terry
and their remarkable families*

Multima Corporation
John George Mortimer
Founder, President & CEO

President
Suzanne Simpson
*Multima
Supermarkets*

President
James Fitzgerald
*Multima Financial
Services*

President
Douglas Whitfield
Multima Solutions
(Formerly Multima Logistics)

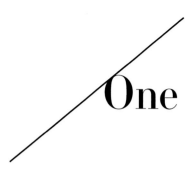

One

A rundown hotel, Quito, Ecuador.
Early morning, Thursday March 10, 2016

Howard Knight felt his pulse quicken as he glanced down at his watch. All hell was about to break loose in New York. His secretary would tell the waiting FBI agent something like, "It's probably just a traffic delay. Mr. Knight is always punctual and will be here soon for your scheduled meeting." Likely, she'd also offer coffee, and no doubt make small talk while they both waited.

In a few minutes, she'd give up and call Knight's spouse at home. His wife would repeat the exact lie he told her the day before while his limousine sped towards Page Field in Fort Myers, Florida. She'd tell his secretary Knight wasn't actually in New York. He was away solving some sort of business crisis in Brazil. Almost certainly, his assistant would become alarmed and immediately contact the pilots of the company's jet.

It might take her some time to reach them. Both the pilot and co-pilot would be gradually recovering from a period of incapacitation but would eventually tell the secretary what little they could remember. They wouldn't have much to divulge though, and would remain groggy throughout the rest of the morning.

Within minutes, The Organization would also learn Knight was missing. They'd hear something mysterious was happening with an annoyed FBI agent pressing for answers. They'd launch a search for him, but they'd do it as discreetly as possible. The Organization abhorred publicity. So, their inquiries would all be through a back channel of resources around the world. The FBI would also be careful. They might have some suspicions, but Knight was confident they'd find scant hard evidence.

This rundown hotel should be okay, he thought. If his calculations were correct, the next few days would be the most crucial in their escape. When he arrived, he didn't notice any security cameras in the lobby. He said as little as possible, speaking Spanish with an Italian accent. The bored front counter employee asked only his name and how long he would stay, as Howard counted out enough US dollars for two nights and completed the check-in ritual.

Once inside his assigned room, Knight first checked the small digital safe crudely embedded in a cupboard. It functioned. Then, he tested the locks on the door, including the metal doorstop, to be sure they all worked. Satisfied, he carefully inspected the entire room for any recording devices. These precautions complete, he took money belts bulging with US dollars and three different South American currencies from his backpacks and jammed them into the safe.

From the same bags, he took socks, a change of underwear, a shaving kit and two pairs of night-vision goggles. He put them all in the bottom drawer of a rickety old bureau. He stashed a disposable cell phone and a new computer tablet under the mattress.

Then, he dragged a heavy chair in front of the door and tilted its back under the knob to slow entry in the event of an unwelcome intrusion. He knew it wouldn't stop them but could provide a valuable second or two to react. Finally, he checked to be sure the semi-automatic handgun was loaded, then slid it under the second pillow on his bed. It would be close should he need it.

Relatively relaxed, he undressed and carefully hung his pre-washed jeans, traveler's vest, and short sleeve denim shirt in a small closet. Then, he stepped into a scruffy plastic stall for a hot shower that left him feeling only marginally cleaner. Dried, but completely exhausted, he stretched out on the bed. There, he calculated the number of hours since he last slept and was surprised such a simple task took much longer than expected. Eventually, he deduced it to be about twenty-nine hours.

The fateful day had started with a three o'clock wake-up call for his flight to Fort Myers to attend an emergency meeting of the board of directors at Multima Corporation. The dramatic intervening hours had been well beyond stressful. He couldn't think of a more confounding day in his entire life, and the drama was now starting only its second act. From this point on, there could be no mistakes. Even a tiny miscalculation could cost him his life.

His elaborate scheme to oust John George Mortimer, CEO of Multima Corporation, started to unravel with his first telephone call in the wee morning hours. His contact at The Organization reported that no one could locate Wendal

Randall – a development of serious concern to Knight. To engineer the election of Multima Logistics' wayward division president to the post of CEO of the entire corporation, he desperately needed Randall at the meeting.

Events worsened. By mid-day, Knight learned that Randall would not appear at the meeting at all. Instead – at the same time as all the other company directors – he was shocked to hear the FBI had arrested Randall and was holding him in custody, charged with multiple serious crimes. Knight might still have had a chance to carry out the Mortimer coup successfully until a subsequent startling revelation proved all his efforts would be in vain.

John George Mortimer, more devious and cunning than Knight ever imagined, had somehow finagled an exchange of corporate shares. He'd found a way to convert some Multima shares from one class to another. The shrewd maneuver instantly shifted the corporation's balance of power entirely in Mortimer's favor. Knight's plot had no hope of success with the new equity structure.

Instead, he found himself trapped in a rapidly unfolding disaster. A decade earlier – on his recommendation – The Organization had invested a billion dollars in Multima. And just the previous week, Howard had knowingly put that billion dollars at precarious risk with his scheme to remove John George Mortimer and seize control.

And it was all because Knight overlooked one crucial piece of information. Years before, as he meticulously researched Multima and developed a long-term strategy to seize control of the corporation, he missed one obscure notation buried deep in the garble of financial reporting. That provision in very fine print changed the entire calculus and would now change his life forever.

Knight knew immediately that there was no alternative. He had to escape from the Multima board of directors meeting before The Organization became aware of that woeful miscalculation. His only hope was to get a head start. In desperation, just after lunch yesterday he put into motion a standby plan he had carefully plotted years earlier with a long-time friend in West Palm Beach, Florida.

Fidelia Morales was really far more than a friend. She was the only person who had been allowed to retire from The Organization. Most died of natural causes, unwilling or unable to extricate themselves. Others made mistakes and paid the ultimate price. A few just disappeared. But, Fidelia had been unquestionably loyal to The Organization and was superbly adept in her role. To everyone's surprise, the compulsively secretive leadership acquiesced to her request to leave New York and live quietly in Florida.

It probably helped that she occasionally slept with the most powerful of them all. It wasn't an affair or anything like that. Rather, it was a relationship of convenience where she provided sexual services from time-to-time. Over the past decade, such requests had reduced in frequency as younger and younger women caught the fancy of that supremely influential man.

And, such a reduction in demand was alright with Howard, for it was he who found the sexual favors humiliating and abhorrent. Nevertheless, he had patiently tolerated the awkward situation for more years than he could remember. In fact, Howard and Fidelia had been discreet secret lovers for longer than many people stay married.

Knight made the call to Fidelia on a disposable cell phone immediately after he left the Multima offices, while his chauffeured limousine sped towards the nearby jet port. She instantly set in motion a scheme they had fine-tuned for years. Only the part from Fort Myers to West Palm Beach required some quick improvisation, but they had even laid the foundation to permit minor adjustments during their furtive conversations over several years. Neither had doubted a daring escape would eventually become necessary at some point in one of their lives.

Once the private jet reached cruising altitude that afternoon, Knight moved forward in the cabin where he banged loudly on the cockpit door, then collapsed in a heap on the floor. He was careful to fall several inches from the door so the co-pilot could open it, see an apparent medical emergency, and rush to his aid.

The co-pilot responded exactly as expected. Knight's still-prone body prevented him from fully opening the cockpit door, so the burly aviator leaned heavily against it and forced it to open wide with a loud grunt of exertion. Knight continued to squirm on the floor, tightly gripping his chest and breathing with apparent difficulty.

"My heart," he gasped, clutching his chest even tighter.

The co-pilot assessed the situation: Knight's flushed face, his frantic irregular breathing, and the way he grasped his chest with both hands.

"Stay as calm as possible," the co-pilot instructed. "Let me loosen your collar and help."

Freeing one hand, Knight reached into the pocket of his jacket and produced a small container. He thrust it in the face of the co-pilot who noted 'emergency' printed in bold red letters with a toll-free number imprinted on the plastic cover. Inside the lid, the co-pilot discovered a single capsule.

"Call them," Knight gasped.

The co-pilot returned to the cockpit and described the emergency to the pilot as he dialed the toll-free number on the container. Concerned, the pilot briefly glanced over his shoulder at Knight who continued to writhe on the floor in apparent pain and distress.

"Good Samaritan Medical Center," Fidelia Morales announced in an official-sounding tone.

"This is Vincent Young, co-pilot of VCI corporate jet KBY724F calling. We are in flight, and I was given this number by our passenger, Howard Knight. He appears to be having a heart incident."

"Let me pull up his file. You said Night, n-i-g-h-t, correct?"

"No. It's Knight with a K," the co-pilot calmly clarified. "Mr. Knight is president of Venture Capital Inc. in New York, and he appears to be experiencing extreme chest pain and some difficulty breathing."

"OK, I've got it. Mr. Howard J. Knight. He had surgery here at Good Samaritan a few months ago. Does he have a container with a blue capsule in it?" Fidelia inquired.

"Yes."

"Administer that medication immediately with some water, please. I'll hold on the line while you do that," the voice instructed.

The co-pilot grabbed an open bottle of water from the pouch beside his seat and returned to the cabin. There, he raised Knight's head, popped the capsule into his mouth, then touched the water bottle to Knight's lips telling him to swallow hard.

"You'll be alright, sir," he said. "I've got your hospital on the line, and we'll get you some care as soon as possible. Try to remain calm."

Picking up the phone again, he resumed the conversation. "Mr. Knight swallowed the capsule. What should we do next?" co-pilot Young asked with a pilot's typically exaggerated calm detachment.

"The capsule was nitroglycerin. In a few minutes, the patient should start to relax and breathe more easily. But he has a precarious heart condition," Fidelia replied. "You said you're calling from the air. Are you near an airport close to a hospital?"

"We're over Central Florida. Let me check our current settings," Vincent Young said as he returned to the cockpit. "We'll be over Orlando in seventeen minutes. Shall we ask permission to land there?"

"Perhaps. Give me a moment. I'm trying Mr. Knight's cardiologist on the other line." About a minute later she returned. "Would it be possible to change your routing to West Palm Beach, instead? Dr. Weinberg would really like to treat Mr. Knight here."

Vincent Young conferred with the pilot who calculated a landing in West Palm would take only five minutes longer at maximum flight speeds. "We could re-route to PBI if necessary, ma'am. ETA about twenty-two minutes," he advised.

"OK, good. How is Mr. Knight doing, now?" Fidelia asked.

"He's started to relax, and his pain appears to have subsided somewhat. He's still breathing with some difficulty."

"That's normal," Fidelia Morales replied. "Please re-route then. I'll arrange an ambulance to meet you. Ask air traffic control to give you priority and proceed directly to the NetJets terminal. We have an agreement with them for emergencies. Taxi to the northwest corner of the airport and there will be a Medi Wheels ambulance waiting beside the building. I'll keep this line open until you land, just in case you need more help."

"Roger that, ma'am," Young replied as he signaled his partner to change course for West Palm Beach. "By the way, ma'am, may I have your name for our records here?"

"RN Susan Hunter, ID number 137564," Fidelia Morales calmly responded as Young scribbled the information on a notepad. "Let me know if you need anything before you land."

No further assistance was necessary, and Knight appeared to stabilize. Air traffic control quickly approved changes to their flight plan and then confirmed their requested emergency priority for descent into West Palm Beach. In precisely twenty-two minutes, wheels touched down, brakes screeched briefly, and the aircraft started to decelerate rapidly on the runway.

Three minutes later, Vincent Young spotted the Medi Wheels ambulance and pointed it out to his partner. It was parked on the tarmac about two hundred yards from the NetJets terminal right next to a large, blue, and mainly unmarked Bombardier Global 5000 private jet.

When they came to a stop, two paramedics stepped out of the vehicle and ambled towards the rear door as the jet engines wound down. Both wore oversized sound-deadening headsets, large sunglasses, surgical masks, and white helmets with a red cross displayed on the front. They removed a stretcher from the rear of the ambulance and casually waited for the cabin door to open.

As soon as the co-pilot lowered the stairs and signaled an all-clear for them to enter, their demeanor changed. The paramedics pounced like athletes in a competition. They quickly mounted the stairs, two steps a time, sharing the weight of the stretcher with one hand each as they gripped the railing to pull themselves quickly upward with the other.

"Would you move into the cockpit to give us space?" one calmly requested as he approached the door.

"Thanks, guys," he continued as he popped his head into the cockpit. Then, without warning, he quickly reached forward and sprayed a fine mist directly into the faces of both the pilot and co-pilot. Before either could react, the lead paramedic quickly jabbed a needle into the right arm of the standing co-pilot, then quickly pulled another from the front of his coveralls. He forcefully pricked the needle into the pilot who was trying to rise from his chair, momentarily blinded by the mist.

Next, he eased the fainting co-pilot into his seat, pushed his head against the high seat back, and buckled the straps, including the shoulder harness. Then, he yanked it as tightly as possible. Within seconds, he did the same with the unconscious pilot before flicking off all radio controls. While this was happening up front, the second paramedic laid the stretcher flat on the floor in the cabin.

"Climb on sir," he said. "I'll strap you in for the ride over."

Without a word of reply, Knight quickly scrambled onto the apparatus, then made himself comfortable. He laid on his back, both arms crossed over his chest, as the paramedic secured straps over his shoulders, waist, and knees. Within thirty seconds, the two burly paramedics were effortlessly carrying him down the stairway.

At the bottom, they shifted their cargo for a better grip and headed towards the ambulance's rear door. However, instead of hoisting Knight into the vehicle, they passed the open truck doors and advanced the few remaining steps towards the parked blue aircraft, its engines already idling, stairway lowered, and a pilot waiting at the door.

"The cash is already on board," one paramedic explained to Knight as they climbed the steps. "Passports, six prepaid disposable phones for South America, and some clothes are all on top of the money in the backpacks. You'll find the rest of the stuff inside a black trash bag. The crew will change ID on the plane when you stop. She also said to tell you she'd be there as planned. No calls, no email in the meantime."

"I'll need both your company-issued and personal cell phones," he continued as they removed the straps once inside the aircraft. "Any questions?"

"I'm good," Knight replied as he surrendered both handsets, then chose a seat near the front and buckled his seatbelt.

Wordlessly, the paramedics left the cabin and descended the stairway two steps a time. On the ground, they first went back to the VCI plane and folded the stairway back into the jet, closing – but not locking – the door. Then they ran to the rear doors of the ambulance and threw the stretcher inside. One slammed both doors shut. The other scurried around to start the vehicle.

Once both were inside, the ambulance sped away with tires screeching and red emergency lights flashing. As Knight looked out the aircraft window, he noticed one paramedic glance back as the large, blue, long-range Bombardier jet's door closed.

Moments later they were airborne. The privately-owned Bombardier 5000 business jet had sufficient range to its destination without stopping for fuel, but a direct path would have been much too easy for inquisitive minds to track. So the pilots first set course south towards Philip S.W. Goldson International Airport in the tiny Central American country of Belize.

When the aircraft touched down about six hours later, the jet taxied directly to a large, gaping hangar tucked away in a remote corner of the airport. A 'mechanical issue', they told air traffic control, with time on the ground estimated to be less than one hour. Inside the hanger, the pilot parked his jet in a vacant corner which could not be seen from either the control tower or the public sections of the airport.

A co-pilot came out of the aircraft with what appeared to be a large plastic sign. It displayed a series of letters and numbers in white on a blue background, the same sky-blue color as the jet. He handed it to a worker who then scurried up a ladder to the top of its tail, on the right side. There, he affixed the 'sign' after carefully cleaning the plane's surface. Instantly, the aircraft sported new identification on one side of the jet, using technology no more complicated than the magnetic-backed plastic signs real estate agents routinely attach to their luxury cars. Identification would change on the other side later.

As instructed, the incoming team disembarked and planned to wait in the hangar for thirty minutes after the plane took-off again. Then, they would ride with a service worker to the main passenger terminal where they'd eventually board a regularly scheduled commercial flight to Miami. When questioned later, they would know only the numbers and letters affixed to the right side of the jet.

A new pilot and co-pilot took the controls. When the aircraft taxied to a runway, only this fresh crew was aware of their next destination and air traffic control could see just the left side of the plane as it passed the tower.

When the flight touched down in Panama City, Panama just over two hours later, the crew repeated the entire process with the left side of the aircraft, now doctored to display an aircraft identification number that matched the one installed earlier in Belize. The result? As the Bombardier 5000 business jet left for Quito, Ecuador, both sides of the tail showed identical ID numbers. They were identifiers that didn't appear in any registration directory, with a sequence of numbers and letters that would change three more times over a two-day period and three subsequent crews.

With his accomplice Fidelia, Howard Knight had meticulously researched and selected the destinations, potential teams, service workers and identification numbers several months earlier. They couldn't know in advance precisely where an escape might originate. Regardless, they intended to include West Palm Beach in any route. They invested accordingly, and significant amounts of money ensured all participants would stifle their curiosity, able to recall only their individual and insignificant roles in the charade when questioned later.

As a passenger, Knight occupied himself with housekeeping for the next stage. He emptied a large black trash bag on the floor beside his seat, stripped off his business clothes and put them in the empty bag. He counted the money and stashed it into individual money belts, one belt for each currency.

Around his waist, he strapped the one holding US dollars, before neatly inserting each of the remaining belts into one of the sixteen pockets and compartments of the traveler's vest or backpacks. Next, he wrapped the night-vision goggles inside pieces of clothing and carefully placed one pair in each bag. Satisfied both were secure, he opened the draw-strings of a leather pouch and inspected two nine-volt batteries before trying out their connections with a jack of a car cell phone charger. Both passed the test. They'd be able to recharge phones and GPS watches, even if there was no power available.

In the bathroom, he examined a new electric shaver, something he had used only for minor grooming over the past twenty years. With one last wistful look of admiration, Knight grimly smiled as he began to shave off his full beard. It took a while.

Clean-shaven, he washed his face, then started his next important task – hair coloring. After a few more minutes, his former hair color, black with a few speckles of gray, transformed into a reddish-brown shade that blended well with his olive-colored skin. It also made him look at least ten years younger, he thought.

Later, he memorized all the names, countries and other details for each of the counterfeit passports before they, too, were organized in separate pockets and compartments. He checked and re-checked all of the contents of the two backpacks to be sure they hadn't overlooked even a minor detail.

For hours he studied maps, guidebooks, and all the travel information Fidelia had included in the package. There wouldn't be any time for sightseeing for several weeks, but intimate knowledge of the terrain might help them blend in as wandering, backpacking tourists rather than fugitives fearing for their lives.

Exhausted beyond belief, Howard Knight still found sleep elusive. Fear proved to be a powerful stimulant, and the more he assessed his immediate risks, the more apprehensive he became.

He knew The Organization intimately. He was keenly aware of the steps his former colleagues would take and even people The Organization would probably recruit for their search. Despite reassuring himself they'd planned every step of their escape as thoroughly as possible, a new variable now weighed heavily on his mind.

They had never dreamed the FBI would become a potentially lethal wild card in their calculations. For that reason his eyes remained fully open, his mind churning with possibilities, and his heart still beating far too quickly.

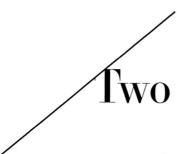

Two

A modern office in Chicago suburb Hoffman Estates.
Thursday March 17, 2016

"Nice work closing that EZ Mortgage acquisition," James Fitzgerald heard his boss John George Mortimer say towards the end of their call. "I'm impressed you were able to bring it together in less than thirty days, but I suspect you may also want to buy your friend Jones a nice dinner."

'Jones' was Chuck Jones, a Chicago-based director on the board of Multima. It was he who first suggested acquiring EZ Mortgage Inc. as part of a grand corporate strategy Mortimer had outlined right after squelching a rebellion led by Howard Knight during their February board meeting.

"Absolutely," James replied. "More than a dinner is in order. Not only did he help us buy an excellent little company at an attractive price, but the management team we acquired is impressive. Those people will be great assets as we launch our new home mortgage program."

"Yes. I saw the resumés you sent over as part of the purchase briefing. I'm glad you decided to retain their president, Whiteside, and have him lead your new operation – especially after I picked young Whitfield for Multima Logistics."

▪ Damn right, James thought. Whitfield had been his rising prodigy – the logical successor to put his own retirement strategy in place – before Mortimer unexpectedly snatched him at that infamous board of directors meeting. Now, his star was managing the Logistics division of Multima Corporation while Fitzgerald initially had been crestfallen with Mortimer's decision.

But his outlook brightened immediately after starting negotiations to acquire EZ Mortgage. Norman Whiteside, its president, appeared to be genuine superstar material. Within days, James had recommended his appointment to lead the new home mortgage initiative approved by the board.

"Well, I appreciate all your support to get the deal done, John George," James replied, preparing to end their conversation.

"You're welcome, James. You know it was the least I could do under the circumstances. I'm expecting big things from this new mortgage initiative. If your projections are right, within a few years Multima Financial Services might very well be generating more revenue and bottom-line profit than all our other businesses combined. Not a bad legacy when your retirement eventually comes along."

"You know you've got me for the next two years anyway, John George. We'll see what happens after."

"I know, James. And I truly appreciate your agreement to postpone it to guide your business unit through this transition period. But I also have another favor to request," Mortimer said. "Do you recall that woman, Janet Weissel, who works with Hadley in corporate and investor affairs?" Mortimer asked.

"Vaguely. I think we met a couple times in Fort Myers," James responded.

"Corporate security is convinced she's connected in some way to both Howard Knight and that outfit known as The Organization. They want me to fire her, but I think it's better not to. Do you remember that expression Michael Corleone used in *The Godfather*, 'Keep your friends close and your enemies closer'? Until I can figure out The Organization's interest in Multima, I think it might be better to move Ms. Weissel away from her current position at headquarters. I'd like you to find a job for her up there in Chicago, in a role where you can keep a close eye on her. I'm thinking maybe in your carefully concealed business intelligence unit," Mortimer suggested without missing a beat.

James smiled as he listened to the request and careful choice of words. Indeed, wily John George Mortimer may be aging, but no one could hide much from him. He was exceptionally cunning, seemingly aware of everything that went on in his company. Until that moment, James had been quite confident no one at Multima knew anything about his covert team of special resources, buried for many years deep in his marketing department. That team's purpose? Collect information that might impact Multima Financial Services from sources both inside and outside the corporation.

But he decided to concede nothing. "If you want to retain this person, I guess marketing would be a reasonable place to keep an eye on her. What should I be looking for?" he replied.

"First, I'd make sure she can't access too much information you'd consider confidential. But, it would also be good if someone there could sort of monitor her activities and maybe keep track of her external conversations.

Someone with excellent technology skills and a person you trust implicitly," Mortimer explained.

After only a moment's consideration, James replied, "Yes. There's someone I can trust to keep an eye on her. I'll set the wheels in motion here. When would you like this to happen?" James asked.

"As soon as possible. I'll work with Hadley to break the news of her transfer. Let's try to do it soon. Thanks again for your help with this, James. You know I appreciate it. And be careful. I hear she's a handful," Mortimer ominously added to end their conversation.

James felt a chill creep down his spine as they wrapped up the call. John George Mortimer didn't pass on warnings lightly, and this whole issue with The Organization concerned him. What little he knew about that outfit of hoodlums was all bad. And now, with a mole embedded in his team, his favorite resource in business intelligence would need some extra guidance for this delicate assignment.

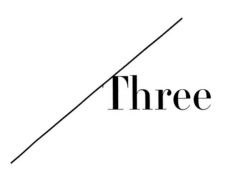

Three

Fort Myers.
Monday March 21, 2016

John George Mortimer slowly opened his eyes from fitful sleep. Even that mundane activity caused almost intolerable pain as he adjusted to the bright morning light. He couldn't remember his body ever feeling such continuous aching, seemingly in every muscle and from every pore.

He took a quick inventory. Nausea still felt powerful even lying in bed. The throbbing of his headache had not subsided overnight, nor had the stiffness and constant soreness in his back, legs, and arms. Sitting up, he placed his feet on the floor and immediately recoiled from an intense burning sensation as he applied pressure to the bottom of his feet.

Worse still, those distasteful side-effects seemed to be intensifying. When John George started chemotherapy a few days earlier, they'd warned him about possible adverse reactions. Nothing he couldn't handle, they'd assured him. They'd been at least partially right, he thought ruefully. The side effects appeared just as predicted, but their confidence in his ability to cope seemed increasingly in doubt.

Of course, it was all necessary. The surgery to remove the lump growing in his breast had been successful. The oncologist was confident he had removed the tumor, but they didn't see male breast cancer often enough to be sure it wouldn't return. So, they'd take no chances. He'd follow a treatment plan of chemotherapy every second day for ten days, followed by a week of recovery. Then, he'd receive three weeks of daily radiation to protect cells around the mastectomy against any potential recurrence.

With a disheartened grimace, he realized it was the first day of what they called a recovery week. It was time to start his daily preparation and try eating before setting out for a few hours at the office. Eating and drinking were still uncomfortable, and thoughts of either made his nausea worse. But he knew he needed some energy to manage even a few hours at his desk.

Initially, he'd intended to work some portion of every weekday despite the chemo treatments. Cancer would not define his life, he declared to himself. Nobly, he started his undertaking by returning from the chemo sessions to his home, resting for a few hours, then driving to his nearby office for two or three hours. That lasted for only three days. On the fourth day, John George decided to work from home for a few hours instead and maintained his executive presence by phone, email, and sporadic access to the company's technology networks.

By the start of the second week, even that became too laborious. Unable to fully concentrate during conversations, dizzy at times, and always coping with pain and nausea, he temporarily abandoned his ill-conceived attempts to maintain his daily responsibilities as CEO of Multima Corporation.

He'd asked his executive assistant to handle all issues she could and to delay those beyond her authority by referring them to Alberto Ferer, Multima's chief legal counsel. He was a master of procrastination and could easily keep the lid on any simmering issues until John George's return to the office this week.

Now, return he must. Multima Corporation demanded his time, focus, and leadership – even if he felt purging his insides was only a breath or two away.

The whole arduous process took an hour or so, but he finally found himself shaved, clean, dressed, and ready to tackle the breakfast his housekeeper had prepared. He was grateful she had volunteered to stay with him rather than returning home each evening as usual. She seemed to sense just how miserable he felt and tried to nourish him with food he could retain. This morning it was piping hot oatmeal with a bagel and strong black coffee.

"Good morning, John George," she greeted with a bright smile. "Is there any improvement this morning?"

"Not at all, Lana," he replied. Then, he quickly grinned with a strained effort to be positive.

"Maybe some food will help. Would you like some fruit or cheese with the oatmeal?"

"No, thanks, Lana. What's here is perfect. Your robust coffee should get me functioning well enough to get me through the morning," he replied. "I can't thank you enough for staying here with me over these past two weeks. You've been a great help. But I know your family misses you. I should be fine tonight. Why don't you go home at the end of the day?"

"Okay, if you think you can manage. Let's see how you feel when you come back. By the way, Alberto will be here in fifteen minutes. He insisted on picking you up. Said he'd like to discuss some things on the way to your office."

"I sense a little collusion," he replied with a tiny smile. "Alberto probably thinks my driving creates a legal liability for the corporation, and these days you watch over my every action just like a mother hen. But, today I'll acquiesce."

He knew their concern was well-founded but didn't want that kind of coddling to become a habit. Without further discussion, his full attention shifted to a waiting newspaper and breakfast. He ate, forcing himself to swallow small amounts after a little chewing. Even that simple activity hurt his mouth and throat and seemed to do little to settle his churning stomach.

Alberto Ferer arrived precisely fifteen minutes later. John George was stuffing some final papers into his briefcase when Lana rushed to open the large, carved-wood front door. Moments later, he had squeezed his long legs into Alberto's little sports car and was ready for their short commute to Multima Corporation's headquarters.

He noticed Alberto's cheerful greeting and warm smile fade to a look of concern, perhaps even foreboding, as he buckled up.

"Is everything okay?" John George asked while Alberto nimbly steered his sports car in a tight circle to change direction in the spacious driveway.

"I should be asking you," Alberto responded carefully. "Are you sure you feel up to working in the office today?"

"Even if I do look like death warmed over, I feel marginally better. It may not be a full day, but I'll manage for a few hours. Any developments we need to cover while we drive?"

"Yeah. A lot is going on. Where should I start?" Alberto wondered aloud as he collected his thoughts. Remaining silent, John George braced himself for some bad news.

"I got a curious phone call again yesterday from Sebastian Folino, my legal counterpart at Venture Capital Inc. He wanted to know if we had heard anything from Howard Knight. It seems Knight still hasn't returned to New York. It's been almost two weeks now since he disappeared from our board of directors meeting, and his wife is reportedly distraught. Plus, the FBI has been poking around the VCI office almost every day. They've apparently installed wiretaps on the phone lines of Knight's office and home. People there are really spooked."

John George listened intently but made no effort to respond.

"Folino wanted to give me a heads-up. People around VCI are starting to talk about naming a new CEO who would also replace Knight on our board. Apparently, there are some who don't expect to see him alive again. Some think he may have jumped off a bridge or something. Folino mentioned general disbelief among VCI management that Knight was spearheading an attempt to remove you as CEO. Apparently, some think he may have had a mental breakdown. Regardless, Folino expects we'll get a call from a new VCI CEO within a week or so, but he has no idea who that might be."

John George processed this information silently for a few moments. "Legally, do we have an obligation to appoint someone from VCI to our board?" he asked.

"Legally, I don't think so," Alberto replied as he considered the issue. "Howard Knight remains a director of the board of Multima Corporation until he resigns, dies, or the remaining directors vote him off the board."

"If he has died, must we appoint a replacement director from VCI?"

"Wow! Interesting question. In the final document that we negotiated to issue their preferred shares, we agreed to name Howard Knight as a director. We mentioned him by name, not as CEO of VCI. I remember that clearly. In fact, I remember Knight specifically demanded we rework a draft version to appoint him personally and delete a reference to his position," Alberto said. "But I guess there may be some moral obligation to consider. After all, VCI is still the second largest shareholder in the corporation – by far."

"I know your memory is flawless, my consigliere," John George said with a faint outline of a smile. "But check the document when you get to your office. I'm leaning towards recruiting an entirely different independent director – one with no affiliation to VCI."

"Sure. I'll do it first thing," Alberto responded despite some trepidation. As he veered into the parking lot, he felt a dull sensation in the pit of his stomach. If John George Mortimer continued to pursue this adversarial path – and the rumors he'd heard linking VCI to The Organization were correct – his role at Multima might soon become extremely uncomfortable. In fact, not only his job might be at risk; it could be his life at stake. Those folks didn't fool around.

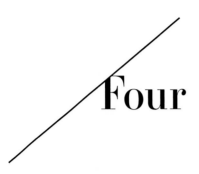

Four

Atlanta, Georgia.
Tuesday March 22, 2016

The president of Multima Supermarkets slipped away from a meeting with her direct reports at the silent bidding of her executive assistant. Suzanne Simpson made a point of personally taking every call from the office of John George Mortimer, even if it usually was Sally-Ann Bureau, the woman who organized the CEO's office, just calling to relay some information from their leader. Intuitively, Suzanne understood well the deep pool of goodwill her small professional courtesy created.

Frequently, an innocuous question or two, followed by a comment reinforcing Suzanne's genuine interest in a subject, encouraged Sally-Ann to divulge more information. Those additional minor details often gave crucial insight into Mortimer's thoughts on an issue. In turn, that deeper understanding directly influenced decisions that helped Suzanne manage interactions with her boss more effectively.

However, today's call had produced little more than its singular purpose, Suzanne mused ruefully as she set the phone in its charging cradle. Before returning to the meeting next door, it might be useful to take a deep breath, lean back, and think more about this latest twist in the increasingly perplexing affair.

Her team assembled in the conference room was finalizing presentations for senior management. The next morning they were scheduled to take the company jet to Fort Myers. There, they were to join a monthly meeting with the board of directors of Multima Corporation. More accurately, until just a few seconds earlier, they had been scheduled – past tense – to make the trip. Sally-Ann Bureau was polite, but not quite as friendly as usual, as she informed Suzanne there'd be no meeting in March. They'd try to get together in April, but she didn't yet know dates or a location.

Suzanne's usual inquisitive banter went nowhere that day. Sally-Ann divulged only the essential facts and seemed unusually pressed for time as she quickly wound up their call. Suzanne understood the woman was only the messenger. Any decision to cancel their meeting was certainly Mortimer's, and her team would now be very disappointed. After all, this event was supposed to be their opportunity to bask in the glory of their accomplishments over the past month. And what accomplishments they were!

Exactly one week after the board of directors authorized them to proceed, the Multima Supermarkets team had negotiated and signed a binding agreement to purchase Price Deelite, a chain of discount stores in the Southeast. They'd completed the deal well within the financial parameters approved by the board, with enough left over to comfortably pay for the major store renovations needed to accommodate a new focus on healthy foods.

They'd also already developed and approved comprehensive drawings for new store layouts. In fact, contracts had been awarded to begin construction in thirty-five locations in the greater Miami area in the coming month. Southwest Florida outlets would follow in June.

Gordon Goodfellow, her former director of marketing, was completing a transition to his new role as president of Price Deelite and managing the integration of this attractive new acquisition. Phil Archer, the son of Price Deelite's previous owner, had already replaced Goodfellow and was settling into his new role as marketing director with aplomb.

Suzanne's director of operations was set to announce they'd found adequate office space and ordered all necessary new equipment to accommodate the board's other significant directive. Employee relocations from their sister company Multima Logistics in Miami – to join her team in Atlanta – would begin the first of May and finish by the end of June. To her relief, more than ninety percent of those employees identified for relocation had accepted transfer offers. There would be little disruption to the technical support those valuable resources provided.

Of course, John George Mortimer already knew all that. Suzanne had consulted with him twice and kept his team in Fort Myers in the loop as each issue evolved. There were no surprises. But she also knew one of the reasons Mortimer invited her people to join the scheduled meeting of the board of directors was to draw attention to their extraordinary efforts and formidable successes. A few words of praise from the charismatic CEO carried significant weight with her team. Such recognition, combined with congratulations from other influential members of the board, would be worth as much to her cohorts as hundreds of dollars in bonus money.

But, they'd cope. Suzanne would find some other way to celebrate the team's outstanding accomplishments. Hopefully, they'd still get their moment of glory with senior leadership later.

She could only speculate about his reasons for canceling such an important meeting. But she knew the chemotherapy was challenging John George Mortimer more than expected. His absences from the office had grown longer and more frequent over the past month. Responses to emails and phone messages were slower. Some days, even his speech pattern seemed to be affected. On those days, he spoke more slowly, appeared to have occasional challenges organizing his thoughts, and more than once deferred making an important decision until he "felt a bit better".

All those indicators suggested John George was having a tough time during his treatments, and her people would understand that.

She too would need to be patient and understanding. That would require some extra willpower because she probably had been looking forward to this session more intently than anyone on her team. Praise and congratulations were not her motivators, though. For her, it was far more personal.

Nagging concerns lingered from her last personal and dramatic encounter with John George. Furthermore, Suzanne still needed more – and better – answers that only he could provide.

It was after the last tumultuous meeting of the board of directors that Suzanne Simpson realized her relationship with John George Mortimer might be something more than boss and subordinate. That meeting took place only a few days after she returned from Quebec City, where she had coped with her mother's sudden death from a massive heart attack.

Suzanne first learned of her mother's heart crisis during a refueling stop in Anchorage, Alaska as she returned from a business trip to Asia. She immediately diverted the executive jet towards Quebec City but didn't make it there in time. Once officials at the hospital confirmed Louise Marcotte's death, the news of her mother's passing proved far more devastating than imagined. Alone in a Quebec City hotel room, she had wept uncontrollably for hours.

Still grieving, Suzanne finalized her mother's estate only days after her passing. Monsieur Marcel LaMontagne, her mother's *notaire*, the one in whose office the heart attack occurred, helped her navigate documentation and details related to a cremation and the disposition of her mother's financial matters.

During that process, the *notaire* explained his investigation into some curious deposits to her mother's bank account over a period of years. She also discovered that her mother secretly held share certificates for a Canadian numbered company, an entity which the *notaire* ultimately found to be a hidden subsidiary of Multima Supermarkets. Both developments perplexed her and frequently caused her to revisit all the puzzling evidence.

Three days after finalizing her mother's affairs, Suzanne had found herself embroiled in a bitter internal battle at Multima's corporate headquarters. One director's attempt to persuade the board to depose CEO John George Mortimer – together with all the related corporate drama around that meeting – prevented her from solving the mystery. There had simply been no opportunity for a meaningful conversation with the man.

Adding to her suspense, just as she was leaving the corporate office that day, Multima's CFO had whispered, "How fortunate our leader was to tuck away that small company in Canada." As she understood it, Mortimer had used that small business in Canada to thwart the attempted coup in some way and thus retain his ownership control and CEO position.

After that extraordinary meeting of the board, Suzanne could think of nothing else as she traveled from the corporate offices to the private airport to meet her jet. Seconds before boarding, she had changed her mind and impulsively decided to visit Mortimer at his home – completely unannounced – to get some answers before flying back to Atlanta.

When she arrived at his mansion, a petite, friendly housekeeper with a welcoming smile ushered Suzanne into John George Mortimer's living room. She took a deep calming breath, but paid scant attention to the finely decorated surroundings in a home she was visiting for the first time. Instead, she focused intently on her boss.

"I imagine you have some questions," Mortimer started with an unusually soft tone as he met and held penetrating contact with her eyes.

"You're right. I need some answers," Suzanne responded through clenched teeth, as she felt her body grow tense despite efforts to remain calm and collected. "Answers about curious share certificates issued without my knowledge by a company that I manage. Explanations about cash deposits, totaling thousands of dollars, to my mother's bank account over several years. Some insight into your involvement with all of this."

After a pause, John George said, "All of them are fair questions, and I owe you an explanation. I'll spend all the time you want, and I'll try to deal with your concerns. But, please have a seat. It will take some time. Lana has prepared one of her excellent meals. We can have dinner while we talk. May I suggest she call your pilots and let them know you'll be a while?" he asked, taking her arm and guiding her towards a table already set with expensive fine china.

It was evident he had been expecting her. With a nod, Suzanne concurred, sat in the offered chair, and accepted a glass of red wine. John George took a seat at the end of the table only a few inches away and raised his glass. He made no comment but took a long sip before he said, "First, I must tell you something I should have shared with you much earlier."

There followed an uncomfortable pause, while he appeared to be searching for the right words, before he said simply, "I'm your father."

Shocked, all color immediately drained from Suzanne's face, and her thoughts became a confused muddle. She had already concluded that Mortimer might have known and probably had some connection to her mother, but she hadn't – for more than a few fleeting moments – conceived that John George Mortimer might actually be her father! She was speechless.

"I know this comes as a surprise, perhaps even a shock. But I assure you it's unquestionably true. May I tell you the story?" he asked. Suzanne wasn't sure, but thought she detected some pain in his eyes and resignation in his tone.

Still unable to speak, she nodded again, took a deep breath and another long sip from the glass of wine.

"Back when you were president of Countrywide Stores, and we first met to talk about selling your company to Multima, I immediately noticed you bore a remarkable resemblance to a woman I recalled meeting years before. Because it was so long ago, I had to think about it for some time before her name eventually came back to me. Louise Marcotte. We met in the seventies. I was taking a brief vacation in Quebec City and met her by chance in a hotel lobby. We connected instantly. Our relationship was not a one-night stand, but there was just a single weekend.

"It's probably more information than you care to know, but over those few days, we made love passionately for hours at a time. They were some of the most pleasurable few days and nights of my entire life. I saw almost nothing of Quebec except glances out the windows of my suite at Loew's Le Concorde Hotel," he said with the trace of a smile.

"From the background materials you included in your pitch to us, I learned you grew up in Quebec. Your resumé also mentioned your maiden name, Marcotte, and your marital status, divorced. Nothing triggered at first, but I retained that reference in my mind, concluded Simpson was your divorced husband's name, and became curious about a possible connection to Louise.

"I did the math and realized your age and birth date were about nine months after that weekend vacation. When I returned home after our meeting, I checked some old agendas, and the timing seemed even more precise than I imagined. Intrigued, I covertly ordered a DNA test.

"Do you recall when we insisted you'd need a full medical check-up before we could close our deal to buy Countrywide? That physician obtained samples from you that we subsequently used for testing with my DNA. The results showed a perfect match. One hundred percent according to the lab reports."

Mortimer paused to let Suzanne process the startling news. But her brain was responding much more slowly than usual. Of all the scenarios she had imagined since she first became aware of those cash deposits and mysterious shares, none seriously included a possibility that her boss might also be her father.

Disbelieving, she was reluctant to say anything. Fortunately, Lana provided some precious time to collect her thoughts by entering the room to serve Suzanne, then Mortimer, a bowl of soup. "A delicious vegetable broth I made fresh today," Lana announced with pride, apparently sensing extreme unease in the room and trying to project both levity and warmth.

After Lana had served the soup, she shared smiles with both and expressed her hope they'd enjoy the first course before she returned to the kitchen. Suzanne knew a response to Mortimer's shocking announcement was necessary. She cleared her throat, drew another deep breath, and asked to see the DNA report.

"Of course," John George replied. "After dinner, I'll make a copy you can take with you. And, if you'd like to have another test for further verification, I'll be happy to provide samples to whatever testing agency you choose. But be assured, I too had multiple tests completed before I was convinced. There is no doubt about our relationship."

"Why…why did you never share this information with me?" Suzanne blurted out as tears welled in her eyes. "How could you keep it secret from me for more than ten years?"

Mortimer's eyes dropped as he took an unusually deep breath before trying to explain. "At first, I thought it best to say nothing until we had worked together for a few months. My impressions of you when we first met were extraordinary. You amazed me with your poise, your knowledge, and your accomplishments so early in life."

Suzanne listened to the story intently, her eyes probing John George's for understanding. But she didn't interrupt because she wanted the full story.

"As soon as I became sure you were my daughter, I decided I wanted to groom you to replace me at Multima eventually. But, I knew it would be much harder for you if people knew of our relationship. People might attribute every advancement you made to your unique status as the CEO's daughter. Respect of your peers might have been immeasurably harder to earn.

"Plus, to be brutally honest, I wanted to be sure you truly had all the qualities necessary to succeed. First impressions of you were overwhelmingly positive, and I thought you had what it takes to be a great leader. But, I wanted to watch you and get to know you better before sharing my secret. It was foolish; I know that now. But there just never seemed to be an opportune occasion to tell you. Time passed. I continued watching every aspect of your management style and learned much about your thought processes and reasoning.

"My fondness for you grew, both professionally and personally. Little doubt remained about your ability to lead a sprawling organization. Still, I postponed a discussion that I knew I should have with you. I make no excuses. I handled it poorly. I understand if you're angry and disappointed. And I can only beg for your forgiveness and understanding," John George whispered.

Suzanne could see uncharacteristic sorrow in his eyes as he tried to explain. She sensed his humility and expected he was looking for immediate acceptance. *But it won't be quite that easy*, she thought.

Instead, she focused on the soup. Eyes downward, silent, and working furiously to process and make some sense of these revelations, she simply didn't buy the logic. Why would someone keep such crucial information to himself for so long? What did it matter if colleagues might associate her career advancement with a special relationship to the CEO? And, by the way, where was he for the prior thirty or so years while she was growing up and getting her education? She decided to start there, completely ignoring his request for forgiveness and understanding.

"Okay, you felt you had some reasons not to divulge the information. But, let's go back to the beginning. Assuming all this is true, why did you abandon my mother and leave her to raise me on her own?"

This time, it was Mortimer who was saved by Lana's entry to take away the empty bowls. They both digressed to compliment her on her homemade soup.

"I didn't know," he resumed as the housekeeper left the room. "In the seventies, it was fairly common to enjoy relatively casual sexual adventures. Unprotected sex was common then, too. Guys assumed their partners were using birth control pills and usually gave little thought to reproductive implications. That was certainly our case. While we had an unbelievably great weekend of intimacy together, we both knew it was only temporary.

"Your mother spoke just a few words of English. At that time, I spoke no French at all. Our relationship consisted mainly of smiles, wine, dancing and delightful hours in bed. It was beautiful, but we both knew our relationship ended with my departure from Quebec. And I never heard a word from your mother again," he added.

Lana's arrival with the main course, a platter of rice with different types of fish and vegetables, provided time for Suzanne to absorb the implications once again. Fair enough. Her mother might have had reasons to withhold information about her birth from Mortimer, but she knew her mother struggled financially all through the years she was raising Suzanne. Why didn't she seek financial help, especially from one of the wealthiest men in America?

"But you felt guilty about me and the burden I placed on my mother, so you started sending her money thirty-some years later – even though you couldn't share information about our relationship with me?" Suzanne asked.

"No, I felt no guilt. Rather, I wanted to do something to thank her for raising you so well. After I realized the significance of our relationship, with the help of a private investigator, I was able to learn a lot about Louise Marcotte," Mortimer replied. "I was impressed. One thing I learned: she probably never intended to contact me.

"To be honest, I'm not sure your mother ever knew my last name. We didn't introduce ourselves formally and used only our given names when we spoke. I knew her surname was Marcotte only because I caught a glimpse of it on some ID she showed at a disco in the hotel.

"The private investigator reported that acquaintances remember her as a fiercely independent young woman who felt no need for a man to care for her or support you. They remember her thrilled with your birth and confident she could manage quite nicely on her own," he said as his face brightened and smile grew broad. He paused for a forkful of rice and cut a small piece of fish before he continued with his story. Suzanne just waited.

"I learned that your mother struggled to cope financially as you grew up, but never left you wanting any of the necessities of life. She was a hard-working woman who saved carefully and devoted all of her time, attention, and money to be sure you would enjoy the best life possible. I admired that.

"But I think you can understand why I also felt a need to be careful, not only as it related to you, but to your mother as well. Sometimes people change when exposed to significant amounts of wealth. Frankly, I was apprehensive that others could influence Louise Marcotte. I was afraid she might try to acquire a substantial amount of my financial worth if I made contact and divulged the information I had discovered."

Suzanne was tempted to challenge him on that point, while he paused for some more of the fish, but decided to absorb the information a little longer.

"I struggled with that dilemma for a while, then made a decision. I would secretly use my own money to finance the purchase of Countrywide Stores. So, I made a personal loan to Multima Corporation. Then, I created several companies to conceal my involvement. One of those companies issued the preferred shares your mother held. Those shares had value only when triggered by a particular event – my death," John George calmly explained. Then he observed Suzanne to gauge her reaction.

She was determined to reveal nothing. Instead, she lowered her eyes again and silently focused on her meal. Mortimer did the same. After a few mouthfuls, Mortimer apparently concluded Suzanne was content to let him continue with his story.

"Naturally, we meticulously structured the companies to make it almost impossible for her to learn about my involvement. But the net result of all this was to ensure that should I die, she would be an owner of a large chunk of Multima Corporation. I was reluctant to leave a corporation to which I'd devoted my life entirely to charities. I have no other family. Given all the information I learned about your mother, I was confident she would work to put you in charge of Multima and eventually leave her ownership position to you. I thought this arrangement would avoid potential legal disputes and ultimately leave much of my company and fortune in good hands."

Suzanne was touched. Still grieving from the sudden death of her mother, she felt tears welling up but was determined to avoid any show of emotion. With a fork, she picked at her meal, made no comment, and avoided eye contact with Mortimer. She didn't want to betray her whirling sentiments in any way.

Both chose to eat their meals silently for a few awkward moments. Then, Mortimer seemed to feel a need to continue his explanation.

"The monthly cash deposits to your mother's bank account were a small way to help her. You might note the amount our secret company paid her each month was the same as she received from the Quebec pension fund. I thought that amount would double her standard of living but remain modest enough that she – or an ambitious lawyer – would not be curious enough to try to solve a mystery about the source of the money. Or take legal action to get even more should they somehow discover my involvement," he added.

Suzanne was mystified by the conflicting emotions she felt. John George Mortimer was explaining this life-altering information with about the same emotion, language, and patience he would use to describe a business deal. His manner seemed methodical and calculating. But under this veneer of corporate-speak, it was evident he felt responsibility for imprudent actions from a carefree period in his life and thought he had found a way to balance the scorecard somewhat. If this story was true, and Mortimer had died before her mother, Louise Marcotte would have inherited billions! And there was no doubt about it; eventually, her mother would have passed on the entire amount to Suzanne.

She could no longer just eat her dinner. Politeness demanded a response, and she knew her next words might powerfully influence her longer-term relationship with the man who appeared to be her father. She swallowed a small morsel of fish, then chose her words very carefully.

"You had some feelings for my mother. I can see that," she began. "You also felt something for me. Here's what I'm having some trouble reconciling. If you were prepared to leave a significant portion of your wealth to my mother, and ultimately me, how could you remain silent for so long?"

"I'm not sure I can give you a satisfactory answer to that," he replied, wiping his lips with a white linen napkin.

As though on cue, Lana arrived to take away the dinner plates. As she moved about the table, she apologized. There was no dessert to serve, but she could bring some fruit or an after-dinner drink if they wished. Both confirmed that wine would suffice, and Lana scurried from the room laden with all the dishes. There would be no more timely interruptions.

"Great wealth carries enormous responsibility, Suzanne," he said, furrowing his brow and looking at her intently. "I could manage quite comfortably with far less wealth than I have. Look around. You see that I indeed live well. I think you also know I forego much of the luxury and frivolous expense characteristic of many people with far smaller fortunes. But I feel an obligation to increase my wealth. Shareholders demand it. Every day, stakeholders in Multima Corporation look for indicators of progress.

"Folks buy and sell shares in our company based on what they can learn, good and bad. If there is bad news like a lawsuit or scandal, they could react negatively and the value of Multima declines. That hurts me, of course. But it impacts thousands of other people far more. Individual shareholders and pension funds all feel pain. Our employees are affected. If a scandal is severe enough, our customers turn away and create even more angst for everyone involved.

"So, I've always tried to weigh the impact of my actions – or failure to take action – with a possible impact on Multima Corporation and the thousands of people who depend on us. Every time I was tempted to have a good talk and reveal everything to you, a heavy weight of obligation blocked me. Whenever I fantasized about reconnecting with your mother, the reality of circumstance outweighed the desire to explore a potentially rewarding personal outcome. I know that may seem trite to you, but it's the best explanation I can give," he finished with a husky voice that seemed exhausted.

Once more, Suzanne tried to buy some time to formulate a response and took a long sip from her glass of wine. She understood John George's quandary on an intuitive level but felt intense discomfort. With this man, business needs had apparently always taken priority over personal needs. Was she cut from the same piece of cloth? For the first time, she was seeing a man far more calculating than she had experienced in their decade-long working relationship. How would this shocking new development affect their ability to work together? Should they even have a future working relationship?

"Where do we go from here?" Suzanne murmured.

"I'm not entirely sure," Mortimer replied. "I feel strongly about you and want to get to know you better as my daughter. I also feel strongly about you as president of Multima Supermarkets. I need you there and hope you can be comfortable in that role given our new relationship. Still, I'm mindful we both need to manage this circumstance carefully."

"Does that mean you *still* want to keep all of this secret?" she gasped with incredulity.

"Until we figure out how to manage it, I think it best we keep it between just us. You know how terribly Multima's market value dropped with the news of my cancer, and share prices are just starting to recover. I start chemotherapy next week, will probably lose my hair, and appear a little ghost-like for a few months. I'd prefer to not further alarm investors with any surprises. Can you live with that for a while?" he asked hopefully.

In response, Suzanne just nodded, folded her napkin, and stood up from the table. "I really should leave now. You're tired, and I need to get back to Atlanta. Please send me the DNA test summary, and let me digest all this," she suggested as they walked together towards the entrance of his home.

"Of course, Suzanne. I know this is all very confusing and stressful. It is for me, too," John George replied. "When you come back for the board of directors meeting next month, why don't you plan to stay the weekend here in Fort Myers? I'd like for us to spend some time together."

"Sure," she said with her usual charming smile. "Let's do that."

Then, without warning, John George Mortimer reached out, and his arms completely encircled her. He held the embrace for a long moment. For the first time, she briefly felt a warmth and affection she had never before experienced. When she looked up, she realized they both had a bit of unexpected mist in their eyes.

Lana appeared in the corridor where they stood, opened the door for Suzanne, and bid a friendly farewell. Steps away, a car and driver were waiting to whisk her to the Multima Supermarkets jet parked at Page Field.

Just over two hours later, she arrived back in Atlanta with her mind still whirling from shock, bewilderment, and unease. The questions surrounding the timing of her mother's death – and apparently fortuitous timing in Mortimer's maneuvers to save his job – continued to dangle uncomfortably.

It was that deeply troubling issue she had hoped to resolve during her planned weekend with John George in Fort Myers. With the meeting now canceled, Suzanne had little choice but to consider the possibilities endlessly in her mind. But that, too, would need to wait for private time. First, she had to return to the meeting with her direct reports, putting their needs ahead of her own.

Five

An office tower off Biscayne Blvd., Miami, Florida.
Tuesday March 22, 2016

With a clenched fist, Douglas Whitfield thrust his arm high into the air and suppressed a strong urge to shout *"Yesssss!"* The call to delay this month's scheduled meeting with John George Mortimer and the board of directors was the best news he'd received since he started this job.

A few weeks earlier he was basking in success, leading a team that won management approval to create an entirely new business model at his previous home in the corporation, Multima Financial Services. His skillful leadership caught the attention of his CEO and the board. They were so impressed with his accomplishments they immediately rewarded him with a huge promotion. Now, Whitfield feared he had plummeted from corporate hero to his current uncomfortable position as an overwhelmed executive with embarrassingly little to show so far.

His new role leading Multima's technology and logistics division had not started at all spectacularly. Appointed president of the unit at the last board meeting, Whitfield replaced one of America's best known and highly respected technologists, Wendal Randall. All Douglas knew about the demise of his predecessor was that Randall had become embroiled in multiple FBI investigations and was in jail awaiting trial on several serious criminal offenses.

Whitfield's most notable achievement in the new job involved the transfer of about half his employees to a sister company, Multima Supermarkets. Since that staff was entirely devoted to the business activities of Supermarkets, the board decided they should become part of that division and physically move from Miami to Atlanta. Whitfield had no say in that decision. It was presented as a *fait accompli* when Mortimer offered him the job. Subsequently, he had managed issues related to the planned relocation as a priority.

By the end of April, they'd be starting their moves. By June, only a few hundred folks would remain to focus on core Logistics activities and the exciting new software assignment. In the meantime, virtually nothing had crystallized with the product's launch.

With the potentially hazardous meeting delayed, he assumed the technology gods must now be starting to look favorably upon him. CEO John George Mortimer had charged him with the task of commercializing an ingenious new software application. Although, ironically, it was developers working in the Multima Supermarkets division who originally wrote the code for it.

When hackers penetrated Multima Supermarkets' computer system a few months earlier, corporate security and the FBI pinpointed the culprits within only a few days. Their success was entirely due to this remarkable new technology. Impressed, Mortimer decided to build an entirely new business around the highly innovative security software and chose Whitfield to bring the new product to market.

Because of the staff relocations and settling into a new role, Whitfield had made only a few telephone calls which he thought represented limited progress. This unplanned delay bought him another few weeks to make something positive happen before the next meeting of the board.

He understood the business culture of Multima Corporation well. Management expected success and didn't accept excuses should it prove elusive. Mortimer always said that division management owned all successes as well as any failure. Headquarters was there to support success, not drive it.

In fact, he had spoken with John George just once during the past month. The CEO called to see if Douglas was settling in alright, and did he need any help? In response, Whitfield joked that he no longer got lost finding his way back to his office from the restroom! They both laughed, knowing the sprawling labyrinth of tiny cubicles created a maze in the layout of Logistics' headquarters, and might easily pose such an initial challenge.

He assured John George all was progressing well and asked for guidance on how he might get the division's name changed.

"The first thing everyone here told me was a little unusual. Our name, Multima Logistics, is confusing to many of our customers," Douglas explained. "Apparently, Wendal Randall first created that name when most of our clients were transport companies and warehouses. Now, since most are really technology users, people here would like to see the name changed to Multima Solutions."

"The idea has merit," John George conceded without hesitation. "What do you think it would cost to rebrand your signs, letterhead, and all those details?"

"Probably a couple million," Whitfield replied.

"As division president, you have the authority to spend up to a million per year in capital expenditures without board approval. If you can do the rebranding over two years and stay within that budget, it's your call," Mortimer said. "Run your idea up the flagpole with Alberto and Wilma. If our legal counsel and CFO have no concerns, it's up to you."

That conversation was typical of a management style tilted towards guidance rather than instruction and gave subordinates an opportunity to show their mettle without constant interference. In turn, he knew Mortimer expected results. And, he knew the CEO measured results by progress, revenues, and profits – not how diligently management was working.

This meeting delay offered a reprieve from his considerable unease on the corporate front, but he still had unsettling issues at home to deal with. Back there, things were going very poorly.

––––––––––

There was one glaring reason that relations soured between Whitfield and his wife. It had been very late the night he arrived back in his Chicago suburb, only hours after the board of directors meeting in Fort Myers that made him a new division president. Mortimer had offered him the job, then expected a decision. Unwilling to show any hesitancy about such a great opportunity to move ahead, Douglas Whitfield accepted the proposed offer on the spot. At home, he needed to elicit support from his wife and kids.

"What would you think about moving to Miami if a good opportunity came along?" he expectantly asked his wife as he pulled the cork from a bottle of wine that fateful evening.

From the sparkle in his eyes as he posed the question, Marleen immediately sensed there might be more to his question than the words implied and cautiously responded, "Why? Is there something going on at work?"

"Yeah," he grinned. "I've been offered a fantastic opportunity. Division president for Multima Logistics. A big promotion. Tons more money. A real resumé enhancer. Unfortunately, we'll need to move to Miami."

"You've already accepted the position, haven't you?" she immediately countered, her face contorted with either shock or anger.

Surprised at her reaction, Whitfield knew he'd need to proceed with caution. "I've tentatively accepted the role. I had to give an indication of my interest immediately. But, we have time to discuss it and get everyone comfortable. Otherwise, I won't accept the job."

"You asshole! How could you?" she shrieked, bursting into tears as her face turned scarlet. "How the hell could you accept a job that requires us to uproot our children and leave all we have here? How could you possibly do that without even talking to us?

"And how could you do such a thing when you know the company *I* love has just promoted *me* to the job of *my* dreams?" she sputtered.

"I already said that I've tentatively taken the job. There really wasn't an alternative. Mortimer wanted an answer. But like I said, we have time to discuss this and get everyone comfortable. Otherwise, I won't accept the promotion," Whitfield repeated. As soon as he said it, he realized his lips were pursed together a little more tightly than he would have liked, and his tone suggested waning patience.

"Bullshit! You know fucking well you do not intend to *talk about it,*" she responded mimicking his tone. "If you cared at all about your family, you could have asked for five minutes to call and discuss it on the phone before you answered. No company would object to that. Instead, you were so supremely confident about your ability to convince me to leave my job and tear your children away from their schools and friends that you didn't even consider us!"

What followed had not been enjoyable for either of them. Although Douglas scrambled to reframe the discussion, change tactics, and assuage concerns, Marleen remained focused on the expected damage to her career and his apparent insensitivity to her circumstance. They both consumed wine while they argued, often swallowing amounts better described as gulps than sips.

It continued that way for about an hour – with bitter, hurtful insults and countering accusations – until they both ran out of words and two bottles of wine lay empty on the bar. After a few moments' silence, she announced her decision.

"I want you to leave," she said, her tone cold and impersonal. "This is the final straw. Your damned career ambition has no limits. You've demonstrated that unfortunate fact too many times, and I no longer want to be part of it. The children and I will stay here. You'll stay somewhere else. Take the clothes you need. Find an attorney. Have your lawyer contact me to arrange the next steps."

———————————

That was the way they'd left it the last time they spoke, almost two weeks earlier. Despite his several attempts to connect with her, she was neither answering her phone nor responding to emails. However, he still hadn't contacted a lawyer. It was better to let some time pass, he thought. After a while, perhaps she'd soften.

In the meantime, Whitfield would need to keep focused on the matters at hand with his new job. He knew Mortimer was battling breast cancer, had already undergone surgery, and was receiving chemotherapy. Regardless, he doubted that distraction would temper the CEO's overall high expectations.

It was with this sense of urgency he had earlier summoned the half-dozen most influential members of his new team to a meeting that would start in just a few minutes and last until he was satisfied they had a strategy to jumpstart this new software sales effort during the coming thirty days. He was determined to make the most of this reprieve because his continued upward trajectory in the corporate hierarchy demanded it.

He glanced at his watch. Before that crucial session started, there was just enough time to make a quick call to Fort Myers. Given how poorly things were going with his wife these days, maybe he could connect with that sexy young fox in corporate and investor affairs back at headquarters – the one who had suggested it might be fun to meet up someday. A guy couldn't work all the time.

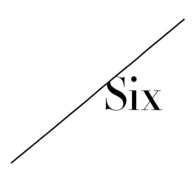

Six

Ste-Foy, Quebec.
Evening, Wednesday April 13, 2016

Roland LaMontagne was surprised when his father called just after dinner to ask if he could drop by for a brief chat. They seldom got together these days.

Only a few months had passed since the Church hierarchy assigned the young Catholic priest to his new role in the *Paroisse Ste-Foy*. Initially, they preferred to send young priests to parishes well away from their families and hometowns. But, the decline of the Church had been so dramatic – and the shortage of clerics so extreme – they made an exception with Roland.

After all, his father was an esteemed *notaire* in adjacent Quebec City, a respected professional, a man they presumed would not interfere with operations within the parish. They also had a word with Monsieur LaMontagne in private, asking him to avoid contact with his son as much as possible for the first year to better let him settle into his demanding responsibilities as pastor.

Monsieur LaMontagne understood the importance of such a request and had carefully kept his distance, communicating only once a month by phone for a few minutes, and studiously confining the scope of their conversations to family news. Roland surmised there must be some issue of critical importance to prompt this visit.

When he arrived, Roland initially noticed his father looked haggard. He had lost some weight, and his pallor was ashen. However, the gregarious man grinned broadly with eyes twinkling as he spread his arms wide, squeezing his son tightly into his usual bear-hug greeting.

"How is my son the *curé* doing?" Monsieur LaMontagne asked playfully, releasing Roland from his tight grip to make a long and affectionate assessment.

"Your son, the priest, is doing as well as can be expected after ten hours of visits to troubled people all over the parish," Roland replied with a smile of resignation. His dad understood well the weight of responsibility his son felt on days of visitation to hospitals and homes of the ill or injured. Generally, he loved his role as pastor and had always been acutely sensitive to people experiencing pain or suffering. Years of training in the cloister hadn't lessened that tendency.

"I know it's hard for you," Monsieur LaMontagne sympathized, his smile quickly disappearing. "But you do your job admirably. Scarcely a day passes I don't have someone tell me what a wonderful priest you are, and how you've helped them overcome some tragic circumstance. I know you'll focus on the positive, the good you do, the service you provide to help people cope with unexpected and unwelcome challenges."

For a few more minutes, as Roland opened a bottle of wine and poured a glass for his father, they exchanged similar banter, with his father displaying predictable pride in his son and the unique calling he had followed. Once they settled comfortably into two plush recliners, his father's manner turned unexpectedly sober.

"Son, I'm carrying a heavy burden I need to share with you, a situation I'm extremely reluctant to talk about. But I want you to know, just in case anything should happen," Monsieur LaMontagne started.

"How can I help, Papa?" Roland calmly replied.

"You know I've always tried to live my life consistent with the teachings of the Church. And I think I do that most of the time, but there's been a recent tragic failure and I feel terribly about it. I need to talk with someone, and you are the only person I can trust with such a shameful secret."

"You know I'm willing to listen. And, of course, I'll keep our conversation between us," Roland said.

"Thanks, son. That's important to me because I have sinned and sinned badly. I'm not asking you to absolve my guilt, or even understand the reasons for what I did. But I need you to be aware of the whole story," his father explained with a pained expression.

"I've got all night," Roland replied with an empathetic smile.

"I have a problem caused by gambling," Monsieur LaMontagne started. "It began with online poker, then frequent trips to the casino in Montreal. At first, I managed to cover my debts. Then, I needed to borrow to meet the obligations. I kept believing my luck would eventually change, but my habit grew stronger. After a few months, I was forced to borrow large amounts from some unsavory people."

"Gambling is a far more common problem today than you may realize, Papa. There's help available. I can put you in touch with groups where you can get help anonymously," Roland replied in a calm, hushed tone of empathy.

"I know. But my gambling is not the only information I want to share with you. It's what came later. A few weeks ago, one of my clients suffered a fatal heart attack in my office," Monsieur LaMontagne told his son.

"How awful for you!" Roland interjected, reflexively covering his mouth with his hand to hide the horror.

"No son. How awful *of* me is more accurate. You see, I directly contributed to her death."

Perplexed, Roland took a breath and studied his distraught father for a few seconds before he cautiously asked, "And why do you feel that way?"

"A few weeks ago, a man I borrowed money from demanded a meeting, right away. I owed him more than five hundred thousand dollars and hadn't been able to repay him anything for more than a month. My luck at the tables just got worse. I couldn't even pay him the twenty-five thousand interest charge for the month. My bank account was empty, and I couldn't let your mother find out that all our savings were gone. Or that our house was entirely mortgaged again, with our credit cards above their limits. I had no choice but to meet with him," his father said as he nervously and repeatedly tapped his left foot.

"The man told me that if I couldn't pay the twenty-five thousand due that day, I had two options, either I could help him with another important matter or he could call the 'collection department'. They would start by creating enough pain to get my attention and give me a greater incentive to find the twenty-five thousand," Monsieur LaMontagne explained.

Aghast, Roland asked, "What did you do?"

"Well, I asked what he meant by helping him. To my amazement, he told me I had an appointment scheduled a few days later with a client named Louise Marcotte. He said someone was going to prick her with a needle as she walked along the street, just before she came into my building. After she climbed the three flights of stairs and arrived in my office, she would soon faint from the drug and the exertion from climbing," the elder LaMontagne continued.

Roland squirmed in his chair and looked at his dad in shocked amazement until his father resumed after a short pause, punctuated by a deep sigh.

"He told me my job was to simply reach inside her top and apply a small patch to her chest. He showed me where to place it. I was to leave it on her skin for precisely one minute. Madame Marcotte would remain unconscious, and then she would start to have a heart attack. At that point, I was to remove the patch and immediately flush it down the toilet in my office. Can you imagine? He even knew I had a toilet in my office!"

Roland interrupted his father. "Dad, are you sure you should be sharing this story with me?"

"I know the risks, son. I'm a *notaire*. You'll do whatever you feel you need to do with this information, but I must tell this horrible story. I haven't slept in weeks. I'm at my wit's end. I have to let someone know what a terrible thing I've done!"

"So, you applied the patch as the man asked you to?" Roland asked.

"Yes. I had to do it. The alternative was too awful to consider. When Madame Marcotte fainted in my office, I immediately made her comfortable on the floor and shouted for my secretary to call 911. Then, I asked her to run downstairs to fetch a defibrillator. When I heard her footsteps going down the stairs, I applied the patch exactly as instructed. Within a few seconds, her breathing was erratic. It became worse and worse. After sixty seconds, I removed the patch and flushed it down the toilet. When I came back to Madame Marcotte, her body was undergoing significant trauma.

"My secretary came back soon with the defibrillator. Of course, neither one of us could remember how to use it! We were just reading the instructions when the emergency responders arrived. They took her to *Hôpital Laval*, where she died a few hours later," Monsieur LaMontagne finished with a whisper.

Roland didn't know how to process a confession so shocking. His brain seemed numb. Time stood still. There was total silence in the room as each tried to digest the importance of the words and implications of the deed. Neither spoke for several minutes.

Eyes closed, his father held his head in his hands, leaning forward. He displayed exhaustion, guilt, and remorse. He couldn't look at his son. The magnitude of his sin seemed just too burdensome for him to bear. Roland instinctively moved towards his father and wrapped an arm around his slumped shoulders.

"We'll find a way to deal with it, Papa," he whispered. "I'll help you if I can."

He listened to his father sob quietly, holding his head in his hands, his shoulders slumped. With a squeeze of his father's right shoulder, Roland resumed their conversation by asking, "Did the police come to your office?"

"Yes. Two officers arrived right after the paramedics. Of course, they questioned both my secretary and me, separately. I told them she just fainted, then suddenly seemed to have trouble breathing. I told them about trying to use the defibrillator and the paramedics saying she had a heart attack. After the police left, I went to the hospital and stayed there until she died," his father said with a shrug and resigned tone of voice.

Then he paused once more, drew the form of a cross on his heart, and bowed his head for a few seconds.

"I contacted her daughter," he resumed after clearing his throat. "She was in Alaska when I gave her the news about her mother's heart attack. Suzanne Simpson is a high-powered executive with Multima Supermarkets and immediately flew here on her private jet, but she arrived too late. I met her at the airport later that evening, then helped her with all the final arrangements. I spent the better part of two days assisting her with her mother's affairs. She's a beautiful and kind lady. Then, Madame Marcotte's body was cremated two days later."

Roland listened for several minutes while his father recounted more seemingly minor details about their two days together wrapping up loose ends related to the woman's death. It appeared to Roland that guilt consumed his father because his voice wavered with more tears threatening to erupt at any time.

His father was apparently most concerned with the sin he had committed. There appeared to be little or no concern about the police or possible legal action. As he listened to his father speak, it became evident the paramedics and police treated the episode without suspicion, just another heart event so unexceptional with senior citizens. For Roland, the issue was a moral one. How should he proceed with this alarming but sensitive information that could destroy his father and his family?

"You've heard nothing further from the police over the past few weeks?" Roland asked his father.

"Nothing. But it's not the police that worries me. Someone wanted Madame Marcotte dead. The fellow I owed the money to said so. His boss told him it had something to do with Multima but wouldn't say more. I'm sure the daughter isn't involved. I see no reason at all for her to want to kill her mother. Madame Marcotte was a woman of limited means. Her daughter has far more wealth and it appeared they had a genuine, loving mother-daughter relationship.

"There's little in the estate. The only things I found of possible value were some share certificates for a numbered company in Ontario. And that's why

I want you to know the story. You see, I was investigating some mysterious transactions with Madame Marcotte's bank account – not withdrawals – instead there were deposits to her account, and over a period of several years."

"Did you solve the mystery?" Roland asked his father when he paused to collect his thoughts.

"Partially. With the help of some contacts in Toronto, I learned that a company ultimately owned by Multima Corporation made the deposits. But someone went to great lengths to keep that ownership secret and almost impossible to discover. There are at least a dozen legal entities that form a barricade. It was precisely that information I planned to share with Madame Marcotte when she was coming to see me on that fateful day," the *notaire* said, shaking his head from side to side before adding his final thought.

"Someone at Multima didn't want that meeting to take place. And, someone was apparently so determined she not learn the information I planned to share with her that they had her killed," Monsieur LaMontagne whispered.

"But couldn't this person just demand that you not tell her? Or, perish the thought, eliminate you to prevent you from sharing the information with her?" Roland wondered.

"Exactly! I can see no reason for killing Madame Marcotte. I am the one with the information. Unless…" Monsieur LaMontagne hesitated. "Unless they planned to eliminate her for some other reason first, then kill me to cover their tracks."

Roland was speechless. The logic was sound. His father's thought process seemed carefully reasoned and unemotional, but the situation felt almost surreal. How did his father ever get into such a position? More importantly, how could they resolve this potentially lethal predicament?

After several poignant moments, Monsieur LaMontagne spoke again, his voice tired and resigned. "Son, I feel horrible dragging you into this mess. You can be sure I thought long and hard before deciding to share this information with you. For obvious reasons, I can't go to the police. What you do with the information I leave entirely up to you and your conscience.

"But, in case something should happen to me, I want you to know the facts. I may need you to take care of your mother. And I want you to promise me you'll just let the matter go if should something occur. I know you. I know your natural curiosity and your sense of justice. Promise me you won't try to dig deeper into this mystery. It would only put you and your mother at risk. That's the last thing I want to happen. Promise me."

Roland bowed his head as he processed the request. He knew he was in shock and wasn't comfortable making any big decisions, or making any promises. With a silent prayer, he asked God to forgive him as he replied quietly, "OK, Papa. I will. But we need to find a way to be sure that my promise stays hypothetical. We've got to find a way for you to get out of this."

For the next half hour or so, Roland quizzed his father, again and again, to be sure he understood all the facts. He wanted desperately not only to grasp everything that had transpired; he also wanted to know all the players and where they might fit. Most urgently, he searched for a way his father could extract himself from this dangerous quagmire.

Monsieur LaMontagne calmly and patiently responded to every question. Every answer was delivered carefully with succinct details. Most importantly, Roland noted that every response was consistent. There seemed to be no variances or confusion. His father had seemingly analyzed every aspect, from every perspective, as one would expect of a *notaire*.

Only after they said farewell, and he finished his glass of wine in the silence of his parish home, the possibility finally occurred to him. If the people in this drama were truly as professional and devious as his father suspected, they might have followed his father there this evening. They could already be aware of the meeting with his father. And that just might mean his own life was now in jeopardy.

Seven

Cusco, Peru.
Friday April 29, 2016

Weeks earlier, Howard Knight had mysteriously disappeared from the Multima board of directors meeting. Now in Peru, he looked like a carefree backpacking tourist. Over the weeks, he'd grown back facial hair. This time it was a neatly-trimmed goatee which he dyed reddish-brown each time he colored his hair. He wore a long-peaked souvenir cap and large round sunglasses that shaded his eyes and covered much of his upper face.

Jeans and t-shirts were his only attire. He had two pairs of each and rotated them daily as he guessed most tourists might. He wore his single pair of hiking boots everywhere and always carried both backpacks. Usually one was strung from a shoulder, the other snugly strapped to his back.

He spent most of those prior weeks 'sightseeing' in Quito, the capital of Ecuador. Their plan called for him to blend into a metropolis where he was not expected to be. For this purpose, Quito was ideal.

He first selected a downtrodden hotel in the southern part of the city near the Quitumbe bus terminal. There, hotel room rates and meals were very cheap, and residents posed few questions if they spoke at all. Then, he learned to navigate the north-south local bus lines so he could travel throughout the city for a pittance. He changed hotels every three days as he thought most tourists might, gradually working farther north to the more affluent parts of the city. As his goatee grew in and his physical appearance evolved, he also seemed to fit the stereotypical profile of a wandering backpacker more and more.

To blend in, he used city tour buses to check out the landscape, locate most attractions, and watch the behavior of visitors. It was useful. On the first bus tour, he learned information he thought might prove helpful later. Surprisingly, the famous *Museo del Banco Central*, Ecuador's most famous museum, had been closed since February for major renovations expected to take about a year. That might be important to know if questioned by authorities. Every day, he made a point of visiting a well-known tourist attraction after asking directions from a hotel clerk to reinforce his image as a vacationing traveler.

When he was a youngster, Knight's Italian mother had nurtured interest in arts and culture. It was a passion he retained. So, he gladly used his time in Quito to visit sites popular with visitors. He went to *Casa de la Cultura* to admire the art and returned several different evenings to watch dance or music performances from inconspicuous seats in the back rows. He visited magnificent churches like the *Iglesia de la Compañia*, one of the most beautiful in all the Americas, as well as popular tourist attractions like *La Virgen del Panecillo*, the imposing statue perched on a hilltop and visible from almost everywhere in Quito.

He rode the *TeleferiQo*, the second-largest cable car in the world, to gaze at the *Pichincha* volcano towering over the city. Like the tourists, he marveled at the view and was so enthralled that he returned on three separate sunny days to admire the six other volcanoes dominating the horizon.

One of the tour operators guided him towards *Mitad del Mundo* or middle of the world. To get there, he took a local bus to a point just outside Quito, where scientists first proved that Earth was indeed an oblate spheroid. Twice, he spent several hours entranced by the bounty of floral beauty in the *orchidaria*. And every day he spent time chatting in different coffee shops, improving his basic Spanish as he fine-tuned the story of his supposed background and life as a retired Italian businessman.

Now, more than ever before, Knight was grateful his mother insisted they speak Italian at home. He was equally thankful that every summer until he finished college, she would send him to stay with his grandparents in Rimini on the Eastern coast of Italy, just minutes away from the principality of San Marino. He knew the locale there intimately and conversed in Italian perfectly. He had little doubt about his ability to apply enough accent, speaking either English or Spanish, to convince even the skeptical of his new identity.

But every moment of every day, he remained watchful for any sign of either The Organization or the FBI. Walking, he would occasionally change direction to avoid eye contact with police officers. In cafes or restaurants, he always chose tables with his back against a wall and a view of the entrance. Returning to his hotel room, he would perform the same security rituals, inspecting for any signs of entry, attempts to open the safe, or evidence of recording devices. So far, it looked like this geographic diversion had bought some time.

He also realized that it would be necessary to move further underground to avoid the vaunted reaches of either The Organization or the FBI. Capture by one would result in immediate – and probably agonizing – death. Arrest by the other would mean a life of expensive legal defense and probable incarceration. Neither alternative appealed to either Knight or the special lady he was about to meet up with again. That's why he had headed farther south to Peru.

To get to Cusco, the route was complicated. It started out with a bus ride to Mariscal Sucre International Airport in Quito for an early-morning departure on flight LA1449 to Lima, Peru. The two-hour and twenty-minute flight was pleasant, with its crew announcing their aircraft that day was the first painted with the newly rebranded colors of LATAM Airlines, created through the merger of former Chilean airline LAN with Brazilian carrier TAM. Their breakfast celebration included a glass of champagne with the usual cereal.

In Lima, he collected his baggage, cleared immigration, and took a taxi to a nearby hotel where he told a clerk he wanted to sleep a few hours before continuing his journey to Santiago, Chile. Inside the hotel room – after completing his ritual inspections – Knight changed luggage identification tags, pulled a new passport from his traveler's vest, and then shaved his goatee to assume the clean-shaven appearance and Canadian citizenship of Hector Wilson. He replaced his current money belt with one that carried a large stack of Peruvian *nuevo sol*, the currency needed for the next stage of his escape.

Later, he showered, changed his clothes, and prepared to return to the airport. He asked the front desk clerk to arrange another taxi driver saying he didn't find the earlier one polite enough. Moments later, a new car and driver arrived. As Knight gathered up the two backpacks and moved towards the car, he made a point of telling the hotel clerk he felt much better after his nap. He emphasized how happy he was to be cleaned up and refreshed for his long trip to Santiago.

Check-in at Jorge Chavez International Airport for flight LA 2075 to Cusco was uneventful. The airline clerk barely glanced at his passport and appeared not to bother comparing the document photo with his face. Rather, she was engrossed in conversation with a nearby colleague about the previous night's enjoyable time with friends at a hot new downtown club.

A little more than an hour after take-off from Lima, the plane landed, and Knight was walking on the tarmac from the aircraft into Alejandro Velasco Astete International Airport in Cusco. There, he would meet Fidelia Morales. Her flight from Rio de Janeiro would arrive shortly, and this realization brightened his mood instantly. He felt a new spring in his step and a broad grin form on his face.

It had always been that way. He couldn't recall a single time a thought of meeting up with her soon didn't produce the same exhilaration. It was like an adrenalin rush, a natural high with no comparison. And he was never disappointed when they did eventually meet and touch each other again. Today would be the same, he was sure.

Indeed, they might have the threats of both The Organization and the FBI hanging over their heads, and their escape might not be permanent. However short their time together was to be, he knew he wanted to spend the rest of his life with the beautiful and passionate woman he loved more than anyone – or anything – in this world.

Eight

On a flight towards Cusco, Peru.
Friday April 29, 2016

It was a fact. Fidelia Morales had been Howard Knight's secret, ardent lover with their lives intertwined intimately for more than twenty years. It was also true she'd been a full-fledged member of The Organization until her retirement only a few months earlier. Her story was remarkable all the way back to her childhood.

Growing up in Puerto Rico was difficult. Her family lived in an undesirable quarter near the core of San Juan. They weren't as poor as some, but Fidelia remembered missing meals often because there was no food. And memories lingered of wearing the same ugly clothes for years, not months. But she had been lucky. Her brain worked well – apparently very well compared to others.

She attended schools operated by the Catholic church, and her parents made sure she attended every class, every day. Even if she was hungry, ill, or extremely uneasy with a particular teacher, her mother always preached the same refrain: "Get a good education to make something of your life. And to get a good education, you must never miss a class."

So Fidelia went to school every day, liked most of her teachers, and was considered the top student in her class. When she graduated from high school, her grades were not only the highest among her peers but also the best ever achieved at that school according to the religious sisters in charge.

Because she attended her classes so faithfully and accomplished such out-standing scholastic results, the priest in their parish had taken a personal interest in her future. It was he who brought her standardized test scores to the attention of a government official with relatives in New York. Those people knew someone at Columbia University. That academic contact, in turn, brought her situation to the attention of the alumni association. Impressed, the reviewing committee awarded a fully-funded scholarship to cover Fidelia's undergraduate studies and later her years at the law school.

There, she ranked among the top five graduates when she accepted her honors degree in law. Well before her graduation, one of the largest firms in New York proudly offered her an entry level job as a junior attorney.

Things started alright at the law firm. But after only a few months Fidelia realized she was continuously assigned mind-numbing documentation reviews that seemed to stretch to eternity. Male lawyers – even a couple from her graduating class – were assigned cases that required court visits and resulted in visibility that came with favorable large settlements or lawsuit awards. That pattern continued for a few years despite conversations with partners, the firm's human resources department, and colleagues. She even slept with two persistent senior partners, based on rumors she'd heard about the only way for a woman to move forward in that firm. It was all to no avail.

More frustrating than her monotonous workload was her inability to move forward financially. New York was an expensive place to live, and it was all she could do to keep up with her rent, living expenses, and minimum payments on credit cards. She tried to limit the use of those cards to clothing purchases but still needed hundreds per month to keep her wardrobe fresh and stylish.

Then, there were the wire transfers she sent back to her parents in San Juan. They'd never asked her to send money, but she felt an obligation to send a few hundred dollars each month despite the way they had treated her. She knew it made a huge difference for them.

It wasn't until she passed her five-year anniversary with the firm that her fortunes started to improve. Fidelia remembered the turning point as clearly as if it had happened yesterday. She had been commiserating with her friend, Julia, a junior attorney with another law firm in the same office tower, over a glass of wine in the bar downstairs.

"I know," Julia had gushed in sympathy. "It's impossible to survive in this city on the pittance these legal firms pay women. If I didn't have my date money, I'd never manage all the bills."

"Date money?" Fidelia had asked, arching her eyebrows.

"Yeah, date money. I go on dates once or twice a week with guys who pay me for my companionship. It gives me about a thousand dollars more a month. Maybe that's something you should consider. With your drop-dead good looks and incredible body, you could probably make a fortune!"

"Do they expect you to sleep with them?" Fidelia asked.

"Of course," Julia replied. "They're not just going to pay to play video games with us! But you know the law better than I do. They're only going to pay us if we put out, but we can avoid prostitution charges if we call it a date and do only a limited number from home. Nobody knows, except for the guys I meet and the woman in charge of our service. I'll bet even you didn't suspect that I earn date money."

"Isn't that dangerous?" Fidelia asked.

"Not really. This woman screens all my dates. They're usually stockbrokers, lawyers, or businessmen. Sometimes it's the same ones every week. Other times, they're from out-of-town. It's in my contact's best interests to charge as much as she can. She collects the date fee and keeps twenty percent for herself. I get the rest in cash. No receipts. No tax returns. You know, with boobs like yours, some guys might pay five hundred or more for a date!"

And that was the way it started. Fidelia had no apprehension about having sex with multiple partners. She knew it was considered a sin by the Church but imagined that God must be somewhat understanding on that one. For it was actually His loyal servants who first coached Fidelia to use her hands and mouth to most deftly create sexual ecstasy. Regularly, two celibate priests and a wayward nun had each paid her small sums to keep secret their regular clandestine sexual liaisons.

Julia was right about her body, too. While Fidelia had always considered herself pleasantly cute, it seemed some people found her ravishing. Julia's contact offered to pay her five hundred dollars per date the first time they met. Then, it turned out that American men, and a surprising number of women, were more than fascinated with her larger-than-normal breasts.

Those breasts, combined with her trim waistline, seemed to make her 'package' very marketable to both sexes. Within weeks, she was earning a thousand dollars a date and worked most Saturdays and Sundays. After about three months, Fidelia realized she was making more money 'dating' than she earned as a junior lawyer. Did it really make sense to continue her career in law?

She thought about it for a few weeks. Dating, she was making about the same amount on weekends as she made the rest of the week at the law firm after all the deductions. The only path she could see to earn considerably more money at the law firm was to get on track to become a partner. That was not a realistic prospect with the rubbish files they continued to shove her way.

Julia's contact was also starting to press her to accept more dates. She pointed out that Fidelia was missing out on thousands more every year by limiting her dating to weekends. She did the math and calculated that if dating opportunities were as frequent as her contact suggested, she'd make about double her current salary as a lawyer. She decided to retire from law.

After a year or so in the dating game, Fidelia realized most of her customers were regulars. She negotiated to reduce her contact's commission and gradually raised her fees for the get-togethers.

She learned that her dates were fascinated with more than her breasts. They also seemed to find her a very satisfying partner. Very early on, she decided that she liked her line of work and found the variety of partners and their different sexual appetites stimulating. She'd perform any act they requested and willingly met any demand they made in bed. But, she firmly insisted there would be no alcohol or drugs involved, ever. Her dates seemed to accept this, and only rarely a new client might briefly explore the potential to stray from her stringent rule.

Fidelia seldom gave any thought to the morality of what she was doing, never considered what impact her dating might have on the personal relationships of her dates. She never became emotionally attached. And, she didn't seek intimate relationships with anyone other than her clients.

She dated, saved astutely, invested her money in blue-chip corporations that paid dividends, and enjoyed her lot in life until she met Giancarlo Mareno in the mid-1990s. Her dating contact introduced him as the most powerful man of all in The Organization. She should take special care of him because he could bring her good fortune, the woman insisted. There were some very wealthy people in The Organization whose tentacles crept into every stratum of society in many countries around the world, she'd explained. And none was richer or more powerful than Giancarlo, she repeated for emphasis.

At the end of her first night with Mareno, he asked her to make herself available every Wednesday. He'd pay her three thousand dollars per week to be available to him exclusively that day every week. A few months later, immediately after they finished a long and exhaustive session in her bed, he asked her to work for him full-time.

"I'll pay you a million dollars a year to start," he said. "And five percent of all the income we generate."

The million-dollar salary caught her attention. "Working with you, how?" she remembered asking.

"I want you to find other women just like you – charming, exquisitely beautiful women who truly like to satisfy their customers. We control thousands of women around the world and have a constant supply of new ones," he continued. "I want you to select the best of those women, train them, and manage them to earn hundreds of millions of dollars for The Organization."

Fidelia quickly did the math. Five percent of one million was fifty thousand dollars. If The Organization generated one hundred million, that meant she would earn a cool half million in bonuses. And he'd suggested income in the hundreds of millions, hundreds with an 's'. She accepted his offer immediately.

It was a "no-brainer", as her lawyer colleagues used to say, and her rise within The Organization was nothing short of meteoric. Salary and bonuses stretched into the millions of dollars each year, and most found their way to numbered offshore bank accounts. Soon, she lived in the lap of luxury in downtown Manhattan or at five-star hotels around the globe.

Whenever she was in New York, Giancarlo Mareno required her to be available every Wednesday night, and she willingly complied. One week, he called with a special request. He couldn't come over that evening but would like her to do him a favor instead. He wanted to send over one of The Organization's bright young financial stars. And he'd like her to personally reward the fellow for his work acquiring a great new company. It was going to be a superb investment for The Organization, and she should make the night extra-special for Howard Knight.

To this day, she didn't fully understand why. But when Howard first walked through the door that evening, his tie a little askew, an embarrassed grin on his face, and a suit jacket slung over his shoulder, she felt something she had never experienced before – with any man or woman. It took her breath away with an excitement that caused her heart rate to surge. She suddenly felt light-headed and bizarrely carefree. It took only a few minutes to realize she had fallen blindly and desperately in love with him.

Maybe it was because Mareno had been her only sexual partner for months. It might have been Howard's shy and retiring manner. Perhaps it was no more than what they call chemistry, but it quickly became apparent that Howard Knight was equally smitten. Their lovemaking that night was tender, passionate, and constant until the first light of morning.

With dawn, their new dilemma gradually registered. First, Knight was married to the daughter of a Mareno associate in The Organization. Not only would a divorce be out of the question, but any discovery of marital infidelity would certainly draw the ire of that associate and could be fatal. From Fidelia's perspective, until that day, Mareno had made it very clear her million-dollar-per-year salary, plus bonuses, also required her to abandon the dating business and reserve herself for him exclusively.

Despite those precarious risks, over the past two decades Howard and Fidelia had seized every precious opportunity to meet in hideaways that allowed optimum discretion. Usually, it was during trips to Canada or the Caribbean where business activities provided cover. They were extremely cautious and constantly fretted about possible discovery. But their love was like an addiction. They could live without each other only for a few weeks at a time.

In recent years, Mareno gradually relaxed his grip. Content with the hundreds of millions in revenue produced by the dating businesses she managed around the world, he waived his requirement that she only be sexually active with him. He told her he couldn't "get it up as often," and asked her only to indulge him whenever he felt a need. She was sure that newer, younger playthings now attracted his attention, and she was alright with that.

Two months earlier everything in her life had changed, seemingly in the blink of an eye. She was now fighting not only to save the only love of her life; she was scrambling for her very survival. For years, they had known they would need to escape eventually. Neither could bear the thought of living out their final days apart.

Over time, they started planning in earnest. Fidelia's request to retire was another step in their scheme to eventually escape. Although she had made millions for The Organization over her years of service, the only part of their business she knew anything about was the dating operation. Mareno shared few details with her about other activities or associates in The Organization. He always said it was better that way.

When she broached retirement at the end of the year, he appeared to labor in silent thought for several minutes. It was extremely uncomfortable for her. Finally, he said, "Go ahead. You deserve it. Move to your home in West Palm. Spend the rest of this year getting Evelyn ready to fill your place. Then you can leave. By the way, I want you to know that Evelyn is one of your most fantastic finds."

After, he stood up slowly from a plush leather chair, stepped out from behind his imposing desk, slowly approached her, and then embraced her tenderly but firmly. She still remembered the overwhelming warmth she felt at that precise instant. But she also vividly recalled the chill she felt with what he said next.

"You're one of a kind, Fidelia. Evelyn may replace you in your job, but she will never replace you in my heart. But remember, as much as you mean to me, be warned. If you ever breathe a single word about The Organization to anyone. Media. Government. Law enforcement. A casual comment to someone in your bed. Anyone – your life will end immediately and without explanation."

Fidelia shuddered again as the tone of the intimidating threat caused a chill down her spine, just as it had that day. At that point, she knew it would probably be only a question of time. Someone would have a score, real or imagined, to settle with her. Eventually, some negative word attributed to her would reach the ears of Giancarlo Mareno, and he would give the order.

The position of Howard Knight in The Organization was even more precarious. He was privy to the financial dealings of every aspect of its operations. Probably only Mareno knew more. Retirement would never be an option. The laws of probability suggested that at some juncture Knight would make a mistake with an investment.

Unfortunately, The Organization isn't much different from America's private employers. Neither has a tolerance for errors nor patience with middle-aged executives. Lots of bright young stars were always waiting in the wings at The Organization. It would take only one mistake for Mareno to seize the excuse to eliminate Howard. He'd just replace him with a better educated, hungrier candidate. The main difference between The Organization and private corporations is the speed with which their replaced executives die. In the case of The Organization, elimination is usually immediate and total.

So, when Howard's debacle with Multima Corporation occurred, it took only a few seconds for them to agree to escape using their carefully developed plan.

While he used an elaborate plot to work his way out of the USA and gradually towards Peru, she tried to make sure no one made any dotted line connection from him to her. A few days after Howard's escape, she announced to her social media network that she was leaving for a trip to Spain. *Away for a few months to explore my roots*, the Facebook headline read. *Leaving my phone behind and will post only when there's free wi-fi*, she added with a meme picturing a happy woman swirling on a sandy beach.

She stayed in the area around Barcelona for the first week. She posted photos of the *Sagrada Família* cathedral on Facebook and some views overlooking the city from the site of the 1992 Olympic games. She checked her emails, voicemails, and social media every day that first week, just in case anyone was following her movements or trying to connect with her.

After her first week, she posted a new message. *Can't communicate for the next two months. In a convent. No technology.* That message might make it more difficult for someone trying to find her, but the limited number of Spanish monasteries would still let someone find her if they really wanted to.

The second week, she used cash to buy a train ticket to the Spanish town of Zaragoza. That journey took less than ninety minutes. On arrival, she found a taxi and asked to go the short distance to *Convento del Santo Sepulcro*. And, for the past six weeks, Fidelia had enjoyed a lovely stay with the holy sisters at the convent. In fact, she hadn't once ventured outside until just the day before.

She'd double-checked every detail she could imagine wanting to know about the convent before she left. There were no video monitors or closed-circuit TVs. The sisters all retired around eleven each evening and reappeared for breakfast about seven. Doors locked from the inside, with keys in plain view nearby. No one at the cloister had asked her for identification throughout her stay. They merely accepted that her name was Maria, although she had a passport to support that name if asked.

The night before leaving, Fidelia cut her long flowing black hair to a length barely covering her ears. Then, she checked to compare its length with the new passport photo. Satisfied the look was close enough, she dyed her hair blonde, then rearranged her money belts and passports. She slept precisely four hours. When she awoke, she dressed, inserted new contact lenses that changed her eye color from black to brilliant blue, and left her room.

Carrying only a backpack, she unlocked and slipped out the side entrance of the convent just after five o'clock in the morning, then walked for about thirty minutes. She ambled along a street by the Ebro River for a few minutes on her way to the rail station. At a point where street lighting was very sparse, and nearby buildings were mainly used as offices, she found a rock and smashed her cell phone to pieces. Then, she dropped what remained of it into the river, and watched the current carry the parts in different directions.

At the rail station, she bought a one-way ticket, then enjoyed her ride on the first departure that morning. An hour later she arrived in Madrid, hailed a taxi, and soon reached Adolfo Suarez Madrid–Barajas Airport.

To leave an unconnected trail, she bought a ticket to Paris Charles de Gaulle with an open return. Then, she paid using a prepaid credit card issued to the same name appearing on her forged passport. Travel to France was seamless as no immigration scrutiny was necessary, and security staff seemed to pay little notice as they stared blankly at an x-ray machine. Upon arrival in Paris, she immediately visited the Air France counters, used another card for a second ticket, and checked-in for a flight to Brazil.

Yesterday morning, she had arrived in Rio de Janeiro and bought one more air ticket for today's flight to Cusco with a stop in Lima. She used a courtesy vehicle to travel to a hotel near the airport where she paid cash for her room and slept for exactly eight hours.

Rested, Fidelia prepared for the flight to Cusco. She re-organized the money belts, currencies, and passports. The new version of her ID displayed the same short hair length but required dying again. This time, her hair became dark brown, closer to her natural color, and more appropriate to blend in with most women in the coming countries, she thought.

She left the hotel at four o'clock that morning refreshed, rested, and – most importantly of all – excited. She could feel the elation growing by the hour. Her flight left Rio on schedule and arrived in Lima as planned. Her connection to Avianca flight 837 was quick, and they left for Cusco only ten minutes behind schedule. Their pilot made his in-flight announcement about weather conditions, assuring them he would make up the time lost in Lima to arrive on schedule, just after noon local time. It seemed only moments later she heard the whine of the engine reduce and the plane tilt forward to begin the descent.

Glancing at her watch, Fidelia saw only minutes remained until she would see Howard again. These past weeks of diversion and circuitous escape were primarily to shield his abrupt disappearance. It had been long and inconvenient. But now, she felt like a giddy school girl. Her heart rate quickened. She felt flushed and knew her face projected a smile of anticipation that was hard to suppress. But she did her best to remain stoic.

She hadn't seen him for two months, and their last conversations had been unbearably brief. Anticipation was almost too much to contain. As she nervously checked her appearance in the mirror of her compact, she noticed the broad smile extending almost entirely across her face. It broadened even wider when she started to imagine the wonderful things they would do together in only a few more minutes.

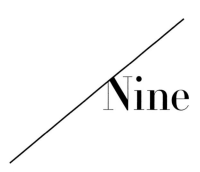

Nine

Multima Headquarters, Fort Myers, Florida.
Monday May 2, 2016

A meeting appeared necessary. John George Mortimer had resisted the overtures of the new chief executive officer of Venture Capital Inc. for as long as possible. VCI emailed a media release to Multima in mid-April announcing that Earnest Gottingham III had been named to the CEO role, replacing Howard Knight who had been missing since late February when he disappeared from the Multima Corporation directors meeting.

The media release gave no other details about Knight, his disappearance, or the reason VCI chose to announce the change at that time. Unusually short, it only declared that Gottingham had been appointed to the position with immediate effect. It also stated that he'd earned his MBA, with distinction, from the prestigious Wharton School of Business at the University of Pennsylvania.

He seemed to have quite limited management experience for a CEO. The only previous employment mentioned in the release was a stint as a financial analyst at one of Wall Street's largest investment banks.

Gottingham tried to call John George two or three days after Multima received the notice. Sally-Ann Bureau let him know her boss was at home for a few days recovering from radiation treatments related to his recent battle with breast cancer. Gottingham knew all about it and used all the right words to express his concern about Mortimer's condition. Smoothly, he assured Sally-Ann there was no urgency, but he'd appreciate her asking John George to call him when he returned to the office.

The next call came to Alberto Ferer from his counterpart at VCI, Sebastian Folino. Somewhat more assertive, Folino inquired about John George's health and was taken aback when Alberto let him know that Mortimer appeared to be recovering well from the radiation treatments. As the Multima executives had strategized, Ferer volunteered that there had been a few rough weeks in March while the CEO received daily doses of radiation. During that time, things virtually came to a halt in the executive suite, he explained. But things were nearly back to normal.

Folino reacted as John George predicted. He asked if there was any particular reason Mortimer had not returned Gottingham's courtesy call several weeks earlier.

"Probably just the heavy workload to oversee all the projects underway since the last meeting of the board of directors," Ferer suggested before he helpfully offered to provide any information he could. "I'll also ask Wilma Willingsworth to call you. Perhaps our CFO can assist with questions and help you become familiar with any financial issues. As our largest investor, it might also be helpful to talk with Edward Hadley, too. I think you'll enjoy meaningful dialogue with our vice president responsible for investor relations."

Over the next couple weeks, both had called exactly as scheduled and got the reaction expected. While Gottingham had been polite, inquisitive, and friendly, there was an edge of anticipation to his tone. Both reported to John George that he didn't make any direct requests about becoming a director of the company, but his unspoken intention seemed quite clear.

As they anticipated, Gottingham tried John George again directly. This time, Sally-Ann followed instructions and forwarded the call immediately to his private line.

"This is John George Mortimer speaking," he answered with a tone both light and welcoming. "How can I help you, Mr. Gottingham?"

"Oh, please call me Earnest. With our difference in ages and your accomplishments in the business world, it is I who should address you with the prefix, mister," Gottingham opened with discernible deference.

"Well, Earnest, I thank you for that, and I want to apologize I couldn't get back to you earlier. Those cursed radiation treatments were truly grueling. I'm sure glad to have it over. But enough about me. Congratulations to you on your appointment to CEO. Are you settling in comfortably there at VCI?" John George asked.

"So far, it's great. This is my first opportunity to serve in the role of CEO, so I have a rather steep learning curve. But everyone here is helping me along," Gottingham replied with a nervous laugh.

"I guess your people concluded that Howard Knight wouldn't be returning to the company?" Mortimer probed, rather abruptly.

"I suppose that's the case, John George. I truthfully don't know too much about the circumstances related to Mr. Knight's departure," Gottingham tactfully responded.

For a few moments, they exchanged several more questions and compliments as each tried to size up the other. John George learned his counterpart was well informed on many subjects, very articulate, and seemed genuinely interested in the goings on at Multima. In return, he volunteered information about recent acquisitions by the financial services and supermarkets divisions and the reorganization underway at Multima Logistics. That allowed him to reinforce the message that a taxing workload had prevented earlier interaction.

"So, I hope you'll understand how hard we've been working to optimize a good return on your investment," he concluded.

"Yes. There's no doubt you and your team have done yeoman's duty. The progress on those projects is very impressive. I'll certainly share this good news with my board here at VCI because they're very anxious to know how our investment is performing. We've had a real vacuum since my predecessor's departure," Gottingham commented hopefully.

"Well, I can certainly understand that," John George replied. "But you, or any of your board members, should feel welcome to contact our CFO Wilma Willingsworth at any time for information. We're very open that way."

There was a pause. Clearly, Gottingham was unhappy with what he just heard and needed to choose the words for his reply very carefully.

"I value that openness, John George, and both Wilma and Edward have been very helpful in our conversations. But I think my board is looking for more than just updates. We've had a seat at the decision-making table for the past decade, and I doubt they'll be satisfied with something less than a directorship going forward," Gottingham stated in a matter-of-fact tone.

"I understand," John George said. "However, the folks here – both board members and management – were a little uncomfortable with Howard's antics just before his departure. He generated a lot of ill-will. The feeling here is that maybe we should rethink both our board composition and its size. We're planning to start that discussion next month."

Gottingham hastily uttered several quick assurances and a profuse apology about Knight's aborted plot to oust John George from his position. He aggressively asserted that kind of action was neither driven nor condoned by VCI's board. And he spent several minutes trying to reassure John George of his admiration of Multima's accomplishments, his board's satisfaction with their return on investment, and the value they could bring to Multima's board of directors with their vantage point in the financial markets on top of their network of connections globally.

"We'll keep all of that in mind as we go through our strategic review of corporate governance. Indeed, we'd prefer our largest shareholder be a happy camper," Mortimer said with uncharacteristic informality, trying to lighten the tone. "But we think it's important to complete our process before I make any commitments to the VCI board."

Gottingham's tone cooled perceptibly. "In that case, John George, I think it better for us to meet in person as soon as possible. If there's a suggestion that VCI wouldn't be at the table for major corporate governance decisions, our board will probably want to undertake a strategic review of our billion-dollar investment. Do I make myself clear?" he asked with a tone just short of menacing. "I think it would be helpful for us to have some face to face discussions before either side makes a decision that might have far-reaching implications."

John George realized he had little choice. If VCI were to bail out of their preferred shares, the market could pummel the already depressed value of Multima's common shares. It could weaken the capital position to the point lenders, bondholders, and suppliers might all panic. He could lose the entire company.

Politely, amicably, and quickly, they agreed to meet in Fort Myers, at Multima's headquarters the week after Memorial Day. Management would set aside a full day to help him better understand the corporation and give them both an opportunity to get to know each other better, John George proclaimed.

However, John George remained undaunted. Although he had consented to a meeting, he still didn't intend to cede his position. No representative of VCI would be welcome as a member of the Multima board any longer. He had only a few weeks to devise a strategy to make that happen without further weakening his corporation.

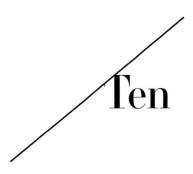

Ten

Ste-Foy, Quebec.
Monday May 2, 2016

When Roland LaMontagne heard the loud knock on his front door, he was somewhat surprised but unconcerned. It wasn't at all unusual for a Catholic priest to receive unexpected visitors. Parishioners often stopped by for a visit. Sometimes they came to chat, occasionally to bring a home-cooked dish, and other times to discuss some issue that just couldn't wait. He had no preconceptions and was ready for almost any eventuality.

However, when he opened the door and realized his visitors were grim-faced police officers, Roland immediately sensed a problem.

"Bonjour!" he greeted them. "How can I help you?"

There was a hesitant pause before the male officer said, "I'm terribly sorry, Father. We must bring you some very difficult news. May we step inside?"

"Of course, please come in," Roland said. "Please forgive my lack of courtesy. Have a seat here in the living room."

"Something has happened to your parents," the woman officer continued once they settled. "There's no easy way to deliver such terrible news, so I prefer to be direct. Both your mother and father have died."

She paused as she looked compassionately into his eyes. Roland heard the words as though they were coming from afar, jarring his brain with a message that what he was hearing must be some horrible mistake.

"What happened?" he managed to blurt out.

"It appears they were killed," the male officer said with unusual candor. "This morning, the woman who cleans their country chalet near Stoneham unlocked the door and found your parents lying on the floor. There were no signs of life."

Roland's mind recoiled, processing information at a crawl, seemingly unable or unwilling to accept it. Utterly bewildered, he looked from one officer to the other.

"I'm so sorry we have to tell you this. Are you alright?" the woman asked. "As a man of the cloth you may be more accustomed to dealing with shocking news than some, but it must be hard regardless. Can I get you some water? Or something stronger to drink?"

Roland declined with a curt shake of his head. "No. I just want to see them," he replied. "I must try to reconcile what has happened."

The senior officer shook his head and said that wasn't a good idea. There was an awkward pause as Roland looked expectantly at the woman first, then again at her partner. The two officers exchanged uncomfortable glances before the male continued.

"You understand that we usually don't share details with surviving family members. But we'll make an exception this time because you're a member of the clergy. They were killed, and the murders were very gruesome. Forensic investigators are trying to determine precisely what took place, but we can tell you this: your mother was shot directly in her heart, at close range. She probably died instantly with little pain," he explained.

"With your father, I'm afraid it was a different matter. It looks like the perpetrator or perpetrators beat him severely before they pulled the trigger. His body is in terrible shape. He probably suffered and may have already died before they shot him in the head. Their murders appear targeted. It's better not to see the bodies," the officer said with a deep sigh of resignation.

"I'm sorry for your loss, and so sorry you have to deal with this. The cleaning lady identified both victims for us. We can probably use dental records to corroborate that identification and save you added grief," the woman offered.

"No, I must see them," Roland insisted firmly.

After a few more moments of polite discussion, with the priest still in shock, they agreed to take him to the morgue. It took only a few minutes and there was no conversation in the police car. The male focused entirely on driving while the female officer scanned the onboard computer with intense concentration.

Roland's experience at the morgue was gut-wrenching. The sight of his father's mutilated body caused him to gag, then vomit on the floor before he could get to a bathroom. He threw-up again as soon as he reached a toilet and his mind went numb as the horror registered.

They gave him time to pray over the bodies and more time to recover in a nearby office, then offered to drive him home. They'd need a formal statement sometime later, they told him. Instead, he politely asked if they would take him to the chalet. Through clenched teeth, he told them he needed to see the scene of his parents' murder.

Initially, they resisted. Police procedures didn't permit visits to a crime scene, particularly while investigators were still working. However, after a few moments of discussion and pointed glances exchanged between the officers, they conceded a man of the cloth could be trusted and probably knew best how to achieve personal closure.

They let him view the main room from an already open doorway. The blood-drenched carpet, furniture in disarray, and scattered bits of what was probably his father's brain on the floor all suggested that his death had been terrible. He prayed they had the decency to take his mother's life first, rather than subject her to the cruelty of watching her husband die in such a miserable way.

After a few minutes, he was ready to leave and asked the police officers if they might just stop at the home of the cleaning lady. She would probably appreciate some comforting words, he urged. Again, after a brief discussion about procedure, they concluded a priest would surely never try to influence a potential witness.

While Roland shared some comforting words with the middle-aged woman, the police officers both remained close enough to hear every word of their conversation. They also bowed their heads in respect as he prayed for the woman, asking God to give her strength to cope with such a horrible event.

Finally, the police officers drove Roland back home, went inside with him, looked around to be sure everything appeared in order, then said their goodbyes. Both shook his hand firmly and once more voiced condolences. Their usually hardened eyes seemed misty, he noticed.

When he noticed it was dark outside, Roland glanced at his watch and realized that he'd been sitting there alone for several hours. His ritual had started with a prayer, the only coping mechanism he knew. Afterward, he wept. Then, he began to think about his last conversation with his father weeks earlier. There could be no other explanation for the brutal murder of his parents. Those unsavory characters his father got involved with through his gambling habit had to be responsible. Nothing else made sense.

He made a mental note to share that information with the detectives when they took his statement. He'd need to think carefully about his father's peculiar confession, though. He wasn't entirely sure how he could avoid implicating his father as a possible accessory to a separate murder.

Then, his father's final admonishment came to mind. "Promise me you won't try to dig deeper into this mystery. It would only put you and your mother at risk. That's the last thing I want to happen. Promise me," he had begged.

It was too late for any concern about his mother's well-being. And even though a promise was sacred, this was one he simply couldn't honor. The animals who committed such a heinous crime had to be brought to justice, but he doubted he could leave it to the police alone.

They were already making a connection to organized crime. Too often, he knew, targeted murders by organized crime remained unsolved because of the extraordinary number of dead-ends police usually encountered. Just recently, Roland read an investigative article in the *Journal de Québec* about their challenges.

Typically, law enforcement officials found themselves dealing with hardened, smart, experienced, and successful criminals. Very few of those cases were ever solved. Consequently, such a probable end to their investigations provided little incentive for police to deploy precious resources to pursue murders with bewilderingly challenging situations. It became a vicious and unsatisfying circle for them.

They'd probably need his help with this one. He knew he wouldn't have any peace of mind until they solved the mystery and brought those vicious thugs to justice. But he also worried that it might be hard to keep secret the damning knowledge about his father's involvement in Madame Marcotte's death. He needed to get involved in the investigation, personally and directly.

It dawned on him where he should start. He'd get a key to his father's office from his parents' home and search for any files about Louise Marcotte. There, he might find a path to the guilty. He might also find out why his father so strongly believed that giant American conglomerate, Multima, was also entangled.

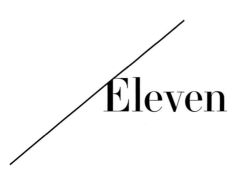

Eleven

Atlanta, Georgia.
Monday May 23, 2016

Suzanne Simpson's deep disappointment about the canceled board of directors meeting in March was offset partially in May. Although she still hadn't talked with John George Mortimer about her lingering concerns related to her mother, she understood the battle he was waging with cancer and recognized malignant cells were no longer his challenge. Rather, it was the vile side-effects of the grueling treatments designed to prevent their return.

His assistant, Sally-Ann Bureau, provided periodic updates, and her reports usually weren't positive. So, Suzanne had followed her intuition to respect John George Mortimer's privacy and let him deal with his health first. Her own need for closure on the mysteries surrounding her mother could wait a little longer.

It was chief legal officer Alberto Ferer who thought a video link solution might enhance communication among management and the board of directors as they coped with their CEO's frequent absences. "Combine the monthly management briefings with the board of director meetings using video," he suggested to John George. "It might temporarily help us manage as you return to work."

Mortimer accepted the suggestion and had Sally-Ann arrange a sophisticated and secure connection between Multima headquarters, each of the Multima operating companies' offices, and the individual locations of each director. It had taken more than a half-day to organize, but the outcome had been superb.

John George Mortimer addressed the entire group first. In a voice that lacked some of its natural warmth and quiet confidence, he thanked them for their patience.

"I know the past few weeks have been difficult – probably more challenging for you in many ways than for me. It's certainly been a struggle to juggle all the competing priorities while contending with the dreadful side effects of the treatments, and for that I'm truly sorry," Mortimer started.

Suzanne guessed that everyone else was scrutinizing his wan appearance as intently as she. It was unsettling to see his bald head. John George had finally shaved it completely rather than display the patchy casualty of chemotherapy that caused some hair to fall out while other strands survived. His skin color looked gray, a shocking contrast with his usual tanned, healthy-looking tones. Everyone could see he was deliberately trying to look strong and confident, his back perfectly straight and head held high. She noticed only a slight tremor of his hand as he gestured for emphasis.

"Thank you all for your patience, and thank you for keeping the company on track in my absence. Now, here's some good news. My treatments are done. The nausea is over. I'm starting to sleep better. And there's no reason for any of you to be concerned. I'm honestly starting to feel like a real person again," he said with his trademark grin. "Every day is an improvement over the one before. My strength and concentration are improving too. I'll even be back to those cursed workouts soon!

"Starting next week, decision-making will get back on track, and well before you want it, I'll be haunting you with far too many questions or off-the-wall ideas," he added with a short laugh.

With that two-minute summary, discussion about his health ended, and he promptly invited James Fitzgerald to update them on developments at Multima Financial Services.

Fitzgerald devoted about five minutes to an overview of the business unit's financial performance for the previous month and year-to-date. Results were all as budgeted and predicted. There were no surprises to report. He then moved quickly to introductions of his team assembled in Hoffman Estates. There were two he highlighted because they were new to their roles. First, he presented Norman Whiteside, leader of the newly acquired mortgage business, who would assume that same role for Multima. He took a few moments to share Norman's resumé highlights for the board.

He repeated the process for Natalia Tenaz, recently promoted from a research position in their marketing department. He explained that Natalia was the mortgage program coordinator between Multima Financial Services and the Supermarkets group – a role they all considered crucial to the successful launch of the new mortgage business. Norman and Natalia would use the rest of the allotted time to outline progress on the project, he explained.

Whiteside started off. Although they'd spoken several times by telephone in the preceding few weeks, Suzanne was seeing him for the first time. He looked much like she had pictured. Great hair and teeth. A winning smile. Definitely fit. Stylist-groomed, neatly combed, blondish hair. He appeared to be at least three inches taller than Fitzgerald who was already taller than most. Both dwarfed petite Natalia seated between them.

Whiteside's presentation was well beyond solid. His performance no doubt reinforced to the board members their wisdom in recommending Multima acquire Whiteside's company before moving forward with the home mortgage project. He was articulate and explained business strategies and expectations with confidence. His initial introduction had impressed, and the smiles of the directors suggested there would be few queries for him in the Q & A session to follow.

He passed the baton to Natalia Tenaz. To Suzanne, she appeared to be a young woman of Latina heritage. Charming smile. Dressed appropriately in a well-cut business suit. Very little makeup but a great complexion. Bright eyes that sparkled when she spoke, and when she started out it was apparent she was nervous.

Suzanne guessed she'd never made this kind of presentation before – and almost certainly would not have addressed such a formidable group of executives. But her confidence appeared to grow as she revealed the strategies developed with Suzanne's team.

Her delivery pace was quick, her sentences short, and her PowerPoint graphics useful. From Suzanne's perspective, Natalia had pushed all the right buttons. First, she complimented the Supermarkets team for their knowledge and expertise, then outlined the comprehensive research both teams had conducted with focus groups and in-store questionnaires. After, she summarized their plans to launch the home mortgage business in just a few sentences.

"Multima One credit cardholders will be our customer base. With them, we'll have the best risk profile as Norman outlined already. Right after the Labor Day weekend, we'll launch an aggressive program to sign more cardholders in Multima stores. We'll offer a 50,000-point bonus to customers who sign up and qualify for a credit card. That's a powerful incentive, equal to about five hundred dollars in benefits," she said as the next PowerPoint slide appeared.

"Between September and December, our goal is to increase penetration among Multima shoppers from the current level of about thirty percent to forty percent. That's ambitious, but we'll support the efforts using third-party salespeople in every store, a massive advertising campaign, a much-expanded social media budget, and colorful in-store banners. We expect to achieve the target before Christmas.

"In January, we'll start to promote the mortgages directly to cardholders. First, we'll target those refinancing. We'll talk about the benefits of reducing overall borrowing costs by switching to our program that processes mortgage payments weekly rather than monthly. Again, we'll offer bonus points to encourage customers to switch to us. And, we'll continue that campaign through the end of March.

"Studies indicate people planning to transfer or relocate often try to time their home purchases around the end of the school year. So, we'll step up the campaign to target customers thinking about making those types of moves in the second quarter. By July, the start of our fiscal year, Multima home mortgages will be firing on all cylinders and achieving the profits projected by Norman and the team," she concluded breathlessly.

For the next thirty minutes, John George Mortimer and a few of the directors posed clarifying questions. As Suzanne expected, none were directed at Norman Whiteside. His message required no further clarification. Questions to Natalia were soft ones, mainly related to the methodologies used in the research, types of media planned, and legal obligations of the third-party sales organization.

Then, it was Douglas Whitfield's turn to talk about his new job at Multima Solutions, the new name chosen for the rebranding of Multima Logistics. And he turned on his charm from the opening comments. Using some self-deprecating humor, he acknowledged that his presentation would not be nearly as glowing and confident. The results wouldn't be nearly so impressive. In fact, as he listened to the previous presentation, he said he felt a little longing to be back in his former role.

Clever, Suzanne thought. Lower expectations, pay a genuine compliment, and subtly remind the audience where all the positive developments they just heard originated. She was sure every director would remember Whitfield's brilliant delivery of the concept his team developed to diversify into the home mortgage business. They would instantly recall that it may well have been Whitfield himself delivering those glowing forecasts had they not approved Mortimer's decision to move him over to Multima Solutions, replacing Wendal Randall.

Whitfield didn't squander the goodwill he generated. Factually and objectively, he reported on the successful transfer of people from Solutions to Supermarkets, also approved at that fateful March meeting of the board. The process had gone remarkably well, Suzanne was obliged to concede. There was little doubt: Whitfield's considerable leadership skills contributed greatly to the smoothness of the transition.

Surprisingly, he also reported one notable business success and managed to compliment the other operating divisions again as he did so.

"Let me update you on the new software," he started. "Throughout March, our security team at Multima Solutions did everything possible to find a weakness in the code. Those brilliant engineers and would-be-hackers tried everything they could think of to penetrate the firewall built by the developers over at Supermarkets. In the end, they grudgingly had to admit they might have met their match and told me we might want to steal some of those programmers from Supermarkets if the opportunity ever came up!"

He paused to let the meeting participants laugh for a moment and enjoy his light-hearted compliment. Blatant flattery notwithstanding, Suzanne found herself smiling broadly with the others.

"Once our engineers assured me the new software was bulletproof, I made a call to an old college buddy. Some of you may know James Fitzgerald's son, Alistair, and I were roommates at Wharton. Alistair now works with Bank of The Americas in New York. In fact, he's one of their most influential vice-presidents with responsibility for technology applications.

"Last Thursday he agreed to undertake a sixty-day assessment on their mainframe servers. If the software performs as well as we claim, he's prepared to buy. He's also ready to work with our marketing team on a joint advertising campaign to tout the security advantages of dealing with Bank of The Americas and featuring our software technology."

Suzanne watched Whitfield pause to let the powerful impact of that statement register with the audience. Bank of The Americas was the second largest bank in the world, with operations in every country where they were legally entitled to do business – more than two hundred in all. Signing a client of that caliber would immediately establish the credibility of the Solutions software product. Having Bank of The Americas' endorsement could conceivably drive demand almost beyond imagination.

Within only a few seconds, Whitfield had masterfully captured the attention of every participant. He knew his mission was accomplished and finished his presentation expressing hope he might have more good news to report next month.

As expected, the board of directors deluged him with questions. The tech-savvy executives wanted to learn more about the testing his engineers had undertaken. The more profit-oriented wanted an idea of income and expense projections. Multima's CFO wanted to know where this development fit in the just-submitted budget forecast for the coming year.

Virtually every director had some question or comment. While the business media may have dubbed Wendal Randall "the Steve Jobs of his era", with just one presentation Whitfield had raised expectations so high that no one in the room gave Randall a second thought.

An interesting strategy, Suzanne thought. In an era when executives usually worked hard to ratchet down expectations, why would Whitfield want to raise them? And not only raise them but boost them to such a high level, at such an early stage of their negotiations? Within seconds, she thought of a half-dozen factors that could easily derail such a potential deal.

Apparently, John George Mortimer had the same concerns. Silent while Whitfield responded to all the questions, he quietly thanked Whitfield for a fine presentation and all the information he shared. He thanked Douglas for noting the excellent contributions of Supermarkets' software developers and wryly praised James Fitzgerald for instilling such good judgment in his son.

Then, he cautioned the participants on the call to treat Douglas' information with complete confidentiality. From his experience, many factors could cause delays or become impediments to a deal. From a forecasting perspective, he thought Wilma Willingsworth and her team should probably not include any potential revenue from Bank of The Americas in the coming fiscal year budgets. It would be far better to surprise the market with an unexpected windfall than report a disappointment.

Suzanne watched heads nodding on her screen. The directors seemingly realized the precarious risks of the deal and quickly sobered to those realities.

Mortimer shifted the focus to Supermarkets and asked Suzanne to bring them up to date. She followed a delivery formula that she'd always found both comfortable and prudent: deliver any bad news first.

"Our April operating results were in line with the budget on the bottom-line, but sales revenues were softer than forecast by five percent overall," she began.

"We achieved targeted profits only because we took in the amount we needed from loss provision reserves. We're still healthy on the loss provision line, and we were comfortable reducing those reserves because theft and pilferage dropped this quarter. I'll be happy to deal with any questions or concerns you may have, but want you to be aware we are reserving at about double the industry standard, with lower actual shrinkage than our competitors."

She paused and watched the monitor to detect any lingering concerns she might need to dispel during her comments or the question-and-answer period. Only Mortimer seemed to be doing the mental math to verify her contention.

"Sales results are on target everywhere but South Florida. You'll recall we have an aggressive renovation program underway. It started in May. We're remodeling thirty-five stores to reflect our new focus on eating healthy. While we do most of the work at night, there are still disruptions for our customers, and the stores aren't as clean and neat as we'd like," she admitted with a grimace.

"That's caused both retail traffic and sales to drop off almost ten percent in some of the Miami area stores. We have intense competition there, and customer loyalty during inconveniences like renovations evaporates quickly. We're bracing for more softness with top-line revenue next month but are planning some flash sales to offset some of the challenges. Fortunately, we expect the retrofits to be complete in most stores by the end of June and should be back on track to start the new fiscal year," she added with a tone of optimism.

"In case there are any concerns about our year-end results," she quickly resumed, anticipating the subject she expected each director would consider next. "Our year-to-date profit results are still ahead of forecast by about two percent. Should the sales performance be weaker than planned in June, Wilma and I have already agreed that we'll bring in the amount we need from vendor rebate reserves. Our year-end results are safe, and we're very excited about the coming fiscal period."

Suzanne said that with her most disarming smile and positive tone, and then watched as faces on the screen relaxed with her assurances. She took about three minutes longer to remind the audience about their major strategic initiatives already underway – the acquisition of discount competitor Price Deelite, reformatting existing Multima Supermarkets to focus on more healthy food choices, and the major relocation of technology resources from Miami to Atlanta.

Then, she turned the presentation over to her team as she usually did. Each of the presenters performed admirably, as expected. And the board of directors seemed unusually impressed with their achievements since February. Instead of asking questions at the end, there was a stream of praise and compliments for her folks. It almost became a little uncomfortable, but Suzanne knew her team would revel in the congratulations for jobs extremely well done.

When the Supermarkets presentation was complete, and feedback appeared to be finished, John George Mortimer made only a few brief comments before he closed the management reporting stage of the meeting.

"It's gratifying to see all of our business units working well together. Your accomplishments over these months have been nothing short of extraordinary. It makes me wonder if I shouldn't just stay out of your way more often!" he said with a quick laugh. Apparently satisfied with the levity he'd injected, he went on.

"I need to caution everybody about two possible clouds on the horizon. First, let's not forget that stern warning the economist Warren Wrigletts from Columbia University gave us at the offsite meeting last year. A severe recession may be coming soon. We don't see it so far, but we seldom have adequate warning before a downturn starts. Usually, we're only aware it's taking place when we start to feel some pain. Indeed, Suzanne's challenge with sales in South Florida may be entirely related to those renovations. On the other hand, it may be an early warning indicator. Let's stay close to it," he said, punctuating each of the last words with a finger-tap on the table.

"My last caution relates to the unusual amount of time I've had to watch television while coping with these damned cancer treatments. To me, this year's presidential election seems weird. I can't think of a better word to describe it than 'weird.' There are probably a lot of people out there who are uncomfortable with both the election tone and possible direction. I've never seen anything like it in my entire career.

"Let's all be very careful. I've learned that when we encounter some phenomenon for the first time, it can be very disruptive. People may not behave as we expect. Rules may change quickly. And we all need to be alert to even the most minute shift in economic direction to be sure we're reacting appropriately. Let's not be alarmed, but let's all be wary."

On that sobering note, John George ended the meeting with a suggestion they all plan to meet by video connection again in June. Sally-Ann would reconfirm the dates.

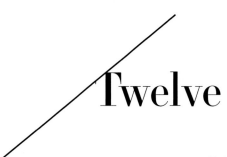

Twelve

Driving from Fort Myers to Miami, Florida.
Saturday May 28, 2016

Janet Weissel couldn't help but think about it as she drove across Florida's *Alligator Alley* early that Saturday morning. It was frigging unbelievable. The whole thing. First, Howard Knight's mysterious disappearance from the board of directors' meeting more than three months earlier without a word to anyone. Then, when the meeting was almost finished, she learned the FBI had arrested Wendal Randall. On top of that, Mortimer announced he had fired Wendal. Douglas Whitfield would replace him as president of Multima Logistics effective immediately. It was all frigging incredible.

Only because of extraordinary good luck, she overheard gossip about all those developments from a bathroom stall just before the tumultuous meeting ended. She'd had only enough time to finish up, then dash from the bathroom down a corridor where she managed to intentionally bump into Whitfield as he was leaving a conference room with Suzanne Simpson.

The bump was surprisingly graceful considering her lack of preparation, but she still made it appear to be an accident. And it undoubtedly produced the desired result. She distinctly caught Whitfield's eyes discreetly take in her carefully arranged cleavage as soon as they both regained balance and exchanged hurried apologies. With Suzanne Simpson right beside him, she'd only been able to say sorry, quickly introduce herself, and give him her million-dollar smile.

Apparently, that was enough. When Ms. Weissel learned he'd be working at the Multima Logistics offices in Miami, she sent an email letting him know that it might be fun to meet up sometime. Sure enough, a few days later he replied. If ever she was in Miami, she should call. He included a private cell phone number at the bottom of his message.

When she googled his name, she was surprised at how much personal information she found about Douglas Whitfield. She learned he was born in Barbados to a black mother and an unnamed white father reputed to be a pillar of the business community somewhere in New York. Later, she came across published stories in a small weekly newspaper about a decision to send Whitfield to an exclusive private school in Canada from the age of six.

Pickering College, a sedate boarding school in Ontario for a few of the globe's very elite, accepted a significant number of foreign students each year. The institution had also been extremely diligent about updating the records of its well-off pupils.

Using only basic hacking skills, Janet tracked many of Douglas' experiences living and learning in Newmarket, a small town north of Toronto. The private school's records especially drew attention to his numerous awards and achievements. Successes ranged from being captain of the soccer and field hockey teams to citations for excellent grades, debating, entrepreneurship, and community service.

She learned his twelve years in residence there prepared him to later graduate from the prestigious Ivey Business School at the University of Western Ontario before he headed south to Wharton Business School in Pennsylvania for his MBA. She was amazed to discover his close friend – at both universities – was none other than the son of James Fitzgerald of Multima Financial Services.

She read that Douglas interned with that division for three summers before he accepted a job right out of university as an assistant vice-president in the credit card group. After a few research sessions, she concluded this chance corridor meeting might become most opportune.

Of course, she strategically waited a week and a bit before she made the two-hour drive to Miami on a Friday evening. Upon arrival, she called the private number and he responded almost immediately. Sure, he'd love to meet up with her. Did she have plans for dinner?

Dinner was even more fabulous than she had imagined. Douglas was the best-looking guy ever. Tall, brown-skinned, and muscular, he stood apart from everyone in the swank restaurant. His smile lit up the entire room. And he was far more charming than Janet dreamed. They ate, talked, and drank expensive wine for more than three hours. They were the last patrons to leave, and she couldn't have answered faster when he invited her back to his room at the Hyatt Hotel downtown.

It was a spectacular view from his suite. His home away from home until he found an apartment, he told her. He'd find a place near the office soon. His wife and kids wouldn't be moving, he recounted wistfully as he poured more drinks.

Then, they silently gazed out their window at millions of sparkling lights on the Miami skyline. Thankfully, thoughts of family and home didn't last very long. Within mere minutes she had successfully distracted him from those potentially precarious topics to refocus on her mission. It had been surprisingly easy.

Their first sexual encounter had been unrestrained, passionate, and incredibly long. Several times, he brought her to over-the-top orgasms and seemed to have an almost limitless appetite for her body. Both were surprisingly rare occurrences. During her many past sexual adventures, her partners usually showed limited affection, with little time to waste. They'd do their thing, and, once satisfied, most times would just leave with scant concern for her needs. She immediately decided to try to hold onto this one.

Their first night had gone almost flawlessly. Except for that incident with the phone. That could have been a total disaster, but she managed to contain it.

At some point near morning, Douglas had left the bed and headed towards the bathroom. More observant than most, he noticed her illuminated cell phone partially concealed behind a towel on the bureau at the foot of the king-size bed. Instantly, he realized it was in video mode, capturing images reflected from the large mirror above the bureau. He didn't say a word.

She watched him casually pick up her phone and take it with him to the bathroom. Seconds later, she heard a loud crash and knew he had just smashed it to pieces. Without hesitation, she moved to damage control.

Forcing herself to sob loudly and convincingly, she ran to the bathroom and immediately pleaded for forgiveness. With fervor, she cried that she'd never intended to do anything with the pictures and begged him to let her explain. He appeared furious, but apparently was also still thinking more with his penis than his brain, so he let her go on.

In just two or three minutes, she tearfully explained her awful past. Why it had been necessary for her to accept paid 'dates' to work her way through college. How the fifty thousand per year tuition of Columbia University almost bankrupted her poor parents, prompting them to throw her out of their home to fend for herself.

She left out most of the salacious parts but let him know she only started filming sex acts for her protection, and reminded him there were some really weird people out there. Without divulging anything close to all the details, she pointed out that one even tried to choke her to death as he climaxed.

Then, she delicately brought him around again, reassuring him that she was ashamed of that part of her life and swearing she didn't do things like that anymore. She'd even played her ace, tearfully expressing her expectation that he would probably not want anything further to do with her, and how sad that made her feel. She had even managed to sob somewhat genuine tears for a minute or two. As daylight came up, they were drinking Bloody Marys from the minibar and had enjoyed two more sensational lovemaking sessions before breakfast.

Since that life-altering night, she'd been back to Miami five times. Each trip included experiences that seemed other-worldly from a sexual perspective. She found herself really liking this guy and becoming more sentimental than she would have expected. That was the reason for her tinge of unhappiness on this drive to Miami.

There was sadness and also some concern. Actually, there was a lot of concern. Howard Knight was still missing and rumors coming from New York were scary. His secretary had called four times to see if she had heard anything from Knight. There were whispered suggestions he'd run away somewhere. Others at Venture Capital Inc. thought he might have committed suicide, and his body would soon surface. Others maintained he might secretly be in the custody of the FBI like Wendal Randall. Regardless, her usual contact with The Organization wasn't around to give her advice.

A few weeks earlier, when her boss Edward Hadley invited her to his office, and a woman from human resources joined them, her political antennae instantly sensed danger. She found their message curious. They were reorganizing Multima's corporate and investor relations department. Her position had been eliminated in the new structure. But the management team had such high regard for her skills and knowledge they wanted to find a new role for her in the corporation.

She would need to relocate. The position available for her skillset was in Chicago, in the marketing department at Multima Financial Services. She'd work in marketing research and development, reporting to Natalia Tenaz. Her salary in the new position would be ten thousand dollars more per year, the company would help with relocation, and they'd like her to start June 1st should she choose to accept the role.

There was no opportunity to consult with Knight, and their message seemed clear. Should she not take the offered position, there was no job for her at headquarters. With feigned enthusiasm, she immediately welcomed the opportunity, thanked them for their confidence, and promised to be in Chicago by the required date.

Douglas had taken the news very positively, more positively than she expected. He recommended a nice area to find an apartment in her price range and promised to give her the lowdown on her new office and the people where he used to work. He cheerfully assured her this could all work out well. His wife had finally agreed to visitation with his children every second weekend, so he'd be in Chicago to visit his kids and could spend time with them during the days, then she could join him at his hotel for nights of pleasure.

He even offered to fly her to Chicago on the company jet. He just couldn't pick her up in Fort Myers because too many people at Page Field would recognize the plane and could make the connection. Of course, they must not let news of their secret relationship get back to the corporation.

For all these reasons, she was driving towards Miami. There, she'd meet him at a car delivery service depot that would arrange to transport her car to Chicago, stuffed with all her belongings except an overnight bag. Monday morning, they'd deliver it to her new office at Multima Financial Services.

Douglas promised to meet her at the transport depot. Together, they'd drive to the private jet section of Miami International Airport. From there, she intended to make their flight to Chicago one that Douglas Whitfield would never forget.

Janet distinctly recalled a casual observation their first night in bed in Miami. He'd never joined the 'mile high club', he said. Despite her worldliness, she'd never heard that expression before. After she googled what the term meant, she decided that great sex at thirty thousand feet might be a magnet strong enough to hold his attention through this unpleasant transition. Now, she was anxiously looking forward to giving him the most sensual experience of his life, doggedly determined their relationship would stay on course despite this hurdle.

Thirteen

When Earnest Gottingham III and Sebastian Folino of Venture Capital Inc. arrived for their scheduled meeting, John George Mortimer was running longer than expected on a video call with the new Prime Minister of Canada. Fortunately, Multima's team had foreseen this possibility. The young and charismatic politician had already established a deserved reputation for pushing the envelope of expectations in his discussions with executives.

CFO Wilma Willingsworth and Sally-Ann Bureau met their visitors at reception, welcomed them, and profusely apologized for Mortimer's delay as they walked towards the huge conference room next to John George's sprawling office. The setting was far too large for a small gathering, but it would do while the video call wound down, and Sally-Ann fetched coffee for the guests.

Their wait was short. John George extricated himself from the call at the first opportunity. Then, he made a point of checking his reflection in an office mirror, straightening a tie he wore that day as a measure of professional courtesy. He wasn't pleased with the image reflected. During the chemo treatments, he'd lost about fifteen pounds from an already lean frame, and none had returned. His clothes were fitting loosely, and that sagging skin also looked too big for the rest of his body.

He noticed his skin tone was still a little colorless. His eyes appeared dull and more gray than brown. The dimples in his cheeks cut deeper and sagged as he smiled rather than perk up as they did before. Encouragingly, there were tiny traces of hairs starting to sprout from his bald crown. Regardless, it was what it was. This appearance would be his new normal for a few weeks at least.

"Good morning, gentlemen," he gushed as he rushed into the large conference room with his widest smile and the most enthusiasm he could muster. "Welcome to Multima. It's great to have you both here. Please accept my apologies for the delay. Let's move to my office where we'll be more comfortable."

With exaggerated friendliness in their handshakes, broad smiles, and body language that projected welcome and camaraderie, the meeting participants bantered informally as they made their way next door and settled into a fashionably designed cluster of leather chairs and sofas. It was there Sally-Ann delivered coffee, prepared just the way each had requested.

"I'm sure Wilma explained my delay, but I had a Prime Minister twisting my arm for some investment. He asked us to build a new distribution center somewhere in Canada. To encourage artificial intelligence capabilities up there, they'd help us with costs should we buy Canadian robotics. Then, he sweetened the offer if we also installed solar panels on the roof to make it independent of the power grid. That fellow's really into technology!"

"No worries, at all," Gottingham assured him. "Your team made us feel right at home, and we understand one can't rush a head of state on a mission. Plus, there's not much we like better than hearing the term government subsidy."

"Yes," Mortimer responded, matching Gottingham's hearty guffaw. "That's true; those government incentives usually enhance the bottom-line nicely. His timing may be right, too. We'll see. There's a reasonable argument for re-investing our Canadian profits there rather than repatriating them and paying corporate tax here. Our team at Supermarkets will look at it for sure. But let's talk about your visit," Mortimer quickly shifted. "Here's what we've planned if you agree.

"Both Wilma and Edward Hadley, our corporate and investor relations vice president, will spend the next few hours with you. They've prepared a presentation to guide you through our recent performance, the challenges we face, and our strategic plans. We'd like you to get a good picture of our current status before we have our discussion about VCI's role in the company direction," Mortimer outlined, choosing his words carefully.

"OK," Gottingham responded. "But we have a dinner meeting scheduled back in New York for seven. I'd like to be sure we're in the air again by 2:30 this afternoon, just in case there's heavy traffic when we arrive."

"Perfect. Let's reconvene here at noon. I'll ask Sally-Ann to arrange some lunch while we talk. There should be plenty of time for us to discuss any concerns," Mortimer said rising from his chair to signal the close of that phase of their visit.

John George had studied the mannerisms and reactions of Gottingham and Folino intently as he spoke. He noted a slight tightening of the lawyer's jaw as he outlined the schedule. A little disappointed they would not do battle immediately? Gottingham, however, betrayed no emotion. His face and stature remained impassive, suggesting he had already anticipated the tactic.

For the next few hours, Wilma Willingsworth took charge of their presentation and discussions. Considered one of America's most influential businesswomen, she artfully organized the subjects and presented her message with clarity and passion. Mundane financial statements came alive as she painted a portrait of the company's enviable financial position. Operating results developed a personality as she explained how each Multima division generated its revenues, controlled expenses, and held on to profits for shareholders.

Wilma welcomed questions as she spoke. To her, interruptions were not a challenge, rather she thought of them as a teaching opportunity and always answered with patience and grace before resuming her message.

When she completed the corporate overview, she passed leadership of the session to Edward Hadley who extolled the virtues of Multima's business philosophy. He drew attention to their long-term commitment to managing the corporation for the benefit of all stakeholders. Customers, employees, suppliers, and the communities where they did business were all just as important as shareholders, he had emphasized.

The VCI executives responded well and became fully engaged. They asked questions, challenged assumptions, and demonstrated all the usual hallmarks of investors or analysts. Their inquiries were predictable. Throughout the session, their reactions reflected a healthy skepticism and their manner remained polite and cordial.

Although John George Mortimer was not present at the meeting, he was aware of all this because Sally-Ann briefed him on the entire morning session with a fifteen-minute overview. Just before noon, when the questions appeared to be winding down, Sally-Ann quietly entered Mortimer's office with her notepad and shared her observations of the morning meeting, complete with assessments of body language and mannerisms.

She had covertly observed the entire meeting on closed-circuit TV from a private cubicle beside the conference room, and Mortimer had absolute confidence in her report. After all, Sally-Ann had honed this skill over more than thirty years.

When they reconvened around a large, circular glass table in the corner of John George's expansive office – the corner farthest from his desk – the table was adorned with bowls of salad and plates of sandwiches. Set with fine china and silverware, it had a bouquet of flowers in the center. Stems of the flowers were intentionally cut short so diners could talk easily with no one's view blocked, the better to assess facial expressions, Mortimer's staff knew well.

John George invited Wilma and Edward to join them for lunch. While they ate, he asked questions about the visitors' meeting that morning and welcomed their queries in return. Conversation was polite, amicable, and formal as all participants knew they were ambling towards the real purpose of the discussions. It was apparent everyone wanted to choose his or her words carefully to give nothing away before the main event.

Alberto Ferer, Multima's legal counsel, had also joined the discussion at John George's request. They had plotted their strategies and roles at length well before the meeting. When John George gave a barely detected nod after everyone finished eating, Alberto knew it was time for his initial question.

"Do you have any corporate governance questions for me?" he asked. "I also serve as secretary of the board of directors."

Gottingham appeared momentarily startled that it was Ferer who introduced the contentious subject and not Mortimer, but he recovered instantly and shifted his gaze back to the CEO.

"I think we've made our concerns about the composition of the board very clear to you, John George. Have you had an opportunity to consider our request?" he asked, shifting his body slightly to look directly at Mortimer.

John George broke eye contact and glanced towards Alberto, signaling that he should continue with the plan they had created.

"Allow me to answer that one for you, Earnest," Ferer interjected. "John George mentioned your concern about representation on the board and asked me to conduct a survey. I'm afraid the response was not very favorable. Almost unanimously, the directors indicated a preference to reduce their number. Some requested we decrease the size of the board dramatically to make meetings more productive and efficient.

"There's also a desire to make the composition of the board more diverse – racially, by gender, by geography, and with less representation from large shareholders and more from other stakeholders. It's not a desire to specifically exclude VCI from the board. Rather, the board thinks we should replace several current directors with candidates who better reflect the corporation's values and mission statements."

"Those might be worthwhile goals," Gottingham replied, again shifting both his gaze and body away from Ferer, directly confronting John George. "But here's the bottom-line. Our company has more than a billion dollars at stake. We required a seat on the board of directors as a condition of making that investment, and we need to see that continue. Although Howard Knight is no longer with us, we need to have a seat at the table when you make decisions. It's only prudent to protect our investment."

Ferer immediately drew attention to the clause in their agreement naming Knight a director and emphasized Multima's intention to appoint an individual who would add value, not satisfy a requirement. That statement, of course, immediately drew VCI's legal counsel into the dialogue. For several minutes, the group around the table watched Folino and Ferer verbally thrust and parry as they dissected the contentious clause. With each oral volley, passion grew – especially with Folino – who became more animated, his face increasingly red.

Before the temperature of the debate become too heated, John George interjected, "I think it's clear we have a disconnect with our interpretations here, and I expect we'll also probably need to agree to disagree on the intent of the clause in our contract. But I understand your desire to keep close to your investment. If it would help your board of directors get comfortable with our direction, we're prepared to schedule a meeting like this morning's every month. We could do it here or in New York if you prefer. And, we could do it right after each board meeting."

"I appreciate your suggestion, John George," Gottingham replied. "But I don't think my people will consider a briefing the day after a board meeting to be quite the same as voting on specific actions. Frankly, I doubt my board will be satisfied with anything less than a full directorship."

They'd planned for such a retort, so Ferer was ready to jump back into the fray. "A decision to appoint a VCI representative to our board is not John George's or mine. Even if we recommend it to the board, there's no assurance they'll agree, and our bylaws don't legally require the board to appoint any investor, no matter how important they may be."

Gottingham must have anticipated that Multima might stake out that position. He responded without a moment's hesitation. "Should that be your board's final position, VCI's board will want to undertake a serious review of its holdings," he stated with a calm tone and eyes of steel looking out from a face as unmoving as granite.

"That undertaking could lead to one of four possible outcomes. There's a remote chance our board will accept your exclusion, be satisfied with your offer, and keep our level of investment. But I certainly wouldn't count on it.

"VCI might instead decide to liquidate our investment in Multima Corporation. The last fiasco didn't hurt us at all. Our preferred shares carry a fixed value and didn't drop when common shares plummeted more than twenty percent after that little-known analyst, from an even lesser-known firm in New Jersey, recommended investors bail out of Multima. If our board should decide to sell our preferred shares, anyone could buy them. Multima might find those new owners even harder to work with than us," he declared with a harrumph.

"A third direction could be a short-selling strategy," Gottingham resumed. "Maybe our board will decide to accumulate options on common shares of Multima should some negative news trigger a further dramatic decline in price. With enough shares, we could lobby shareholders for support and changes to the board.

"And I also anticipate our directors might consider lodging a formal complaint with the Securities and Exchange Commission. Our board might test just how curious the SEC could become about that clever little maneuver you made in February to convert equity from that numbered Canadian company into preferred shares in Multima," he said quietly as he leaned threateningly towards John George.

The room immediately became silent. Mortimer knew well that any of those last three alternatives could be painful for his company. On its own, one could dramatically disrupt Multima. Worse, any combination could cause serious financial harm.

"Let us discuss it with our directors at the next board meeting in June," he said. "We'll take your request for representation to the board and seek a formal vote. Then, depending on the outcome, I guess we'll each need to assess our options and let the chips fall where they may," John George said.

Apparently satisfied they had accomplished all they could expect, Gottingham announced they'd leave earlier than planned. With the skies so full of corporate jets these days, he'd like to avoid a line-up for a landing slot in New Jersey. Within minutes, after awkward handshakes showing little personal warmth, everyone said farewell.

John George held a thorough debriefing with his team immediately after the visitors left. When they finished, he called Dan Ramirez in corporate security. They needed to meet at the house as soon as possible.

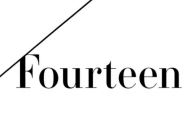

Fourteen

In a bleak, mountainous area near Escoma, Bolivia.
Monday June 27, 2016

When Howard Knight met up with Fidelia Morales in the arrivals section of Alejandro Velasco Astete International Airport in Cusco on the last day of April, he was almost overcome with joy. It had been months since he felt the warmth of her smile, heard the lilt of her voice, or saw the sparkle in her eyes that always lifted his spirit.

They met just outside the immigration clearance center. When they wrapped their arms around each other for a long affectionate kiss, Knight felt tears spring into his eyes as he treasured every second of their reunion. Their separate journeys to this point had been arduous, risky, and stressful. Now that they were together, he intended to savor every delightful second.

After a few moments, they both remembered it essential to avoid unwanted attention and reluctantly parted, still gazing at each other like love-struck teenagers. Hand in hand, they walked to a nearby taxi stand for a ten-minute ride to the Tierra Viva Cusco Plaza Hotel. Howard had made a reservation from the airport while he waited for Fidelia's arrival after getting assurances a luxury room was available immediately and staff would hold it.

Neither paid much attention to the scenery as they traveled towards the center of the city. They spoke sparingly. And when they did talk, both used soft tones in English sprinkled with difficult-to-translate expressions, making it hard for the driver to hear or understand. Most of the time, they just looked at each other, smiling and touching, taking in the subtle changes each had undergone in the months apart.

As promised, the ride was short. Located on a narrow one-way street that fed into the historic town plaza, the charming hotel looked inviting. As they came to a stop at its entrance, Howard noticed an Italian restaurant on his left and remarked that it should be a convenient place to have dinner.

When they checked in, they used passports created months in advance. Fidelia's was American, showing a photo matching the wig she now wore with flowing dark hair, an address in California, and a name they chose years earlier.

Howard used the same document presented to hotels in Quito. The European Union passport described him as Italian and pictured him clean-shaven although he now sported a closely trimmed dark goatee.

They made a point of chatting with the reception clerk. They were tourists who recently met in Lima and intended to sightsee in Cusco for a few days before they traveled to *Machu Picchu*. "At least that's our plan," Howard exclaimed with a mischievous grin and wink that had everyone laughing jovially.

Once in their room, both performed the usual security rituals, checking the locking mechanisms on the door and safe, then searching for video or recording devices. Both knew they couldn't be too careful and must put those precautions before all else. This time, they also needed to reassemble and hide the weapon made of several plastic parts which Howard had divided between the two backpacks to evade airport screening.

Satisfied the room was secure, they grasped each other almost desperately and locked their lips in passion. As their tongues probed, and their breathing became rapid, they tore at each other's clothes. Their desire was impatient and overwhelming. Within mere seconds, each had the other completely undressed, both anticipating the satisfaction of long-awaited love-making.

Their fervor was almost violent as they squeezed each other as tightly as possible, kissing and thrusting towards each other with abandon until they quickly collapsed in desperate orgasms. The next number of times they made love (for neither could remember precisely how many) their sessions stretched for hours and were more deliberate, sensitive, and tender. They completely forgot about the Italian restaurant across the street, and it was well into the next morning before they finally awoke.

Their plan called for them to spend time in Cusco for three reasons. Foremost, they were concerned about the altitude. They read that the Andes were higher than people realized and many experienced nausea from the reduced oxygen. Almost everyone lost energy and stamina the first few days. Furthermore, because neither Fidelia or Howard had experience in mountainous regions, they thought it best to acclimate before continuing their journey.

Sitting at more than 11,000 feet, the ancient capital of the Andean empire was perfect for this kind of transition. Fidelia remembered several comments on Trip-Advisor that reinforced her impression: three days in Cusco should serve their purpose perfectly.

As always, they feared someone might pick up their trail, so establishing a diversionary intention to visit *Machu Picchu* was important. Travelers to Peru hike to the popular sacred site from a couple separate departure points using a few possible routes. Some paths took hikers up to a week to complete. If someone should be on their tail, they would hopefully think it necessary to check out all the alternative paths which might buy some valuable time.

Their last reason for choosing Cusco was practical. They knew when it came time to leave the beautiful old capital, future accommodations would be unlike any they would enjoy there. Their intended home for at least the next several months was to be a tiny tent strapped to Howard's backpack, or on rare occasions a room in some dilapidated hotel. There would be nothing approaching the comfort and luxury of the Terra Viva Cusco Plaza.

For three days, they walked everywhere around the city laden with their backpacks. Security was one reason for carrying them, but conditioning was equally important. For Cusco was a magnificent old town with long steep hills. While they looked like curious tourists exploring the sights, they were also building stamina and fitness to cope with the challenging trip ahead.

As they visited cathedrals, museums, and souvenir shops, they felt the weight of the altitude and the sacks that carried their meager possessions. Each day, they'd trudge from *Plaza de Armas* near their hotel up narrow sidewalks with hundreds of steep steps to *San Cristobal* church at the summit of a hill with a magnificent view of the picturesque city below. They'd rest awhile, then make the thirty-minute descent using a different route each time.

When they were too tired to continue, they'd return to their hotel for a nap. Refreshed, they'd make love again before going out once more for conditioning. Their moods shifted subtly over the days as they realized how dramatically their lives had already changed, and would continue to change in the days ahead. They touched each other often, held hands for hours as they walked and looked longingly into each other's eyes when conversation lapsed.

The evening before they left Cusco, they spent more than fifteen minutes with the hotel clerk, rechecking bus schedules and tour arrangements for *Machu Picchu*. They sought advice about needs on the trails and asked questions about Aguas Calientes, a village at the base of the sacred mountain. They were determined to create the impression of a couple thoroughly excited about their planned visit to the most famous mountain in Peru.

The morning of departure, they paid their bill and reinforced with a new shift clerk their exuberance about the planned trip to *Machu Picchu*. They set their plan in motion and walked towards the bus station, changing streets and directions several times, and frequently checking to be sure no one was following them.

When they arrived at the chaotic terminal, Fidelia assumed responsibility for finding their bus. They'd scouted it out earlier and knew they should expect a cacophony of noise and bustling activity from every direction. Her mission was to listen for a vendor announcing their bus departure. When she heard it off to their left, she tugged on Howard's arm and led him to the shouting man. Fidelia confirmed the tariff for two in Spanish, paid the requested fee, then gestured for Howard to follow her onto the crowded bus.

It took a few minutes to find seats together. The old vehicle was packed, and only a very few single seats remained near the back. Undaunted, Fidelia led the way, squeezed her backpack as she progressed along the aisle, and convinced one needy woman to give up her seat for a small fee. They stashed the bags at their feet and settled in for the eight or nine-hour ride to Puno – precisely the opposite direction from *Machu Picchu*.

They could have flown to Puno in about ninety minutes. But it was time for Howard and Fidelia to assume the nomadic persona of tourist backpackers, their best chance for escape.

They traveled during the day for fear of both falling asleep at the same time. Buses in Latin America were notorious for organized criminals stealing luggage and the personal effects of sleeping passengers. Thieves knew passengers, dozy from the rocking motion and monotony of the ride, nodded off. They also were aware buses – such as the one to Puno – frequently stopped to pick-up and discharge passengers. Often, they snatched belongings from their prey while a passenger slept, usually just seconds before the bus stopped. They made their escape, and the bus was often miles away before an unsuspecting victim awoke and realized what had happened.

So, they diligently rotated responsibility throughout the long, uncomfortable journey. One slept while the other warily watched. However, sleeping was sporadic and depended entirely on road conditions. The route from Cusco to Puno was one of Peru's better-maintained roads. Still, there were forceful jolts from tires meeting pot-holes without warning and often with enough intensity to jar passengers from their hard, unforgiving seats.

They were grateful the weather cooperated. Well into Peru's autumn, temperatures outside the bus were mild – with frequent cloudy periods that moderated the intensity of a brilliant sun beaming in through open windows. A gusting breeze from the speed of the bus also served to decrease the temperature inside, offsetting the heat generated by more than fifty live bodies crammed tightly together.

After testing the English fluency of nearby passengers, and finding there was little, they exchanged murmurs together as quietly as possible, discouraging potentially curious fellow passengers from eavesdropping. They shared their adventures of the previous month, each keenly interested in the other's stories – Howard with his dramatic escape and disappearance to Quito, Fidelia recounting her tranquil days among the nuns in the convent of Zaragoza.

Like typical tourists, they laughed as they recounted minor mishaps, inconveniences, and customs they'd encountered that seemed odd or unexpected. The only subjects of concern they studiously avoided were the FBI and The Organization. There would be time later to reassess the risks, consider tactics both might use to track them down, and further refine their survival plan.

The one constant, Howard realized mid-way, was the way they touched each other continuously, as though a physical connection was integral to their survival. He drew strength when Fidelia was near him, and their closeness buoyed his spirit and nurtured his optimism. Increasingly, he grew confident they would somehow discover a way to make their escape work for many years.

For the last few hours of their bus journey, they took in the scenery, mainly spotting llamas and sheep that dotted the rolling countryside approaching the town. From earlier research, they knew Puno was a vibrant city of more than one hundred thousand people nestled along the shores of South America's largest lake. Upon arrival, they found bustling streets, congested traffic, and a rustic ambiance in an urban setting.

After a day on a bus, both felt sweaty, dirty, hungry, and thirsty. But there was no time to refresh. Their orientation to backpacking was to become even more exhausting, for their day involved still more travel. To avoid showing the identification most hotels demanded on check-in, they decided they should remain in Puno only for so long as it took to find someone who would carry them across the lake to Bolivia that night.

Months earlier back in Florida, they discovered a blog in Spanish that offered tips for finding a few fishermen and tour operators on Lake Titicaca who might be willing to carry passengers across the lake under cover of darkness. Naturally, such folks demanded generous payment for breaking the law, but she had located one.

She used one of their disposable phones shortly after they arrived in Puno. Her conversation was short and entirely in Spanish. After just a few minutes, she confirmed to Howard that someone would pick them up near the bus station in about an hour and transport them that evening. Her contact said they'd make the voyage in two stages and he'd provide all the details when they met. They had also agreed upon a fee of one thousand American dollars in advance and in cash.

Only a few minutes after the promised hour, a short, small-framed man with a quick smile, an outsized handlebar mustache, dark complexion, and confident swagger met them and introduced himself. He gave the name Pedro. Reluctantly, they heaved their backpacks into the rear of a beat-up pick-up truck among ropes, fishing nets, and an odd assortment of tools. All three then squeezed into the front for a ride of about an hour as they jostled along the lake on roads that seemed to be little more than enlarged footpaths.

As they drove, Pedro provided the promised further details about the next stages of their trip.

"We'll embark on my small – but very seaworthy – fishing boat when we get to my home. I'll take you part way across the lake, landing at Llachon, a beautiful village located at the tip of a small peninsula jutting into Lake Titicaca. It will take us about three hours, and we'll arrive just after dark. Lake conditions should be good with only slight winds and gentle waves," he explained in Spanish far more articulately than expected.

"Once we get to Llachon, I'll bring you to a local inn. You should check-in for one night. Be sure to tell the innkeeper that you plan to sightsee in the nearby countryside the next day," Pedro instructed. "That will let him tell any inquiring authorities that indeed guests stayed there but left with no specific destination," he said with a wink. "The innkeeper is my cousin. You can trust him. One more thing, you'll also need to pay him fifty US dollars in advance."

Howard muttered more to himself than Fidelia that fifty dollars would probably also pay the 'cousin' for a room only Pedro would use. Their contact resumed his briefing.

"After your check-in, we'll all go for an excellent meal at a restaurant I know. Be sure to bring your backpacks. We'll take dinner until late in the evening. Then, I'll bring you to another cousin, Juan, who has a bigger boat that will carry you safely to Bolivia.

"Juan's boat has expensive detection devices. You'll skirt around any other boats on the lake. It also has radar jamming technology so that no Bolivian authorities will detect your arrival. You'll land in a quiet inlet near a nice little village called Escoma about two hours before dawn. Your time on the water will be agreeable and there will be no surprises," he assured them with a broad smile and dismissive wave of his hand.

Since neither Howard or Fidelia posed questions, he continued. "Last year we carried more than twenty passengers to Bolivia with no problem. We took three to a town further south just last week. Don't worry. Juan will drop you near the shoreline, and you'll just walk in from there. Then you'll be on your own!" he exclaimed with another wink and smile.

Howard took note that Pedro hadn't once asked why they should want to cross into Bolivia in such an unconventional and entirely illegal manner.

Shortly after he finished his thorough briefing, Pedro stopped at a tiny one-room home where a fishing boat was anchored about twenty feet offshore. Several young children played in the nearby yard, shouting and laughing. They all ran to check out the curious new visitors but were shooed away after quick hugs and kisses from the laughing fisherman.

Cheerfully, Pedro asked if they would like to use the toilet before they set out as he gestured towards a tiny, dilapidated shack a few yards from the house. Fidelia glanced apprehensively towards Howard for a moment before she resolved there was little alternative.

Their ride to Llachon was exactly as described. An introduction to the innkeeper and dinner followed as expected, with a delicious meal that cost a pittance even compared to the low prices of Cusco. Cousin Juan met them as scheduled and their boat trip to Bolivia was uneventful, with waters so calm that Howard and Fidelia successfully took turns napping.

When they arrived on the Bolivian shores of Lake Titicaca, captain Juan dropped anchor about fifty yards offshore in a sheltered, secluded cove. They saw nothing distinctive, only a dark shadow of land. It was deathly quiet, with sporadic moonlight as clouds floated aimlessly above. There were occasional chirps and hums of insects or frogs. Otherwise, all was quiet; even the birds were still asleep.

After assuring them the water was shallow enough to walk from there, Juan helped them from the boat into the water and passed down their backpacks, recommending they carry them just in case they should slip walking in. It would be easier to retrieve their belongings that way, he added. They both entered the water barefoot to keep their hiking boots dry, with jeans rolled up to their knees.

With their first steps towards shore, Juan started his boat engines and immediately veered towards open waters, leaving a gentle wake behind.

The water was shallow, but the lake bed was rocky. Feeling about with his toes, Howard detected stones and pebbles of all sizes and shapes. There was none of the soft, gentle sand found at vacation resorts and their decision to tie their boots to their backpacks and go ashore barefoot soon proved to be an ill-advised strategy.

Some of the rocks were jagged and extremely sharp, making their advance painful. They both tried to walk as delicately as possible, probing for sharp edges with their toes before shifting weight to the advancing foot. For about five minutes, they made modest progress. Suddenly, Fidelia cried out. Reacting to the sudden pain caused by a jagged rock, she instinctively recoiled. As she did so, she lost her balance completely, falling straight backward and landing flat, momentarily submerged under water.

Howard's first reaction was to laugh uproariously. The entire scene struck him as hilarious. But he promptly stretched out his arm to assist Fidelia, who raised her head, sputtering out the water she had partially swallowed, while struggling to keep her backpack somewhat dry at the same time.

The combination of Fidelia's simultaneous actions, poor balance on the rocky lake bed, and Howard stretching to help, all caused him to tumble forward onto Fidelia, further drenching her. Then, she lost her grip on the backpack, while Howard's weight completely submerged his. Soaked, with their packs equally saturated, both realized there was nothing to do but laugh.

They eventually managed to get upright while still giggling, recovered their wet luggage, and put on their very soggy hiking boots. Fidelia noticed a tiny drop of blood on her toe as she pulled on the boot but resolved not to be concerned. Within moments they made their way to shore and collapsed on dry-land, still chuckling in each other's arms.

As their good humor subsided, they realized they had landed in a sparsely populated area but needed to carry on while they still had darkness as cover. The vegetation resembled a combination of swampland and the scruffy, long, brownish grasses and squat shrubs found in America's wild west. There were only a few scrawny trees and no canopy. With light, they could be visible to people in nearby farmhouses or travelers on the highway.

Wet or not, they had to continue. Their intended refuge was in the mountains east of them, just outside Escoma. They set out with water squishing from their boots and dripping from their clothes as they walked. A nearby road was less than one mile away but in the darkness, handicapped by the extra weight of their wet clothes and bags, progress was both slow and tiring.

It took more than an hour to reach the side of the thoroughfare. Howard's GPS confirmed their Google maps research. They had reached the edge of Highway 16, a roadway that appeared to be well-maintained and free of traffic that early morning. To their right, about fifty miles to the southeast, was the capital city of Bolivia, La Paz. To their left, about five miles to the northeast was the village of Escoma.

They ambled across the road and almost immediately started a gradual climb. Soon, they spotted a worn path that held promise and followed it upwards for more than an hour, stopping to rest as needed. With only four bottles of precious water each, Fidelia reminded him to sip only small amounts each time they became thirsty.

By first light, they were about a half mile into the mountains and beyond the crest visible from the road. There were no buildings in sight. They didn't see any sheep or goats. The mountains appeared to be completely barren, with virtually no vegetation or habitation. They listened as they surveyed the terrain in a large gradual circle, then agreed this should do for their first day and night.

From research they'd undertaken online months earlier and confirmed during their dinner with Pedro, they knew they could buy food and water in the village of Escoma. They planned to stay one day in the mountains to rest and remain out of view. They had enough protein bars and water in their backpacks to last two days if they were careful.

They explored the area. After about another hour, Fidelia spotted a plot of soil large enough to pitch their tent. While Howard tossed away a few stray rocks and worked to make the site as flat and comfortable as possible, Fidelia emptied their backpacks and laid out all the contents to dry on nearby rock formations. She used some of the smaller rocks to weigh down their few possessions in the event of a sudden gust of wind. Then, she took off the clothes she was wearing, leaving her shivering in the chilly morning weather.

It was also time to rotate their passports. From hidden compartments in both pieces of luggage, Fidelia retrieved sealed plastic bags which held their stash of identification. She took out the ones that claimed they were a married couple from Canada and glanced at hers to be sure all was in order. She made a mental note of her new name and reminded Howard about his new identity and their new marital status.

She double-checked the photos to be sure each corresponded with their current appearance. Then, she quickly scanned over immigration stamps showing they had traveled from Vancouver south through the United States, Mexico, several Central American countries, Brazil, and Paraguay before landing at El Alto International Airport in La Paz, Bolivia a little more than three weeks earlier. Satisfied the new documents would withstand scrutiny from any probing police or immigration officer, she carefully put the previously used passports back into the hidden compartments.

It took a while, but Howard managed to assemble the tiny tent attached to his backpack. They'd once practiced putting it together during a hiking weekend in Vermont several months earlier to be sure they could sleep comfortably and use a tent for an extended time. Then, they'd put all the bits together, anchored the rip-stop nylon tent securely and spent an entire night that also featured a thunderstorm. Since then, neither had used it. So, it took considerable patience and more than a little fidgeting to make everything fit.

Once they pitched the tent, they decided Howard would try to sleep for a few hours while Fidelia kept watch. The sight of her naked body caused modest arousal, but his tired body won out. It had been about thirty-six hours since they awoke from a good night's sleep in Cusco, and they were both exhausted from travel, walking, and stress.

They thought it prudent to rotate resting with lookout duties for the first day and night to be sure they were alone in their surroundings. Reluctantly, Howard stripped off his still-damp clothes, spread them on the rock formation to dry and promptly climbed into his sleeping bag. Mid-afternoon they reversed roles.

Neither slept deeply during that first day and night in the mountains, but they both slept well enough to offset their initial exhaustion. The second morning, they packed up the tent with all their other belongings and walked towards Escoma.

First, they had to descend the mountainside back to the road. Climbing up, it had been grueling, so they'd expected the downward trek to be easier, not realizing that going down could be more treacherous and tiring. The backpacks added complexity, and they found their balance sometimes shifting unexpectedly as the rocky soil gave way underfoot. The uneven ground demanded caution, but after more than two hours they arrived at the side of the road, turned right, and headed towards Escoma.

Walking along the road was much easier. It took only a little more than an hour to reach the village, while a surprising number of cars, pickups and commercial trucks passed in both directions as they walked.

Howard wasn't sure Escoma should even be described as a village. It was smaller than any he had ever seen. More like an enclave, he remarked to Fidelia. In the center was a large rectangular plaza ringed with shops, apartments, a school, the church, and a few municipal buildings. There appeared to be only a few hundred inhabitants, but it was bustling when they arrived.

Women wore traditional Andean clothes with ever-present coarsely woven shawls. Men dressed in work clothes and wore bright, colorful sweaters to ward off the high-elevation chill of Bolivia's autumn. Youngsters dressed in a variety of garb, both traditional and modern.

As the strangers walked into the plaza, a group of children immediately flocked to see them. They were curious and friendly, while adults watched warily. Fidelia took charge at once. With her perfect command of Spanish, sparkling personality, charming smile, and friendly demeanor, she became an instant celebrity. It seemed everyone wanted to help her with directions, provide advice about which shops were best, and ask questions about Canada or the visitors' impressions of their visit to Escoma.

Surprisingly, more than a month after that auspicious arrival, they were still there, or more precisely, were in the mountains around there. To their relief, people in the village proved comfortable with strangers. Besides the farming businesses, there was a nearby gold mine where many of the men worked. Foreigners frequently came there for quick visits and then spent a few minutes in town to wander around or have a meal.

But Fidelia apparently appealed to the townsfolk on some other level. Howard saw how her magnetism immediately attracted attention from both men and women. And there was something about their story, two retired Canadians wandering across the Americas to explore and learn, that seemed to resonate with the villagers.

The visitors never spent a night in the town. Instead, they trekked back into the mountains to continue their wandering exploration. Two or three times a week, Howard and Fidelia came back into Escoma around mid-day. They'd lunch with some of the villagers in the plaza and regale them with stories about Canada and the United States. In return, the townspeople willingly answered their visitors' questions about life in Bolivia. Occasionally, they'd all just listen to music or watch the children perform. Of course, whenever there was a soccer game, the visitors made a point of attending and enjoyed the local wine or beer, blending into a festive environment.

On those visits, they stocked up with fresh food and other supplies, then left to pitch their tent in the mountains four or five miles from town. So far, everything had gone smoothly, just as they had planned. Howard's Spanish improved daily. Fidelia fine-tuned her Puerto Rican accent to sound more Bolivian, and like sponges, they absorbed every morsel of information about the country and its culture.

They knew their bliss was only temporary. To spend an entire month in such a small village was already a significant risk and they knew they should move on. Their last day in Escoma, they bought a little more water than usual. That was the only change they made in their normal behavior. When they left town, they went in a northerly direction, waving enthusiastically with their usual warm "Adiós!"

That evening, they pitched their tent in a valley only a short distance from the village and slept for a few hours. About midnight, Howard's GPS watch abruptly woke them. They quickly packed up their tent and belongings, then set out in a southerly direction intending to walk five to ten miles to the south of Escoma. There, they would retreat into the mountains before first light and sleep throughout the day. During coming nights, they'd hike along the highway in darkness, then again sleep through the daylight hours, until they eventually arrived in La Paz. There, they desperately hoped to disappear officially.

Fifteen

John George frequently circled back in the conversation to be sure Dan Ramirez completely understood all the issues and reasons he was determined not to appoint any new director representing the interests of Venture Capital Inc.

He held nothing back as he walked his chief of security through Howard Knight's antics and his complicated maneuvers to elevate Wendal Randall to the office of CEO. He recapped their discovery of The Organization's influence on Multima through Knight and the spy, Janet Weissel. He explained his rationale for keeping the informant on Multima's payroll while shuffling her off to the financial services subsidiary. Then, he finished with an update from his meeting with the new CEO of Venture Capital Inc. and Gottingham's subsequent ultimatum to either appoint him as a director or face the consequences.

Mortimer studied his security chief's body language carefully as they held their intense discussion over cups of strong coffee in the secrecy of his splendid home office. Both knew they could speak freely because Ramirez personally inspected the residence every morning to ensure no audio or video recording devices had been planted. They both knew there were few places in America more secure. This chief of corporate security had learned his many skills as he climbed to the most senior ranks of the FBI, and he unquestionably applied them well.

When he retired a few years earlier, Ramirez was one of its five most powerful executives with oversight experience in almost every branch of the FBI. It was precisely such knowledge Mortimer sought when he hired the wily former law enforcement specialist and the reason he paid him an annual salary higher than any of his division presidents. Mortimer had sensed the business environment was changing and expected those changes would eventually require elite know-how to keep Multima employees, customers, and buildings more secure.

Until that morning, it hadn't occurred to him that Ramirez might also play a vital role in his planned resistance to the threats and pressure from VCI.

As implausible as it might sound, the ex-government agent seemed to retain exceptional communication – and influence – with his former cohorts. So, John George wanted to see exactly how his chief would respond to the preliminary information before exploring the risky and far-fetched idea germinating in his mind.

"This is not at all the situation I envisaged when I joined the team," Ramirez said as he drew a long breath, shook his head in exasperation, and leaned back in his chair. "When I was with the FBI we had no inclination that VCI and The Organization were connected. We knew their operational strategy was to infiltrate established legitimate companies, but we usually traced their involvement to businesses on the periphery of the mainstream.

"Hotels, nightclubs, and restaurants were logical extensions of The Organization's illegal trafficking in people and drugs. Payday loan operations made sense with their casino and illicit gambling activities. But we were never able to get enough hard evidence to get a conviction," Ramirez complained. "However, the possibility they might actually control venture capital or private equity outfits never crossed our minds."

"It gives organized criminals a sort of aura of legitimacy, doesn't it?" Mortimer tested.

"Fucking right!" Ramirez blurted as his face contorted with a burst of anger. "If they can invest in start-up companies or steal control of corporations like Multima, eventually it will become almost impossible for us to identify the good guys from the vermin who run those criminal gangs."

John George watched Dan Ramirez unconsciously clench his fists in annoyance and saw his toes start to tap anxiously as his frustration grew. He was also encouraged by the dilated pupils of Ramirez's eyes as he vehemently condemned despicable criminal outfits. Clearly, his security chief was having trouble letting go of a life-long war against scurrilous, undesirable elements. He let the former agent vent for a few minutes more before he was comfortable enough to probe.

"It almost begs for lady justice to tilt the scales in favor of the good guys, doesn't it?" Mortimer asked.

Immediately alert to the possible implications of John George's less-than-subtle suggestion, Ramirez quickly straightened his posture and chose the words of his response very carefully.

"All scales require some correction from time to time. Do you have some specific adjustment in mind?" he asked.

"I've been wondering about Knight's subterfuge to make Randall CEO. It seems to me that just getting Wendal into the role of CEO would not serve their purpose. Even if they also had a few directors they could influence, to me it seems like quite a stretch to exert effective control over the corporation unless they had some other leverage," John George offered.

"I see what you mean. Unless they had something that would ensure Randall followed their bidding, why go to all the trouble of engineering a coup?" Ramirez mused.

"Exactly," John George replied. "Plus, it was Howard Knight who brought me the opportunity to acquire Wendal's little company in the first place. If Randall was also a plant of The Organization, might there also be something else powerful enough to guarantee he'd do their bidding?"

"Makes sense, John George," Ramirez cautiously answered. "What did you have in mind?"

"Perhaps those friends of yours who've got Wendal squirreled away in Miami might change their questioning tactics. Rather than continuing to determine his involvement in the hacking incident and disappearance of our IT employee Willy Fernandez, maybe they would find it more beneficial to focus on Randall's relationship with Knight," Mortimer suggested. "That might lead us to a better understanding of The Organization's desire to give him my job."

Ramirez got the message, and his friends working in a rogue unit buried deep within the National Security Branch of the FBI went to work. It took only a few days of 'unorthodox' interrogation to learn about Knight's blackmail of Wendal since his days in college. They found out the story of him strangling an unidentified woman as he reached an orgasm during a paid sexual escapade, and the damning video of this event that Knight retained.

It took only a few hours longer for them to conclude he had very little useful information about his companion at the time they snatched him – the Russian woman Wendal Randall knew only as Frau Schäffer. And it became evident he had no idea Interpol wanted her for the role she played in human trafficking.

She proved much tougher to break. They needed several weeks of similar interrogation methods to pry useful information from Frau Schäffer. Finally, she furnished a half-dozen names that she maintained was a comprehensive list of people involved in the human-smuggling operation in Europe. Her captors doubted they had the full picture, but they did learn about the roles of Howard

Knight and other key members of The Organization in the sordid criminal activities destroying the lives of thousands of women and girls.

As arranged, the interrogators promptly shared everything they learned with Dan Ramirez who then spent several tense days convincing the excited rogue group to sit on their trove of information for a while. Once John George Mortimer listened to all the collected intelligence, he felt comfortable making the call to VCI's CEO with a response to Gottingham's demand for a seat on the board of directors.

"It's not going to happen," John George said after dispensing with the opening pleasantries. "Our board has made its decision. We'll reduce the number of directors from thirteen to eight, effective the first of August. The board has also decided that several, including Howard Knight, will leave the board, and we'll appoint only two. One director will come from the union representing workers at Supermarkets, and the other will be an eminent economist. There was no support for a director from VCI."

"Very disappointed to hear that, John George," Earnest Gottingham said evenly. "You leave me little alternative. I'll report your decision to my board and determine which option they prefer to implement."

"I understand our decision disappoints and I expect it might fall short of your board's expectations," Mortimer replied. "But before your people do anything rash, I suggest you mention two names to your board of directors. Wendal Randall and Klaudia Schäffer," he said, pronouncing both names slowly and succinctly.

"Tell your people they've cooperated and provided very useful information to some very important folks. Let your directors know those people we're working with have agreed to sit on the information they've learned – for now. But they'll act without hesitation should you implement any of the options you outlined to me. Your only alternative is to accept our decision and then passively maintain your holdings in Multima without any shenanigans. Anything short of that, and they will start proceedings."

There was a long pause. Longer than a few seconds. John George tactically remained silent, patiently waiting for a response.

"I don't know the people you've named. However, I'll relay your message to the board. Thank you for calling. Goodbye," Gottingham muttered as he abruptly ended the call.

Sixteen

Wendal Randall cursed the cruel irony. It was Independence Day 2016. Instead of celebrating the holiday in a friend's backyard somewhere, his government was holding him hostage illegally in a high-security compound on foreign soil. How had things gone so horribly wrong?

More than three months earlier, they surreptitiously snatched him after arriving in Miami by private jet. Wendal and his companion, Frau Schäffer, climbed into a limousine they thought would take them to his home in Coconut Grove. Once the vehicle was in motion, the driver flashed an FBI badge, locked the doors, and drove them to a secluded warehouse near the airport. There, they were surrounded by armed men, separated, beaten, and held in unfurnished rooms until Wendal eventually succumbed to some form of mental breakdown.

He remembered how they restrained him with a straight jacket, the kind they used with violent, mentally ill patients. He recalled lying on the floor for several hours, wet and dirty with urine and feces. Sometime later, a pair of new faces entered the room and forced him to strip off his clothes. Then they led him down a short corridor to a bathroom with a shower. When they brought him back to the room, he saw that someone had set up a folding bed and provided a pail he was supposed to use to relieve himself. They'd left some toilet tissue, a toothbrush, a comb, and fresh clothes on the bed.

The new faces didn't look at all like FBI agents. Both were males, wearing khaki shorts and ragged t-shirts. Their boots were military issue, but they had scraggly beards and long, unkempt hair. They spoke politely and more softly than those who restrained him earlier and promised to have a doctor look at his broken fingers.

For the next three days, they questioned him for extended periods of time. He had no watch and no way of knowing how long the sessions were, but each interrogation left him confused and exhausted. Frau Schäffer seemed of great interest to them. They asked dozens of questions about her.

What was their relationship? How did they meet? What did they do together in Europe? How did they know Howard Knight? Wendal answered all their questions patiently and truthfully, but they never seemed satisfied. Different interrogators used various methods. Some were friendly, others downright hostile. But his answers never seemed to satisfy their cleverly phrased questions.

Every time he tried to complain about his detention or raise the subject of his legal rights, an interrogator would remind him things in America had changed since 9/11. It was a matter of national security. His rights were whatever they decided.

Late one night, while the moon shone brightly outside his room, two of the captors woke him from sleep, ordered him to dress, and escorted him to a waiting SUV. Frau Schäffer was already inside the vehicle, her hands cuffed in her lap, her seat belt very tightly fastened.

Watching the brightly lit digital clock of the dashboard, Wendal could see their drive took less than an hour. He realized they had headed south towards the Keys but turned off the highway in Homestead. There were no flashing lights or sirens. They entered what could only be an Air Reserve base, then went around behind the darkened buildings to a running helicopter. The door to the chopper opened the moment the SUV stopped. Their escorts pushed them up the stairs into the aircraft, bundled them into rear seats, snugly buckled them in, and slammed the doors shut.

Within seconds, the helicopter engine revved to higher speed and slowly took off. They rose gradually to a height of several hundred feet, then they were thrust back into their seats as the jet engine of the helicopter surged forward. Within moments they were over water with the only light a bright moon in a cloudless sky. It was eerie. An illuminated sky above, black water below, and the roar of the helicopter engine all combined to give Wendal a sense of penetrating fear.

Frau Schäffer appeared equally bewildered. Her face was pale. Her usually long, thick hair was now cropped short, almost like that of a young boy, and looked equally unruly. Her facial expression was taut, her lips held tightly together as she stared straight ahead. She rigidly avoided any eye contact with Wendal and conveyed a stoic spirit.

They continued that way for the entire flight – more than an hour Wendal guessed – until the aircraft touched down on a helipad in the center of a sprawling compound. Several heavily armed military people were waiting on the ground, weapons at the ready. Still handcuffed, Wendal and Frau Schäffer were led to a processing center and almost immediately separated.

Intensely focused army personnel roughly searched Wendal, including all his body cavities, then watched as he showered and dressed in the new garb they handed him. They accompanied him to a cell with a single bed, a toilet, and a small bureau for personal effects. He sadly noted that he had no personal effects to store away.

When he looked out the tiny window at eye level, he saw a fenced-in area with people aimlessly walking around the perimeter. They all looked to be foreigners, most with long, unkempt beards. Their demeanor appeared subdued, with body language that projected defeat. It finally dawned on him; incredibly, he was inside the notorious American prison for suspected terrorists at Guantanamo Bay in Cuba.

More than three months had passed since the fateful night they brought him to this disreputable hell-hole. Every day, his captors questioned him at length about Howard Knight, about Wendal's business in Europe, about Frau Schäffer, and what he knew about human trafficking, of all things!

Anytime Wendal tried to ask why they were holding them at Guantanamo or treating him like a terrorist, the interrogators ignored his question. "Just worry about good answers to *our* questions," one or the other usually snarled.

Eventually, Wendal and Frau Schäffer were allowed to meet for about an hour each day in a supervised courtyard. They seemed to think the pair were friends and encouraged them to play games, get some exercise, and relax. Frau Schäffer had almost immediately spotted and pointed out the hidden microphones as she whispered that everything they said was being recorded.

Over time, Frau Schäffer gradually became Klaudia, and their relationship shifted from wary adversaries to cautious friends. Always aware they were being watched and recorded, they carefully guarded every conversation. Gradually, their mutual interests – music, movies, video games, and technology – became the focus of their sessions. The more they talked, the more Wendal realized they had in common. Sometimes, their conversations were punctuated with humor and laughter as they developed code words to complicate the mission of their captors and provide relief from their unimaginable plight.

To their mutual surprise and delight, at one point their captors presented them with a Microsoft Xbox and allowed them to game with each other for two or three hours every evening. It turned out that Klaudia was an excellent video-gamer and far more competitive that Wendal expected. Their gaming provided a welcome diversion from the interrogations and dire circumstances. Then, just last week, everything changed.

An important-looking official in a business suit disembarked from a helicopter early one morning. Behind him, dressed casually, six younger people stepped down and followed the official into the nearest building carrying what appeared to be laptop cases. Wendal and Klaudia were summoned to meet with them in a large office with several guards watching. The room immediately fell silent as they were led into an office and offered seats across a huge desk where the new man-in-a-suit was waiting.

"We'll get right down to business," he said without introducing himself or offering any form of identification. "You're both in terrible predicaments. Randall, we've directly linked you to a computer that stored data received from your missing and presumed deceased colleague Willy Fernandez. We've got enough evidence to go before a grand jury and seek a charge of murder. On top of that, we've got those charges of hacking into the Multima Supermarkets IT system and stealing private information. Finally, we can charge you with sheltering a fugitive by bringing the charming Frau Schäffer into the United States with you," he said, perhaps expecting the sarcastic taunt about the woman to evoke a response.

"Even if you can hire some brilliant attorney to save your ass, we think we can make enough charges stick to keep you behind bars for at least forty-five years with little chance of parole. Reflect on that for a while," he said, leaning forward menacingly before he shifted his gaze to Klaudia.

"As for you, Frau Schäffer, our friends at Interpol can hardly wait to get their hands on you," the large man said, starting to read aloud from a paper in his hand. "Wanted by police in Germany for human-trafficking in more than one hundred individual cases. Sought by police in Romania as a person of interest in a matter of thirty-five women missing over the past five years. Wanted by police in Kazakhstan as a person of interest related to the disappearances of more than ninety women missing over the past nine years, and three separate murders – one involving torture and mutilation," he intoned. Then he paused to see the effect these revelations were having on the pair.

"Allow me to continue," he resumed after again glaring at each of them for a moment. "Pursued by police in Azerbaijan as a person of interest in the disappearance of more than three hundred women in just the past two years.

Or perhaps you'd like to think about the police in Uzbekistan who would like to chat with you about more than five hundred missing women and girls – some as young as ten years old. They also maintain you were involved in at least five murders – again involving torture and mutilation. Once they finish questioning you, they think you'll probably want to confess to even more!"

Wendal and Klaudia sat silently without saying a word. He was simply speechless and appalled to learn the alleged despicable crimes of his companion. Frau Schäffer flinched but seemed to think it unwise to make any comment at this stage. Both stared straight ahead at the man-in-a-suit whose every voice inflection and body mannerism oozed menace.

He stared back wordlessly for several minutes. Then he sipped from a water bottle before asking, "Are you both getting a clear picture of what's in store?"

Terrified, neither Wendal nor Klaudia spoke, but both nodded their heads once in the affirmative.

The man-in-a-suit continued. "I have two last pieces of information you might want to consider. Yesterday, a very trusted informant in New York let us know that someone who goes by the name of Giancarlo Mareno is looking for you. Does that name mean anything to either of you?"

Both Klaudia and Wendal immediately shook their heads no.

"Well, let me tell you a little about Mr. Mareno. He's a wealthy and powerful man who we think is the head honcho in America for a secretive but nasty bunch known as The Organization. It seems he'd really like to find both of you. So much so, he's apparently offered a bounty of two million dollars to anyone who can capture and bring you to him. That's one million dollars each if someone brings you to him alive. I understand the amount drops to only five hundred thousand each if they simply kill you. Now why do you suppose he might like to pay double the amount to have a word with you?" he hissed in a mocking tone as he leaned even more intimidatingly towards them.

Klaudia gasped, either in shock or with a realization of the seriousness of their situation. Wendal watched as all color drained from her face and thought she might faint on the spot. There was no doubt. Their plight had become something more than ominous.

"I told you I have two last pieces of information. You might also want to think carefully about this, too. Mr. Mareno is also willing to pay five million dollars to anyone who finds and kills either Howard Knight or someone known as Fidelia Morales. Five million each," he emphasized.

In shock, Klaudia instinctively raised her hand to cover her mouth, shaking her head in apparent disbelief at what she was hearing.

"That tells us that Knight and this woman Morales must be much more important to Mr. Mareno than either of you," he continued. "Because they are more crucial to him, you might have a chance to redeem yourselves and save your lives.

"Personally, what I have to say next absolutely disgusts me. I'd love to return you, Frau Schäffer, to a police force in one of the 'stans' we just talked about. I'd enjoy watching their interrogation methods extract real justice before you ever got near a court. Frankly, I think you deserve to die a most horrible death," the man-in-a-suit said in a stage whisper.

"And you, Randall. My conscience would be entirely clear letting you wither away in some nice federal facility with other scum who don't deserve to see the light of day. Unfortunately, though, I've been ordered to offer you a way out."

From the corner of his eye, Wendal could see Klaudia trembling as she listened. She seemed on the verge of tears. And her normally staid facial expression now conveyed acute distress. But, like Wendal, she remained silent as the threatening individual stared at them with an expression of disdain and distaste.

"Here's the deal. I'll explain it one time. There will be no negotiation. If you agree to work with us and accept our terms, you will sign the document I have in my hand. And you'll sign it right now. There will be no more time to think about it. So, listen carefully.

"We know you're small fries compared to the truly potent leaders in The Organization. That's who we want – Mareno and his partners in America, Europe, and around the globe. We think Knight and Morales can provide us the information we need to build a solid case against Mareno and his friends.

"We understand both of you are some sort of computer geniuses, and we want to harness your technological abilities to find Knight and Morales before Mareno and his cohorts can kill them.

"My superiors are prepared to admit you to the FBI witness protection program if you'll agree to testify in court. Wendal, you'll commit to telling a court all the information you shared with us about your interactions with Knight and his blackmail with the video," he announced, looking intently at Wendal, then shifting his attention after a long moment.

"Frau Schäffer, you'll agree to tell the court everything you gave us about Knight and the other people in Europe. In return, we'll relocate you both to a secret location in the United States, give you new identification, and provide protection from any retaliation by The Organization. We do this very well.

"But my superiors also want to give you an incentive to work hard. We need you to find both fugitives very quickly. So, they'll give you contracts to provide computer consulting services for the next five years and pay you a fee of two million dollars per year. But the consulting contract only kicks in if you find Knight and Morales and we can capture them before Mareno does," the man-in-a-suit said as he started to pace back and forth in front of them.

"If you accept our offer, you'll work with these six people," he said, gesturing to the young team. "They'll work in shifts – around the clock if you like. One of them will be with each of you whenever you're near computers. They will immediately report to me if you try any tricks, divulge your location, or communicate with anyone. If there is a violation, our deal is off. We'll transport you back to the mainland and release you – right after we tell our informant exactly where he should go to earn a quick two million dollars.

"We strongly suspect Knight and Morales are on the run together. And we've pieced together some useful information that suggests they are somewhere in South America. These folks with me all speak Spanish fluently and are among the brightest technologically inclined minds we have in the FBI. They all have clearance to use our most sophisticated software applications, and you'll have access to the same technology through them," he explained as he stopped pacing and faced them again.

"My superiors think a combination of your reputed knowledge and expertise, together with our systems' capabilities, can lead us to the fugitives. If they're right, and you're as good as people claim, you'll not only get a chance to live a protected life; you'll get at least ten million dollars for your trouble.

"Do we have a deal?" he asked, dropping a single piece of paper in front of first Wendal, then Klaudia.

They took one quick look at each other and said "Yes."

The remainder of the meeting took only a few minutes as both read and signed the simple, life-saving agreement. The man-in-a-suit disappeared immediately after gathering up the signed documents. They could hear the helicopter rotors whine as it lifted only moments later, just as a young woman stepped forward from the group of six and introduced herself. "I'm Maria Gonzalez. I think we should begin work right away."

Seventeen

La Paz, Bolivia. Afternoon,
Monday July 7, 2016

Two days after leaving the beautiful village of Escoma and the warm welcome of residents there, Howard Knight and Fidelia Morales came to an abrupt realization that they would need to change their carefully devised plan. To their dismay, La Paz would no longer work as a long-term destination to hide from either the FBI or The Organization.

The first day out had been uneventful. Using a strategy of walking at night and sleeping by day, they set out following Highway 16 southward towards La Paz. They walked briskly and arrived at the outskirts of the tiny village of Carabuco just before dawn.

On plan, they changed direction and walked farther inland about a mile to a mountain range. There, Howard pitched their tent out of view and they both slept soundly until mid-afternoon. By now, both were comfortable sleeping in the fresh air of the great outdoors. They'd also adapted to resting with only sleeping bags cushioning their bodies on the rough rock surfaces. Furthermore, their arduous amount of walking each day usually drained any remaining energy by the time each campsite was ready. That first night south from Escoma, sleep came quickly.

Awake again about eight hours later, they ate a breakfast of sunflower seeds and walnuts, then performed their daily rituals. Within an hour, they repacked their tent and resumed the march towards the village refreshed and ready for another ten-to-fifteen-mile walk. From her research back in Florida, Fidelia remembered that Google Maps listed the population of Carabuco at about four hundred people, so she had few expectations for the village.

A late afternoon sun still shone brightly in a picture-perfect blue sky. There wasn't a cloud in sight. As they entered the village, Fidelia took a deep breath, looked around, and was immediately smitten by the brightly colored collections of homes and buildings nestled between Highway 16 and Lake Titicaca.

To her delight, Carabuco looked peaceful, romantic, and welcoming. Her mood brightened, and she felt unusually good vibes from the town. Almost idyllic, she thought. For a few moments, she savored the karma of the pleasant surroundings, her new-found fitness, and resurfacing warm thoughts about her lover. It seemed perfect – until Howard Knight abruptly smashed her euphoria.

"Shit!" he exclaimed as he stopped suddenly and slapped his forehead with his palm in an expression of unconcealed exasperation. Fidelia watched his face suddenly blanch before he turned towards her and said, "It's too risky for us to settle in La Paz."

She was speechless and looked at him inquisitively.

"I don't know how I could have forgotten it when we were making the plan. But I did. The Organization owns shares in a huge mining conglomerate. They control its management and have infiltrated the communication chain of the company thoroughly. They took over a small gold mining company in Bolivia last year.

"Do you see that sign we just passed back there? The one that says *Empresa Minadoro. Turn left 5 KM*? That's the company they bought. They own that mine just outside Escoma, and I forgot all about it until I saw that sign! They have a direct link to The Organization. They can easily learn we're in Bolivia," he moaned, covering his face with his hands.

"How?" Fidelia asked.

"I remember they had concerns about protesters. Apparently, there's a significant population in Bolivia that hates the gold mining business and its impact on the environment. So, the company monitors the whole town with security video. They want to be able to identify outside agitators and help police round them up. I saw dozens of security cameras spread around Escoma. I remember now. Empresa Minadoro has an elite team that uses face recognition software to identify outsiders."

"So, you think they'd report us to the Bolivian police?" Fidelia asked.

"No. If The Organization sent photos of us to any of their contacts around the world – including Empresa Minadoro – it would be a basic computer search of video records to compare with our photos and find a match. Your wig and my goatee instead of a beard won't be enough. Within minutes, they can capture our identities and learn we've been in Escoma. They'd just narrow their search to Bolivia and surely assume we would eventually visit La Paz."

"Right. That's a complication we didn't foresee," Fidelia said calmly. "Do you think there is any possibility they haven't put our photos out to their network of contacts?"

"Very little," Howard replied. "Look, it's been five months since my escape from that board meeting at Multima. Four months since you left for a vacation in Europe. We both know Giancarlo Mareno. He's probably more than pissed by now. My guess is he's pulling every string he can."

Within moments, they decided to minimize their time in the quaint village of Carabuco. They'd buy enough food and water for a week, then retreat to the mountain range outside the town. There, they'd regroup and decide how to modify their exhaustively crafted plans to deal with this ominous new complication.

They spent the afternoon talking through options. By evening, they reached two conclusions. First, La Paz would no longer work for more than a quick visit. Even if more than two million people lived in the region, it would be almost impossible to live without leaving a security video footprint somewhere. More importantly, they needed to find a way to alter their physical appearance significantly. Video monitoring could also be a risk in any small town or village. They'd need cosmetic surgery, they decided. Surgery had risks as well, but they saw no alternative under the circumstances. Once that was decided, they only had to figure out where and how.

To travel anywhere they could undergo cosmetic surgery safely, they'd need to pass through La Paz. They decided to risk visiting the city but only to get to its international airport. As they worked their way south, they'd choose where to fly from La Paz and how they could safely navigate that city without detection.

In the meantime, they planned to become even less visible for a few days. Google Maps showed an unnamed road leading in an easterly direction from Highway 16 to connect with another unnamed road heading southward towards La Paz. A check of their replenished food and water supply assured them they had enough.

After dark, they put on their night vision goggles again and set out along the highway for about three miles. There, they found the eastbound road and walked until the first sign of dawn. As usual, they searched for a nearby campsite hidden from the road. They found one within minutes and pitched their tent and slept through the day.

For six nights and days, they repeated that process, hiking along the two unnamed roads until they connected again with Highway 16 just north of the Bolivian village of Achacachi. There, Howard's GPS watch indicated they were hiking at an elevation of 12,644 feet, causing both to marvel at how drastically their physical fitness had improved as they acclimated to the elevation and built endurance with their daily walking.

While they trudged through solitary darkness those long, quiet nights, they talked for hours about their circumstances. They considered dozens of options and plotted to find a new survival plan. When they found holes in one idea, they immediately moved to another and talked that one through.

Fidelia realized Howard's oversight about video surveillance was a potentially fatal mistake but rationalized that neither of them had more than functional expertise with technology. Still, he should have told her about the mining company in Escoma months earlier. She felt strongly about that. Regardless, it was imperative they devise and implement a meticulous new strategy.

As she thought about those conversations – especially the ones about cosmetic surgery – she realized the pair had fused even closer together. Thoughts of capture and an almost certain horrible death should The Organization find them were always present but never discussed. The possibility of being snatched by the FBI and separated by incarceration was also real, and far too painful even to contemplate. Although unspoken, she was sure Howard shared her determination to find a way to buy more time together.

One week after leaving Carabuco, as they approached the village of Batallas – thirty miles or so from La Paz – they finally settled on a new plan. It wasn't perfect. Nor was it easy to implement. It would involve considerable sums of money and risks for them both. But it had a good chance of success.

On arrival in the town of Batallas, they determined where and when the next bus to the city would pass and prepared themselves for a flurry of activity when they arrived in La Paz. From the roadside, they finally detected cell phone signals which they used to locate a hostel near the airport. Then, they checked airline flight times and prices. Finally, they discussed how they might find a place to stay when they arrived at their new destination.

As they wrapped up details for their brief pause in La Paz, the bus arrived. It was about an hour later than expected, but neither was overly concerned. Both travelers had long acclimated to the vagaries of Bolivians' concept of time. Far less precise than Americans, a given hour was usually a mere approximation of when something might occur.

As they also expected, the bus was almost full. The route originated in the larger town of Copacabana, so many passengers had already embarked there or at the several stops in between. Prepared, each paid the driver cash, found seats in separate parts of the bus, and settled in for the two-hour ride to the stop near Hostal Austria a few miles from El Alto International Airport.

The bus ride was uneventful. A friendly and helpful driver stopped at the intersection of Avenida Mariscal Santa Cruz and Cochabamba in La Paz, just a ten-minute walk from the hostel, and their room was ready when they arrived. They paid for one night with Boliviano and performed their usual hotel room security precautions before going to work on a hostel computer.

For several days, Fidelia had agonized over their next step. She knew it was a risk to contact anyone from their former worlds, but they desperately needed to find a discreet plastic surgeon who could safely transform their facial features. There was one other person who she could trust with her life.

That woman lived in Belgrade, Serbia. Fidelia knew her friend had personally undergone cosmetic surgery after a particularly violent night with one of her clients. Several years earlier, that friend located a surgeon in Argentina who was superbly qualified and could be trusted completely. It was rumored – but never proven – that he had transformed the faces of dozens of felons and political refugees over the years.

It would be expensive. And it would be risky to travel to Buenos Aires and stay there for a few weeks recovering from surgery. But they couldn't think of a better alternative, so she made the call.

While Howard continued to research information on the hostel's internet connection from a cubby-hole off the lobby, Fidelia returned to their tiny room with twin beds and bright yellow walls. She reached into her backpack for another disposable cell phone to replace the one they discarded in Carabuco. The first one she grabbed looked like it didn't have enough battery life for an international call, so she chose another and dialed.

Her friend was delighted to hear from Fidelia and asked no questions about her whereabouts. She understood the need immediately, again with no questions. Then, she offered to make the necessary appointments for precisely two weeks later. She also knew of a safe house where they could stay and meet the surgeon for a consultation. She'd used it herself. An American who wouldn't ask questions owned it, and the Serbian friend could rent the apartment for a month, paying for it by Western Union. There would be no records. Fidelia could settle with her sometime later.

Within minutes, they agreed Fidelia would call back in two days for confirmation of both the surgery and the apartment plus any additional instructions. With tender expressions of mutual love, the women reluctantly ended their conversation.

Eighteen

Aboard a Bombardier Challenger 300 jet to Chicago.
Evening, Friday July 15, 2016

Janet Weissel finally had a few minutes to appreciate the sumptuous luxury of the Multima Financial Services corporate jet. She loved the smell of leather and plush texture of the seats. She also enjoyed sharing the newfound swagger of success her boss projected earlier that morning. She was starting to think that she might eventually tolerate working with this woman she usually thought of as the Bitch.

Of course, she never used that term aloud, but their relationship had not started at all well. It began when she showed up for her new assignment in Financial Services and first met Natalia Tenaz. The Bitch showed her to an assigned cubicle, one with virtually no privacy. There were only three-foot walls on two sides of her workstation. The rest of the cubicle was open, and the Bitch had a direct sight line to everything she was doing. Every time she looked away from her computer screen, the woman seemed to be watching.

A few hours later that same first day, her new boss summoned her into a small conference room near their work area and closed the door. Then, for about a half hour, Tenaz read her the riot act. They had a dress code there. She described it in tedious detail and then told Janet she was expected to follow those rules, effective the next morning, even if she needed to go out and buy a new wardrobe. Provocative clothing would not be tolerated in their offices. Period.

Then, the Bitch outlined Janet's role in the group. She must have used the word 'team' a hundred times in that half-hour and emphasized that supporting her teammates would be Janet's most important responsibility. It would also be the primary factor upon which Tenaz would evaluate her work on a quarterly basis. More humiliation followed.

"Personal phones are not permitted in the office at any time," the woman told her. "Leave yours at home. Here's a new Samsung for you to use. It's company property and should be utilized primarily for company business. But you can use it for making personal calls or surfing the web if you do so reasonably.

"You must understand. All communication with your Samsung phone and desktop computer will be recorded automatically by sophisticated software that is regularly monitored by management. Improper use of communications equipment is grounds for immediate dismissal. Sharing any information classified as 'confidential' with anyone outside Financial Services – even in other divisions of Multima – will also result in immediate termination of employment," the Bitch said with a stern look on her face and body language that suggested she was secretly hoping for an opportunity to wield her newly delegated power.

It continued that way for several minutes until the woman finally got around to their actual work. That was the only thing that prevented Janet from walking out of the meeting and resigning from Multima. The Organization could just go to hell, she remembered thinking at one point.

Instead, by waiting a little longer, she learned they would be handling communication and project liaison for Multima Supermarkets' launch of the new Financial Services home mortgage business. Tenaz described how they would interact with senior management over at Supermarkets, including Suzanne Simpson, the most powerful woman in the entire corporation.

In the following weeks, Janet was surprised to be included in almost all meetings and conference calls. Natalia Tenaz often asked for her opinions and ideas. She also frequently assigned important tasks with critical deadlines. In fact, it was becoming harder to think of her as the Bitch. Instead, the woman seemed to be gradually winning her over.

A few days ago, her boss got a sudden inspiration. "Would there be merit to offering the new home mortgage program to the employees of Multima Supermarkets before everyone else?" Natalia asked in a meeting with their project leader. "Would it be a good idea for Supermarkets' employees to see how easy it is to apply and receive approval? Wouldn't it be helpful to have Supermarkets' employees see how smoothly the weekly payments work and realize how much they could save over the term of a mortgage?"

Norman Whiteside, the senior vice-president in charge of the mortgage initiative, thought this was a stroke of absolute genius and immediately contacted Suzanne Simpson to get her thoughts. Their conversation was broadcast to the entire meeting room from the speakerphone. Simpson was equally effusive and saw immediate benefits for her employees. She recognized how powerfully it could help with the home mortgages introduction and perhaps also assist with another issue she needed to raise with their labor union.

It was then the influential division president suggested Natalia and her team join her for discussions with the workers' representatives. Suzanne would arrange a meeting to introduce the idea and win the union's approval for this change to their collective agreement. That's when Whiteside offered up the jet for Natalia and whomever she needed to accompany her to Atlanta.

When they met at the private aviation section of Midway Airport early that morning, Natalia Tenaz was clearly in awe of the company jet. It was her first time on a private aircraft, and her mannerisms showed she was genuinely impressed both by the luxurious interior and executive comforts.

Janet suppressed a knowing smile as she thought back to her own recent first experience on a company jet. Douglas Whitfield's plane was smaller but equally luxurious, she thought. Wistfully, her thoughts drifted back to their sensational flight from Miami to Chicago just a few weeks earlier. It had been her introduction to the mile-high club, and she remembered their sex was over-the-top spectacular.

Despite her best efforts, her mind lingered on that flight. She could almost feel the heat and lust of Whitfield's kisses and caresses after they reached cruising altitude that day. Whitfield knew right away what she wanted to do and undressed her completely within minutes. She had never felt better about herself as she watched him hungrily kiss every part of her before he drew her completely on top of him in the plush leather seats.

They made love twice before a pilot came out of the cockpit and caught her on top of Whitfield with his penis deep inside her vagina. She smiled at him and even twisted her waist a bit so he could have a glimpse of her bare breasts. She thought it never hurt to advertise a little. After all, one never knew when another liaison might be helpful. She caught the pilot's grin of appreciation before he averted his eyes and dashed into the toilet.

Her flashback to their mile-high sexual escapade ended that morning when the private jet reached cruising altitude and Natalia suggested they review their PowerPoint presentations one more time before arrival. It was Janet's first opportunity to present some of the information to an external audience, and Natalia wanted to be sure everything went smoothly.

When they arrived at the meeting, Janet was grateful for the extra rehearsal. She was shocked to see more than twenty people in the large conference room with a long, oval table and projection screen at one end. Half the contingent was from the Multima workers' union, and they were casually milling about the room drinking coffee or eating pastries as they introduced themselves to the management participants.

Suzanne Simpson's arrival at precisely the official nine o'clock start seized Janet's attention and held her entranced. She was watching the executive operate in a meeting for the first time and was amazed at how the woman changed the atmosphere simply by entering the room. Her smile was radiant. The expensive business suit, tasteful hairstyle, and touches of makeup expertly highlighted her extraordinarily beautiful features.

Suzanne first strode confidently towards Fernando Disputas, president of the syndicate, and greeted him with a warm hug. A hug! Whoever heard of a company president welcoming a union representative with a hug? Surprisingly, they actually seemed to like each other as they exchanged greetings with easy laughter and carefree gestures.

Suzanne seemed to know all the people representing labor and greeted each by first name as she gracefully completed a maneuver that included a brief hug while shaking each person's hand. Janet watched her make direct eye contact with each member of the union team and consistently flash her dazzling smile.

Suddenly, it was their turn. "It's so nice of you to join our meeting today, Natalia," Suzanne gushed as they warmly embraced. "Everyone is so anxious to hear your proposal!"

"Janet," she continued, "I feel like we've known each other for months. I'm really looking forward to hearing your suggestions on employee engagement."

She performed this ritual for about ten minutes as she made her way around the table for brief personal contact with every participant in the meeting, including the handful from her own Multima Supermarkets management team, before reaching her seat. It was located precisely in the middle of the row of chairs on the side facing towards the window, directly across from the union president.

From the moment Suzanne Simpson formally welcomed her guests, until the meeting concluded mid-afternoon, Janet was in awe of the skill Suzanne used to engage every participant in the meeting. She had started with a very brief background overview before she asked Natalia to introduce the proposed employee home mortgage program.

Natalia outlined how the plan would work, starting with the benefits to employees. Then, she explained how employees could apply and qualify to transfer their mortgages from a current lender to Multima Financial Services. After, she described how the new loans would operate, particularly an innovative new weekly payment requirement. Then, she used PowerPoint examples to show how much employees could save. She even talked about the flexibility they envisaged for employees, including an option to choose automatic deductions from their paychecks for required payments.

When it was Janet's turn to explain how they proposed to introduce the program to employees – and the role the union might play – she was nervous at first. But her anxiousness quickly evaporated as she watched the first skeptical facial expressions of the union people warm to smiles and active listening questions. Her segment was designed to take about ten minutes. But, because Suzanne encouraged her to take questions as they went along, the time stretched to almost an hour. She handled most of the queries, but Natalia had jumped in to clarify a technical issue or two that she couldn't immediately answer.

Once Natalia and Janet had finished their segments, Suzanne masterfully took control of the meeting. She asked Fernando Disputas for feedback and listened intently as he posed a few questions about the anticipated timing. Then Suzanne went around the table seeking comments from each of the participants, including her own team. Intrigued, Janet watched as she encouraged members to voice criticisms or concerns. Then, was amazed to see the executive clarify each possible resolution, noting that she always phrased her answers with another question like, "Would something along these lines make you more comfortable?"

The discussion was always calm. They expressed objections or concerns with respect and decorum. Before Janet realized it, Suzanne Simpson was summarizing her understanding of the consensus they had reached. She spoke at a measured pace and didn't refer to any notes. Then, she asked Fernando Disputas if she'd accurately summarized all the details and adequately addressed the union's concerns.

"As usual, you've summarized the discussion very articulately, Suzanne," the cagey union negotiator replied. "But I think we need to know what you're asking in return before I say more. I've been around long enough to know if Multima Supermarkets is offering a new employee benefit part-way through a contract, you must want something in return."

"You're right," Suzanne replied. "I need the union's support to start testing automated check-outs right away, not when we negotiate a new contract in two years. Here's what I propose. I'd like to start testing automated check-outs when we do renovations in the Southwest Florida stores. That's thirty-five locations. We plan to remove four traditional checkouts and replace them with eight automated stations. We'll use one employee to oversee the eight machines for each shift. We'll restrict the test to those stores until the current contract expires, then share our observations with you and discuss whether we want to expand the program at that time." Then, she waited for his response.

"A headcount reduction," Disputas responded, his tone suddenly cooler. "That's all I heard from your short speech. And we've made it abundantly clear before that we're not prepared to support reductions in staffing without other major offsets. Market-testing Multima's new home mortgage program doesn't offset lost wages and union membership."

Janet watched the body language of both Natalia Tenaz and Suzanne Simpson. Natalia appeared crestfallen. Her shoulders slumped. Her smile disappeared. Silently, she started to wring her hands, concerned her idea – and all their work – was about to be torpedoed by the objecting union president.

On the other hand, Suzanne appeared completely relaxed. Her smile even seemed to brighten. She crossed her legs and shifted her seating position slightly to fix her gaze directly on Disputas.

"I hear your discomfort, Fernando," she responded warmly. "Your members surely don't want to see terminations or a reduction in their hours. We get that. And I think you know Multima management well enough to know we share your concern for our employees and their job security. We don't make changes to headcount or working hours unless it's absolutely required.

"We also understand the union's dilemma. We realize any reductions in either hours worked, or numbers of employees, directly impact the income you receive. We get that too, and we're not looking to create financial challenges for your local.

"But we must adapt to the changing marketplace, or we'll lose sales. If we lose revenue, we'll certainly have to reduce employee hours and probably headcount. And, if our sales decline is dramatic, it will impact our ability to make a profit and lead to store closures or more drastic actions that could be even more painful for our employees," she said and stopped selling again to give Disputas a chance to respond.

"Why is this suddenly an urgent issue? Why can't we deal with it in the next round of negotiations?" Disputas wondered.

"I think we can deal with the broader issue of technology in the next round," Suzanne conceded. "But we need to do the test. Piggly Wiggly stores in Southwest Florida have already started using automated check-outs. We hear that Best Foods will install some equipment next month. Our store managers are reporting that a few loyal customers are expressing a preference for the convenience of the technology and sales have already dipped.

"Here's what I suggest," Suzanne calmly offered. "Let's agree to move forward with the test as I described. I'll give you my word. We won't reduce either the number of employees or the number of hours they work during the next twelve months. Let's see how customers react to the test. Let's study the economics of the technology. We'll share our results with you before we start the next round of negotiations. Then, we can both negotiate with facts rather than fear."

The union president asked for a few minutes to huddle with his team before responding, and Suzanne agreed without hesitation. She invited the management team to her office for a coffee while Disputas discussed her proposal with his colleagues. There, Suzanne again thanked Natalia and Janet, complimented their excellent delivery of the presentation, and told them not to worry. She'd find a way to get agreement from Disputas and the union.

Surprisingly, they hadn't finished their coffee when Suzanne's assistant came in to let her know the labor representatives were ready to resume discussions. More shocking to Janet, Disputas was laughing and joking with his negotiating team when they returned to the meeting room.

"We'll need your undertaking in writing, Suzanne, including your offer to share all the results of the automated checkout pilot test," he started. "We'll also need a commitment that you won't expand the test or install automated checkouts in more stores than Southwest Florida until the next contract negotiations. If you accept those conditions, we'll support the test."

"Fair enough, Fernando. We'll do that before you leave," Suzanne replied. "But let's both remember one principle neither of us can change. Technology will continue its relentless march whether we want it to or not. And companies or unions who fight progress are doomed to failure. You know that for almost half a century John George Mortimer has been steadfast in his loyalty to our employees, your members. You also know I share his passion.

"But bear with me while I rant about one fundamental reality. The only way to assure job security for our employees and your union is to help us to grow our sales and our share of the market every day our team comes to work. If you continue to work with us to instill and reinforce that fundamental responsibility among your members, I have no doubt our company will continue to succeed. If we can continue to expand, we'll treat current employees fairly. But we can only do that if our workforce is committed to growth," she finished.

As they wrapped up their meeting and returned to the corporate jet, Janet continued to be completely in awe of Suzanne Simpson. She had never seen a woman lead so skillfully and was impressed with her negotiation skills. Particularly, she was fascinated that someone could create such a positive, even warm, atmosphere throughout the session. Plus, it was the first time she could recall really admiring another woman!

Nineteen

Roland LaMontagne gingerly eased his small, silver Fiat 550 up a narrow, dark, and winding underground parking ramp to an attended booth at ground level. There, he was shocked to learn the fee for three hours parking in the Royal Bank Tower was forty-three dollars.

Compared with the usual ten or eleven dollars – certainly no more than fifteen – he might pay to park in a similar building in Quebec City, he questioned the attendant three times to be sure he had not misunderstood. He knew his command of English was limited, but he finally conceded to the exorbitant charge when the lot attendant brusquely pointed to a lighted digital monitor above the left front fender of the car. It displayed the same amount, so he paid.

Muttering to himself about such an unfair cost just for parking, Roland waited for a gap in the constant stream of passing pedestrians before he could join the one-way flow of traffic onto the street his GPS instructed him to follow. Several more minutes and a few turns later, he found himself nervously driving along the Don Valley Parkway with several thousand other vehicles.

As he headed northbound towards Highway 401, the car's speedometer sometimes registered just below the limit. Moments later, brake lights would suddenly flash red, and the pace reduced to a crawl. Sometimes they came to complete stops. It quickly became very tedious and annoying.

Roland soon found his thoughts drifting back to all the circumstances leading up to his just-finished, unpleasant, and unproductive meeting with the attorney Roger Liveenwel at the Toronto headquarters of Berister Law LLP. He had arranged the meeting soon after discovering the lawyer's name and contact information in the stacks of files left behind by his murdered father.

Almost immediately after his father's death, Roland decided he should do all his digging into Madame Marcotte's files without the aid of his father's secretary. To quickly eliminate all possible expenses related to his father's business, he let the woman go immediately. Later, he regretted his haste as he discovered her filing wasn't up to date. In fact, he found hundreds of bits of paper stacked on surfaces around the office.

His father had a propensity for scrawling notes on small post-its and either tucking them in files or sticking them on surfaces to remind him to file them away later. Often, Roland couldn't determine which was the case as he sat in his father's swivel chair for hours trying to match scrawled notes and comments with folders from his large metal cabinet.

Madame Marcotte's file was not a thick one, so Roland concluded his father had not devoted much time or energy to the project until quite recently. The notes he finally thought might correspond to Madame Marcotte's concerns were usually vague and oblique, often with punctuation that suggested frustration or even irritation.

It was clear that someone didn't want the true source of the funds discovered. It was equally evident that someone had spent a lot of money creating companies and legal blockades to prevent discovery. His father had concluded that it must be someone at Multima, but his notes never explained how he reached that conclusion.

The slip of paper that led Roland to a decision to meet with the attorney in Toronto was one that didn't seem to fit with either the information his father shared before his death or other scraps of paper in the file.

> *02-29-2016 Call from Mme. Marcotte. Distraught. Received 4 calls from same stranger last week. No identity given. Phone company told her a blocked number in USA.*
>
> *Each time, caller offered to buy her share certificates in numbered company. Last offer for $500K! Seeks advice <u>urgently</u>. Agreed we'd meet 03-04-16 @ 2 p.m.*

Was this a hint of the reason someone wanted to kill the woman? There was no indication his father investigated the calls any further. Nor could Roland find an explanation for either Madame Marcotte's distress or the reason she wouldn't want to sell her shares for such a large sum of money.

Although *notaire* LaMontagne and that source seemed sure a subsidiary of Multima Corporation was the mysterious entity depositing three thousand dollars per month in the bank account of his deceased client, Roland wanted conclusive evidence of the facts from someone representing the company.

Now that the meeting with the lawyer was over, Roland found it frustrating on many levels. First, he had worked so hard that day and went away with so little information of real benefit. Travel to Toronto started incredibly early. His alarm sounded at three o'clock in the morning, disturbing the almost total silence in his Ste-Foy bedroom. Rushing to prepare, he was in his car and on the road by three-thirty. A departure that early was essential to avoid the expected crush of rush-hour traffic congestion as he passed through Montreal.

His travel strategy worked. By about six-thirty that morning, he was successfully past Montreal and stopped at the first service center beside Ontario's Highway 401. There, he enjoyed two cups of coffee with his Tim Horton's donuts. He smiled as he thought about the irony. His first stop in anglophone Ontario was at the same fast-food outlet he saw on seemingly every second street corner in Quebec.

On the road towards Toronto again, he continued to gather his thoughts for the meeting, and the drive went smoothly. With only a couple more stops for snacks and fuel, he had sighed in relief as he maneuvered into the Royal Bank underground parking before one o'clock that afternoon. After his car was parked, locked, and checked twice, he followed a painted pathway from his vehicle three levels underground to an impressive marble lobby in the massive office tower.

Minutes later, an equally well-appointed elevator stopped in front of the impressive entrance to the offices of Berister Law LLP. Featuring more marble, polished brass fixtures and plush carpet that was deeper than he had ever seen in an office lobby, the ostentatious display of wealth did not impress him.

After a receptionist had called the office of Roger Liveenwel to announce his arrival, the beautiful and very expensively dressed young woman offered Roland a seat and cup of coffee. For the first few minutes, he had been quite comfortable. He mentally reviewed again all his research and details of the complicated subject he planned to discuss with the attorney.

Later, when a glance at his watch indicated the meeting should have started more than twenty minutes earlier, Roland walked across the spacious lobby to inquire if there was a problem. Apologetic, but apparently not surprised, the woman called to Liveenwel's office again and then relayed that the extremely busy lawyer was delayed for another few minutes with a meeting that ran longer than planned. Could she offer him another coffee?

To Roland's chagrin, it was almost a half-hour longer before another woman came to greet him and usher him into the even more elegantly decorated office of Roger Liveenwel. He rechecked the time and was annoyed to see it was just a few minutes before three o'clock – more than an hour later than scheduled and twelve hours since his long day began!

Apparently surprised to learn he was meeting with a priest, Liveenwel signaled that he was not of the Catholic faith. As he sputtered out apologies and excuses for the delay, he also asked if he should address his guest as 'Father' or 'His Excellency' or some other honorific. With a natural grin, Roland had assured him no formality was necessary: just his given name would be fine.

They got down to business after Liveenwel's rather hollow expression of condolence about Monsieur LaMontagne's murder. "I was sorry to learn of your father's death. I only met him once, but he seemed like a very nice man," the attorney began. After only a brief pause, he continued. "In our telephone conversation, you told me you wanted to discuss information I may have shared with your father. Where would you like to start?"

"I'm trying to better understand the relationship between my father's deceased client, Louise Marcotte, with this big American company, Multima Corporation. It seems very odd that a woman like Madame Marcotte would receive monthly payments for so many years without knowing why she was receiving them or from whom," Roland LaMontagne said.

"I'm not sure I can be of much help to you with that. I only know Multima Corporation because of their supermarkets. My wife shops there. I don't have any relationship with management at Multima. But, why would payments *to* Madame Marcotte be a concern for you?" Liveenwel asked.

Anxious to not divulge any of the sensitive information his father imparted before his death, Roland tried to approach the subject more obliquely. "I'm the executor of my dad's will. That includes communicating with his clients about the status of their affairs with my father at the time of his death. Suzanne Simpson, president of Multima Supermarkets, is listed as a client. The notes in my father's file indicate she seemed unaware of any relationship Madame Marcotte may have had with Multima. She asked my dad to investigate on her behalf and let her know what he could learn."

"Yes. You mentioned that when you called to make an appointment," Liveenwel responded tersely. "But I told you then I didn't expect to be much help to you."

Their circular conversation continued in that vein for a few more minutes. Roland probed from at least five different angles only to have the unflappable Roger Liveenwel deflect all queries politely but firmly. He tried to appeal to the lawyer's emotions, suggesting Suzanne's need for closure. Then, he fished for information appealing to Liveenwel's sense of fair play. He probed the legality of such payments. All his attempts met with a wall of resistance that Roland could not penetrate.

In desperation, he finally divulged his concern that there may be some connection to his father's murder. At that point, Liveenwel straightened in his chair, folded his arms across his chest, and said, "I'm very sorry about your father's passing and wish I could be of more help, but we'll need to end our conversation there, Father LaMontagne."

Then, he promptly stood up to punctuate the finality of his comment. With an abrupt, formal handshake, Liveenwel ushered Roland to the door of his office, with perfunctory good wishes for a safe return to Quebec City.

He continued to digest their conversation again as he coped with Toronto's rush-hour traffic. Roland thought about Liveenwel's carefully managed mannerisms as they spoke. With his keen eye and grasp of body language, he was certain the lawyer was hiding something. Now, how to get that information?

He continued to consider his quandary as traffic thinned and speeds gradually increased. He noted that he was veering onto Highway 401 and once again was about to cross the sprawling suburban areas of Toronto, with still another eight or nine hours to think about it all as he drove towards home.

As Roland LaMontagne settled in for that long drive back to Quebec City, he had no way of knowing that Liveenwel tried to make a call within moments of his departure. Unfortunately, after three rings, an automated attendant prompted him to leave a voicemail message for the person he wanted to reach. The message the lawyer left was succinct: "We need to talk. Urgently."

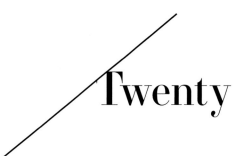

Twenty

Multima Headquarters, Fort Myers.
Early Evening, Wednesday August 17, 2016

The hair stylist held a large mirror at different angles so they both could inspect her work. His head was now almost entirely covered with gray fuzz about a quarter of an inch long. She did the best possible and said she thought he looked terrific. Her effort to at least make the length consistent would have to suffice until more grew in, they agreed.

Chemotherapy and radiation treatments had ended more than two months ago, but his hair seemed to be growing back in again very slowly. His oncologist advised patience. Everyone reacted differently to treatments, and he was sure John George would be fine and look great within a couple more months.

The stylist was equally confident. She claimed to have worked with dozens of clients who lost their hair during cancer treatments. It almost always grew back in again, though usually a little less densely. He'd be ready for television interviews on CBNN within weeks, she cheerfully assured him.

It wasn't an obsession, but John George realized his appearance was a crucial component of his role as Chief Executive Officer. Early in his career, he learned that good acting skills were part of the job. And one's appearance directly impacted one's ability to act. Truly successful business leaders learned to camouflage real emotions, maintain an aura of confidence, and project authority without creating fear. To do all those things well, he believed an image that implied good health, fitness, and a zest for life was essential.

As he dealt with the ravages of cancer surgery and treatments over the past few months, John George had little doubt his wan appearance had negatively impacted his image with his subordinates and others with whom he had contact.

The issue with Venture Capital Inc. was probably a case in point. He had taken a strong position with their CEO, Earnest Gottingham, denying him a place on Multima's board. John George wondered if both the new CEO and the people behind him had tried so assertively to fill the director position left vacant by Howard Knight only because they expected the cancer and its treatments might weaken his resolve.

John George also wondered if his own strong reaction, including the thinly veiled threat to VCI about using information obtained from Wendal Randall and Frau Schäffer, was also influenced by factors related to his health. That style of negotiation was not his standard *modus operandi*. Regardless, it seemed VCI had backed away from its original demand and was not following through on any of Gottingham's overt threats.

But John George expected this reprieve was temporary. Dan Ramirez shared his view. In fact, during their meeting earlier that day, his chief of corporate security spent more than an hour reviewing information he had received from his contacts in that secretive branch of the FBI. They were the folks not only holding Randall and Schäffer illegally at Guantanamo Bay but incenting them to use their vaunted technology skills to help the FBI find Howard Knight and his companion, Fidelia Morales.

Ramirez learned things were going well. As expected, Randall and Schäffer had accepted a deal, given verified statements to interrogators, and started working with FBI technologists with enthusiasm and apparent skill. The FBI was intrigued with the pair. "Brilliant" was the word they used to describe their input.

But, it was Frau Schäffer who was the real surprise. The FBI people knew about Randall's technological expertise but didn't realize the woman was a genius too. It seemed she graduated from a Russian university with the equivalent of a doctorate in computer sciences. But she abandoned her field for a life of crime with The Organization when they offered twenty times the salary she was earning as a programmer in the civil service. Now, she and Randall were working together like life-long collaborators!

The FBI apparently was astounded at the applications and depth of new knowledge both captives had already imparted to the six technologists assigned to work with them. Ramirez's contact told him they had implemented more than a dozen new programs monitoring telephone systems, airport security videos, and social media sites.

They still didn't have a precise location for the fugitives, but two intercepted calls between Eastern Europe and Bolivia suggested the fugitives were in Argentina. Police there were cooperating, and the FBI was growing more confident that either Knight or Morales would make a mistake soon.

John George took satisfaction in the way the FBI responded to Ramirez's suggestion and was equally pleased the results seemed positive. He never doubted that Randall would have the knowledge and expertise to tilt the odds in favor of the FBI. But he understood the risks.

For his scheme to succeed, the FBI had to find the fugitives soon. If The Organization located them first, Mortimer's own life might be in danger. It was also impossible to calculate the magnitude of impact The Organization might have on Multima's future. They could not only seize the company: they could also destroy it.

The whole morass was unfamiliar terrain for John George. And the way he was acting was completely out of character. By nature, he didn't usually break the law. He deplored secrecy and had worked a lifetime to encourage open communication and collaboration throughout his company.

Now, he found himself digging deeper. Of necessity, he was forced to compartmentalize communication. Only certain people could know fragmented bits of information. It was better for others to remain in the dark as much as possible. Wilma Willingsworth, for example. He had to tell his CFO about the huge amount he agreed to donate to the Internal Revenue Service.

"I'd like you to reserve ten million in the public relations expense account," he told her that morning. "There's no need to pay it until year-end, but I'd like that amount earmarked for payment as a corporate donation, with a request the IRS distribute it specifically to the FBI for technology research."

"The FBI? Technology research?" Wilma asked as her eyebrows arched. "I'm not even sure that qualifies as a *bona fide* corporate expense."

"Well it should, and I'd like you to find a way to do it. I think those reports we hear of cyber espionage by the Russians are a big issue. It's not only the impact they could have on our elections. It's also the vulnerability of our company computer systems that concerns me.

"If you think we might have a challenge with this, maybe you could work with Hadley. Find a way to gain some positive exposure. With the right spin, I think Fox Business News or others would jump all over it," John George had elaborated with his most sincere expression.

Reluctantly, the CFO accepted his instruction, but not before adding that he would also need to deal with Hadley. Ten million was a big amount, and there was no cushion in the overall budget. John George should explain why the vice-president for corporate and investor affairs would need to cut ten million somewhere else, she had insisted on her way out the door.

Later in the day, during his meeting with Alberto Ferer, he divulged Ramirez's interference with the FBI. The corporate legal counsel needed to know.

"I realize I should have discussed it with you before I took action, not after." John George apologetically broached the subject. "But we needed to act quickly, and I knew you'd have some reasonable concerns."

Alberto put down his notepad and pen, then tilted his head upwards in a posture of full concentration. John George didn't miss the signals of apprehension as he continued.

"You know Ramirez worked his contacts at the FBI to get Randall and the woman held secretly on a pretense of national security risks after we learned the Feds scooped them up at the Miami airport. You probably don't know the secret branch he works with has transferred them to Guantanamo Bay," John George said, noting Alberto's uncomfortable shift in posture and partially suppressed sigh.

"Don't worry. Ramirez assures me they aren't being tortured or anything like that. In fact, the FBI has worked some sort of a deal to drop their charges and protect them if they become witnesses. So, we won't need to worry about any lawsuits from Randall or demands for compensation. Apparently, he's satisfied with whatever the FBI came up with," he elaborated.

Despite the casual justification, Alberto protested. "John George, you know it's wrong. Not only is it in violation of several state and federal laws, but it's also just not right to violate the rights of an American, no matter how urgently we need information."

John George thought about the admonishment a moment before he quickly changed the subject. "Your concerns are noted," he replied coolly. "Have you heard anything more from your contacts over at VCI since I formally turned down their request to make Earnest Gottingham a director?"

"None," Alberto replied. "I haven't heard a peep since your call. I keep in regular contact with the SEC, and they haven't mentioned any concerns. We haven't detected any unusual trading in Multima shares. It's hard to imagine, but maybe The Organization has decided not to push the issue with VCI."

"It's not only hard to believe, Alberto. You and I know it's impossible. It's inconceivable they'll accept our position in the long term. Have you started those strategies we talked about to communicate effectively with shareholders in the event they take a run at us or try to sell off their preferred shares?" John George asked.

"Positive on both counts, John George," the corporate counsel replied. "I'm working with Hadley and his team to accumulate and maintain lists of email addresses for every shareholder. We've discreetly talked to investment bankers with enough heft to handle any deal VCI may try to make covertly. They all know we'll pay big incentives for information about any secret trades. And I've asked Whitfield over at Solutions to set up a monitor of the shady exchanges on the dark web. I think we're covered."

Despite his colleague's assurances, John George remained uneasy. The people running The Organization were just too obstinate to accept Multima's position as final. He wanted desperately to see the FBI, Randall, and Frau Schäffer succeed with their search in the coming days. Otherwise, John George expected he would continue to have trouble sleeping at night.

Added to all that, there was the lingering issue of Suzanne Simpson. For almost six months he had avoided meeting with her in person, unsure he could maintain secrecy as she drilled down on his excuses and explanations. He was also painfully aware her safety might become jeopardized should the wrong information inadvertently fall into unfriendly hands. Altogether, it made his feeling of guilt profound.

Today, he finally succumbed and agreed to meet with Suzanne. She was coming to visit and would stay at his home after an offsite company meeting at the end of September. It would make that encounter far more enjoyable if these unseemly issues with The Organization could be out of the way.

Twenty-One

Multima Financial Services, Hoffman Estates, Illinois.
Monday August 29, 2016

As planned, Multima Supermarkets and its employees' union jointly announced the new home mortgage program benefit in mid-August. But a new problem had just come to James Fitzgerald's attention. During a routine courtesy call with Suzanne Simpson last Friday, she mentioned that several employees in Alabama had complained about the Multima home mortgage program for employees. Was James aware the employee offering was not yet approved in the state of Alabama?

He certainly was not aware. Moreover, how did such a major oversight slip through the cracks? Immediately after his conversation with Suzanne, he summoned his new head of the home mortgage business, Norman Whiteside. He learned they had not sought approvals in Alabama, thinking the team would focus first on the states of Florida and Georgia where ninety-five percent of the employees lived. Alabama would come later when they had more time.

James stopped him right there. They needed to do a reality check.

"You're new with us Norman, so I'll take entire responsibility for this oversight. Apparently, I failed to convey to you a fundamental pact we have with our employees. It's in our DNA. It's the Multima business culture," James began.

"Let me explain. Every leader in this corporation – from John George Mortimer down the line – is expected to treat every employee equally. Every program we create must be available to every colleague at the same time and impact each team member fairly. It's not just a policy. It's also the way we think, live and work here," he emphasized.

"Apologies for the oversight, James. I just didn't realize the importance. I'll try to see that it doesn't happen again," Whiteside offered.

"Good. As I said, I'll handle any repercussions this time. But I want to underscore another important trait of our culture here at Multima. We encourage risks and know people make mistakes. But we expect everyone to learn from a mistake and never repeat it. And, on that note, I'll let go of my little lecture and return to our issue at hand," Fitzgerald said with a warm smile returning to his face.

"If we overlooked approvals for Alabama, how about our Canadian employees?" James wondered.

To his chagrin, the answer was negative. Like Alabama, the home mortgage business team planned to deal with a program for Canadian employees at a later stage, after the intense workload from the initial introduction settled down. Concerned, Fitzgerald continued his probe.

What about the snowbirds? Had they considered how many residents of New York, Illinois, Ohio, and other northern states lived part of the year in Florida, but maintained their primary residences elsewhere? Had they considered how many Canadian customers shopped at Multima Supermarkets in the winter months and might want to sign-up for a home mortgage program?

He was appalled to learn that Whiteside and his team had paid scant attention to all those concerns. It was essential to treat this situation as a learning opportunity and ensure his new business leader's team grasped Multima's underlying view of customer service. Like it or not, they would start to live it.

"I'll repeat it. You're still a relatively new guy here, so I'll assume responsibility for the gap in our communication. Clearly, I didn't convey my earlier messages succinctly. But I need you to correct this immediately, and start to instill in the home mortgage team an absolute requirement that we think from our customers' perspectives on every issue, every time," James explained with a soft tone, but a chopping motion of one hand into the other palm to demonstrate his passion for the subject. He paused for a moment to let the message sink in before he continued.

"I know it's Friday afternoon. Your folks probably have plans for the weekend. But I must insist on this. You'll need to change those plans, and start correcting this potential debacle before we lose control. First, I want you to meet with your direct reports. Review the program with them and ferret out all – and I mean *all* – those approvals we still require to legally sell home mortgages to people living in every state in the USA and all provinces in Canada where we do business."

"You're looking for a legal opinion on the scope of regulations we need in order to satisfy all fifty states?" Whiteside asked, his face ashen.

"All fifty states and at least six Canadian provinces: that's right. And I want you ready to discuss your conclusions on Monday morning. Here at nine o'clock. Bring whichever team members you think appropriate," he added.

"At that meeting, we'll review the extent of the challenge. Then we'll prioritize the states and provinces to ensure we're completely ready to do business with Supermarkets' employees in Alabama, Georgia, and Florida, by Labor Day. We'll need Eastern Canada and the remaining states compliant by the end of September. We can set aside the western Canadian provinces and territories because Suzanne has no immediate plans to expand farther west," James decreed.

"I understand the sense of urgency, James, but it will take hundreds of person-hours to pull together that level of data," Norman Whiteside protested.

"Tell me how many additional people you need. I'll get them from credit card operations, and you can hire outside attorneys if that will help. But I want us to have a comprehensive roadmap of how we get from a bad situation to complete resolution before lunch hour on Monday. I'm scheduling an employee town-hall meeting for two o'clock that afternoon and want to lay out for them the magnitude of their task over the coming few weeks," James insisted.

The mission required extraordinary work by seventy-five people, thirty-five of them from credit card operations and twenty from independent law offices across the USA and Canada. More than 2,500 grueling person-hours were expended on the weekend to compile the information before Monday's nine o'clock meeting. Discussions during that three-hour summary meeting occasionally became tense as James demanded firm commitments from Norman Whiteside and his direct reports point-by-point, leaving no wiggle room or tolerance for excuses.

But they managed to complete the task on schedule, James Fitzgerald thought, as he stood on a makeshift stage constructed of folding tables in the cavernous lobby of their building. Hundreds of employees were assembled, standing shoulder-to-shoulder, filling all available space. Their voices silenced as he turned on the microphone and asked for their attention.

"I'm the ogre who ruined weekend plans for many of you. So, go ahead and boo or groan or express your displeasure some other way, right now!" he proclaimed with a broad grin. "Let's get it out of the way," he continued as more than a few employees half-heartedly responded to their popular leader's invitation.

"I asked many of you to work on the weekend and asked all of you to attend this town-hall so we can candidly discuss the most pressing challenge this company has faced in more than thirty years.

"Since April, we've been welcoming the folks from EZ Mortgage to our team and helping them become familiar with our business culture as we launch a home mortgage program based upon their excellent experience and deep expertise.

They've done a great job over the past few months getting the program ready, and I ask you to give them a rousing round of applause!" James shouted into the microphone as he led off the hand-clapping.

"They've developed a great product that will revolutionize our business here in Financial Services, but we need to get the introduction absolutely right. And that creates a challenge for each one of us. You see, Norman Whiteside is leading a small team – an excellent team but a small one. You know how I like to keep our expenses low," James said with a self-deprecating aside that drew a few smiles from the crowd.

"Until last week, they intended to roll-out the home mortgages in stages, starting with Florida and Georgia. That approach is an entirely logical and efficient way to get a business started gradually. But it's a strategy with a downside as well – not all Multima employees and customers are treated equally.

"You know I have a problem with any strategy that falls short of equity and fairness for *all* our colleagues and customers. That's the reason I asked Norman and his team to modify their plans. It's also the reason I asked many of you to work so hard over the weekend. This morning we identified all the known challenges we must overcome, and the steps needed to resolve them," James said before pausing to theatrically look around at the audience.

"And that's why I've asked all of you to come down here this afternoon. For the next five weeks, each of us will need to spend time helping the home mortgage team prepare for a launch that is timely, fair, and equitable – for our colleagues over at Supermarkets and the customers they serve.

"Your leaders will be asking some of you to assist, even if you work in administration or credit card services. That means some of you might not be able to get your usual work done on time. So, I need to ask each of you to work a few extra hours every day. I know this will be a disruption to many of you, and we're prepared to make exceptions in cases where people are unduly inconvenienced," he continued, raising both hands in a gesture of surrender.

"But we'll pay overtime to hourly employees, and we'll grant later time-off for salaried employees who aren't eligible for overtime. Plus, at the end of September – when we have it successfully finished – we'll organize a special barbecue lunch with live entertainment, so we can all relax and enjoy a great party outdoors for a few hours!" James shouted into the microphone again, his enthusiasm prompting whistles and applause.

"Are you with me?" he shouted into the microphone again, thrusting his right arm high into the air. Their applause grew even louder as many cried out "Yes" while others continued their whistles and cheers of support.

James knew it was important to take questions to make any town-hall session successful. Today would be no exception. For precisely thirty minutes, he welcomed questions about their mission to introduce the home mortgage program and anything else his audience chose.

As always, there was a broad mix of issues, and James answered each with patience and good cheer. As he wrapped up the session and his team found their way back to cubicles and workstations, the mood was jovial. He knew he had successfully tapped into a deep reservoir of goodwill carefully nurtured over the years. And the new folks would have a much clearer understanding of the role customer satisfaction had to play as they made decisions in the future.

Twenty-Two

Hilton Hotel, Quebec City, Quebec.
Monday September 5, 2016

It all started exactly one week earlier with a seemingly innocent telephone call screened in advance by her executive assistant.

"Hello, Madame Simpson. My name is Roland LaMontagne. I'm the son of your *notaire* Monsieur Marcel LaMontagne," the man said.

"Yes, Roland. My assistant told me. How can I help you?" she responded.

"First, I must share with you some news," he continued. "Since you last met with my father he has been murdered."

He paused to let this news sink in, and Suzanne fell speechless. There were several seconds of silence as she tried to process the shocking news. Murders of any kind were rare in Quebec City. That such violence should befall an acquaintance was almost inconceivable!

"I am so sorry, Monsieur LaMontagne. Please accept my heartfelt condolences for the tragic loss of your father," she replied after recovering from the initial shock.

"Actually, they killed both my mother and father … and please call me Roland," he said. "It happened a few weeks ago at their cottage in Stoneham. The police apparently have no leads so far."

"That's terrible," she replied. "Do they know what happened?"

"My mother was shot in the heart, and they tortured my father before they killed him. Other than those details, the police are unwilling to share any information, either publicly or with me privately," he told her.

"But I should explain the reason I'm calling. I've learned my father was doing some research for you and I've uncovered some information you probably need to know. It's not safe to talk about it on the phone. Instead, I'd like to meet with you in person," he suggested.

"Sure," Suzanne replied. "Would you like to make an appointment to meet here in my office?"

"I can't do that easily, Madame," he replied. "I am a priest, and the small salary I earn doesn't permit me to travel to places like Atlanta. Would it be possible for us to meet in Quebec?" he asked.

Suzanne hesitated. Her corporate security training instilled caution, and her intuition was flashing bright warning signals. First, she posed a few questions to determine if she could extract any more information while they talked. That tactic was unsuccessful. Roland LaMontagne seemed genuinely concerned their call could be intercepted and firmly refused to divulge any information.

Alternatively, she explored the possibility of paying for his air ticket to meet her in Atlanta. He also politely declined that suggestion, explaining that he was the sole priest in his parish and was only permitted to travel with adequate notice for his superiors to arrange a replacement. That might take weeks. Finally, she agreed to think about his request and took a number where he could be reached.

Suzanne summoned her assistant immediately after their call and asked her to do some research. "Scan the media in Quebec City for the past couple months to see if there are any published news articles about the *notaire* Marcel LaMontagne," she instructed. "Then check out his son, Roland, a priest. Confirm he really is a priest and where his parish is located. He'd like to meet in Quebec, and I want to be sure he's not a security risk."

"His story checks out," Eileen reported back the next morning. "Several newspaper articles confirm the double murder and support the scant details he shared. It was easy to establish his role in the *Paroisse Ste-Foy,* and his biography on the church website seems legitimate. Everything cross-checks with info from the diocese. And people there think highly of him."

While Suzanne was cautious about the situation, she was also intrigued. Worryingly, John George Mortimer was stonewalling her attempts to meet and settle the issues surrounding her mother's death. It looked like they were finally going to meet privately after an upcoming offsite event. But it would be helpful if the priest from Quebec could shed more light on her concerns or give her something more to probe in her conversations with Mortimer.

She called him back, tried once again to ferret out some information, then reluctantly agreed to meet with him. It had to be in a public place, she insisted. He acquiesced immediately, and within a few moments, they settled on the Allegro Bar, on the ground floor, just off the lobby of the Quebec Hilton, at nine o'clock Labor Day evening.

She spent most of that holiday in her Atlanta office addressing pressing issues before boarding her company jet at Fulton County Airport. She planned to arrive in Quebec, have a good meal at the Quebec Hilton, and then talk with the priest. The pilot and co-pilot could keep an eye on her interaction with the priest in the bar. After, she'd get a good night's sleep, then travel early the next morning to Toronto to join a meeting with Multima Financial Services at the office of attorney Roger Liveenwel. The timing would work perfectly.

Indeed, all went smoothly until her meeting with the priest. She was mortified when Roland LaMontagne claimed her mother's death might not have been from natural causes. He seemed confident about the accuracy of his information but repeatedly refused to divulge his source.

"I've learned a sophisticated drug may have been used to induce a heart attack," he whispered as he glanced furtively around the sparsely populated bar. "I also found evidence that suggests someone at Multima Corporation was involved to a much greater extent than simply sending money to her bank account."

"Who at Multima?" she asked, also keeping her voice low.

"I still don't know. But you must be very careful. Whoever is involved has extensive contacts in prominent places. The police confided that my parents' murders looked to be the work of professionals. And there's a very well-known lawyer in Toronto who seems to know a lot but refuses to cooperate with me in any way," he warned, again refusing to divulge either names or details.

Their conversation continued along those lines for almost an hour until she concluded the priest had nothing else he was willing to reveal. She politely thanked him for sharing his thoughts with her, promised to keep in touch, and agreed with his advice to be very careful.

Back in her room, she reconfirmed morning departure plans with both pilots, thanking them for their surveillance support, as she dismissed them for the night. Minutes later she was reading updated reports from Multima Financial Services to prepare for legal discussions the next day. She fell asleep with the last page of a thick update memo in her hands. A little after three in the morning she awoke with a start. There was loud knocking on the door of her room.

"It's the police, Madame Simpson. Please open the door immediately!" she heard a woman's voice call out in French.

Still half-asleep, she grabbed a nearby hotel robe and wrapped it around herself as she stumbled in the darkness towards the door. Through the security eye, she saw two detectives in business attire displaying their badges.

Alarmed, she wrapped the robe more tightly and said, "It's three o'clock in the morning! What do you want?"

The female detective stepped closer to the door and held her badge close for ease of identification. "It's important we speak with you privately, Madame Simpson. Please open the door, and let us in."

With trepidation, Suzanne slowly opened the door and allowed the pair to enter. Still trembling, she asked, "What is this all about?"

"Madame Simpson, did you meet earlier this evening with a priest, Roland LaMontagne?" the male inquired.

"Yes. Why do you ask?"

"You may be the last person to have seen him alive. We found his telephone in the wreck of his car and learned he had an appointment with you only minutes before we received reports of a car catapulting down Cote Gilmour end-over-end. His little Fiat was destroyed beyond recognition, and Father LaMontagne was dead," the male detective replied.

"Initial indications suggest the vehicle's brakes may have been tampered with," the female added. "We need you to come to the local station to answer some questions for us."

"No. I'm not going anywhere in the middle of the night," Suzanne defiantly responded. "I am the president of a large corporation and know nothing about tampering with brakes. If you have questions to ask, allow me to dress, and I can answer any questions you have right here."

"My colleague can wait outside while you dress, but I must watch you at all times," the female detective advised. "We have rules of evidence and detainee security that must be followed."

Annoyed to be stripped of her privacy and forced to disrobe before another woman, Suzanne also became very wary. Once dressed, the female invited her colleague to return. He glanced quickly around the suite as he re-entered the room. It appeared all was okay.

Then they started asking questions – questions that immediately caused her alarm. Why was she in Quebec? Why was she meeting with the priest? How long had she known him? What did they discuss? Was she willing to take a lie detector test? Why not?

It was at that point Suzanne realized she should get an attorney without delay and so informed her interrogators. With knowing glances between them, the detectives agreed it was her lawful right. However, if she insisted on formalities, they would require that the interview move to the police station. Adamant, Suzanne declared she was going nowhere unless they were prepared to arrest her and divulge the charges. After several minutes of back-and-forth with the investigators, they agreed she could make her call before they went to the station.

She woke Albert Ferer from a sound sleep at his Fort Myers home, but he was alert the instant she outlined her situation. Annoyed, he asked to speak with one of the detectives. After a short exchange, the male detective handed back the phone, and Alberto filled her in on their conversation.

"Don't answer any more questions. I'll get on one of the corporate jets as quickly as possible and fly there to meet you. I'm not familiar with Canadian law, or criminal law for that matter, but I'll find a defense attorney while I'm in flight and should see you in about four hours. In the meantime, say nothing.

"I've already told them what I'm telling you," Ferer continued. "And they've agreed to wait with you in your hotel room. I suggest you order up coffee and some food for all three of you, then just check emails on your phone or something until I get there. I'll check in every hour and don't hesitate to call my cell phone in the meantime if you need me. Why don't you also call the company pilot and ask him to come sit with you in the room. That might discourage any police monkey business," he ended with a feeble attempt at levity.

The police agreed it would be okay to call the pilot in his room. Suzanne summoned him in calm tones that belied her unease. "Sorry to wake you, Tony. Alberto Ferer suggested I call you. There are two police detectives with me in my room. Yes, that's right. They want information about Roland LaMontagne. He died in a car crash after our meeting. Alberto would like you to sit with me until he's here in about four hours. He asked us not to answer any questions before he arrives. Can you come?"

Twenty-Three

A ground-floor apartment, Buenos Aires, Argentina.
Monday September 5, 2016

For the first time, Fidelia mustered the courage to look in a mirror. For more than a month, she had studiously avoided all mirrors – even brushing her teeth at the kitchen sink – to prevent an inadvertent glance at her ugly complexion left behind from the surgery. Now, her face appeared to be starting to heal. The pain had subsided, and the itchiness of her skin was more tolerable.

The cosmetic surgeon was certainly a good one, she thought, as she leaned into the mirror for closer inspection. It was hard to see any scars on her face and neck. As promised, she looked twenty years younger. She saw no evidence of the broken nose, cropped to become shorter and wider. Maybe her look hinted towards Asian ancestry, she thought.

The treatment around her lips made them less full, exactly the opposite of procedures used by some to make their mouths appear sexier and more inviting. To appear sexier was the least of her concerns. No, all this painful surgery was for a singular purpose – survival.

The alarm was triggered when Howard Knight remembered The Organization might have photos of them in Escoma and be able to place them in Bolivia. That realization reminded them other interested parties might also use facial recognition software to track them down.

It took almost two weeks after they arrived in Buenos Aires to discreetly connect with the cosmetic surgeon recommended by her friend in Belgrade. Then, there were furtive consultations in the privacy of their rented apartment on three different evenings. Finally, they concluded there was no alternative. They had to visit the surgeon's office for the procedure. Attempting to perform them in a private apartment involved too many unacceptable risks.

It took a lot of money and protracted negotiations, but they finally persuaded the surgeon to do both procedures at night with no other staff present. He also reluctantly agreed to pick them up from their apartment after dark, drive them to his office, perform both procedures alone, and then return them to the apartment.

It was almost light when he dropped them off outside the high, locked gate that opened into a courtyard just off their suite. They wore hats and covered their bandaged faces with scarves. With heads down, they quietly walked along the short path, staying as close to plants and shrubs as possible.

Howard had their key in hand, ready to insert. With two quick turns, they released the security door-lock and dashed inside. Since that night, they hadn't left their five rooms. Although the apartment was comfortable, even with touches of luxury, it was a stark and confining contrast to their previous months of freedom outdoors in the rugged mountains of Bolivia.

As part of the exorbitant fee they paid him, the surgeon called on them weekly. With his visits, he brought fresh fruit and vegetables to augment the food supplies Howard stocked up on before their surgery. One time, he even agreed to bring bottled water as they were starting to run low. But his primary purpose was to ensure his patients were healing properly.

When he dropped in the last time, he pronounced them both fit and his work almost finished. From his bag, he took long-haired wigs, one blonde and the other brunette. He shot passport photos of each. Starting with Fidelia, he captured her image with her current short hair and each of the hair pieces, then made notes confirming which photos applied to each of the Canadian, European, and American passports he would produce for her.

With Howard, the doctor took pictures of his current short dark hairstyle as well as a longer-haired blonde wig that he pulled from his bag. Then they waited while Howard dyed his hair a reddish-brown for a third photo. Satisfied he had everything needed for the final stage of his work, the surgeon recommended another few days to let their skin tones return to normal. "Just a precaution. You don't want to raise suspicions with a curious security official or an astute immigration agent," he counseled as he swept out into the darkness.

With a final glance in the mirror at the new Fidelia, she decided it was time to discuss the next stage of their escape once again.

"I'm still uneasy about the Baltics," Fidelia said as she wandered into the living room at the end of their suite. "Neither of us speak the languages. Neither of us has visited there before. And our knowledge of all three countries is really limited to the research we've been doing on the Internet."

"I understand your concern," Howard replied. "It has risks. The main attraction for me is the general character of the people. Everything I read tells me people in all three countries tend to stay apart from visitors. They may not be completely welcoming and friendly, but that also means they're somewhat aloof, tending not to pry too deeply into affairs of others. That's the kind of environment we need for a long-term hideaway."

"But, Howard. Aren't you concerned people will find it odd that we rent a house in a remote area of Lithuania with no jobs, no family, and no ability to communicate? It will take months for either of us to be fluent in Lithuanian – maybe years. We need to leave here soon. It's already been two months. Even though we've been careful, we might be traced."

"You still prefer Spain, don't you?"

"Spain has advantages," Fidelia replied. "First, I think we can both ease into the community in Marbella. Lots of British ex-pats live there, and there's a significant population of seasonal English-speaking tourists. We're unlikely to arouse suspicions. We can create a plausible cover," she suggested before pausing to give Howard time to think about it.

"We could make you a retired businessman with a passion for writing and me your newfound girlfriend," she added. "We can explain that we're both trying to escape from unpleasant previous relationships that we prefer to not discuss. Our Spanish will serve us well with locals. Most important, from Spain we can travel freely throughout Europe. No passports. No border controls. No prying immigration officials. And hopefully, no encounters with law enforcement. It just makes more sense to me."

"Fair enough," Howard conceded. "Let's get everything arranged to be out of here Saturday. I'm also uneasy about the amount of time we've been here."

Without further discussion, they started to work. Using one of the new identities they would assume, Fidelia focused on finding a place to live in Spain. Howard explored the cost of a circuitous travel route taking them to four countries before the final Barcelona-Malaga leg. They'd take a train the last few miles to Marbella and the new villa Fidelia was arranging.

It would take more than three days of travel and cost thousands of dollars, but it would buy them more time. By dawn, they completed all their arrangements, prepared a checklist, and were giddy with anticipation. As the first light started to peek through the Venetian blinds, they looked at each other, grinned and raced towards the bedroom where they made love until both were completely exhausted.

As she closed her eyes and pulled closer to him, Fidelia thought about her lover's new look. Although they chose it together, she wasn't sure the wider nose, hollowed cheeks, and lost dimples would suit him over time. Regardless, her last satisfied thought was how lucky she was to have Howard Knight and how desperate she was to keep them both alive.

Twenty-Four

As the women walked at a brisk pace from their downtown hotel to their first appointment that morning, their phones announced the arrival of emails at precisely the same time. It was Natalia Tenaz who glanced downward to read the message as they navigated pedestrian traffic on the busy sidewalk.

"Oh no! Suzanne won't be at our meeting this morning," Natalia exclaimed. "Detained in Quebec for some reason. She doesn't say why, but we're to go ahead without her."

"How should we handle it?" Janet Weissel asked.

"I'll carry the ball. You just provide moral support. I'll need it," Tenaz replied tersely. That was one of the reasons Janet Weissel continued to think of her boss as the Bitch. The woman always wanted to be in control.

That was probably one of the reasons she let her mind wander to fantasize a bit. Roger Liveenwel attracted her attention from his first flash of a charming and charismatic smile. Janet sensed interest and instantly moved into seduction mode. She might be at the Toronto headquarters of Berister Law LLP to learn more about how Canadian laws might impact their rollout of the Multima Financial Services home mortgage plan, but her return flight wasn't until the next morning. That left a full night for fun and games.

The Bitch took charge of the meeting. So, Janet focused on her potential quarry in the opening minutes, while Natalia Tenaz summarized what they wanted from the meeting. Liveenwel played his role perfectly. While Natalia spoke, he leaned forward, cocked his head to project keen interest, and locked his eyes with hers as she outlined her concerns from her notes.

His full head of hair suggested robust health and was almost long enough to touch his shoulders. Subtle head movements caused the slightly disheveled styling to flip and sway, attracting Janet like a magnet. When he smiled, engaging dimples cut deep into the smooth texture of his skin, highlighting a strong jaw before angling upward to his sky-blue eyes. When he casually ran his hand through his hair, the gesture seemed almost sensual.

Her eyes fixed on Liveenwel, Janet still tried to concentrate as Natalia emphasized the importance of the program launch for Multima and the urgency of resolving all outstanding issues during their meeting. She continued watching as he made notes, clarified issues with Natalia and frequently leaned back in a sumptuous leather chair to ponder what he was hearing.

Every time Liveenwel glanced in her direction, she was ready. A mischievous smile the first time, and then a slight parting of her lips the second peek. Straightening her shoulders to highlight her breasts, or brushing back her long hair, each gesture evoked the same subtle response. He held her gaze for just a fraction of a second longer than necessary, letting her know the interest was mutual.

Fortunately, the Bitch seemed oblivious to it all. Instead, Natalia furiously made notes and asked follow-up questions to almost every comment Liveenwel made as they discussed the challenges, province by province, for every legal jurisdiction in Eastern Canada – six of them in all. Almost too far into the meeting, Janet realized she too should be taking notes because the complexity of the matter was growing exponentially.

She finally refocused her attention when Liveenwel told them the shocking news. Legal costs to obtain approvals from each of the provincial governments would exceed seven million dollars, and the time required to complete the project would probably be more than six months. It simply couldn't be done quicker!

The room suddenly became very still. After his definitive pronouncement, Liveenwel and his three associates sat back in their chairs and waited. Natalia looked desperately to Janet for support and she responded with what she hoped was a blank expression and a shrug of her shoulders.

"Okay. We get the magnitude of the challenge," Natalia calmly replied as she turned to face Liveenwel. "We understand you'll need to work with regulators in six different Canadian provinces. We get that you need to do everything in both English and French. We know the province of Quebec will demand that we market the mortgage plan there with a French name. We get all that. Now, I'd like to discuss how we can deal with each of those challenges much more quickly. We don't have six months to spare."

"I'm sure you were hoping for better news from us today," Liveenwel replied. "Here at Berister Law, we do our best to deliver the results our clients need. We certainly have the resources, and you probably know our enviable reputation for access to decision-makers. But I can't sugarcoat the enormity of this task. We're aggressive when we say six months. It could well take even longer if the bureaucrats don't cooperate. But the main issue is the cost. The quicker you need the project completed, the more hours we'll need to bill."

For the next five minutes or so, Liveenwel walked them through the intricacies of the firm's billing policies and various fees they usually charged clients based on attorney seniority and experience. Then he promised to blend those rates to create an average of about seven hundred dollars for each hour billed, suggesting this would be a better deal for Multima than precisely tracking all the individual hours and rates for each attorney.

His monologue then switched to an overview of the many steps the firm would take to win the coveted approvals in each province. With the fervor of a salesperson, he took several more minutes to make the process seem as arduous and complicated as possible before he paused to let it all sink in.

Janet watched the Bitch absorb the pitch and think about it. The mood in the room became a little uncomfortable as no one spoke for a while. The associates even shifted nervously in their seats and someone coughed. After what seemed like a few minutes, Natalia finally responded with a question.

"Let's look at this differently, shall we? How much time would you estimate it will take for us to get everything gathered and submitted for approval in Ontario?"

Liveenwel looked towards his associates and they exchanged a few whispered thoughts before he responded. "It seems Ontario might be doable in a month or so. We can start immediately, and our firm has an excellent working relationship with the regulators. It will take some extra hours, but we should be able to get approvals within a month or two."

"Now let's look at Quebec. What's the situation there?" Natalia asked.

"Quebec is more complicated. We'll need to use some resources from our office in Montreal. Even if we started today, with the complexities of French and the civil code – not to mention the notorious Quebec bureaucracy – we'll probably need ninety to a hundred and twenty days to obtain approvals there," he added.

"Well, how about Nova Scotia?" Natalia wanted to know.

"Our office there has done some research and thinks approvals can be completed in a timely way, but the provincial minister responsible is currently on extended leave due to illness. Apparently, getting any kind of decision is taking an enormous amount of time and effort," Liveenwel responded.

"Okay," Natalia answered with her pace of delivery deliberately slowed. "I think I hear that you can do Ontario in about the time we require. Quebec is a challenge, but you can't see any immediate solution to get it done quicker. And, Nova Scotia is a problem because a government official isn't well and that complicates the process."

"It's not quite as clear-cut as you suggest," Liveenwel sputtered. "But you've highlighted the essence of our challenges."

Again, it became uncomfortably quiet in the room. To Janet, it seemed she was part of a drama with tension, emotion, and frustration building. She had no idea where there would be common ground. She saw no solution to meet the demands of James Fitzgerald, with the limitations explained by Liveenwel. The earlier enticing sexual attraction of the attorney was now long lost in the background.

After several uncomfortable moments, Natalia was first to speak again.

"Mr. Liveenwel, I know Douglas Whitfield holds you in very high regard, and our company appreciates the excellent service your firm has provided since he retained you as our legal counsel for Canada. Also, I value the findings of your research and the advice you've provided so far in our meeting today.

"But you need to understand the importance of this project to Multima Financial Services transcends all that. We're going to take a break now. Janet and I will go down to the lobby and update James Fitzgerald about the current situation. He's taking a personal interest in the matter and has instructed me to complete all regulatory approvals by the end of September, taking whatever action I think necessary to achieve that goal.

"We'll return to this conference room in one hour," Natalia said, leaning forward with her teeth clenched.

Then she looked directly into his eyes and said, "When we return, I'd like you to provide me with the plan of action you'll put in place to get approval from all six provincial regulators by the end of September. I expect to hear how our project will become your number one priority in every Berister Law office from Ontario to Newfoundland.

"If we are not satisfied with the steps you're taking," Natalia continued, "we'll withdraw our retainer and immediately hire a law firm who *will* make our project their top priority and at an acceptable price. One final thing, Mr. Liveenwel. The total cost for this project will not exceed five million dollars, regardless of the billing time it takes you to get it done. Do we understand each other?"

The silence that followed lasted only a few seconds this time. Attorney Roger Liveenwel got it. The petite young woman was an adversary to reckon with, and the Multima business generated millions per year for his firm.

With a sigh and a broad smile, he responded, "There's no reason for you ladies to wait in the lobby. My team will make all the arrangements. They really don't need me to muck up their great work. We heard you. They understand what you need. Now, why don't the three of us have some lunch?" he said with a nod to include Natalia and Janet. Then, he gestured dramatically towards his colleagues.

"My folks will spend the next couple hours putting together the information you seek. It might take an hour or so longer, but we'll be able to give you complete information and assurances. Can that work?" he asked.

Without hesitation, Natalia nodded her head and quietly said, "That's fine."

Liveenwel turned to his team and gave them very general instructions. "You all know the importance of Multima's business to our firm. You've heard our client's requirements. Let's find the resources we need to complete these regulatory approvals by the end of September. Sally, why don't you take the lead on this one and put together a PowerPoint summary of the steps and timeline for two o'clock?"

Finished, Natalia rose from her chair, thanked everyone for their support, and asked Liveenwel where she could find a restroom.

Twenty-Five

Really, she just wanted to cry. Suzanne felt her tear ducts welling up, and her emotions becoming more volatile, but was determined her colleague Alberto Ferer would not see a single tear. The last thing she needed was a male peer thinking of her as weak or emotional because of her ordeal over the past several hours.

They were now at cruising speed in American airspace flying towards Atlanta. She finally started to feel some relief. Less than an hour earlier, Quebec City police detectives finally agreed to her release after keeping her at the Hilton Hotel for hours. With the frenzy of activity after Alberto arrived at the suite, she lost track of how long she was confined, but the entire episode was fraught with stress and concern.

The Quebec police suspected she knew something about the circumstances surrounding the priest, Roland LaMontagne, who died shortly after meeting with her at the Hilton. First, she had to deal with surprise and unease when police knocked on her hotel room door demanding she let them in. After, she felt shocked as she tried to process the information that a man she had met just hours earlier died in a suspicious automobile crash.

It seemed inconceivable to her at first, then she had to cope with two surly detectives who treated her with obvious suspicion.

Corporate counsel Ferer had been like a rock since her call to him in the middle of the night. He took charge immediately as she hoped he would. Within minutes, he persuaded the detectives not to take her to a police station for questioning. That helped to avoid potential cameras or unwanted reporters.

Then, he persuaded them to delay interviewing her for a few hours until he could travel from Fort Myers to Quebec on a corporate jet. During the flight, he'd checked in periodically to be sure she was alright and brought her up to date on anticipated next steps. But things really started to happen after he arrived at her hotel room with a hastily assembled entourage.

To her relief, John George Mortimer had also instructed Dan Ramirez, his chief of corporate security, to accompany Alberto. She knew the respect and influence he carried with police everywhere.

Alberto introduced her to a criminal lawyer from Montreal who had driven to Quebec City in about the same amount of time it took Alberto to fly from Florida. The criminal lawyer then presented two other men. One he described as a senior official in Canada's Royal Canadian Mounted Police. The other was an executive with the Canadian Security Intelligence Service. Speaking French, this last one immediately took charge of the meeting.

"Jean-Claude Gagnon. Bonjour," the CSIS man said as he stepped forward and shook hands rather stiffly with the detectives. "Here is my business card. Before we start, I suggest you call your chief. He can be reached right now at the number I wrote down on the back of that card."

Everyone remained silent while the surprised male detective called the number – then they all listened as he explained to the chief of police why he and his partner were interested in asking Suzanne questions. After getting a short reply from the chief, the detective summoned the RCMP officer to participate in their call, setting the phone on speaker and retreating with the handset to her bedroom just off the living area before closing the door behind them.

They waited several minutes making small talk quietly, while the police officials discussed what Suzanne supposed was her circumstance. A few moments later, the CSIS official was also asked to join the call in her bedroom. Sometime after that Dan Ramirez, Alberto Ferer, and the criminal attorney were all pulled into the discussion. Meanwhile, she dismissed the Multima pilot and co-pilot who were still in the suite. Then, she waited patiently alone.

After more than an hour, Alberto Ferer left the telephone conference and returned to the living room to advise Suzanne there would be some more interrogation. But he and the criminal lawyer would be present to advise her about any questions she was not required to answer.

"Tell us, Madame Simpson," the older detective started as he pressed a button on a recording device. "How do you know the deceased priest, Roland LaMontagne?"

"He called me last week. He introduced himself as the son of Monsieur LaMontagne, a *notaire* who handled my mother's affairs. I only met the *notaire* at the time of her death a few months ago. Roland told me he had sensitive information that he preferred not to discuss on the phone and asked if it was possible to meet in person. Because I had a meeting scheduled in Toronto today, I decided to leave Atlanta one day earlier, meet with him, and stay here for the night."

"So, you met Father LaMontagne here in your room?" the woman detective asked.

"No. We met in the Allegro Bar downstairs. Again, I told you this last night when you first inquired," Suzanne replied a little testily.

Before the detective could follow up, her criminal defense lawyer quickly interjected, "Officers, respecting my client's earlier cooperation, may I request you focus your questions on areas you haven't already covered?"

"OK," the male detective replied with a brief flash of annoyance. "Maybe you could tell us exactly what information Father LaMontagne gave you."

"There wasn't much really. Nothing I could treat as a fact. The information was more accurately a collection of theories, rumors, and suspicions. I found it curious."

"I understand, Madame Simpson," the female added. "But, just let us decide if what he told you was fact or suspicion. That's our job."

"Well, as I explained, he thought the deaths of his parents were somehow related to my mother's death, but he never told me the reason he thought they were connected. Apparently, he met with a lawyer in Toronto to try to find out more about this perceived connection. But Roland didn't trust him and believed he was withholding information from him. He wouldn't share that attorney's name either."

"Did he mention the name of the company you work for in any of your conversations?" the male detective asked.

Suzanne quickly glanced towards Alberto Ferer who immediately interjected. "That question sounds like you're fishing for information, detectives. Do you have something specific about Multima you would like to ask Madame Simpson, or are you just expecting her to recall any incidental reference to Multima that might have crept into their conversation?"

The male detective glared at Suzanne with stone cold eyes and clenched teeth as he repeated, "I asked you if Father LaMontagne mentioned Multima Corporation or its subsidiaries in any of your conversations."

Suzanne again glanced quickly at Alberto who nodded almost imperceptibly. "He said he thought someone at Multima might be involved in some way but wouldn't tell me why. Nor would he give me a name. It seemed to me just an unfounded suspicion."

"Tell us exactly what you remember him saying to you," the female insisted.

Suzanne hesitated for just a second before she replied in a tone little more than a whisper, "He said he found evidence in his father's files. He wouldn't tell me what the evidence was, but he felt someone – somewhere in Multima – was involved. He asked me to be very careful because the deaths of his parents bore all the hallmarks of a killing by a professional."

"If you're not involved, Madame Simpson, who do you think he was referring to?" the female detective asked.

"You don't need to answer that question, Suzanne," her defense lawyer advised. "And, detective, you know that's not an appropriate question. My client will answer your queries that involve facts. But I will not permit you to require her to speculate. Your question about Multima was already borderline, and I'll advise Madame Simpson not to respond to any more questions along that line."

There was an awkward moment of silence as the detectives seemed to process this admonishment and decide next steps. Apparently, they decided not to challenge the attorney's mettle. Instead, they posed dozens of new and different questions that dissected seemingly every minute of Suzanne's time in the city and every word she exchanged with the priest. It lasted for the rest of the morning.

Finally, the male detective said, "OK. We'll leave it there for now. But we may want to speak with Madame Simpson again." He turned to face Suzanne. "We want you to stay in Quebec until further notice."

"On what grounds?" the defense attorney blurted in exasperation. "Madame Simpson is a respected business leader whose job demands that she travel continuously. You have no reason to keep her here in Quebec."

"We want her to be available when we have more questions," the female detective responded calmly.

"Then ask her to make herself available," the defense lawyer demanded as he sprung to his feet set for battle. "If she agrees to your request, let her carry on with her business. If you can't accept that, let's get your chief on the telephone right now. I will not allow you to restrict her movements without any charges or even evidence to suggest she is in any way involved!"

"OK," the male detective conceded. "But, Madame Simpson, be advised. If you fail to respond to any requests for further interviews, we'll issue a warrant for your arrest, and extradite you from the USA if we must. Then, you'll most certainly have some negative publicity to deal with."

Suzanne humbly acknowledged her understanding of the request, and the interview lasted only moments longer.

Shortly after, the entire entourage was following the pilot and co-pilot at a brisk pace from the hotel to waiting cars, then to the aircraft at Quebec's Jean Lesage International Airport.

On the corporate jet, still trying to make sense of the past twenty-four hours and manage her fragile emotions, she retrieved her telephone from her bag. Once she had a wi-fi signal, Suzanne clicked an icon she used only occasionally, one for the electronic version of the French-language newspaper *Journal de Quebec*. To her amazement, a bold headline screamed,

"Notaire LaMontagne. Mafia Hit?"

Twenty-Six

Multima Solutions Headquarters. Miami, Florida.
Wednesday September 7, 2016

"The sonofabitch raped me!" Janet Weissel screamed into the phone. "I agreed to have a drink with him after the meeting, and he slipped something into it. I woke up this morning in a strange hotel room, completely naked, with his disgusting semen all over my body and bed sheets."

Douglas Whitfield listened without a word and took several seconds to process her message. "Who raped you? Where? When?" he finally asked.

"Liveenwel. That friggin' lawyer you recommended to give us advice on the home mortgage expansion to Canada," she replied. "You told me he was an old friend, so when he asked me to join him for a drink before I flew back to Chicago, I thought no problem. I met him in the bar at my hotel. I remember having a couple of drinks. The next thing I know, I'm waking up alone in a darkened hotel room feeling totally violated. I could kill the bastard!"

"Wow! I don't know what to say, Janet. Are you OK now? Where are you?"

"Back in Chicago. I woke up early and was able to catch United's nine o'clock flight back with Natalia. I'm OK now, but I'm pissed."

Starting to grasp the implications of this accusation, Whitfield felt a tightening in the pit of his stomach. "Did you report this?" he asked.

"No, of course not. I didn't report it to anyone. Do you think I would ever subject myself to further rape by the friggin' legal authorities?"

"OK. Look, I'm really sorry this happened. It doesn't sound like the Roger Liveenwel I know at all. But I'll make it up to you. It's not my weekend to visit the kids, so why don't you fly down here on a commercial flight? We'll go to the Caribbean for a couple nights. We'll talk about this more. I'll find a way to make it right for you."

There was a long pause while she thought about it. "Sounds like a plan," she finally responded. "I'll book a flight and let you know when I get in. Should we meet at the private jet lounge at MIA?"

"Perfect. Plan to arrive anytime after five. I've got meetings scheduled 'til then. I'll get my assistant to book us something. St. Barts sound OK?" he wondered.

"Of course," she replied in a tone that seemed slightly remote as they said their goodbyes.

Without setting the phone back in its cradle, Whitfield pressed the speed dial for Liveenwel's mobile and connected on the third ring.

"How did the meeting with Financial Services and Supermarkets go?" he asked when the pleasantries were out of the way.

"Simpson didn't show. Apparently, she was detained in Quebec City for some reason. But I'm going to need you to send me some profitable business from Solutions to recover the fortune I'm about to lose. That bitch who ran the meeting for them demanded an unrealistic deadline and then placed a cap on the fees at five million. I'll lose about two on the deal. She was a real ball-breaker!"

"You're talking about Natalia Tenaz?" Whitfield wondered.

"Yeah. She demanded that we get all the regulatory approvals by the end of this month. I'll need to hire temporary resources in a few provinces and can't hope to recover all my costs. It's a good thing I got to bonk the other slut as partial compensation," Liveenwel said with a leering tone.

"That slut, as you call her, is suggesting she was raped," Whitfield replied dryly.

"What? Oh. No! Don't tell me the one I bonked is one you've been doing? Sorry about that, man!"

"Who I'm doing is none of your business," Whitfield responded. "But it seems you're still thinking more with your dick than your brain. I don't believe she's going to report you, but she claims you drugged and raped her."

"Just like we did back in college, Dougie. She eyed me all through the meeting. Practically had her tongue hanging out. No big deal, a little Special K sprinkled in her wine – just like we used to do in the good old days – and her legs were wide open. But, if she's one of yours, I'm really sorry, man!"

"Well, Rog, it's no longer the good old days. Women are reporting it now. And we can't afford to have legal authorities poking around investigating date rapes. Cut it out. Keep your dick in your pants or something worse than losing money on a business transaction is going to happen. Are we clear?" Whitfield demanded coldly.

"Got it, Doug," Liveenwel responded meekly. "What can I do to make it up to you?"

"Send me a check for the ten grand it's going to cost me to soothe some ruffled feelings this weekend. And stay focused on business."

"OK. I got it. Speaking of business, I don't suppose you spend a lot of time down there monitoring French-language newspapers, but the *Journal de Quebec* is running a front-page story today speculating the Mafia might have been involved in the deaths of a notary public named LaMontagne and his family. It looks like the info is coming from inside the police department there. You might want to let your friends know," Liveenwel said.

Twenty-Seven

John George Mortimer's home, Fort Myers, Florida.
Friday September 9, 2016

He needed some time to think, to process it all. The past seven days had generated more peaks and valleys than he'd experienced in a long time. The peaks seemed higher, but the valleys were much deeper than usual. Exactly one week earlier a climb to one emotional peak started. John George Mortimer awoke that Friday morning with an impulsive inspiration.

"Would you like to visit your family in El Salvador for a few days?" he casually asked his housekeeper Lana as she served his morning cup of coffee on the lanai.

"I always like to visit my family, John George," she smiled. "But I won't have enough money saved up until Christmas. If you agree to give me the time off, I would like to go then."

"You can have a vacation at Christmas. But I was thinking about today. Would you like to go this afternoon for a few days?"

"Of course!" she replied. "But how?"

"I'll ask Sally-Ann to book a commercial flight for both of us to San Salvador this evening. It's a long weekend. If she can't find us commercial flights, I'll ask her to borrow a jet from one of the division presidents. They can't all be planning to work on the Labor Day holiday," he exclaimed with a laugh.

Sure enough, Sally-Ann found a flight from Miami to San Salvador with Aero Mexico. By late evening they were celebrating their arrival with a dozen or more of Lana's family and friends in a small town just miles from the capital.

All weekend he basked in the glow of a happily reunited family. His impulse to reward Lana this way proved uplifting to her, her family members and himself. He'd watched and listened from the periphery as they reminisced and told stories of earlier times together. He glowed as he watched the hugs and kisses Lana showered on her siblings, nieces, nephews, and cousins.

For two days, they ate copious amounts of food, drank wine, and spoke Spanish. John George could not remember a time he felt that relaxed, and Lana thanked him profusely at every opportunity. He was sure the mist in her eyes reflected tears of joy and gratitude. From that satisfying emotional peak, he was suddenly swept downward by the unexpected crisis with Suzanne Simpson.

Only hours after he had gone to sleep on Monday evening, there had been a call to inform him of Suzanne's detention by the police in Quebec. There wasn't a moment of doubt as he heard the news. Alberto Ferer needed to travel to Quebec immediately to help. John George felt pleased that he had flown commercial, leaving a company plane available to whisk Alberto and Dan Ramirez up to Canada.

But it had been difficult to return to sleep that night, and he remained uneasy until Alberto called again from the corporate jet as he came back from Quebec after securing Suzanne's release. His subsequent conversation with Suzanne was an awkward one.

"I'm grateful to you for making it easy for Alberto to help me in Quebec, John George," she told him in a tone he didn't recognize. "But I'm horrified by the death of that young priest, and I need to understand all of the circumstances surrounding Multima's involvement with my mother and her estate. I imagine there is a very good explanation. But I need to hear it. I need to hear from you. And I need to hear it soon."

During their short conversation, John George had been haunted by the tinge of desperation in her voice and the sharp edge to her demands. He reminded her that he was still planning to devote the weekend after the offsite meetings exclusively to her concerns. Without pushing back too forcefully, she'd agreed that she could live with that. They'd broken off the call cordially, but he made a mental note to schedule some additional time to anticipate her questions and craft some compelling answers.

He'd also need to make time to process the unfortunate new development with Venture Capital Inc. Immediately after he returned from El Salvador, Alberto had requested a meeting to update John George on his most recent call with his counterpart at VCI.

"It looks like they're going to use the annual general meeting as a platform," the chief legal counsel warned. "They'll try to pass a resolution from the floor to remove the entire current board of directors if you don't give Gottingham a seat on the board before the AGM."

John George thought he had bought more time with his threat to use Wendal Randall and Klaudia Schäffer to expose VCI's relationship to The Organization. A willingness to challenge John George now signaled that they must be close to capturing and killing the elusive pair. He couldn't imagine a scenario where The Organization would allow Gottingham to risk exposure of their activities merely for a seat on the board of directors of Multima.

It was good that Ramirez had agreed to follow up with his contacts in the rogue unit of the FBI. John George needed to know exactly how they were progressing in their pursuit of the fugitives everyone wanted to find. He was still hopeful the FBI would be first, but it was a challenge to be optimistic.

Although Suzanne's circumstances and VCI rearing its ugly head again represented emotional valleys, his earlier calls with James Fitzgerald and Douglas Whitfield scaled the peaks again.

His Financial Services division president enthusiastically explained they were moving forward their launch of the home mortgage program. Now, it was scheduled to begin in October and was looking better all the time. Employee acceptance of the plan had been overwhelming, and Fitzgerald was elated that Natalia Tenaz had negotiated so forcefully with the lawyers in Canada. They'd now be launching the project everywhere – and all at the same time – he had crowed.

Whitfield's call reported multiple early successes with the new software. The market test with his buddy Alistair Fitzgerald – James' son – over at Bank of The Americas had proved successful. Hints of the bank's endorsement had already generated enough other indications of interest to make Multima Solutions' new software product viable by the end of the year, should they all sign purchase agreements.

John George allowed himself a few moments of satisfaction for decisions well taken on both projects. As he gazed out over the Caloosahatchee River and sipped from a glass of young Pinot Noir, he calculated the projected revenue from the successes. Those two projects alone would double the size of his company over the next five years. Planned expansions at Supermarkets would add another fifty percent growth. It was all truly the stuff of mountain peaks.

But now there was another emotional valley. Yesterday's follow-up meeting with the oncologist seemed routine. John George was feeling great. His appetite had returned. He was exercising regularly. His skin color had improved. His hair had almost grown in again. All indicators were positive. But the follow-up tests were still necessary, the oncologist had insisted.

This morning, John George's cell phone rang before he arrived at the office. "You'll need to come in again. I'd like to make it Monday morning, and we'll need more tests and some discussion. It looks like it's back," the oncologist said quietly. "There are traces of cancer on your left lung. We'll have to act quickly."

Twenty-Eight

Buenos Aires, Argentina,
Saturday September 10, 2016

Fidelia felt something about the driver was not quite right from the moment she spotted him leaning against the small white van as they locked the door to leave the apartment. Her unease was compounded by their need to disassemble Howard's gun and spread the parts throughout both backpacks before they left the apartment.

"He's too well-dressed, too well-groomed for five in the morning," she whispered as they gathered their bags from the ground.

"You're just a little nervous, Fidelia. He looks okay to me," Howard Knight replied softly. "We'll keep a close eye on him on the way to the airport."

Her antennae keenly alert, she gazed intently through the darkness and watched as the driver took a last, long draw on a cigarette before casually tossing it in the street and squishing the remaining glow with a practiced movement of his left foot. He looked at them as they approached the wrought-iron fence just feet from the vehicle, then smoothly opened the rear compartment to store their bags when they arrived. His smile seemed tentative. Did he appear uncomfortable or uneasy? Or, was it just her imagination?

After Howard opened the inside gate release and motioned for her to pass first, she stepped onto the uneven sidewalk outside their protective fence and waited for Howard. As soon as she heard the loud clang of the gate closing and locking, she turned again towards the van and driver. It was then she noticed a sudden blur of movement behind Howard's back.

Before she could cry out a warning, a large muscular hand holding a wadded cloth pressed violently against her mouth and nose. It smelled strongly of some gas. And someone was doing the same to Howard from behind his back! Panic set in, and she struggled to free herself from the putrid odor of the cloth. But her arms were locked, restrained by a grip far more powerful. She tried to kick out in defense but found she had no strength.

Sometime later as she struggled to clear her head and wake fully, the room started to come into focus. She was in a building that seemed old. The walls of the room were stone and felt damp. Maybe she was in a basement? There were no windows. The ceiling was quite low, she noted as she sat up on the cement floor. Everything was dark and musty.

"Howard? Are you there?" she called out, then listened for a reply. There was none. In fact, there were no other sounds at all. No breathing. No hum of a furnace or air conditioner. No sounds of traffic. Just total disquieting silence.

Fidelia felt around in the darkness as her eyes adjusted. There didn't seem to be any furniture. As she swept her hands around her on the floor, there was nothing. She tried to stand up. With a little boost from her hands, she lifted herself from the floor and maintained her balance, though she felt wobbly. She took a few tentative steps and thought she saw the outline of a door. As she approached it, she started to discern a door handle and reached for it. She tried to turn the handle in both directions. There was no movement at all. She tugged at the handle. Again, with no success.

Fidelia felt a chill as she realized she was locked away in a room somewhere, in total darkness, completely naked. Whoever put her here had taken every piece of her clothing. This realization intensified the chill she was feeling.

Was it the driver whose image was slowly returning to her memory? If so, he surely had companions. She started to recall the cloth, the gaseous odor, and Howard under attack all at the same time.

Worried, she touched herself. Had they raped her? Were there indications of semen? Deftly, she moved her index finger around her vagina. There were no signs of liquid or the stickiness of semen. She didn't feel any pain or discomfort in either her vaginal region or her breasts. They probably didn't rape her while she was unconscious.

She suddenly felt a need to relieve herself. Stooping forward to touch the floor, she walked unsteadily using broad, sweeping gestures to determine if there was a toilet, a pail, a tin can or anything suitable in the room to urinate in. She covered every square foot of the floor and found nothing. Not even a light switch. Her need for relief grew with each passing minute. Finally, she worked herself to one corner of the small room, squatted, and felt the release of a long stream of urine falling around her and puddling onto the cement floor.

It was at that point panic started to set in. Who had seized them? What did they do with Howard? Where was she being held? As her knees buckled, and she slumped to the floor, reality started to settle in. If the police had snatched them, treatment like this was unlikely, even in Argentina. Her captors were probably working with The Organization. That meant the coming hours might become more horrible than anything she could imagine.

Twenty-Nine

Hoffman Estates, Illinois.
Friday September 16, 2016

"Remember my former college roommate who works in corporate security at headquarters? The one who tipped us off about John George Mortimer's cancer and The Organization?" Natalia Tenaz asked.

They had just dispensed with the morning pleasantries, and the newly minted executive didn't want to waste any of James Fitzgerald's valuable time. He nodded wordlessly, but she already knew he would remember. It was he who got her friend the new job in corporate security after those discoveries.

"Well, she contacted me again last night," Natalia continued. "It seems she's up to her old tricks again. But before you rush to judgment, let me confess that I'm more than a little guilty this time. May I explain?"

"First, let's go downstairs and take a short walk outdoors on this beautiful autumn morning," Fitzgerald said as he stood from his chair and guided her towards the door. His demeanor quickly signaled to Natalia that her explanation should wait until they were in an environment where recording devices or other subterfuge would find it harder to listen in on their discussion. Neither spoke as they waited for Fitzgerald's private elevator, traveled to the ground floor, and walked about two hundred yards from the building.

"What have you and your friend been up to?" he asked when they were a comfortable distance from the building.

"I know it's illegal and the penalties are severe if we're ever caught, but I encouraged my former college roommate to continue covertly monitoring Janet Weissel's private cell phone line," Natalia said delicately.

"Let me quickly add that I did so only because the surveillance you authorized on her company phones wasn't producing any useful information at all. She took so seriously my first-day warnings that she used them strictly for business, just like I demanded. I remembered the unique software code my friend wrote to tap into her conversations the last time – the one that operates like the systems the CIA uses. So, I asked my friend to use code words like Multima or The Organization. But I also asked her to add names like Natalia, James and several other people working in our company."

"And what turned up?" Fitzgerald asked with a tinge of impatience in his tone.

"On a hunch, I had my friend add the name Roger Liveenwel. You know, the lawyer we're using in Canada for the new mortgage program?" she asked. Fitzgerald nodded again so Natalia continued.

"I don't know exactly why, but I just had a feeling that we should add his name before we went to meet with him in Toronto. My friend just got around to checking her monitoring updates yesterday and discovered there was a hit on Liveenwel."

Fitzgerald stopped walking and turned to face her with a quizzical expression. "Liveenwel's name came up in one of her private conversations?" he asked.

"Yeah, in a private conversation the morning we returned from that meeting. A private conversation with Douglas Whitfield," she said, watching her boss intently for any reaction. There was none, so she continued.

"She called Whitfield to tell him she was raped by Liveenwel the night of our meeting, apparently sometime after we left his offices. I had no idea …."

Fitzgerald's brow furrowed and manner softened before he quietly said, "Tell me about their whole conversation."

"I'll play it for you," she replied as she took her telephone from her bag. She watched his reaction while they both listened to Janet's claim of rape and Whitfield's reaction of surprise followed by his offer to make amends with a weekend in the Caribbean. Despite Fitzgerald's well-established ability to conceal his emotions, she detected signs of both disappointment and concern.

"How long have they been having an affair?" he asked.

"I don't know. We didn't have Whitfield's name programmed for recording. She did speak with him a few times on the company lines, but I checked. The conversations were always legitimate company business. I couldn't detect any unusual pattern or codes."

"From what we know of the woman, we shouldn't be too surprised she found herself involved in an extra-marital affair," James said. "But, I'm disappointed with Whitfield. I heard that he and his wife were having problems, but I had no idea one of our staff might be entangled. As for Liveenwel, when his people finish the mortgage program at the end of the month, get rid of his firm. I'll let you have the pleasure of doing it."

"As much as I'd like to get rid of the scum, might it be better to keep the relationship with Liveenwel a few more months in case we have any legal challenges?" Natalia wondered.

"It might be more practical," James conceded, "but it's not better. From my experience, once a rotten apple has been identified, it's better to throw it out before others are spoiled. I feel the same way about people."

"Should we continue monitoring Janet?"

"I can't counsel you to break the law," he replied. "But, what you and your friend do on your own time is beyond my control. Let me just say that I value your friend's information, and it's safe with me."

Natalia made a mental note to suggest her old college roommate expand the scope of her monitoring. It should include incoming and outgoing calls for both cell phone and office landlines of Douglas Whitfield.

Thirty

He didn't ask for a wake-up call, Douglas thought when he heard the intrusive ring of a phone in his room at Chicago's Westin Michigan Avenue. He felt a little groggy. Reaching out, he noticed the time – just before two o'clock in the morning – and groaned.

"Hello," he grunted into the phone.

"Just answer yes or no. Do you recognize my voice?" the caller demanded.

"Yes," Douglas Whitfield responded after a moment to collect his thoughts.

"Is it raining in Brooklyn?" the caller asked.

"I don't know. I'm not a surgeon," Douglas replied.

After a pause of several seconds, the caller continued. "Black BMW seven series. Southbound on Michigan. Five minutes. Not a word to the broad."

There was a click to end the call before Douglas jumped from the bed to start picking up and putting on clothes strewn across the floor. In fact, there had been only a few hours bridging some earlier eager sex with the just-received intrusive call, he thought as he felt his heart rate quicken.

Janet stirred from her sleep. "What's happening, babe?" she murmured.

"Nothing. I just need to run downstairs for a minute. Go back to sleep. I'll be back for another round with your tempting body before you know it," Douglas whispered, as he gently stroked Janet Weissel's nude body for a few seconds.

Slipping on his shoes, grabbing his phone and wallet, and buckling his belt – all at about the same time – Douglas dashed towards the door. Despite the room's darkness in the middle of the night, he felt completely awake and alert. Amazing, he thought, as his memory briefly darted back to the two bottles of wine they'd consumed before more than a few sessions of outstanding sex over about two hours.

And there his thoughts lingered while he waited for the elevator. He still found it incredible that Janet delivered such satisfying sex time after time. There seemed to be no limit. He grinned as he stepped through the opening doors.

Once headed towards the ground, his attention jolted back to the call. He had spoken with the caller many times before. But, even if he didn't enjoy that level of familiarity, he could never forget either the unique quality of the voice nor the importance of the man. When he said to be there in five minutes, Douglas knew he couldn't be even a few seconds late. The man's impatience was legendary.

But how did the caller know he was in Chicago? And how did he know there was also a woman in the room? Douglas tensed as he realized he must be under some form of surveillance. That seemed new – and a little disconcerting.

As the door released, he stepped from the elevator and headed towards the front of the hotel. As he walked, he shifted his eyes around the large expanse of the lobby towards the spiral staircase in the corner. There was no one in sight. The front desk was vacant. There were no bellhops. The concierge desk was empty. Even the usually brilliant lights were dim.

Leaving the hotel, Douglas immediately turned southward as directed. After a few steps, he spotted the black BMW about a half-block down the street, quickened his pace slightly, and was there in just a few seconds. The rear door opened just as he arrived, and the driver left the curb before the door completely closed.

There was little formal greeting. The caller offered a huge hand to shake. He squeezed Douglas' slightly smaller one with his usual show of strength and power. There was no small talk or banter. Once Douglas was inside and securely buckled, his caller said, "Sorry to disturb your night of debauchery with the broad but we need to talk. You're off to the Multima offsite management meeting in Naples next week, right?"

Douglas nodded yes.

"Listen carefully. We're about to move into a critical new phase, and it's your turn to carry the ball. Pay close attention to every detail I'm going to share with you. I expect you to deliver the message just the way I give it to you. No more. No less. Memorize it, but don't write it down or make a recording on your phone. And, I want you to make your delivery before the end of your big bash there in Florida. Needless to say, the broad upstairs is to know nothing about your current activities or the message. Are we all clear?" He paused just long enough to get another nod of confirmation before he continued.

"Here's what you're going to tell him."

Thirty-One

Suzanne Simpson concealed her boredom as she discreetly glanced at her watch for what was probably the fifth time in the past hour. The speaker was entertaining, and his subject matter quite interesting, but her desire to see this offsite meeting wrap up overpowered his valiant efforts.

Within an hour it should be finished. John George Mortimer's executive assistant already confirmed a limousine would be waiting for them at the front door of the Ritz-Carlton at noon. Together, they'd travel the 45 minutes or so to his Fort Myers residence. Magnanimously, he'd invited her to stay there for as long as she wanted that weekend and promised her his time exclusively.

But, Suzanne was more than a little apprehensive about their upcoming conversation. She had finally accepted that he was her father. DNA tests were almost infallible. But several disturbing unanswered questions lingered about his relationship with her mother. Roland LaMontagne's contention that her mother's death was not accidental preyed on her mind. His assertion that someone at Multima was involved was worrisome, too. Then, there were the horrible unsolved murders of the entire LaMontagne family. It was all very troubling, and she desperately sought satisfactory answers.

Then there was the lack of sleep. Uncharacteristically, she had slept very little and was wide awake before dawn even after turning in well after midnight. Considering the previous day's grueling schedule, she had expected to fall asleep quickly and soundly.

The company jet had taxied down the runway of Atlanta's Fulton County Airport at precisely five thirty in the morning for its two-hour flight to Fort Myers. She chose to park the aircraft at Page Field instead of Naples for the weekend, to be close to Mortimer's residence in case she decided to leave early. The pilots would stay in nearby Fort Myers Beach, available to fly with only a half-hour's notice.

A limo driver met her and five colleagues at Page Field and ferried them to the hotel in Naples for the scheduled eight o'clock group breakfast. They arrived just in time to greet their colleagues from other divisions and join a line-up for a scrumptious buffet outside their private meeting in the hotel's ornate ballroom.

All day, they had listened to presentations with only a half-hour lunch and two fifteen-minute breaks. John George Mortimer led them off with a rousing thirty-minute pep-talk about the purposes of the get-together including leadership's need to offset the current adverse effects of the nasty presidential election spilling into the workplace. His preferred antidote: lots of employee communication and encouragement.

The remainder of the day was a parade of experts on subjects currently of interest to Multima management. Months earlier, Sally-Ann Bureau had solicited opinions from John George Mortimer's direct reports. From their input, she hired the best and brightest in every field to share their wisdom and ideas with the corporation's entire management team.

The Internet, e-commerce, social media, artificial intelligence, logistics, and distribution – there seemed no limit to the range of subjects. Like most other Multima executives, Suzanne was usually intrigued by these topics and valued Mortimer's willingness to spend thousands bringing informed and influential personalities to expand their knowledge or to keep them current with significant developments. She never knew exactly when she'd use the information, but past sessions had always proven valuable at some critical juncture.

Warren Wrigletts was the only disappointment. For the second year, he predicted economic gloom. Suzanne just didn't buy it. Despite the unease many Americans seemed to be feeling, and the foul mood surrounding the presidential elections, business seemed healthy. Everything she read suggested a plodding, upward trend in the economy. She detected no indicators of the impending economic crash Wrigletts had been predicting for more than a year – and continued to promote in his speech to the group.

She vowed to remain cautious but intended to maintain her course with store renovations and the new healthy food focus they'd just launched. If Wrigletts proved right after all, renovations could always be delayed or promotional activity curtailed.

Chatting with all the speakers had been fun. Although the lunch break was short, Mortimer's practice of asking presenters to sit with his division presidents gave time to pose a few good questions and get to know each of them better. Of course, they'd all exchanged business cards. The speakers always hoped for more paid speaking engagements or opportunities for consulting fees. The division presidents liked to expand their network of contacts they might draw on for information or assistance when a later need arose.

Despite absorbing and processing thousands of words on dozens of different subjects over the two days of offsite meetings, Suzanne knew the most illuminating part of the events was often the two-hour cocktail meet-and-greet before dinner the first day. There, her keen political antennae could detect subtle shifts in direction or simmering issues that might suddenly become crucial. She always expected to glean valuable nuances as people relaxed and talked.

Yesterday's session didn't disappoint. Both incidents involved Douglas Whitfield. Suzanne had mastered the art of seemingly devoting one hundred percent of her attention to any conversation. However, as she talked and listened, she remained surprisingly alert to most activity around her. Even she was sometimes amazed at her ability to detect subtle movements or gestures in another conversation or between people several feet away.

At one point, she realized Whitfield had monopolized the attention of John George Mortimer for almost an hour. That was extremely rare. She always considered Mortimer a master at working the room. Usually, he found a way to spend five to ten minutes with every person attending receptions. He had the knack for fully engaging in a meaningful conversation quickly and just as rapidly extricating himself to move on to the next person.

So, Suzanne was a little intrigued about the matter Whitfield was discussing which could hold Mortimer's attention so intently for such a long time – and at the expense of his usual mingling routine.

A few moments later, she hoped for an opportunity to probe a little when Whitfield interrupted Suzanne's conversation with Natalia Tenaz.

"How is the home mortgage program launch going, ladies?" he asked with a broad grin and curious tilt of his head. "Is my favorite project working out as planned?"

It was an innocent question. Everyone knew Douglas led the team that created the home mortgage concept for Financial Services before a big promotion to his current role. So, why did Natalia suddenly become slightly tense and her usual smile disappear for an instant before she quickly recovered?

"You did such a great job creating the program that its implementation is really the easy part!" Natalia gushed with a disarming smile and gentle touch of his forearm. "And you know Suzanne's team," she added, shifting her attention towards her. "Everyone's so focused and professional. We're all grateful for their outstanding support."

Suzanne saw both intensity and kindness in Natalia's eyes and thought the warm-hearted comments the younger woman directed towards her seemed more genuine than her tone of voice seconds earlier as she flattered Whitfield. All three shared comments about the mortgage project launch for the next few minutes until Whitfield subtly changed direction.

"I heard about the complications with regulatory approvals in Canada," he said. "Did Liveenwel's people get everything cleared up okay?"

Suzanne was surprised to see how intently he studied Natalia as they both watched her suddenly tense again, physically stepping back slightly from Whitfield as she answered.

"Most of the provinces are finished. They assure me we'll have the last two approvals on Monday," she replied rather tersely.

"I'm sorry those issues cropped up at the last minute like that. We probably should have covered them better in the development stage," Douglas admitted with what appeared to be a look of genuine apology. "I hope that rascal Liveenwel didn't make it too difficult for you."

"No. Janet and I were forced to push a little harder than I would have liked to meet the deadline and had to pay far more than James Fitzgerald wished," she added with a playful wave of her hand. "But Roger finally saw it our way."

Suzanne noticed Natalia's lips purse tightly and smile disappear as she looked directly into Whitfield's eyes with an intensity that caused Whitfield to blink and tense momentarily. There was far too much subtext in this conversation, Suzanne thought as she considered excusing herself for another group.

"Well, I'm glad it all worked out in the end," Whitfield quickly replied as he recovered both his smile and control of the dialogue. "I'll make sure he makes amends for any grief he gave either of you."

Again, Suzanne noticed Natalia's body language almost recoil with another slight defensive step backward. "That won't be necessary. We've got it all under control."

Then, quickly excusing herself, she spun on one heel and immediately set off for another corner of the room. Suzanne was left to recover the conversation and used a few minutes to query about the move to Miami, how his family was doing, and other banal questions to perhaps diffuse the tension.

As she studied his tone and manner, she decided it would be too gauche to pry into his conversation with Mortimer then. So, as soon as she thought a decent amount of time had elapsed, Suzanne too, sought to escape and engage with someone else. She noticed that Whitfield headed towards Fitzgerald, probably anxious to smooth over any remaining ill will James might harbor about the regulatory fiasco. He was politically smart enough to know that if Natalia was upset about something, Fitzgerald was probably even more unhappy.

Glancing away from her next conversation for an instant, she noted that Fitzgerald hadn't welcomed Whitfield into his ongoing conversation with Alberto Ferer. Instead, he had subtly shifted his body specifically to exclude him from the conversation. Something was going on between the Financial Services and Solutions groups.

Suzanne thought about those dynamics throughout the evening. Mortimer's executive assistant, Sally-Ann Bureau, had organized a marvelous dinner after cocktails. An ensemble from the Naples Symphony played throughout the four-course meal, and a former late-night television personality told stories that had everyone in the room laughing uproariously for more than hour. It was a typical, first-class affair, carefully designed to encourage fun, relaxation, and harmony.

As usual with these events, as the evening ended, Suzanne returned to her suite and welcomed one knock on the door after another. Her entire entourage was there within fifteen minutes. They took places on the sofa or in chairs that circled a short oblong table holding several bottles of water. She invited them to serve themselves and asked who'd like to start.

For the next hour, each of her entourage summarized their takeaways from the day, issues that needed attention, and concerns that might have surfaced. They all knew the routine and came prepared. Suzanne listened intently while each of them summarized impressions and findings.

As they were leaving, one of her subordinates asked for a word privately. Once the others had left the suite, her shy colleague hesitantly relayed a message.

"I have a friend in corporate security who asked me to share some information with you. It's rather cryptic, but she said to tell you some new issue with Howard Knight and VCI has resurfaced."

"That's all she said?" Suzanne demanded.

"She also mentioned that James Fitzgerald has been spending an unusually large amount of time recently with both her boss, Dan Ramirez, and Alberto Ferer in legal affairs."

Something big was going to happen soon. She could just feel it. There had been no information about Knight's disappearance nor changes to the board of directors. She heard new murmurs of lingering uncertainty among staff about John George's future. It was all rather unusual for Multima.

Unfounded gossip relayed at cocktail parties was certainly not a source of information Suzanne usually heeded. But this time, someone's effort to get a message to her through an intermediary struck her not only as odd but in some way intriguing.

As a result, in addition to a high level of anticipation about her upcoming meeting with John George Mortimer, Suzanne had been distracted by unsettling thoughts about VCI all through the morning's session. Why would Fitzgerald be interested in the private equity company? What could a major shareholder have done to attract the interest of corporate security?

And then there was the curious long cocktail conversation between Mortimer and Whitfield, followed by Fitzgerald's subsequent snub of Whitfield a few minutes later.

Relieved the corporate event would end soon, she guessed her coming private conversations with John George Mortimer might assume even more importance. Now, what other important pieces might she be missing?

Thirty-Two

Guantanamo Bay, Cuba.
Friday September 23, 2016

It had been almost two weeks since someone snatched Howard and Fidelia from the sidewalk outside their temporary apartment in Buenos Aires. They'd been held captive somewhere near the Buenos Aires international airport, then put on an unmarked private jet where four guards released their hands but not the feet restraints. With a surly reminder not to try anything foolish, one guard shoved them into adjoining seats near the door.

Whispering, they compared their fates. Him, they treated reasonably well. Solitary confinement meant very limited human company and no exercise, books, or entertainment. The food was barely edible. But, other than some rather rough handling while transporting him to the secluded location, there was no violence.

He knew Fidelia had not been so fortunate. Tears sprung to his eyes again as he listened to the tales of terror she recounted. Her newly altered face looked horrible. It was obvious; they beat her severely. Her nose remained broken and smashed to one side. There were purple and blue bruises on her cheeks and jaw. Several teeth were broken or missing. And lacerations were apparent seemingly everywhere on her arms and legs.

"The worst was the first day," she told him with tears flowing down her battered face. She made no attempt to wipe them away as she continued.

"A brutal female guard came into my cell, screaming at me in Spanish. She shouted for me to get up off the floor. Called me a filthy whore and struck me across my back with such impact it knocked me to the floor again.

"When I tried to get up, she forcefully drove her truncheon up my ass. Blood spurted out everywhere. When I screamed in pain, she slapped my face repeatedly demanding I remain silent or she'd drive her club into my cunt the next time. Then she asked me dozens of questions about our activities in Argentina," she explained through sobs and tears. "When she didn't like my answers, she struck me again and again."

Howard tenderly reached out to comfort her. But she pushed him away.

"It's not The Organization who has us," Fidelia continued. "This jet belongs to the FBI. That miserable guard told me the Americans agreed to let her and her colleagues 'have some time' with us before the FBI took us away. She said it was the price the Argentinian police had stipulated in return for cooperation.

"It was horrible, Howard," she cried. "When the female guard finished with me, they let male guards come in and rape me. They took all kinds of pictures. Called me terrible names. Yelled obscenities at me while their companions laughed or cheered. Later, another female guard came with more questions and more demands for information. That horror started the first day and continued until last night."

With a gasp, Fidelia collapsed into his waiting arms. Sobbing uncontrollably, her entire body shook as she desperately clung to him with both hands, her face buried in his chest. They both wept wordlessly for several long minutes.

"I could hear it," Howard said when his tears subsided. "They held me in a nearby room. Most of the time I was bound and gagged so I couldn't call out to you, but I heard your screams and felt your pain. I'm so terribly sorry."

Fidelia didn't reply. But they both seemed to come to the same realization at the same moment. If the FBI were indeed their captors, these hours en route to America might be their last hours together for many years, maybe forever.

For the rest of the more than twelve-hour flight, with a stop for refueling, Howard tried to comfort her. But for the first time he could remember, she resisted his caresses. Neither slept. Instead, she only listened while he whispered occasional words of love and comfort, and savored their closeness.

When they landed, it became apparent that more than the FBI was involved. They had expected to arrive in Miami. When they saw the notorious complex with military personnel everywhere, both realized that something much bigger and more sinister was underway.

As soon as their feet touched the ground, they were separated. Two female guards in army fatigues gently led battered Fidelia away from the jet into a building Howard supposed was a clinic or hospital. Two burly soldiers roughly shoved him in another direction.

At least five people were sitting in a semicircle on wooden, hard-backed chairs as he entered the room. The guards pointed Howard towards a single chair facing them and released the handcuffs they had locked on the jet just before landing. A very bulky man wearing a casual shirt and blue jeans – seated in the center – was first to speak.

"Welcome, Howard Knight. No doubt, your flight was long and tiring. We'll let you relax in a few minutes. First, we're going to give you a few things to think about while you rest," he said with what seemed a mocking tone despite his civil manner.

"My name is Les. That's the only name you need at this stage. I'm your assigned case officer. I work in the department of justice, and I'll be spending a lot of time with you over the next few days. That is, we'll be spending a lot of time together if you and Ms. Morales decide to cooperate with us fully.

"If you choose not to cooperate, our time will be very short. Should you choose not to help us, Ms. Morales will be cleaned up and given a few cosmetic repairs. Then, we'll put her back on the same jet you came on and return her to the same friendly folks where she spent the past two weeks. They're really miffed about the role she played in the disappearance of more than one hundred Argentinian young women – some as young as twelve. They were pissed when we told them we needed her alive and well enough to assist us," he said firmly, then waited for the message to register.

"Who are you, and what is it you want?" Howard asked meekly.

"That's not important right now. At this stage of our discussion, we'll focus only on the consequences should you decide not to cooperate with us. As we said, Ms. Morales will need to fend for herself with the Argentinian secret police. You, on the other hand, may do some more traveling, too. There's an outfit called The Organization who seems very interested in you," the man whispered.

"Should you choose not to cooperate, we'll make one phone call to let them know exactly where at Miami International Airport you'll be arriving. And, we'll be sure to let them know the time someone will open a helicopter door and push you down the stairs to the tarmac before taking off again. We think those people in The Organization will be very grateful to us. They'll do whatever they might want to do, and we'll save them the five-million-dollar reward they've so generously offered," he finished with a slight smile.

"What kind of cooperation are you looking for?" Howard asked.

"No. It's too early in our discussions for that," the big man replied. "We want you well rested before we get into those kinds of details. We don't want you to suffer any lapses in memory due to fatigue when we talk, do we? No. For now, you'll just rest and think about the consequences should you choose not to cooperate the next time we chat, a few days from now."

With that thought firmly planted in his mind, all the men sitting opposite him promptly stood up and left the room without further comment. His soldier guards replaced his handcuffs and led him towards what appeared to be a barracks.

Sure enough, they took him first to a shower and forced him to undress and clean up while they watched. When he finished, they handed him a plastic bag with clean clothes. Shorts, socks, a t-shirt, and underwear, all the same drab shade of gray. Down the hallway a short distance, they led him into another cell. This one was certainly more comfortable than the last. There was a bed, a sink, and toilet; sunlight streamed into the room. There was even a small television in the corner.

"Someone will bring you food within the hour," one of the soldiers said tersely as he locked the cell door.

"Don't forget to do some serious thinking," the other shouted over his shoulder. "The boys will expect your answer to their offer when you meet the next time."

"What fucking offer?" Howard muttered under his breath. All they told him were the horrible consequences should he not cooperate. Who knew what the consequences were if he did help them?

With a shudder, he turned on the television. CNN was broadcasting a loud and hotly contested panel discussion about presidential candidate Donald J. Trump. They were almost unanimous. The man was totally unfit to be a presidential candidate. It appeared not much had changed in the months Howard and Fidelia had been away.

Thirty-Three

Fort Myers, Florida.
Saturday September 24, 2016

It was a disaster. There was no other way to describe it, he thought as he took another gulp from the cup of strong coffee Lana had wordlessly handed him moments before. His night had been almost sleepless. Not only had he failed to mend his relationship with Suzanne, he made matters worse. Instead of enjoying breakfast and pleasant conversation with him this morning as originally expected, she was gone. And there might be even more unsettling news to come.

It was entirely his fault. He realized that. But he still couldn't figure out at what point he'd lost control of the situation.

No doubt, that bizarre conversation with Douglas Whitfield at the cocktail reception rattled him. A subsequent interview with Dan Ramirez in corporate security did nothing to calm his fears. He was literally in shock. Even now, his hands trembled noticeably and there was a dull sensation in the pit of his stomach that refused to go away. At first, he thought Whitfield was playing some sort of grotesque joke.

"I've been ordered to give you a message that I personally don't understand from a person I don't know," he had started, visibly uncomfortable and glancing around to avoid direct eye contact. "After visiting my kids in Chicago this weekend, I was summoned from my hotel room in the middle of the night. The caller said he had information you needed to know and insisted I go down to the lobby and meet him outside the hotel."

John George immediately demonstrated a keen interest in what was to follow, arched his brows and said nothing.

"I was more than a little nervous, but the hotel was well lit, and I thought there would be around the clock security," Whitfield resumed. "So, I went down. Outside the hotel entrance, a large man was pointing a gun at me. I raised my hands in the air immediately. He was wearing a ski mask that covered his head and face completely. He asked my name. When I told him, he dragged me by the collar and pushed me into an alley. He said he had a message for you. He instructed me to give you his message exactly as he gave it to me.

"Tell Mortimer we know all about Suzanne Simpson," he said. "Tell him he has seven days to respond positively to Gottingham's request or bad things will start to happen to her," Whitfield explained as he leaned towards John George using a tone barely above a whisper.

Mortimer could only imagine how he must have looked as he stood there speechless, his mouth agape as he tried to process the disturbing message. After a few seconds, Whitfield continued.

"He told me that I must only give you that message before leaving the offsite meeting and should I contact the police – or communicate with you in any way before this offsite – bad things would start to happen immediately. I was terrified, John George. I'm still sick with fear. I certainly don't wish any harm to Suzanne. That's why I've kept it quiet all week and share the awful message with you only now."

Once he regained his composure, John George tried to learn more, but Whitfield either had nothing more to share or was unwilling to pass on what he did know. He still wasn't sure which was actually the case.

He lost track of time as he posed question after question to Douglas Whitfield. While the division president appeared to consider each of John George's queries thoughtfully – and repeatedly emphasized his effort to recall anything else – he ultimately revealed no additional details. He was respectful and seemed genuinely concerned about Suzanne's well-being but never wavered as more than once John George asked him to repeat the demand. In turn, two or three times Douglas obliquely inquired if the name Gottingham meant anything.

John George avoided answering the questions directly as they parried for information for almost an hour. When he realized how much time he had spent with Whitfield, he dismissed him carefully.

"I know this matter troubles you as much as me. I think it best we both sit on this for a few days. I'll speak with Ramirez in corporate security and get his advice on best next steps. Maybe he can find out what this is all about. I'll let you know as soon as I learn anything," Mortimer remembered saying as he walked away to join another cocktail conversation.

He met with Ramirez later that night, and their talks continued well into the early hours of the morning. His first concern was a provocative question.

Was Whitfield indeed the innocent carrier of the malicious message? Or, did he, too, have some connection to The Organization?

Ramirez ordered a team to dig up information on Whitfield from trusted contacts in multiple police forces and other reliable sources of information. Then the pair dissected all possibilities they could identify. What kinds of 'bad things' might befall Suzanne? Were they talking professional damage? Or could they be threatening personal harm? Was Gottingham likely to be 'in-the-loop'? Or, was this exclusively the domain of The Organization? Why did they contact Whitfield in Chicago? Why not Miami where he spent most of his time? Or New York, where they knew Whitfield spent the day before continuing to Chicago for the weekend?

By the time they concluded their discussions, the sun was rising outside the window of Mortimer's spacious penthouse suite in the Naples Ritz-Carlton. Ramirez's team also came back empty handed. They found no connection to The Organization or other criminal elements.

Ramirez recommended they make Suzanne's security their top priority, and that's where last night's trouble started. As he and Suzanne traveled in the limousine, with the closed privacy divider separating them from the driver, John George broached the subject.

"I know this is not what we planned for the weekend," he ventured tentatively. "But here's the problem. You may have noticed I was in and out of the session several times this morning. I was dealing with a crisis, and I don't know any easy way to say this, so I'll be direct."

He turned to look into her eyes. "Dan Ramirez in corporate security thinks you should take some time away from the office," he said and watched her face express immediate and total surprise.

"We've just received a credible threat. It's still unclear whether that threat is against you, personally, or Multima Supermarkets."

"Have the police been notified?" Suzanne exclaimed with concern.

"They warned us not to contact any law enforcement agencies, or they will act immediately. Ramirez wants you to take refuge somewhere safe, right away, and preferably out of the country, while he attempts to establish a dialogue and negotiate."

"But where? And why now? What is going on? And why am I learning this just now?" Suzanne questioned without waiting for a reply to any of her questions. "For months, now, I have patiently waited until it was convenient for you to discuss the several serious concerns I have about your relationship with my mother and some troubling events surrounding her death. On the weekend we finally have planned for that crucial conversation, you suddenly inform me I am the object of an unknown threat from an unknown source. Now, I need to get out of the country immediately and into hiding. It's unbelievable! I don't trust you or what you are saying at all!" she exclaimed with an intensity John George had never before seen.

John George tried to calm her. He relayed some of the information he received, letting her know about Whitfield getting the demand at gunpoint and suggesting she confirm the threat's validity independently with him. But, he was careful not to mention Gottingham or anything related to The Organization and its connection to Multima. He knew it was not entirely convincing but wanted to shield her from information better left unknown.

He was unsuccessful. Apparently, he had miscalculated the depth of her concerns. She appeared to be unloading several months of intense frustration with words and accusations he had never imagined hearing from her. Every attempt he made to change the direction of their confrontation failed. She immediately twisted every alternative he presented, reverting to her perception that he was unwilling to be open, honest, or forthcoming. She was fed up and used that exact expression more than once in her tirade.

Even the chauffeur realized there was something amiss. John George noticed that he glanced surreptitiously in the rearview mirror several times with some apprehension.

The drive from Naples to his home in Fort Myers was usually less than an hour, but the Friday afternoon traffic north was heavier than usual. As a result, their awkward discussion continued for some time. John George had never seen the extraordinarily tactful and diplomatic woman show such frustration and anger. It truly surprised him. No executive of Multima in his almost half-century of experience ever spoke to him with either the tone or vocabulary Suzanne used. It was very disconcerting.

He was trying desperately to convince her to move out of potential harm's way, while she was fixed only on her perception that he was continuing to evade her quest for information. There seemed no way to bridge the gulf. His considerable management skills hadn't adequately prepared him for such an intensely personal confrontation.

"Let's call a temporary truce here," he said with the most charming grin he could manage. "I'm happy to answer your questions. I understand how much this concerns you. But I'm also concerned for your well-being. I think it more urgent to get you somewhere safe – somewhere far away from here until we can sort out whether this threat has merit."

He watched Suzanne's shoulders stiffen and chin rise as she gave him a look he could characterize only as defiant before she said in an even tone, "I get your message. I'll leave. Please have the driver drop me at Page Field. I'll fly somewhere for the weekend. But I want you to understand that I will spend these next few days deciding if I want to continue to work in such an uncomfortable environment.

"You have withheld crucial information from me for years – more than a decade. For the almost six months since you dropped the bombshell that you are my father, you have evaded meeting with me to answer questions that are essential to my mental and physical well-being. Now, while we are on the road to your home – for long-awaited answers to my troubling concerns – you ask me politely to get out of town. I'm not sure the role of president of Multima Supermarkets fits into my career plans any longer."

At that point, John George realized further discussion was probably pointless. It would be better for her to cool down and for him to think through how best to rebuild her trust and confidence. He lowered the limousine privacy panel and instructed the driver to divert to Page Field.

They remained silent for the last few minutes of the ride. As they turned into the private jet airport, John George was the first to speak.

"I know I've disappointed and angered you terribly," he paused for more than a few seconds as he seemed to search for just the right words. "And for that, I apologize deeply. I have never intended to hurt you in any way, and I make my request that you lie low somewhere outside the USA only because I care so profoundly for your safety. I respect your desire to reconsider your future. I'll say only this. Please take some time before you make any decisions. With time, I think you'll realize what I'm suggesting has only your best interests at heart, and I will eventually be able to put your mind at ease."

"I'll promise only to consider your comments carefully," Suzanne replied as the vehicle stopped at the terminal. "I'll call the pilots, and I'll be okay to wait here until they arrive."

With that farewell, she left the car.

John George immediately closed the privacy panel again and pressed the speed-dial for Dan Ramirez as it closed.

"Dan, Suzanne has decided to follow your advice. I'm not sure where she's headed so I'd like you to contact her pilots. Have the co-pilot fall ill and replace him with one of your guys. She's probably calling them at Fort Myers Beach right now, so act quickly. Make sure it's one of your best people. Be sure your man gets you the flight plan and details about where she's staying. And Dan, I think he needs to be armed," John George added.

For the remainder of the limousine ride home, John George struggled to understand how the circumstance had run away from him. He replayed their conversation over and over in his mind. He thought about the different ways he could have broached the subject of her safety. Most of all, he worried about the ability of Dan's man to protect her while they sorted out the other issue.

In the heat of their strained conversation with a less than satisfactory outcome, he had also completely forgotten the other matter he intended to mention to her: the cursed news about the return of his cancer.

Thirty-Four

*On an American Airlines flight towards Chicago.
Sunday September 25, 2016*

Janet Weissel could barely hold back the tears. She had been sobbing on and off since she left the Hyatt hotel a few hours earlier. At first, the heartbreak was so intense her body had shuddered completely while she screamed out strings of violent profanities.

The bastard dumped her. It was that frigging simple. First, Whitfield didn't even take her to Miami on the jet he parked at Page Field in Fort Myers for two days. Oh, no! Instead, he called her room at that damned offsite meeting in Naples and left her a voice message. He couldn't risk the visibility of taking her on the jet with him from Page Field. Could she instead rent a frigging car and drive over to meet him in Miami for the weekend?

So, she did. She left the Ritz-Carleton mid-afternoon Friday and drove across Alligator Alley to the Miami Hyatt Regency, just like he asked. She met him there, and they went out for an excellent dinner on South Miami Beach, then partied in the clubs until the early morning Saturday.

When they returned to the Hyatt, they immediately made love. It started slowly, just as she liked it. He teased her with his tongue as he undid her buttons and reached inside to stroke her braless breasts. She loved the way he alternately kissed the nipples and leisurely circled them, first with one finger, then two as he squeezed ever so gently before kissing them again with his lips and tongue.

It was exquisite! Then, he reached under her short skirt to massage her thighs and gently pry them open with teasing probes to touch her. She loved the way he stroked her clitoris in the same gentle circular motion as her nipples while his tongue probed deeper and deeper into her mouth.

It made her want to respond. So, she did. She always did. As she opened her legs ever so slightly for him to probe deeply with one or two fingers, she would start to stroke his penis. Teasing him the same way, she'd tickle his testicles until he began to squirm a little. As his erection grew, she always found ways

186

to make it grow faster and harder. Stroking. Kissing. Licking it from one end to the other, she'd continue until he begged her for release, and she'd give him a blowjob that left him spent.

They would usually have another glass of wine before they started again. Usually, on the second go, she'd have multiple orgasms. It seemed he could go for hours during the second round, and she always made sure he knew how much she treasured his efforts.

They slept for a while, but she was not surprised when she felt him working gently on her breasts sometime later. Their sexual exploration started again and ended with the same delightfully predictable result.

Saturday, he needed to go to his office for a few hours and left her to sleep late, enjoy breakfast in the room, and then work out in the hotel gym. She knew it was essential to maintain her impressive body. For her, exercise was a tool more important to success than any computer skills or degree from Columbia, so she made time almost every day to work out strenuously.

When Douglas returned to the hotel late in the afternoon Saturday, she noticed something was different. He wanted sex right away. The tender love-making of the previous night was gone. He stripped her naked in moments, barely bothering to look at her breasts let alone stroke and make love to them. He reached down to her crotch almost immediately, well before she became moist.

His touch was rough and rushed. There were almost no words of affection or appreciation despite her two-hour workout on the elliptical in the gym. When she tried to slow him down a bit, he became even more rushed and pressed her back against the bed, forcing her legs apart with his knee. Then, he demanded a blowjob and squeezed her nipples roughly to emphasize his urgency.

She did what he asked. After all, she had experienced all kinds during her exploits over the years. Her performance was good, she thought. She smiled and cooed. She licked and sucked. And when he came, she accepted his full load with enthusiasm and passion.

But there was nothing for her. He cleaned up, showered, and dressed. Then suggested they leave for dinner. Was there any place she wanted to go? In the end, she left it to him to decide.

Their meal was okay. He talked about his new software project and asked her questions about his old stomping grounds at Multima Financial Services. He inquired about a few former colleagues and seemed interested in her stories about the successes of the new home mortgage program. His idea initially; she knew he always had time and interest to talk about its progress.

They decided to forgo the clubs their second night and returned to the hotel shortly after dinner. To her chagrin, when they got back to the hotel, Douglas wanted to watch a college football game on TV. So, they drank a bottle of wine and watched the game for a few hours.

After, he started to show interest again. This time, he began slowly. Like the night before, their lovemaking was tender, long, and unbelievably satisfying. She lost count of the orgasms. All she could remember was the power of each, reaching a crescendo somewhere around number five. It was after three o'clock when she last looked at the clock before drifting off into a fully sated sleep and pleasant dreams of love and passion.

When she awoke around nine, he wasn't there! She checked the bathroom. His toiletries were still next to the sink, and a change of clothes still hung on a hanger in the closet. It was strange. In all the times they'd met up for sex, he had never left their bed in the morning without waking her, telling her where he was going and leaving her with a passionate kiss. "A down payment for later," he liked to say with that impish grin that always sent shivers down her spine.

About an hour later he returned to the room, sweating profusely from a workout in the gym. "Hi babe," he called out. "Why don't you order breakfast from room service while I shower?"

Before she could ask what he might like for his breakfast, he was in the bathroom, and she heard the shower spray. She guessed that he'd probably be satisfied with some variation of eggs. Perhaps an omelet, she thought, and ordered one for herself as well.

Room service arrived quickly – about the same time as he returned refreshed from the bathroom. They ate breakfast with a conversation about the weather, the previous night's football game, and their respective demanding work schedules for the coming week. There was nothing controversial, nothing unusual. When they finished breakfast, the bastard slid his chair back from the wooden table in the center of their room and delivered the devastating news.

"I think we're going to need some time apart, babe. My family issues are getting more complicated. A lot is going on in the company. And I'm going to need to stay focused on the critical issues for a while. Let's just keep in touch. I'll let you know if things change," the bastard said before kissing her on the cheek, gathering up his things, and walking out of the room.

Thirty-Five

Guantanamo Bay, Cuba.
Saturday October 1, 2016

"It's up to you to persuade her," the now familiar FBI agent in a rumpled blue suit had insisted early that morning. "We've already waited five days for her to come around. There's no deal for you if she won't cooperate. We need to toss the folks at Interpol a bone for all their trouble, and only she can give us the details we need. So, the entire offer is off the table if we don't have her buy-in before six o'clock tonight.

"That means if she doesn't agree to give us everything we need, she's on a flight back to her friends in Buenos Aires and at 6:01 you're on a trip to Miami with me. And I'll make sure The Organization knows the exact spot where we drop you," he snarled for emphasis.

"She's a strong woman. I don't know if I can persuade her to take it," Howard Knight replied.

"Well, I guess it will depend on your charm then. There's no deal if she's not in," the agent said, suppressing a grin. "I told you. I don't like this deal anyway. I'd much rather let The Organization have its way with scum like you, and your friend deserves every bit of the torture she'll surely get from the Argentinians."

"Look," Howard replied, a little more boldly. "I'm ready to give you the information you need to convict Giancarlo Mareno and at least a half-dozen of his most influential associates. You'll make a huge dent in The Organization's operations in the US, and I can lead Interpol to some off-shore convictions too. I've got names of people, companies, and banks in a dozen or more countries. Even without the human trafficking piece, Interpol can get lots of headlines and convictions.

"Fidelia was broken by that Argentinian Gestapo you used to seize us. What they did to her was inhumane. I don't know if she can even remember the stuff you want. During the time we had together on the plane, she seemed not just distraught: she was practically comatose. I'll cooperate with you. You and Interpol will get your convictions. Let me carry the load and put us both in the protection program," Howard said.

"There is no fucking way that is going to happen," the agent firmly retorted without a moment's consideration. "You've got until six o'clock to convince her. Not a minute longer."

With that refusal, the FBI agent stood and left the room. Howard's spirit dropped as the guards led him out. He had only a few hours to convince her the protection program was their best chance for a life together. In fact, for any life at all, he recalibrated.

They led him down a new walkway several minutes away from the main compound and the cells where they had been holding them. Until then, they had insisted there would be no contact between the prisoners. Days earlier, Howard learned that not only Fidelia, he, and a few suspected foreign terrorists were captives in the godforsaken place. In fact, there were others, and he was shocked the day guards wordlessly paraded both Wendal Randall and Frau Klaudia Schäffer in front of his cell. Neither wore handcuffs or restraints. Both appeared carefree, laughing and holding hands as they strolled outside the window of his cell.

The message had been crystal clear. The pair were cooperating. It would be better for him to do the same. Sure enough, the very next day the agent in a blue suit offered to waive criminal charges and put them in the FBI's witness protection program if Howard and Fidelia cooperated with both information and testimony that would lead to convictions of The Organization's leadership.

Within hours, he accepted. In his mind, there was simply no alternative. His release to The Organization would mean a slow, long, and painful death. He knew that. He'd witnessed some of them and had no desire to spend his last hours screaming in agony as they removed body parts as crudely and gruesomely as possible.

It would be bad enough for him, but he could never allow them to throw Fidelia to the Argentinian animals who'd treated her so horribly in their custody. With their animosity towards her involvement in human trafficking, he shuddered to imagine how violently they would treat her and for how long they would try to extend the torture.

As they arrived at a cabin near the edge of the compound, the guards removed his handcuffs and feet restraints, told him they'd be outside if he needed anything and assured Howard the cabin was private. No one would intrude, and there were no audio or video devices. He could use whatever means he chose to convince her, one guard said with a suggestive grin.

Their reunion was tearful and tender. Fidelia threw herself into his waiting arms the moment she realized he was there. They clung desperately to each other for several minutes. Both sobbed. Their bodies shook as they grasped each other as closely as possible and stood in the middle of the room wordlessly.

Then, as a realization gradually set in that they were reunited – at least temporarily – their hold on each other changed to a warm and relaxed embrace. Long, passionate kisses followed as each savored the taste of the other. Embraces gave way to extended looks into each other's eyes as they tried to wordlessly divine what had happened to the other over the past few days of confinement and separation. Finally, after some minutes, Howard said, "We have to talk."

Patiently, he told her about his decision to cooperate with the FBI and his meeting with the agent earlier. He described to her his understanding of the protection program offered. He emphasized his confidence in the FBI to protect them adequately. And finally, he asked her how she felt about it.

He was appalled to hear her say, "I understand why you accepted their offer, and I want you to cooperate to save your life. For me, it's not so easy. I can't agree. Giancarlo Mareno will eventually find us. The man is the devil incarnate, and there is no limit to his vindictiveness. I remember the look in his eyes when he told me never to divulge details about The Organization to anyone at any time. Despite the horror of my incarceration there, I prefer to take my chances with the Argentinians," she added.

"He might find us, Fidelia, I get that. But the FBI might also be able to buy us a few more months or years together. They've done this many times with people like us. Their record is actually quite good."

"Look how quickly the Argentinians found us with the help of the FBI," Fidelia countered. "It took them only weeks, even after we altered our identities and documentation. They might put him in prison, but you know Giancarlo will always find a way to reach us."

For hours, they continued to talk. Patiently, Howard explored one avenue after the other, trying to use logic to persuade her to follow his example and cooperate with the FBI. Fidelia countered every argument, stubbornly insisting they wouldn't be safe anywhere. She rhymed off names and dates of dozens of their former colleagues as proof of Mareno's ability to penetrate any supposed shield of protection. The number of names she could recall, and the intricate details she remembered about each of their deaths, amazed him. Might the FBI find her even more valuable than they realized?

He changed his tact. Rather than appealing to logic, he subtly shifted to a more emotional plane. With so many people hurt and killed, should they now perhaps think about doing good and making restitution for all the harm they and other members of The Organization caused over the years? Could they make right some of their wrongs by cooperating with the FBI?

Fidelia humored him by listening for a while but eventually drew the conversation to an end.

"You know I love you more than anyone. I treasure our time together. But I can't do what you're asking. The Organization may not be perfect, but it has treated me very well. I'm not prepared to betray Giancarlo and his people. What I'm going to do is hard for me, very hard. But you'll see in time that it's better for you too.

"I'm quite sure they're recording this conversation, and probably they're also listening to us as we speak. So, this message will be for you and everyone else involved. I will not become a witness for the state. As much as I love you and wish for nothing more than to spend the rest of my life with you making love in some secluded place, I have never believed in fairy tales. And I don't believe this one. You and the FBI can do whatever you choose to do. I have nothing more to say."

Howard knew that he would remember the cold shock and bitter sadness that immediately enveloped him for many months. But he realized further discussion was pointless. He had seen her firm and immovable will before. In desperation, he wrapped his arms around her back and drew her closer to him. Tears sprung to his eyes as he accepted the reality of her words.

"I love you, Fidelia," he whispered. "I always will. And I hope with all my heart you'll find some way out of this mess."

They shared one last lingering kiss. As they broke away, Howard heard the tropical stillness of the afternoon suddenly shatter. He recognized the sound – a nearby executive jet starting its engines, preparing for departure. Seconds later, the door to the hut opened, and the approaching guards reached out with handcuffs to secure his wrists again.

As they led him towards his cell, he turned to look back and started sobbing intensely as he took in the scene. Two female guards were escorting Fidelia towards the idling aircraft. She, too, looked back over her shoulder but only for an instant.

Thirty-Six

In a Bombardier Global 5000 corporate jet flying over Florida.
Friday October 7, 2016

After her eagerly-anticipated meeting with John George Mortimer was aborted three weeks earlier, Suzanne had been livid. From the moment he left her at the entrance to the Page Field terminal, she took immediate action.

First, a call to Dan Ramirez in corporate security confirmed Mortimer's story about a threat that involved her, even though she knew he and Mortimer had adequate time to harmonize their stories. As expected, he supported Mortimer's story and encouraged her to confirm it with Whitfield. More importantly, she should leave the country for a while. Even a week or two might help, he implored.

She refused. She did not intend to be intimidated by criminals. That could be the end of her career. She accepted the security chief's help, though. There was no reason to be foolish. That explained the two burly escorts who now accompanied her everywhere.

The more experienced one, a male who towered over her by more than a foot, was in charge and made sure he inspected every room before she entered. They temporarily discontinued visits to company stores due to his discomfort about her safety in congested public environments. Suzanne trusted the man and listened carefully to his quiet counsel.

The female – a very muscular woman – was about her height but probably packed on an extra thirty pounds compared with Suzanne's trim figure. Despite the woman's size, she moved quickly with grace, and walked everywhere about a step behind Suzanne. Around the office, one or the other always sat discreetly in the background as Suzanne conducted meetings with colleagues or suppliers. The sole exception was the private bathroom of Suzanne's luxurious executive suite. Evenings, both bodyguards occupied their own separate rooms in Suzanne's spacious home.

It was a lifestyle she didn't want for any length of time, and it added to her intense discomfort with her entire situation at Multima. Few women in America earned more money or wielded more influence in their jobs, but gnawing concerns continued to weigh on her mind day and night. Who could ever have imagined that more than a decade after joining the company she would discover her boss and CEO of the company was her father?

Who could ever have imagined the death of her mother would uncover secret monthly payments to her bank account from a company ultimately owned and controlled by a subsidiary of the very company she managed? And who could ever have foreseen the police in Quebec detaining her for questioning related to the mysterious death of a priest whose parents were killed in tragic circumstances – also possibly related to her mother's sudden death?

It was all too much for her to absorb. Further, her boss and apparent father had stonewalled her numerous attempts to get some answers and closure for several months.

The mysterious threat delivered by Whitfield compounded the tension of a bewildering puzzle. Whitfield confirmed the story about the threat when she called him from Page Field. He professed extreme discomfort to be put in such an untenable position and forced to deliver such an unsettling message.

However, she remembered his tone seemed a little rehearsed and flowed a bit too smoothly for someone supposedly equally rattled by the circumstances. Further, over the past months, Suzanne had become uncertain about Whitfield from a few different perspectives.

It started with his bizarre behavior in that teleconference several months earlier. She remembered finding it odd that he would stoke sales expectations unreasonably high after only an initial contact with a prospective customer for the new software his division was charged with developing and promoting.

Then, there was the curious oversight related to their introduction of the home mortgage program with Multima Financial Services. Everyone knew the concept developed under Whitfield's supervision. If he was indeed such a business genius that Mortimer and the board rewarded him with the presidency of Multima Solutions, how could such brilliance overlook a glaring need for regulatory approvals in more than a dozen states and several Canadian provinces? Did Mortimer reward him for entirely different reasons she hadn't yet discovered?

Questions like these plagued Suzanne every moment she wasn't focusing on her business responsibilities. So, for the past three weeks, she devoted inordinate amounts of time to her job. Her schedule and pace of work were already legendary among her staff, but even they had remarked about her lengthened days in the office and the copious amounts of work she completed overnight. It was truly her relief from a situation she found not only implausible but increasingly frightening.

Normally, she loved her job. She loved the people in her division. And, she was thrilled with her accomplishments in the business world. But she was no longer prepared to function in an environment where her boss withheld crucial information, perhaps even life-altering facts, and created a mysterious shroud of doubt around everything of value to her.

Worst of all, there was no one she could approach. Who would believe her bizarre story? The police? What police authority would have an interest even should they believe her? Her mother's bank account and the company making payments to the account were Canadian. The murdered *notaire,* his wife, and son were all Canadian. But the police in Quebec were also quick to consider her a suspect in at least the priest's death.

The FBI was unlikely to have an interest as she had scant evidence of possible wrongdoing and what little she had was from another country. A private investigator was out of the question. If ever it was discovered she had hired someone to investigate activities of the corporation that employed her, her career would be finished. No other company would ever hire her.

It all looked very bleak, and Mortimer had suddenly become even less available without explanation. Four times over the past three weeks she called his office, only to learn from his assistant that he was away from the office on private business.

Sally-Ann's manner caused her even more concern. When Suzanne tried to use her usual friendly banter to pry more information from Mortimer's protective barrier, the woman politely – but firmly – deflected every attempt in a business-only tone of voice.

Finally, on the fourth attempt, Sally-Ann offered some hope. John George Mortimer apologized for his unavailability, she explained. And he wanted to make amends. Could she fly to Fort Myers for the weekend? There were some issues of importance he'd like to discuss with her.

Because of that call, she was relaxing as much as was possible in her company jet at thirty thousand feet headed towards Florida. There would be answers this time, she vowed. And, unless Mortimer's answers were extremely illuminating and benign, she would also tender her resignation and negotiate the terms of her departure from Multima Corporation forever.

Thirty-Seven

Lyon, France.
Friday October 7, 2016

Fidelia Morales delicately kissed each of Klaudia Schäffer's cheeks immediately after she stepped into the long-range Bombardier Global 5000 jet, and they exchanged a long, warm embrace once the guards freed their hands from the cuffs.

There were four female guards – two from the FBI and two from the CIA. They warned both captives again. There would be no shenanigans either in flight or when they reached their destination. One of the guards would remain awake at all times. The pilots were securely locked inside the cockpit with no possibility of entry without a secret code only the guards knew.

"Should you make any attempt to escape or endanger the flight in any way, we'll take any necessary action. We'll return to Cuba, and the deal will be off. Do you understand this?" the most senior officer asked coldly.

Both acknowledged the directive and nodded assent. For the first four hours of the flight, the guards conducted more interviews with each captive separately. All wore sophisticated microphones on headsets designed to deaden the sound of the whining engines. Thin black wires drooped from the headsets, connected to tiny devices that recorded all questions and answers.

Neither captive could hear the interrogation of the other. Like in the sessions they had already conducted for several days in Guantanamo Bay, the guards took breaks every hour to review issues and study the answers they received. Then they compared responses for consistency and agreed upon the next series of questions they would pose.

While the interrogators analyzed their data, Fidelia and Klaudia relaxed. A flight attendant, who Fidelia assumed was probably yet another guard, provided them refreshments and entertainment. There was music to listen to or movies to watch while their minders prepared for the next round. Neither woman was

196

surprised. The entire process was consistent with the deal Fidelia had negotiated in Cuba.

When she first saw Klaudia and Wendal Randall aimlessly wandering through the grounds hand-in-hand that day in Guantanamo Bay, she immediately saw her opportunity.

It was evident they were cooperating with their captors. Neither wore handcuffs or foot restraints like she had been forced to wear. She was also certain Klaudia was playing the role expected of her. It was inconceivable she had fallen in love with the guy. But, she knew her to be cunning and shrewd. After all, she was the woman who had managed Fidelia's human trafficking operations for all of Europe.

Fidelia knew all about Klaudia's earlier horrible experiences in Russia. She knew the bitterness she retained about the systemic abuse she suffered from her days in university and onward. The woman had told horror stories about the brutal misogyny, sexual assaults, and cruelty she experienced in her roles with a string of secret service agencies that sprouted up, led by former bosses of the notorious KGB.

She'd also learned about the extreme economic hardship that triggered Klaudia's decision to seek a better life. Her circumstances seemed almost unbelievable in the twenty-first century. Not only was she mistreated at her job, but she also earned only enough money to afford a basic one-bedroom apartment where she was forced to share a toilet and kitchen with ten other families! To Klaudia, an escape to another life – even if it meant trafficking in humans – was the only way out of her quagmire.

There was little doubt. Her former subordinate was probably no more in love with the young American man than she felt necessary to portray for survival.

Within hours of seeing Klaudia, she hatched the idea. Now, they were well on their way to realizing its success. At first, the Americans were slow to see the benefit. However, in the end, they understood her scheme could not just win them points with Interpol, it could also tip the global political balance in ways they might only have dreamed about before.

In Guantanamo, she had never been alone with Klaudia. Her captors just wouldn't allow it. Still, through the intermediation of the senior FBI agent in charge, Fidelia had successfully communicated her intentions. Immediately, her former subordinate in The Organization bought in and the individual interviews started.

Their flight earlier today was in an entirely different direction than the Argentine destination they wanted Howard Knight to believe. Fidelia worked tirelessly to help the FBI understand her insistence that her safety could only be assured if Knight thought she was dead. Otherwise, even if they were in witness protection programs, she was vulnerable. They finally got it.

Instead of a flight to Argentina, they crossed the Atlantic and landed first at the international airport in Düsseldorf, Germany. There, they were directed to a secluded parking slot at the extreme end of the terminal.

A plain black Mercedes-Benz met the aircraft. Only Klaudia and her handlers disembarked and entered the limousine. Fidelia and the other guards remained on the plane as it refueled. The car headed to a Deutsche Bank branch in the small city of Ratingen, no more than twenty minutes from the airport.

They arrived as the bank opened for the day and a nervous manager was waiting for them as arranged. After he closely inspected the promised German court order from a *Richter*, the young man led them to a room secured with sturdy steel bars and filled with dozens of locked safety deposit boxes of all different sizes.

The guards escorted them to the back of the cavernous room to the largest box. It was digitally locked, and only the bank manager and Klaudia knew the combinations. She entered her secret code first and stepped back as the manager moved forward to key in his six-digits. The door swung open and the guards reached inside to remove eighteen large binders. Each binder was a different color, and each contained pages of data. One guard carefully inserted each of the binders into an empty duffle bag they brought for the purpose, while the other kept a wary eye on both Klaudia and the squirming young bank manager.

As discreetly as they arrived, the women departed with a perfunctory thank you for the manager's cooperation. Minutes later they re-embarked on the jet, this time joined by two more agents. No one introduced them or explained their role, but Fidelia assumed they were new European 'hosts'. French accents reinforced her suspicion. Within moments of their arrival, the aircraft door slammed shut, and they were airborne again.

Less than an hour later they arrived at Aéroport Lyon-Bron, a terminal for private aircraft on the outskirts of Lyon, France. There, two black Renault limousines were waiting. Fidelia and her guards climbed into one. Klaudia and her keepers used the other for the half-hour drive to Interpol Headquarters on *Quai Charles de Gaulle*.

Their limousines stopped in front of the impressive entrance to the massive complex where more 'hosts' were waiting. There would be no rest yet. Fidelia and Klaudia were resigned to several more hours of questioning with refreshments provided as needed. Their information-hungry captors had agreed to at least that concession.

Within seven or eight hours, she fully expected they would be satisfied with the meticulously maintained manual records of Klaudia Schäffer. They would find everything intact. Thousands of individual entries detailing names of women and girls snatched from streets and homes across Europe and sold into sexual slavery. They would see the actual dates they kidnapped them. Locations of their disappearances would be listed. Their ultimate fate would be described under a column titled *Anordnung*, always pointing to yet another accomplice.

Of much greater interest to the enthusiastic agents at Interpol, the carefully recorded information included names, addresses, and telephone numbers of hundreds of former colleagues – those who delivered the victims of human trafficking. Finally, they would also see page upon page of entries in the section called *Schutz*. There, they would learn the names of criminals, law enforcement personnel and government officials who provided safe harbor and assured a protective free hand to those engaged in such widespread trafficking.

She thought they would probably be astonished to see the names of some of Europe's most famous and influential government leaders. In fact, they would probably be shocked to see just how high in some states such protection extended. A particularly famous name – the one from Russia that most intrigued the Americans – would probably leave them flabbergasted.

Thirty-Eight

Miami, Florida.
Friday October 7, 2016

"There's a problem," Alistair Fitzgerald said.

"Tell me about it," Douglas Whitfield responded with a touch of impatience. Drama always seemed to surround James Fitzgerald's son, and that was the last thing he needed at this point.

"Our legal beagles found out about my plans to endorse your new software. They were apoplectic. They said the litigation risk is untenable and could bankrupt the bank. They ordered me to cancel our endorsement. Period. End of discussion."

"Wow! What's their rationale?"

"The unique purpose of the software is to track any hackers who copy files from a database. Their concern is what might happen if someone sees my endorsement, buys the software, then gets hit by a hacker who isn't apprehended immediately. Our lawyers maintain that our deep pockets will become a target for any attorney who takes even a cursory look at the situation," Alistair continued.

"Okay. I see. But what's a court going to give them, even if they're successful? The software package only costs a few hundred grand. That's peanuts to the bank. And that's assuming you lose. Our legal guys think that's the worst-case scenario, as unlikely as it is," Douglas replied patiently.

"Maybe for you that's a worst-case scenario. You've got warranties and representations in your agreement that limit your liability. We've got nothing. Some CIO sees your ad with my face and glowing endorsement of the app, buys it from you, and then becomes an unhappy camper. From you, he might get just the amount he paid for the software. From us, he claims damages – all the money his business lost because of the theft. Money lost because he thought he was buying a package that would protect him from those losses. With the big players you're targeting, companies could be claiming damages in the billions of dollars," Alistair countered, his voice rising.

Douglas needed to diffuse the situation quickly. James Fitzgerald's son became stressed easily and unhinged far too fast. He couldn't let that happen now.

"Okay, Alistair," he replied. "Let's just put things on hold for a bit. I sure don't want to see you in any trouble over there. I'll call the ad agency and ask them to hold the launch. Too bad we're not going to see that handsome mug of yours in every business publication later this month as we planned," he said with a hearty laugh.

"Thanks for understanding, Doug. I know this is important to you."

"Hey, not to worry man. We'll think of something. Like I said, the most important thing here is to avoid a sticky situation for you with your people at the bank.

"By the way," Douglas continued. "When I just said we'll think of something, it reminded me of our old friend Liveenwel up in Toronto. That sucker finds a proper solution to every challenge. Have you talked to him lately?"

"No. It's been more than a year since I saw Roger last – a Yankees game I think."

"Do you have any plans for next weekend?" Douglas asked.

"Nothing special. Why?" Alistair asked, his curiosity instantly aroused.

"My calendar shows one of those rare occasions when I have nothing scheduled. Why don't I see if Liveenwel has any plans? If not, maybe I could pick you up next Saturday morning at that private jet airport outside New York, and we scoot up to Toronto. I could drop you off again Sunday evening. What do you think?" Douglas encouraged.

"Sounds awesome!" Alistair replied. "It'll be great to spend some time with you guys."

"I'll call Liveenwel as soon as we finish. A party right in his hometown should interest him too. I'm guessing he'll be available, but I'll send you a text with my expected ETA. You know, he also just might have some ideas you can use to bring your legal folks around," Douglas finished. The endorsement subject was not entirely dead just yet.

Alistair Fitzgerald had never been able to handle a little pressure, he thought and shook his head in disgust as he dialed Liveenwel's office number. That's what made him so vulnerable to drugs. Now, the addict's unfortunate character trait was starting to show signs of unacceptably complicating Douglas' life.

·

Thirty-Nine

More than six months had elapsed since John George Mortimer's revelation that he was her father. Her long-thwarted efforts to resolve the perplexing unanswered questions about their relationship should finally produce results. She was at his home in Fort Myers specifically to get those answers and would be satisfied with nothing less.

Again, he insisted they talk during dinner at his home. She acquiesced, and moments after arriving found him politely leading her into his stylish dining room just like the last time. Determined to control the conversation, Suzanne drew a breath and was about to speak when John George's housekeeper bustled back into the dining room with a steaming cauldron of soup.

With a sigh and requisite smile, Suzanne waited patiently as Lana ladled the broth into each bowl. Finished, she wished *'Buen appetito'* with a customary hope they enjoyed her offering. Then, she disappeared as quickly as she came.

"I'd like to start with the issue of that numbered company in Canada that deposited funds in my mother's bank account for a decade," Suzanne opened. "Exactly what was its purpose?"

"I thought you might like to start there," John George acknowledged with a wry smile. "As I told you already, the entity that made payments to your mother was a non-operating subsidiary of the holding company I created to fund the purchase of Countrywide Stores. That holding company is the key.

"I've always been a little paranoid. Since my parents both died in a car crash when I was in college, I've had a nagging fear that something unforeseen might again dramatically change the trajectory of my life. The greatest of those fears has been that someone might seize Multima Corporation from my control," he said, then took a sip from his glass of wine before continuing.

"When I discovered that you are my daughter, I confided in Alberto Ferer. I told him I wanted to buy the company you ran and would probably want you to succeed me ultimately. As an only child myself, I had no other logical successor, and I was very impressed with you in our initial meetings. I planned to groom you for the role of CEO over time. But, I also wanted a device I could use to thwart any attacks on my control of the corporation. Alberto suggested the scheme. By creating the special share class as a subsidiary of Multima, my personal equity in that holding company would automatically convert to Multima preferred shares," he said, pausing to be sure Suzanne was following. With her nod, he continued.

"By issuing those shares to your mother, if I died or someone took control of Multima, whoever held those shares would influence about one-third of the voting shares of the corporation. In my personal will, Alberto legally granted my preferred shares to you. If I died, you and your mother would own the corporation. However, if someone ever tried to wrest control from me, I could legally cancel those shares issued to Louise Marcotte and convert them to preferred shares in Multima at the time of my choosing. Alberto convinced me this was an elegant way to address my concerns about ownership and control. It also seemed the right thing to do," he ended with a tentative smile.

"Okay," Suzanne hesitantly replied. "But you essentially told me all that the last time. Tell me, how did you get the share certificates to my mother? What was her reaction? What did you say to her?"

"Good question," he started. "I admit it. There was a little deception involved. After a lot of effort, Alberto found a stockbroker in Quebec who once worked with your mother. They had remained casual friends over the years. After Alberto convinced him your mom wouldn't be harmed in any way, and with enough financial incentive, that stockbroker agreed to work with us.

"He told her a story about a numbered company involved in mining exploration in Northern Ontario. After a few conversations, he persuaded her that he had inside information. The company would soon announce a remarkable discovery of diamonds and an investment of one thousand dollars could provide a return of many times that amount. He'd even loan her the money to buy it if she couldn't afford to invest.

"After a few calls, she finally gave in, and he delivered the certificates to her. Every year or so, she'd contact him to ask about the mining company announcement, and he always told her only a few more months should be necessary. The certificate would eventually be worth many times more, he'd always claim." John George finished with a shrug.

"So, you basically lied, misled, and cheated my mother," Suzanne replied looking directly at him.

"That's a fair assessment. Your mom was not an experienced investor. But I hope you understand that my motives were good even if my actions were not entirely above board," John George replied defensively.

Just as Suzanne started to respond, alerts sounded on their smartphones at precisely the same time. Both ignored those intrusions until Lana burst through the door again, this time almost running, with a TV controller in her hand.

"John George. Suzanne. You must see this," she exclaimed breathlessly as she pointed the device towards a television screen on an opposite wall. "It's a Multima store!"

The video images that appeared on the screen shocked them all. A helicopter was capturing scenes overlooking a large store with one side of the building blown out by some terrific force. The gaping hole was right below a large, teetering Multima sign. Black smoke spewed darkly into the sky, and brilliant orange flames danced from the gaping opening.

A voice from the television said the store was in the Boggy Creek Marketplace in Kissimmee, Florida. The wall and roof appeared ready to collapse. Next to the massive hole, a car was partially buried under mounds of bricks, and rubble covered a wide area. As the video angle widened, the camera showed dozens of first responder vehicles with bright lights flashing and people on the ground rushing about in all directions.

John George was first to move. He reached for his telephone, saw the call just missed was from Dan Ramirez and punched the redial button with his forefinger. Within seconds they connected.

"We're watching now, Dan. What happened?"

John George activated the speaker so Suzanne could hear his response.

"There's no question. It was a bomb. My contact with the police force in Kissimmee tells me there's explosives residue everywhere. A number of people are dead, and several have serious injuries," the chief of corporate security replied.

"Was it a terrorist attack?" John George asked.

"They don't think so. It looks too professional. I assume you want to get up there right away?"

"That's right. And Suzanne Simpson is here with me. I expect she wants to get there, too," he said as Suzanne nodded affirmation. "We should bring Hadley along as well."

"Of course. OK if we use Suzanne's jet? There's an airport just a few minutes from the store. We could probably be at the scene within an hour. I'll get law enforcement to meet us there. Suzanne should bring her bodyguards as well. Can you all fit in your BMW, or should I send a car?" Dan wondered.

"We'll find a way to get everyone there," John George replied, already starting towards the door. Suzanne immediately summoned her bodyguards, pausing only to take a bag from Lana as she, too, rushed out the door.

"I threw a few things together. At least you can have a snack on the plane," she said to Suzanne. "You'll need energy."

Mortimer tossed the keys to his BMW Z4 sportscar to Suzanne's male bodyguard. "You two take the car. I'll bring Suzanne with me on the motorcycle," he announced without consultation.

Moments later they were underway. The BMW's tires screeched as the bodyguard accelerated onto the street while a speechless Suzanne clung tightly to John George Mortimer's waist on the bike.

With little traffic, they all arrived at Page Field in about ten minutes and parked the vehicles in front of the terminal. Dan Ramirez had picked up the pilots from a downtown hotel and was already there. Edward Hadley was also standing at the base of the stairs, ready to board.

Inside the aircraft, they immediately shifted their seats into a circle around the meeting table Suzanne used so frequently with her team. They all connected their telephones or other devices to the jet's wi-fi and prepared to learn everything possible about the tragedy in their Kissimmee store.

Throughout the trip, they received messages continually. There were updates from operations staff at Multima Supermarkets' offices in Atlanta. Dan Ramirez received texts every few minutes with more details from his police contacts in Kissimmee. Public relations staff at Supermarkets sought guidance on requests for comments from the media. Suzanne had her executive assistant working with Kissimmee emergency services to determine the extent of deaths or injuries requiring hospitalization. And Edward Hadley was handling the dozens of media inquiries flooding into headquarters.

Their trip was short, less than an hour. Once they landed, two cars from the local police department pulled up beside the jet, waited while everyone piled into one or the other, and then whisked them to the chaotic scene. As they arrived, Suzanne was amazed to see dozens of media people run towards their car, microphones and recorders in hand. Edward Hadley jumped out first, then Dan Ramirez. John George followed them out of the car to meet with the horde.

While he skillfully held the media at bay in front, as they had all agreed he would, the car slowly circled to the back of the store, well away from both the media crush and the horror of the devastation.

Suzanne slipped under the yellow police tape raised by a junior officer and dashed into a door in the warehouse section of the store. It was held open by a Multima employee who instantly recognized her. Suzanne warmly embraced the woman for several seconds, inquired if she was alright, and asked which officer was in charge.

Instantly, she was inundated with strings of disjointed facts from the investigating officers. A bomb indeed caused the explosion – a very sophisticated and powerful bomb. Had there been any warnings? It didn't look like the work of terrorists. That entire section of the store was still too unstable for investigators to determine the exact type of bomb detonated. A coroner was on site, and at least three people had been declared dead. Ambulances had delivered fifteen more people to hospitals nearby, and several remained in critical condition with life-threatening injuries. The fire was out, but the front of the store remained off-limits. They would need to detain all employees until they were questioned.

John George joined her several minutes after the briefing had started and sought her out for a quick private conversation before they both rejoined the investigators.

"I've bought about a half hour with the media," he said quietly. "They understand we've just arrived and want to talk with the authorities before we comment. But it's after ten o'clock, and they're all anxious to have information and video to use on their eleven o'clock newscasts. I told them you run Multima Supermarkets, and you'll talk with them as soon as possible."

"Are you sure?" Suzanne asked.

"Absolutely," John George replied. "I made it clear to them that I'm here to do the same thing I do every day, support you if you need any help from headquarters. Let's get back in there and get fully briefed. Hadley will help you prepare."

Minutes later, they all agreed Suzanne was clear about the necessary facts. She understood the outstanding issues and concerns. She also was aware of the information police didn't want shared. Still, she made a quick call to Alberto Ferer to see if there were any other subjects she should avoid.

Fifteen minutes later than promised by Mortimer and only fifteen minutes before the newscasts would begin, Suzanne stepped out into the blinding lights set up for the TV cameras and strode to a microphone stand Edward Hadley had borrowed. She supposed they'd all agreed to share a recording of her comments.

She couldn't remember a time when she felt so inadequate. Nothing she could say would ease the pain for the people directly impacted by the blast. The media wouldn't be happy with the lack of detail she was going to provide, and they might even become angry she couldn't tell them more. She felt pain and emptiness like she had felt only once before – the night she realized her mother was dead and gone forever from her life. Tears welled in her eyes as she greeted the media and started her comments.

Without any notes, script or teleprompter, Suzanne ignored the cameras, looked towards the clustered media, and then spoke directly to them.

"No words can describe how badly I feel for the people affected by this incident at our Kissimmee store tonight. Authorities tell me three people lost their lives – a child of seven or eight years and her mother. The third person was a long-serving and valued employee I knew very well," she hesitated as she felt her voice falter slightly and the pressure of tears build in her eyes.

"Everyone at Multima shares your shock at this incident, and we're truly sorry for those families who must deal with the grief of losing someone dear to them. We understand the pain each of them must be feeling and want to express our heartfelt condolences.

"We're also saddened that several people have been injured, some very seriously. I know everyone in the Multima organization will be thinking about these unfortunate victims and hoping for their early and full recovery," she said as she became more relaxed in front of the crowd. Still, she took a deep breath before continuing.

"I think law enforcement specialists have already provided you as much information about the people involved in this unspeakable tragedy as they can. They tell me a bomb exploded, but they don't yet know who is responsible. However, they don't think the perpetrators of this crime are terrorists. At Multima, we have not received any threats against any of our stores. None of the employees I have spoken with are aware of any reason someone might have taken this action.

"I've asked our entire team in Kissimmee and back at headquarters to cooperate with the investigators in every way to find out who is responsible for .

this act. I have also instructed our store leadership here in Kissimmee to allow our employees to take whatever time they need to grieve and cope with their horror," she explained before pausing once more for those taking notes.

"We'll close the store to let investigators do their work. Then we'll have experts inspect the integrity of our building structure before we undertake repairs. We'll reopen this store only when we are satisfied everything necessary has been replaced or restored to make shopping in our store completely safe. At this stage, it's impossible to predict how long that will take. So, we also apologize to our customers who are inconvenienced by this tragedy.

"That's all I can share with you at this stage, but if you have questions, I'll answer the best I can," she finished.

There were a few questions, but none as damning as she feared nor as insistent as expected. These hardened gatherers of news seemed to understand she felt as badly as they and was just as powerless to figure out what happened and why. Edward Hadley broke in after the fifth question to close the session and guide her back to the makeshift command center in the tiny storage area.

There was nothing further they could do there, John George told her as the investigators excused themselves to return to their tasks. She knew he was right, but it didn't make it any easier to accept.

"I'm going to make a visit to the hospitals," she told him. "Take the jet. It's late, and you've had a long day. I'll get a room here for the night, and the pilots can come back up for me tomorrow."

He hesitated. For a moment, she thought he might offer to join her for the arduous task of comforting the families of those killed or injured by the explosion. But she could see the total exhaustion in his eyes as he considered the possibility.

Without a single exchange of words, they both knew any further attempt to discuss issues surrounding her mother that night would be pointless. As anxious as she was to resolve them, their importance paled in the shadow of the evening's disaster.

"That's great, Suzanne. Far beyond the call of duty, but I understand it's something you feel you need to do. I just don't have enough energy to continue tonight. I'm not going to be of any help to you if I stay, and fatigue could cloud my judgment or cause a miscue. I don't want to risk either," John George Mortimer explained.

Then, without a word, he spread his arms wide and awkwardly wrapped them tightly around her. For the second time in her life, she felt his genuine warmth before he said goodbye and headed towards a waiting police car.

Another officer drove Suzanne and her bodyguards to three nearby hospitals one after the other. She spent about an hour in each. Her protectors patiently helped her find members of some of the affected families in each facility. She felt her words were hollow as she expressed her sympathies and condolences. Several times she was so heartbroken by individual circumstances, or the condition of an injured patient, that she physically felt pain in her eyes as she fought back tears.

But she was determined to complete her mission before allowing herself relief. About four o'clock in the morning, a police cruiser deposited them at the entrance of the small hotel her executive assistant had reserved for them. Exhausted and hungry, Suzanne checked them all in with her credit card, bought a protein bar from the kiosk beside the front desk, and went to her room.

Despite her abject exhaustion, there was no sleep. The pain of the tragedy wouldn't go away. Sobs and tears failed to wash away memories of the distress and emotion she saw with every family. Thoughts of those killed and injured surfaced repeatedly. And images of tearful parents and distraught family members flashed in and out of her memory over and over again.

Seeking a diversion from the turmoil of her emotions, she mindlessly turned on the television. She increased the volume after recognizing one of the families she met a few hours earlier. She listened as the woman praised her for coming to visit them at the hospital and expressed genuine thanks for Suzanne's thoughtfulness. It didn't make it easier, but it validated her intuition. It was just the right thing to do.

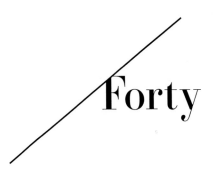

Forty

John George expected her to be deeply disappointed. Suzanne felt strongly about the need to visit with families hurt by the tragedy at their supermarket, and he realized that. He also understood the intense frustration she felt about her inability to fill in all the blanks related to their personal situation. For a moment, he seriously considered following her lead and spending more time together after they did their duty at the hospitals.

But he decided otherwise. Little doubt remained about the cause of the explosion in the Kissimmee store. Law enforcement and his chief of security were one hundred percent certain a bomb was the source. Ramirez agreed that The Organization probably carried out the attack in response to John George's refusal to appoint a representative from Venture Capital Inc. to Multima's board of directors.

While Gottingham from VCI had been silent since their last telephone confrontation, there was little mystery that the malevolent threat relayed through Douglas Whitfield directly related to this incident. The likelihood of a terrorist attack was almost zero. The bomb exploded when the store had the fewest customers of the day, and there had been no threats or warnings. No organization claimed credit for the blast either.

Instead, it appeared the harm to Suzanne mentioned in the warning carried by Whitfield meant malice to her business unit rather than to her personally. For that he was grateful. But, with such despicable action, The Organization showed they were prepared to do almost anything. He had few remaining alternatives.

"I'm running out of time, Dan. How are your FBI contacts progressing with Knight?" he asked as soon as the corporate jet was airborne.

"They're pleased. They've been interrogating him for eight hours a day since he accepted their offer for witness protection. For the first few days, right after they shipped out the women, they had trouble keeping him focused. It was evident he was heart-broken," Ramirez replied.

"I never thought of Howard Knight as a romantic," John George said. "He always projected an image of a hard-working guy, with his head down, fully focused on business."

"Well, it seems his affair with Morales went on without detection for about twenty years. Apparently, even The Organization was caught unaware. But there's no doubt he was still deeply focused on business and well-connected to the most senior leadership. The info he's giving the FBI is phenomenal."

"How so?"

"Once they managed to move him out of his forlorn-lover funk he started to deliver exceedingly high-quality intelligence," Ramirez replied. "His memory is almost photographic. Without notes or records, he's provided the team in Guantanamo with about two hundred names. Most are in the USA, but some are the most senior honchos in Europe, Latin America, and Asia too. They immediately started cross-checking the information Knight provided with the names and details the women were giving Interpol in Europe. Almost a hundred percent match on names and addresses. Unbelievably, about a seventy percent match on phone numbers. All three suspects have far more intelligence than we ever would have guessed," Ramirez said.

"Intelligence in terms of intellect or intelligence in the form of information?"

"Both," Ramirez told him. "Apparently, the FBI teams are overwhelmed with the brilliance of their memories. But the quality of the information they are getting is far better than expected. And both teams are shocked at the penetration of The Organization into society globally. They're deep into human-trafficking, closely connected to the Latin America drug cartels, dominant players in all kinds of gambling and casinos, and in control of some of the world's best-known multinational corporations. They own private equity firms worth billions. They even have people inside major government-sponsored lotteries.

"Some of The Organization's foot-soldiers are already known to law enforcement. A good percentage are in and out of jail on a regular basis and already were suspected of involvement in some form of organized crime. What's surprising is how decision-makers in The Organization's formal structure are involved in everything," Ramirez explained with a tone of amazement in his voice.

"What do you mean when you say 'everything'?" John George asked.

"They've penetrated law enforcement, private businesses, banking, publicly traded corporations, professional sports and governments at all levels. They tell me the number of politicians either actively involved in managing criminal activities or affording protection to them is astonishing," Ramirez explained.

"How soon will they move?" John George asked.

"Not sure. They're still cross-checking all the info received with historical data and building evidence against all the people named by Knight and the two women. It will take months to complete it, but they tell me they need a few more weeks to be sure they have enough evidence to go before grand juries for indictments. They can't move until that's all ready."

"I have to make a decision much sooner than that. We can't allow them to blow up another store," John George said.

"I understand," Ramirez replied with a deep sigh. "But there's another issue. Even if these guys throw in more people and money to pick up the pace of their investigation, there's one other wild card that will almost certainly delay breaking it open."

"And that is …?"

"The elections," Dan Ramirez said. "The FBI director already got himself into a major political boondoggle from that whole issue of emails. The people I'm working with haven't even told him about these new discoveries. Apparently, they're worried that sharing what they have with him right now could put the entire American election process in peril. Evidently, Knight has pointed the finger at more than one name currently on ballots for election or re-election across the nation," Ramirez said soberly.

"That means at least another month, maybe more, right?"

"That's right," Ramirez conceded.

John George immediately picked up a secure satellite phone to call Alberto Ferer and instructed him to meet them at Multima Corporation headquarters.

There, the three men talked until morning light peeked through the windows of John George's office. By the end of their conversation, all three were up to date on the information Ramirez's FBI contacts were willing to share. They also discussed at length and fully understood the implications of naming Gottingham to Multima's board of directors. They'd explored the feasibility of every possible response to The Organization's demand from every perspective they could imagine. With grim faces and slumped shoulders, the trio agreed on a distasteful call Alberto Ferer would make the next morning.

Forty-One

Hoffman Estates, Illinois.
Wednesday October 12, 2016

"I just received some new information from my old college roommate, the one you helped get a job in corporate security at headquarters. I thought I should make you aware of it as soon as possible," he heard Natalia Tenaz say. "Can we meet outside?"

James Fitzgerald immediately understood the simple code. She had information she should share only outdoors, well away from possible recording devices and distorted by the noise of background sounds like traffic. He agreed to meet her on the usual walking path in thirty minutes.

"My friend in Fort Myers tells me a lot is going on at headquarters this week. Her boss had her checking all sorts of sites to get information about Venture Capital Inc. Apparently, John George Mortimer has a big, secret meeting planned with VCI this weekend in New York," Natalia said.

"Some of the corporate folks meet with Gottingham every month. What makes her feel this is something special?" James asked.

"It's the type of information they wanted for the meeting. Things like a list of every company they hold shares in and the extent of their holdings. A summary of all the companies where Gottingham holds directorships and how long he's been a director. They even wanted to know about his education and people he sees socially, going back to his university days!" she explained.

"Did she learn why Ramirez wanted information like that?" James wondered.

"No. He just said Mortimer wanted to be well prepared when they met."

"Okay. Makes sense. Gottingham's the new CEO of a major shareholder, and remember how much trouble the last one caused."

"Maybe, yeah. It seems Gottingham attended Wharton Business School at the same time as your son, Alistair. In fact, her research found that he, plus Alistair, Whitfield, and Liveenwel – that lawyer we used in Canada – were all in the same fraternity at the same time. Does that sound right to you?"

"I knew Whitfield was there. It's through Alistair that we came to know Douglas. They were roommates, and Alistair asked me to find him a summer job as an intern. He was so extraordinary that we hired him right off campus. I don't recall them ever mentioning the others, but I guess it's certainly possible they knew each other," James responded. "I'm still not sure I see why your friend red-flagged this for you."

"She didn't. It was Dan Ramirez who asked her to give you the heads up."

When he didn't respond to this information, she continued. "But my friend also thought you should know a copy of the entire file she prepared went to somebody with the FBI in Miami. She only discovered that when she received an acknowledgment from the anonymous email address where she sent the info."

"I see," said James, suddenly deep in thought.

"There's a bit more," she added. "We added Whitfield to her special monitoring with that software, the one like the CIA uses. It seems your son, Whitfield and Liveenwel are all getting together for some sort of reunion in Canada this weekend. She didn't know if that was important or not."

"Thanks, Natalia. I'll think about all that. I'm still not certain how useful the information is, but be sure you thank her for sharing it with you. How about that Weissel woman I asked you to keep an eye on. Anything new?"

"Only that she has become a model employee since the offsite management meeting in Naples. When she returned to the office after our company event, she became a new woman. Since then, she's wearing a whole new wardrobe. No more exposed cleavage. No more short, short skirts. Every day, it's a business suit with a conservative style, fashionably long.

"Her work ethic has changed dramatically too. It's almost a little weird. She's becoming the consummate team player. Everything is collaborative. She volunteers for more assignments and offers to help others on the team. Everyone's talking about it!" she said with a lighthearted laugh.

"Anything unusual with her communication?"

"Only one thing: since the management offsite there has been no communication with Whitfield. I don't know if he dumped her or what may have happened, but they haven't communicated a single time. We've monitored both landlines and cell phones," Natalia told him.

From there, James abruptly switched their conversation to the new mortgage program launch with Multima Supermarkets' employees. He figured he might as well learn something that could be of use from this conversation. The intelligence shared so far didn't seem to be all that valuable.

Forty-Two

Toronto, Ontario.
Friday October 14, 2016

Since John George Mortimer relayed the ominous warning communicated by Douglas Whitfield, Suzanne had been very busy. Of course, the everyday demands of a company president continued unabated during the turmoil. Most days, she arrived at her office before six o'clock in the morning. That's when she caught up on reports, briefing documents, and emails before the stream of meetings started.

Generally, there were people in her office from about eight o'clock until the dinner hour. Lunch was usually a sandwich or salad at her desk while a staff member continued discussing the subject of the moment. Her time was meticulously scheduled by her executive assistant Eileen, who shepherded guests into her office at the appointed hour and reminded Suzanne when only a few moments remained for each discussion underway.

Such precision management of time and schedules allowed her to process massive amounts of work in a day but gave her little time to deal with her personal unease. Eileen had noticed Suzanne's growing discomfort over the weeks and was appalled to learn there had been threats towards her. She asked if there was anything she could do to help.

From that late evening conversation a few weeks ago, their quest for more information began. Eileen volunteered to help Suzanne track down more details. She offered to bring her own laptop to Suzanne's home for a few evenings. There, they could probe websites for information and insight.

Surprisingly, she showed remarkable research skills that Suzanne didn't realize she had. In fact, Eileen proved to be extraordinarily adept with technology. Once she learned Suzanne's concerns and goals, she quickly guided her through the complexities of the worldwide web.

First, she taught Suzanne to surf the Internet 'incognito' and helped her create more diversions to mask her identity. Gradually, she introduced her to the dark web and the murky world of information hidden from all but the most computer-savvy.

Every evening was a new adventure, but Eileen led her through their mission with bubbling enthusiasm and good humor. Hours passed before they realized it. On a couple occasions, Eileen decided to crash on a sofa for a few hours of sleep before returning to work at the office, only to drop back in again after work. And their efforts bore an unexpected bounty.

To suggest that Suzanne was uncomfortable with the role Douglas Whitfield supposedly played by relaying a threat to her personal safety from an unknown source would be a major understatement. A shiver had shot down her spine the moment John George relayed the ominous information to her. Her whole body shuddered.

Her conversation with Whitfield to confirm Mortimer's version proved even more disconcerting. He seemed sincerely concerned for her safety. But there was an edge to his tone that raised her suspicions. Something that suggested his replies were just a little too polished, a little rehearsed. It gave her pause.

Also, when she thought more about the remarkable start to sales of the new software his division had recently introduced, the pieces didn't quite add up. Regardless of how amazing the new technology might be, major global corporations like Bank of The Americas seldom made such far-reaching decisions so quickly.

Who ever heard of a major company moving from a first introduction to purchase – plus a willingness to endorse the product – in less than a month? It usually took more time than that to get an appointment with a decision-maker at such a mammoth bank!

These inconsistencies added to Suzanne's unease and prompted the flurry of private investigation. It also led directly to a trip to Toronto.

Store visits provided cover for the journey. Early that morning she left Atlanta with her usual entourage plus the two reluctant bodyguards. They landed at private Buttonville airport – just north of Toronto. Over the following eight hours, they had productive and informative visits to six different Multima Supermarkets locations in the Greater Toronto Area.

Their last visit was to an experimental urban model store in the heart of the city. Once they finished their inspection and discussions, Suzanne released her staff to unwind from the week for a few hours in Toronto's vaunted entertainment district. While they had drinks and dinner, she held her secret meeting.

One bodyguard had already left the entourage to make her way to the place where the lawyer agreed to meet. The other accompanied her and would return to the bar after dropping Suzanne off. They'd both find discreet places to observe and protect Suzanne while she met with Roger Liveenwel.

The large, black SUV stopped only long enough for Suzanne to alight directly in front of the entrance and be sure she entered the building. From the corner of her eye, she could see the vehicle leave as she tugged open the large wooden door to the entrance.

As her eyes adjusted from the outside light to the darkness and sedate leather interior of the trendy watering hole in Toronto's financial district, she spotted him waving from a booth near the back of the bar. Within moments, they had greeted each other and exchanged banal small talk about this return to her old stomping grounds.

The pretense for the informal meeting was her request for him to brief her on the regulatory issues he'd resolved for Multima Financial Services to facilitate the introduction of the home mortgage program in Canada. For about half an hour, Liveenwel controlled the narrative with a polished recap of the issues, the challenges they experienced, and the supreme accomplishment of his fantastic team to get everything completed before the deadline.

Suzanne listened intently and showed more interest than she felt. As she had hoped, the process seemed to energize him, and with each glass of scotch on the rocks, he appeared more relaxed. She thought it was time for her real mission.

"Tell me something, Roger," she said with her most charming smile. "I know Douglas Whitfield recommended you handle Multima Financial Services' legal work in Canada. How do you know each other?"

"We didn't really know each other that well before we started working together. We both went to U. Penn about the same time. He was in business at Wharton, and I was at the law school. But I was active in campus politics and student activities, so I guess he remembered me when Multima needed some legal advice. I'm delighted he called. It's been a great relationship," he replied warily.

"That's really interesting," she leaned towards him, conveying false interest as convincingly as possible. "What led you to the University of Pennsylvania? I thought all Canadian lawyers-to-be preferred the law school here at the University of Toronto."

"Yeah, I thought about that for a while. But U. Penn made me an offer I couldn't refuse. I was lucky. They offered me a full scholarship and a chance to hobnob with some of the American elite. For a young guy from a modest background in Nova Scotia, that was too good to turn down," he explained. "I made some great contacts like Douglas as a result, and some of those contacts have been very good for business."

For another few minutes, Suzanne continued her charade. As with the answers to each of her initial questions, all the others were equally false. From her late-night research with Eileen, she knew Whitfield and Liveenwel were far from casual acquaintances in college. They were fraternity brothers. They lived in the same house for two years, and their friendship extended back to private school where they were roommates for three years before they both attended the University of Western Ontario and shared a house with James Fitzgerald's son, Alistair.

Furthermore, there was never a university scholarship. Liveenwel's tuition and college expenses were paid for entirely by his father, one of the wealthiest industrialists in Canada. With a glance at her watch, Suzanne was ready to leave. She pasted on her most beguiling smile and reached out to touch his arm.

"I'd love to learn more about your university days. They seem far more exciting than mine," she gushed before smiling even more mischievously. "But I don't want my team drinking too much before our flight home. I was supposed to meet them fifteen minutes ago, so I really must run. Thank you for the briefing on the regulatory issues. And the next time I'm in town we should plan to have dinner or something."

"I need to leave, too," he said as they both rose from the comfortable leather chairs to shake hands. "I've got dinner plans with a couple old friends at seven."

She held his hand just a moment longer than necessary, and his farewell smile showed he appreciated her signals of interest. That convincing performance required every one of her considerable acting skills. Her intuition seldom failed her. This man was a real danger. But she still didn't know precisely why.

Forty-Three

Fort Myers, Florida.
Saturday October 15, 2016

It seemed that he had lived a lifetime in just the past month. Thirty-four days earlier, his oncologist had delivered the news. He had a microscopic malignant tumor on his lung – a form of cancer that was inoperable. There was no cure yet, either. But he wasn't going to die immediately. According to the specialist, there was a very slight possibility he might eventually die from something else if the treatments proved entirely successful.

This cancer was different. It was progressive, but they would try to manage it with immunotherapy. This time, there was no chemotherapy or radiation. Instead, they recommended John George become part of a clinical study and start a treatment to build up his natural immune system. It wasn't entirely proven yet, but results so far were promising, with few reported side effects.

Every day for two weeks he would receive a concoction of substances made in a laboratory. Then he would stop the treatment for two weeks to let his body adjust and recover. This process would continue for as long as he lived or until researchers discovered a better treatment. The prognosis was somewhat hopeful. If his body responded to the treatment, John George would probably survive several more months. He might even manage a few years, the oncologist told him with a blend of candor and optimism.

At first, the news was devastating. That first night he wept for the first time he could remember. The oncologist's message was clear. Time remaining was limited. For the following few days he felt lethargic and depressed. At the age of seventy-one, he was facing death far earlier than he had imagined. And there remained so much to do.

His succession wasn't yet settled. His relationship with Suzanne was still murky. The corporation was undergoing massive changes in both the financial services and supermarkets businesses. And Whitfield over in Solutions hadn't even scratched the surface of a technology application poised to harvest billions over time. He wasn't at all ready to die. The timing seemed so unfair.

He grieved but not for long. By the end of that week, John George had reluctantly accepted the ominous diagnosis and the grim reality it produced. "It is what it is," he told Lana as they sat together for a glass of wine before she left for her home that day. He could see she was in shock as she bravely struggled to hold back her tears and listen to his requests.

"No one else is to know. I'll break the news when the time is right," he said. "Promise me that you'll keep this entirely to yourself. Cancer will not define my remaining time. It's there. I understand it's messing with my body. And I realize I will die sooner than I would like. But, I'll continue to live my life to the fullest. And I want you to help me do that every day. Push me if I seem lazy. Remind me to smile if I lose my good humor. And don't let me feel sorry for myself – ever!"

He held her hands for a few minutes that evening as she finally sobbed as quietly as possible sitting beside him on the lanai. Well after a spectacular sunset ended, her tears subsided, and she bid him goodnight.

"Thank you for letting me know, John George. You know I'll be with you to the end – whenever that is. I hope it is many years from now, but I will treasure every additional day I can spend at your side. You are the gentlest man I know. And the wisest person I've ever met. It is a pleasure for me to serve you, and I will do everything you ask for as long as you ask," she managed to say before she turned and swiftly left the room.

Every day since then, she kept her word. Along with his challenges, occasional discomfort, and unexpected side-effects of the powerful treatments, Lana always maintained her sense of humor, positive outlook, and unfailing support. It made the whole thing much easier.

But his life was still in turmoil. The morass with Venture Capital seemed without end, and the stakes had been raised dramatically with the bombing of the Multima supermarket in Kissimmee. In his half-century doing business, it never occurred to him that one of his decisions could cost the lives of an employee and two customers. But that's what happened.

As soon as Ramirez told him the FBI needed more time to build its case against The Organization, John George knew he had to reverse his position on Gottingham's appointment to the board of directors. If they weren't going to play by normal rules of business, he simply couldn't further endanger either his employees or customers. He'd never be able to live with himself, however short that period might be.

Of course, the employee he felt most badly about was his daughter. More than six months had passed since he had revealed the truth about their connection. He was acutely aware of the angst she felt and the many questions she must have. It pained him that every attempt they made to reconcile her concerns fell apart. He certainly was not prepared to put her life in more danger with a stubborn refusal to acquiesce to The Organization's demand.

Indeed, he had thought about the negative aspects of his relationship with The Organization with regret. He should never have accepted Knight's offer to help buy Wendal Randall's struggling technology company. A decade earlier, he sensed something amiss and then realized it more profoundly later. But he always rationalized that he, not The Organization, was in control and their investment was no different from any other.

That was wrong. Clearly, The Organization was stretching its ugly tentacles into his company to control it eventually. They were patient to a degree, but they were also ruthless. The senseless bombing deaths and injuries were compelling proof.

So, Alberto Ferer carried the message to Gottingham that Multima would reverse its decision. There must be no further attack on any Multima business or person working for the company. At the December meeting of the board, John George would propose a new board structure and recommend Earnest Gottingham become one of the new directors.

Gottingham said only that he would discuss that information with his board and get back with a response. One day later, he called. "My board will be satisfied with that proposal only if the intended meeting and invitation to join the board occur on or before the third of November. Call a special session of the board if you must."

Alberto had handled the curt response as well as he could. He tried to buy more time with different proposals, but Gottingham was adamant. The best Multima's general counsel could achieve was an undertaking that the VCI president would make himself available for an extensive interview with the board's selection committee.

Gottingham understood Multima's need to present a pristine image to other board members, shareholders, and regulators. He was delighted to spend as much time as they wanted on the fifteenth of October.

It was from that meeting John George had just returned and was decompressing on the lanai of his home with an excellent California Pinot Noir – desperately trying to discern how to get his personal life back on the right track with Suzanne.

Forty-Four

Miami, Florida.
Saturday October 15, 2016

Alistair Fitzgerald was waiting inside the terminal at Teterboro Airport and bounded out to Whitfield's company jet as soon as the door opened and stairs lowered to the ground. He was dressed in designer jeans and a long-sleeved shirt with a leather overnight bag hanging casually from his shoulder as he mounted the stairs to greet his long-time friend.

Almost ceremoniously, the pair exchanged long-rehearsed flamboyant hand motions culminating in their fraternity handshake. They also gave each other a hug, then Douglas motioned for his old buddy to take one of the posh leather chairs that circled a polished mahogany table in the center of the passenger area. A gorgeous 'flight attendant' offered Alistair a drink before he was completely seated.

For the fifty-minute flight to Billy Bishop Airport on Toronto's Centre Island, Douglas regaled his guest with stories. His ability to tell jokes was legendary when they were at Wharton. Now, Alistair's constant and raucous laughter proved that he still had the knack. Douglas remembered how much his friend liked to laugh and the hours they wasted in their free time talking nonsense. His own smile was genuine and warm.

They parked next to the Porter Airlines terminal at the airport and found an underwater walkway to the mainland. The quick-moving sidewalk greatly accelerated their walking pace, so they arrived at the Toronto shoreline in only a few minutes. From there they walked to the Westin Harbour Castle Hotel where Roger Liveenwel waved to them as they entered the elegant lobby.

They repeated their elaborate handshake ritual again while bemused onlookers glanced briefly, then rushed past. The ceremony finished, all three sauntered towards a bank of elevators. There was no need to discuss their dining choice. It was the same every time they met up for these little reunions.

Douglas pressed the elevator button for the thirty-eighth floor, and a moment or two later they stepped into the entrance of the Toula Restaurant and Bar, a magnificent rotating restaurant with the Italian fare they all enjoyed.

"My treat tonight," Douglas said as the host distributed their menus. "It's been a while since we had a chance to do this. So, the entire night will be on me – dinner, drinks and whatever mischief we can find later," he elaborated with a hearty laugh and wink to Roger Liveenwel.

His friends didn't scrimp. First, they ordered shrimp cocktail costing twenty-seven dollars each. Then, Liveenwel asked for the chef to come to their table where the group negotiated a price of one hundred and seventy-five dollars for an extra-large Chateaubriand for three instead of the usual serving for two. Of course, they also needed a good wine to accompany the meal. So, Alistair settled on a delightful nine-year-old *Casina Adelaide* Barolo. They devoured two bottles at two hundred and fifty dollars each.

And they all had a great time. Douglas entertained with his latest repertoire of off-color jokes and stories. Alistair laughed so hard that people at other tables took notice. And, as usual, Liveenwel paid more and more attention to their server and any other female who happened to walk into or out of the restaurant. They all knew he considered it his personal mission to size up and rate on a scale of one to ten every woman who passed.

The bill totaled more than one thousand dollars once those notoriously high Canadian taxes were added. Douglas paid with his black American Express card and added another three hundred dollars as gratuity when he signed the chit.

Undeterred by the expense of dinner, Douglas asked Liveenwel where they should go next.

"Elements, man. The hottest women and high, high energy."

"Anything else there?" Alistair inquired, arching his eyebrows.

"Everything, man. I guarantee we'll all be very satisfied puppies in a few hours!"

Douglas watched as his friends continued to overindulge. Liveenwel hit on every woman who didn't ignore him while he consumed generous quantities of scotch whisky. At least six glasses, Douglas noted. Meanwhile, Alistair had found a source. No less than four times, he wandered off to the restroom and his eyes were more glazed with each return.

By midnight, it was time to escape. When Alistair came back to their place at the bar after his most recent visit to the restroom, Douglas told him he was leaving.

"I'll meet you for breakfast tomorrow morning. Let's make it ten thirty in the Mizzen Restaurant at the Westin. I've got rooms reserved for all of us back there. Just get your key at the front desk," he shouted over the din of the music and noise of the celebrating crowd.

Minutes later, he tracked down Roger Liveenwel dancing with a beautiful young woman who looked barely of legal age but was attached to the lawyer as though she would never let him go. He shouted the same directions into Liveenwel's ear, then headed for the exit.

When Douglas stepped out onto the street, he waved off the first cab to honk and decided he would walk. He still had thirty minutes, and a little exercise would unclutter his head for what came next.

Both friends had been utterly predictable. There was no doubt that Liveenwel planned to be foraging in a bed somewhere with either the beautiful young thing currently attached to him or a similar facsimile should that one not work out as hoped.

Alistair Fitzgerald was already gone. He probably even forgot the message already and who knew where he might turn up in the morning? They were good friends, guys he really liked. But both had too much history and serious flaws.

About ten minutes after leaving the club, Douglas walked down the escalator to the moving walkway for Billy Bishop terminal on Toronto Island. He was alone at that hour. The walkway wasn't operating, but he was still able to complete the journey in less than twenty minutes.

As he climbed the steps of the immobile escalator into the terminal, he used a cheap disposable cell phone to make one last required call before leaving the city.

Precisely on schedule, Douglas walked out of the terminal to the jet, its engines already idling. He could see the pilots completing their final checks in the lighted cockpit. As he came closer to the aircraft, a smile formed on his face. The beautiful flight attendant stood at the top of the stairs with a sensuous smile and her arms wide open. She was wearing absolutely nothing at all, precisely as he had requested.

Thoughts of his friends evaporated instantly. As soon as the door to the aircraft closed, the pilot revved the engines and prepared for departure. Douglas had no concerns about possible flight crew curiosity or interference with his plans. Before they'd arrived in New York, he let them in on his own intentions. The mile-high sex with Janet Weissel had been such a great experience he wanted a repeat performance all the way back to Miami. To be sure the pilots stayed happy, he let them use her earlier, in a hotel room, for the few hours he partied with his friends.

Freshly showered and smelling of seductively fragrant perfume, she started taking off his clothes as they taxied towards takeoff. By the time they were in the air, he was inside her. She was a professional in every sense. For the entire three-hour flight to Miami, she kissed, caressed and massaged every square inch of his body – most parts more than once.

As the pilots announced their preparation for descent, she brought water and a towel from the aircraft bathroom and washed his body clean, then presented him with his neatly folded clothes. As he pulled up his pants and tucked in his shirt, he reached for his cell phone and brought up the website for Toronto's tabloid newspaper, *The Sun*.

As a young man attending private school north of Toronto, he'd always enjoyed *The Sun*. The back page featured beautiful, young and sexy women in provocative poses. Their luring images often provided stimulation for the sexual relief of a lonely expatriate teen in the dormitory of a private school.

But, this time it wasn't the back page he sought. *The Sun* was more than beautiful women. They also had excellent contacts on the Toronto police force and often had crime information before other news outlets. As the aircraft touched down and taxied to its assigned parking spot by the private aviation terminal, he scrolled until he found the column.

The newspaper's police reporter wrote that Friday night had been a particularly violent one in the city. There had been two shootings, both in the downtown core. One victim, a black youth, appeared to be gang related. The other, a prominent Toronto lawyer killed in a dark alley near Elements nightclub, was possibly the casualty of a love triangle, police speculated.

Drug use also continued to be a growing problem in the inner city. A New York man was found dead in the sheltered entrance of the Dollar Store on Adelaide Street. It appeared to be an overdose, and police suspected that Fentanyl might also be a factor. That was all the news Douglas sought. With only a tinge of remorse, thoughts of their good times together were erased by a harsh reality. There had been no alternative.

As the plane came to a stop, he headed for the door after slipping ten one-hundred-dollar bills into the hand of the now-dressed flight attendant. She gave him one more sensuous kiss before he ducked his head and dashed down the stairway.

He still had much more work to do as the project entered its next delicate phase.

Forty-Five

An undisclosed location somewhere in Europe.
Wednesday October 19, 2016

Fidelia Morales considered herself a survivor. No more, no less. From a life of bare subsistence as a child in Puerto Rico, she amassed a small fortune. She last estimated that she had more than twenty-five million squirreled away in offshore bank accounts around the globe.

Unquestionably, she loved Howard Knight on a certain level. She honestly treasured the times they spent together – some of the most enjoyable days of her life. Their love-making had always been tender and extraordinarily satisfying. He was a bright man who conversed with her on any subject at any time. He was thoughtful and always treated her with respect. What more could a mature woman expect in her twilight years?

When she abandoned her life of retirement in West Palm Beach to help him escape, there had been no doubt. She fully intended to spend the rest of her life with him – no matter how long or short that time might be. But, to her consternation, that all seemed to change from the moment he overlooked The Organization's connection to the Bolivian mining company with facial recognition technology. That simple oversight stirred buried concerns and started to play games with her mind.

As she suffered excruciating pain and degrading humiliation in a prison cell in Argentina, she started to wonder more intently if he deserved her confidence. With the years of discussion they had devoted to planning their eventual escape, how could he overlook such a fundamental piece of information? What other crucial information might he have also overlooked?

The agony of the Argentinian torture magnified those doubts. She was just recovering from the anxiety of major cosmetic surgery to change her identity when they started the merciless beatings. Repeatedly, the female guard raised a truncheon and swung it forcefully at Fidelia's head. Whenever she successfully used her arms to protect her face, the sadist rammed the weapon into other parts of her body. The physical damage was awful.

And it was all the result of Howard Knight's stupid mistakes. His first grave errors were the several miscalculations in his bid to wrest control of Multima Corporation from John George Mortimer. Of course, such incompetence left him no alternative but to run. The Organization never tolerated ineptitude.

That forgotten piece of information about the mine in Bolivia compounded their circumstance, forcing her to undergo the pain of surgery, followed by the misery of torture. Argentina was never in their original plan because they always considered its government too unpredictable. They may have hidden a few German fascists after the second world war, but they also returned other escapees to extreme punishments in other countries. As she thought about her terrible predicament from the Argentinian cell, her doubts and concerns magnified by the day.

That's the reason her thought process shifted radically once she arrived in Guantanamo and heard the FBI's proposal. As soon as she understood what the Americans really wanted, she saw a glimmer of hope.

Almost immediately, she decided she had no interest in their offer of protection, living in some remote town in Idaho or wherever they created new identities these days. It would only be a matter of time before Howard made some other colossal mistake that would again put them in danger. She realized that now.

Instead, she plotted to devise another solution. That's when she hatched the idea to use Klaudia Schäffer. She knew the wealth of information the woman had stashed away in Düsseldorf. She recognized the high value the European Union would place on that information and knew, too, the authorities in Brussels would leap at an opportunity to clean up some of the corruption that plagued local member governments.

She realized the key to her scheme was an agreement with the Americans first. If she could get them to agree, they'd force the Europeans to accept the negotiated terms and conditions.

It had been difficult. They argued for hours at a time. Continually, Fidelia had to find ways to entice them and whet their appetite for more. The shrewd American negotiators were extremely intelligent. Their methods were clever. And their leverage was enormous, for she knew well that she could never survive a return to the Argentinians as they continually threatened.

In the end, she helped them realize that Howard Knight could provide them far better information for prosecutions in the USA. Her value was to the authorities outside the country, particularly Europe. At the last minute, they capitulated. Once they learned the identity of the biggest fish they could catch – the Russian – they gave her everything she wanted.

They'd strike a deal and pressure the Europeans to accept it. She and Klaudia would be transported to Europe. Once there, they'd turn over her extensive files with their meticulous details. However, they'd never become witnesses in trials that might take decades to complete across more than twenty different countries and legal systems.

Instead, they would each undergo extensive video questioning for a maximum of ten days. Fidelia and Klaudia would answer every question truthfully and point them to names, addresses, telephone numbers, and events that could be documented individually and collectively. Interrogators would be able to check the veracity of their testimony quickly. Interpol would then assume responsibility for liaising with every individual jurisdiction to get authorization to use their video evidence in that country's legal proceedings.

Fidelia knew there was only one country in the world where she could feel safe and assure Klaudia's safety. Her final demand, the one they found hardest to accept, required that once the interviews were complete, they would be delivered by a helicopter to Kaŝtavar, a remote village in Serbia.

To her relief, Interpol had honored every condition of their agreement. She and Klaudia traveled without any documentation. Interpol assured them no government would know of their route or arrival. The helicopter dropped them onto a vacant field that Fidelia pointed out to their pilot. It was just a few miles from the tiny village where she signaled him to land as close as possible to the unmarked waiting helicopter on the ground.

Reunion with her friend from Belgrade had been joyous. All three kissed and hugged each other for several minutes. When their new pilot confirmed the delivering helicopter was definitely outside Serbian airspace and headed towards France, they climbed into the new chopper and immediately took off in the opposite direction.

Within a half-hour, they touched down in an equally remote field of another nearby country where their Serbian friend had an exceptionally close relationship with that nation's long-serving minister of justice.

Forty-Six

Guantanamo Bay, Cuba.
Sunday October 23, 2016

In the end, his captors didn't ship Howard Knight off to Miami as they had threatened.

As the pain of losing the person most precious to him receded, he concluded Fidelia had chosen a path of certain death by the Argentinians over possible death by The Organization. He surmised that she must have doubted the ability of the FBI to keep her safe to such an extent that she preferred whatever treatment the Argentinians gave her over the torture she feared from Giancarlo Mareno.

This line of thinking created enough doubts that he spent two entire days reviewing the specifics of the proposed protection relocation and a new identity. It was only after the FBI changed its tune and provided precise and intricate details of every step that he agreed to start talking. Still, he realized there were risks of discovery after he testified against The Organization and its leadership.

For his entire life, he'd been conditioned to believe that stoolies were the lowest form of life in society. From his earliest memories, he recalled his father advising him to ignore what he saw and keep his mouth shut. It was a matter of life and death. He'd always believed it, too.

It had all changed with Fidelia. His love for her was so powerful he easily compromised his principles. It took only hours after his incarceration by those FBI thugs in Guantanamo to realize they were more ruthless than he. They left no doubt that they would relish the idea of leaving him on a tarmac somewhere right after they called The Organization to tell them where to find him.

So, he had caved. At that moment, he fully expected Fidelia to surrender with him so they both could retire to some remote farm in Montana or wherever they hide people in the witness protection program these days. He was astounded when she refused the offer and instead let them ship her back to the Argentinians who had so cruelly tortured her while they held her captive for the FBI.

Now, there was no doubt in his mind. She preferred a certain and horrible death over a new life with him in the witness protection program. That she made such a choice stung him painfully, and her loss broke his heart. That day they led her to the waiting aircraft he sobbed for hours after they returned him to his room. The pain of losing her was just too intense.

Their pleasures together had been immeasurable. Everything, from long conversations revealing their most intimate thoughts to countless hours of passionate sex, flooded back into Howard's memory as he cried tears of genuine pain. The agony continued for days. But, once he signed their documents and started talking, the questions multiplied.

They only demanded three or four hours a day for the first week or so, but the sessions intensified dramatically. Recently, the pace of interrogations accelerated even more. They now posed question after question for almost ten hours most days.

Evidently, they were checking every fact Howard Knight gave them in real time, too. On several occasions, they returned after a meal or coffee break to drill down in more intricate detail on a subject they had discussed only a few hours earlier. And the questions were often phrased several different ways before his answers were deemed acceptable.

He was also surprised at the amount of time they spent discussing his relationship with Multima Corporation. While Multima occupied a significant amount of his day, there were other equally large corporations over which The Organization exercised much more influence or control. But he steadfastly stuck to his determination to provide only answers to the questions they posed.

Yes, he had weighed the risks and could live with his decision. Cooperating with the FBI still looked like the better option, even without Fidelia there to share it with him. But the key word to describe his attitude was cooperation. He'd answer their questions. He'd tell the truth. He'd provide the level of detail they demanded. But the FBI investigators would have to work for every morsel of information.

It had been that way for the past two weeks, and it would continue as they summoned him from his cell for yet another grueling session.

Forty-Seven

Miami, Florida.
Friday October 28, 2016

"We'll need to delay the next phase," Giancarlo Mareno said.

Douglas Whitfield was calling on a cheap disposable cell phone, and the sound quality was not perfect. He couldn't entirely discern Mareno's tone, but the message was clear.

"That's disappointing. I did a lot of work and tidied up like you asked," Whitfield responded plaintively. "Is there something missing?"

"No. Nothing within your span of control. You did everything we asked," Mareno responded. "But I decided to hold off for now. There'll be a meeting next Friday. Mortimer will agree to restructure the board and appoint Gottingham as director. We'll give Earnest a chance to get some traction on the board before we move on the other front."

"Got it," Douglas said. "What about my role here?"

"Nothing changes for now. Keep outperforming until Gottingham tells me he can do it," Mareno instructed.

"I'm OK with that, but I need some help. With Alistair Fitzgerald gone, I don't have my big customer for our software. I also don't have his endorsement that opened doors to another dozen good candidates. Never mind Mortimer's reaction. The board will treat me like scum if I have to tell them we don't have any sales."

"What do you need?" Mareno asked.

"At least a dozen multinationals ready to spend five-to-ten million each. I need Gottingham to lean on their decision-makers so we get sales this month. Mortimer canceled the October management meeting, but I'll have to report something at the end of November," Douglas explained.

"That's a tall order. I don't know if he can pull in that many, that quickly."

"If he can't, I'm toast as the company superstar. You'll need to decide how important that is in the total scheme of things. But I can't imagine a scenario where the board will fire Mortimer and replace him with me unless I show some exemplary sales results. We intentionally raised the expectations just like you instructed," Douglas reminded him.

"I know, but we expected to have the whole Howard Knight issue behind us by now. Our people in South America almost had them in Buenos Aires. They even found and dealt with the plastic surgeon who changed their identity. We got pictures of their new looks and everything. By the time our guys got to the apartment they had rented, they were gone. Just fucking disappeared.

"You know, some of those companies under VCI's control still don't completely accept that Gottingham's in charge. They want evidence that Knight is truly out of the picture and some are acting a little like Mortimer. It might not be wise for us to push too hard," Mareno said with a sigh.

"Fair enough," Douglas acknowledged, "but I have five years of time and effort invested here. And a lot of collateral damage, too," he added.

"I know. I can't wait 'til we get our hands on Knight. He royally screwed things up. His half-cocked idea to slide Randall into the CEO role was probably doomed from the start. We tried to tell him it was better to wait for you, but he wanted influence immediately. The boys from Florida supported him, so I had to let him try. I didn't think he'd shoot a complete blank. I thought he could at least get Randall into the role for a few months before we brought you in," Mareno said with some frustration in his tone.

"Since he fucked that up, we'll have to move slower," he added. "But I hear your need. I'll have a word with Gottingham and ask him to do his best to bring you a dozen customers, but you and your Solutions team just might have to find a few deals, too."

"On another note, you need to make nice with the broad from Chicago you jilted a few weeks ago. Her heart's broken, and I don't want any long-term damage. Do you understand me?" Mareno asked with a full expectation that there was only one correct answer.

"Weissel? The slut with Financial Services? She's with us?" Douglas asked.

"We're grooming her for something important. There's a lot of women taking over in the business world now, you know," Mareno replied coyly. "Make her a happy woman again and let's try to keep her that way, alright?"

The next sound Douglas heard was the drone of a dial tone. Evidently, there would be no more discussion on that subject.

Forty-Eight

A Chicago area suburb.
Saturday morning October 23, 2016

Exactly one week earlier, his cell phone rang while he was out for an early morning jog through the state park immediately behind his home. Slightly out of breath, he answered with his usual greeting, "Fitzgerald here."

"Is this Mr. James Fitzgerald?" the caller asked.

"Yes, this is he. How can I help you?"

"Mr. Fitzgerald I'm sorry we need to have this conversation by telephone, but I'm Detective Harry Walker of the Metropolitan Toronto Police force. Are you related to Alistair William Fitzgerald?" James heard the voice ask.

"Yes, he's my son. Is there something wrong?" he asked with urgency in his tone.

"I'm afraid so, Mr. Fitzgerald. I'm sorry. Your son appears to have taken an overdose of drugs last night. We found a body carrying his identification. To be sure, we need you to come to Toronto to identify and make arrangements for his body. Again, I'm sorry," the detective repeated.

James imagined that he would never escape the immediate dread he felt. His only son, dead? It simply wasn't possible! In the minutes after receiving the shocking news, James started to piece it together. Yes, Alistair was in Toronto. Natalia's contact in Fort Myers had relayed that information at the request of Dan Ramirez in corporate security. He was to be there for a reunion with his friends. And it was that precise moment the regrets started to bubble up.

He'd meant to call Ramirez after his conversation with Natalia to find out what the concern was all about. He forgot to make that call. Now his son was dead. As he dejectedly walked the three or so miles back to tell his wife the devastating news, he wept openly. Big, heart-wrenching sobs.

When he arrived home, his wife took one look at him and immediately knew. She cried out "Oh, no!" before he could say a word. Then, she released the most horrifying scream of anguish he had ever heard. It took him almost an hour to share all the details with her. Every time he tried to speak, only a few words would come out before they both broke down in tears once again.

The following few days were fuzzy. A trip to Toronto. The horror of seeing the lifeless body of his son. The arrangements to have his body shipped back to Chicago. The obituary. The visitation. And finally, yesterday's funeral. They all ran together in a dark and ugly blur that left him dispirited and spent.

He appreciated that John George Mortimer and some of his other colleagues at Multima attended the funeral. During the week, he acknowledged calls of sympathy from dozens more executives from both within the corporation and others he interacted with regularly. The call from Suzanne Simpson had been particularly touching, but it all left him feeling hollow and more discouraged than he had ever been.

He tried to start moving on as people told him he must, but he lacked the motivation to do so. Getting out of bed each day had become a chore. Eating· gave no pleasure. His mood remained lethargic with little energy and even less interest in the world around him.

Since that morning's jog was interrupted with the news of Alistair's death, he had no interest in exercise and preferred to just remain in the house, with the shades drawn. Today, he'd already been sitting and listlessly daydreaming for several hours in a La-Z-Boy recliner in the home theater.

He saw little hope. For years, his wife had dreamed of experiencing the joy of grandchildren when Alistair finally got himself straightened out. Together, they had meticulously planned their summer cottage to become a magnificent retirement home on a lake. It was to be a place their son and his future family would be thrilled to visit weekends and maybe for a few weeks of vacation.

They'd be able to fish, hike, snowmobile and go boating as the seasons changed and they'd have a chance to spend quality time that simply hadn't been possible as he devoted thousands of hours to help build Multima Financial Services into a formidable company over the past thirty-five years.

Now, he was asking the most fundamental of questions: What was the point of continuing?

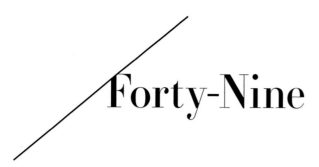

Forty-Nine

Atlanta, Georgia.
Monday October 31, 2016

At last. After more than six months of suspense and frustration, it seemed that in just a few more hours Suzanne would know where her future might be heading. Mortimer had reacted surprisingly well to her no-nonsense ultimatum.

"I must insist that we meet today, John George. I've been patient long enough. This circumstance is not only troublesome; I think it's becoming dangerous for all of us. I can fly there this evening or send my jet to pick you up. Whichever you prefer is fine with me, but it must be today," she told him with uncharacteristic boldness.

She could sense he was taken aback by this newly assertive tone and language by the long pause before he calmly replied, "Fair enough. I've got a full day booked. But I could meet the jet at Page Field about six. That would put me in Atlanta by about eight. Shall we plan for dinner somewhere around eight-thirty?"

"Sure. I'll have a car meet you at Fulton County Airport and bring you to my home. I don't have a Lana, but I'll order in Chinese or something if that works for you," she suggested, trying to create some levity.

"Chinese is fine. But I'll need to return tonight. I've got some things early tomorrow morning that I can't change," he warned.

"I understand. From my perspective, an hour or two should be fine. See you then, John George," she said. "And thank you. I know this isn't easy for you."

Regardless of how comfortable he might be or not be with her ultimatum, she was confident the time had come to take charge of the situation. The information she had discovered in the two weeks since her meeting with the lawyer in Toronto was shocking.

Liveenwel's several obvious lies defied logic. He must have known every piece of information he gave her was not only false but could also all be verified easily. That implied he had no concerns about either damage to his reputation or Suzanne learning the truth.

She had already redoubled her evenings-at-home research efforts with Eileen before she heard the news. Liveenwel had been shot in an alley, not fifteen minutes from where they met only six or seven hours earlier. The police theory about a love triangle seemed just too easy despite his well-known sex addiction.

Then, there was Alistair Fitzgerald's tragic death from a drug overdose. The internal announcement from Mortimer's office didn't make any mention of the circumstances or location, but James tearfully shared more details when she called to offer her condolences. Her colleague at Financial Services was devastated by the news. Several times in their brief conversation Fitzgerald had paused in a futile effort to regain his composure.

"It wasn't a new problem," he revealed after one of those pauses. "The habit started in college. We got him some help, and he was able to graduate, but it came back…"

Another pause after his voice cracked. "There was some powerful influence on his life we could never figure out. Whenever he got help, he'd be okay for a few months. Then, the cycle would start all over again. Counselors told us it was a friend who seemed to be the enabler. We could never determine with certainty who that enabler was …

"I have my suspicions, but that's all I have," he continued after another pause. "For this to happen when he was in Toronto with friends intensifies those suspicions. But they have no evidence it was anything more than an accidental overdose. Naturally, we're both heartbroken. Candidly, I'm not sure I really want to continue working at this point."

Suzanne felt his pain. Her eyes misted as she assured him she'd keep their conversation to herself and repeated the best words of solace she could find.

"I know how hard it is to lose someone so close, although I can only imagine how difficult it must be losing an only child as you have. But time will help. Take lots of time to grieve," she added. "We're all thinking of you and Diane. You know the entire Multima family will support you in any way we can."

Her angst grew when Eileen reported some damning evidence a day or two later.

"You're going to want to hear this Suzanne," she started. "This morning I called Douglas Whitfield's assistant, Marjorie. We talk regularly. I told her we were tabulating the cost of operating the company jet and wanted to compare our expenses. Could she share a copy of the travel log for their last three months so we could see how our costs per hour of flying compared to theirs?"

"She sent it to you?"

"Yes. All thirty-one pages. Douglas Whitfield was also in Toronto the night Liveenwel was shot and Alistair Fitzgerald overdosed. He flew there after a ten-minute stop at Teterboro in New Jersey and arrived at Billy Bishop Airport about seven in the evening, then left again at one in the morning. Here's the curious thing. His return flight to Miami was nonstop, direct. There was no stop in Teterboro. Isn't that curious?" she wondered.

"Yeah. Ten minutes wouldn't be enough time for refueling so he must have stopped to meet someone," Suzanne supposed.

"Or pick them up to join him on the flight to Toronto. If that were the case, he must have either just left that person in Toronto or knew they wouldn't need a ride back," Eileen suggested.

Sure enough, after Eileen contacted a friend in corporate security who called a friend at Teterboro Airport, they learned there was surveillance video of the lobby. After Eileen provided a picture from Alistair Fitzgerald's obituary notice, that person in New Jersey confirmed the person in the photo was there at the same time as Whitfield's company jet was on the ground.

But that wasn't all. On a hunch, Suzanne also invited Dieter Lehren, her director of information technology for lunch. She decided it was time to learn more about that remarkable software his team developed. Since John George Mortimer convinced the board to move that software from her division, where the code was originally written, to Multima Solutions where they would develop a new business selling it, she hadn't given it much thought.

"Why do you think John George got so excited about the potential for sales of the app?" she asked him.

"There's no doubt some companies can discourage hackers just by using it. It's like a home alarm system. Sometimes, posting a sign on the lawn advertising alarm company protection dissuades potential thieves. Same thing with the app. If companies publicize that they use the software and can track intruders, lots of hackers will forego the risks. It's got tremendous potential."

Intrigued, Suzanne asked her IT director a dozen more questions to get reacquainted with the software's features and capabilities.

"Is Multima's selling price competitive?" she wondered at one point.

"Yeah," Lehren replied. "But I hope the folks over at Solutions have fixed the backdoor issue."

"What's the backdoor issue?"

"I told John George this was the most severe limitation to commercializing the software. Once a system has been hacked, it's true we can trace exactly where the software has been copied and by whom. But every time the software is copied, it leaves a trail. If someone uses those same computers that captured the software, a good hacker can find a path right back into our system. That's what we call the backdoor," Lehren explained, then paused to be sure Suzanne was still with him before he continued.

"We wrote this software for our own use. To keep costs down, we left the backdoor open. We needed to manually go into the system and reprogram a few fields to lock it up again. Of course, we secured it immediately after our discovery. We're safe. But I reminded John George that someone would need to rewrite the underlying code to make the backdoor lock up again automatically. I emphasized the importance of completing that before any marketing activities. You could never count on individual companies remembering to take that additional step, and it could pose a massive liability for the corporation if it were ever discovered," the technology expert cautioned.

"I'm sure John George would follow your advice, but why don't you have a discreet word with your counterpart over there?" Suzanne requested.

Two days later, Dieter Lehren reported back to Suzanne that he talked with Ricky Technori at Solutions. To their mutual amazement, the senior technology executive in Whitfield's division was completely unaware of either the issue or any efforts underway to fix it.

That could mean only one of two things. Either John George Mortimer had failed to notify Douglas Whitfield of the problem. Or Whitfield was aware and, for some reason, had not taken the required action to fix it.

Either way, Suzanne was armed with overwhelming evidence that much was amiss within Multima. Her discussions with Mortimer that evening promised to be far more encompassing than the ever-disconcerting issues related to her mother's death.

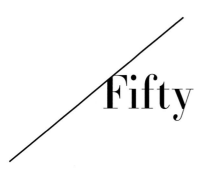

Fifty

"I just spoke with Dieter Lehren at Multima Supermarkets. He's the guy in charge of technology for their division. I think we have a problem," Ricky Technori said.

"Yeah, I remember meeting him. What's up?" Douglas Whitfield replied.

"He mentioned there's a backdoor on the new software that needs to be fixed. You know anything about that?"

"Yeah," Douglas said. "John George Mortimer mentioned something about it when we discussed my transfer to Solutions. It's a housekeeping detail I've got on my list to handle when we have more time. But right now, I need everybody focused on selling a few of those apps to show some revenue."

"I'm afraid it's more than housekeeping, Doug," Technori explained. "Bank of The Americas is at significant risk. We'll have to let them know immediately. We can't let them use the app as is."

"What?" Douglas exclaimed, his voice rising. "We can't stop anything! Letting the bank know we have a little glitch to fix at this stage will kill any further orders this month. If we don't have ten or twelve deals written by the next management meeting, this whole division might be toast."

"I understand the pressure you feel. But we really have no alternative. If someone accesses the backdoor of the app and hacks the bank's system, it would be catastrophic. They could lose billions. The bank could even find itself bankrupt. Our business would also be destroyed. As unpleasant as it may be, we must tell them about the problem," Technori insisted.

"Okay, Ricky," Douglas said calmly, trying to defuse the crisis. "Let's think this through. I understand the magnitude of the problem. You're right. I'll let them know. We'll need to do a full court press to fix the issue if it's as critical as you say. But I don't want to create panic within our team, right?" he said, then quickly added another thought.

"So, let's not spread the word to anyone internally until we have a plan together to fix it. I'd like you to do that assessment personally. How much time do you need to analyze the scope of the project, figure out what resources you'll need, and estimate time and costs?"

"It might take me a couple days to get it all together," Technori said after a few seconds thought. "But, in the meantime, you must emphasize to Bank of The Americas that they have to let us know immediately if any hacking attempt is successful. They can't wait for the system to identify the perpetrator; they must call us immediately. We can close the backdoor and fix the issue quickly to mitigate risk. But timing will be essential."

"Sure, I'll emphasize that to them," Douglas assured with the most confident tone he could manage. "But let's keep this between us for now. Okay? And one other thing, Ricky. Why don't you just work from home for the next few days? You'll have fewer disruptions there, and we'll get it done quicker."

With Technori's cautious concurrence, Douglas ended the call and immediately pressed a speed-dial button.

"I'm running into real time-pressures here," he started. "Did you hear back from the Russians yet?"

"Yeah, we're still talking," Giancarlo Mareno replied. "They're prepared to give us a billion up front but don't want to pay any royalties. I don't want to do the deal if we can't get ten percent of their action."

"We may need to be flexible on the commission. My number two here was alerted to the issue by someone at Multima Supermarkets. The fucking open communication in this place complicates everything," Douglas remarked in frustration. "I've persuaded him to sit on it for a day or two, but I can't keep a lid on it much longer. Maybe we should consider a smaller commission. This access is so powerful that even two percent would net us billions."

"Good point. Are you sure you can keep this contained for a while?"

"I'm sure," Douglas replied. "He knows I have a high-quality but lurid video of a raucous night he spent with a couple fags when he was high on coke a few weeks after I got here. He doesn't want his wife to know. He'll stay quiet."

"Alright. Let me have another go with the Russians," Mareno said. "In the meantime, be sure you keep a lid on it."

Douglas had already determined there would be no call to Bank of The Americas. That would kill everything. Instead, he'd focus on a backup plan if the Russians wouldn't make a deal. If they were prepared to spend a billion dollars to get the technology but didn't want to pay a commission, somebody over there must have already calculated their potential harvest to be many times that. They just didn't want to share. Maybe it was time to shift gears.

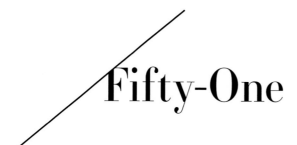

Fifty-One

Suzanne Simpson's home, Atlanta, Georgia.
Monday October 31, 2016

"You remember Jasmine," Suzanne said, extending her arm towards a stocky woman. "She's one of my protectors assigned by Dan Ramirez. She so sweetly volunteered to help serve dinner while we talk this evening."

In an attempt at levity, she added with a smile, "I just don't know if she'll interrupt our conversation at the same critical junctures as Lana."

"You made it quite clear that I shouldn't do that," Jasmine quickly interjected and laughed merrily along with them.

"You go ahead and interrupt whenever you think I need help," John George replied, still chuckling. "Over the past few weeks, you've probably seen just how tough this woman can be!"

As Jasmine retreated to the kitchen, Suzanne turned serious. "Let's have a seat over at the table. Jasmine said she'd open a bottle of wine and bring it for us. I'd like to get started."

Pleasantries about the day's work, John George's flight from Fort Myers and his ride in from the airport were brief as Jasmine poured glasses of wine for both within just a few moments.

"Let's pick up where we left off the last time," Suzanne said, raising her glass of wine in salutation.

"I know it's your meeting, Suzanne, and should be your agenda, but I'd like to ask your indulgence to share some information with you first, if I may," John George replied as he lowered his wine glass, untouched, to the table.

Suzanne shrugged and graciously allowed that would be okay.

"I have some news to share with you about my health. I wanted to let you know before, but the timing just didn't seem right. Unfortunately, the cancer is back. It's attacked a lung this time, and the long-term prognosis isn't good."

Suzanne was shocked by the new information. A return of cancer after such a short time seemed unlikely, and she was immediately skeptical. Was this yet another diversion he was attempting to create? Was he trying to soften up her determination to get information? Was he looking for sympathy? She kept her facial expression impassive as she processed the information and predictably said, "Oh, John George. I'm so sorry to hear that."

"I've known for a few weeks. They detected it from some blood work they did back in September, and it looks like my number will be up sooner than I expected. It's inoperable. They might be able to slow it down, but they can't cure it at this stage. So, I'm taking an experimental immunotherapy treatment as part of a clinical study."

"I've heard about those treatments. They've achieved some great results, haven't they?" Suzanne asked in her most confident tone of voice.

"Yes. The treatments have promise. I had an MRI last week, the first since I started the treatments. There was no growth in the tumor over the past six weeks. That's a good sign. But you didn't call me here to talk about my health. We both know it is what it is, and I'll manage to live with it for a while. Let's talk about your concerns." John George insisted.

Caught off guard by the significant new development, Suzanne was unsure how best to proceed. She started her pursuit obliquely.

"John George, are you at all familiar with an attorney, Roger Liveenwel at Berister Law LLP?"

"Only by name. James Fitzgerald referred to him in a conversation we had about the regulatory snafu he had to fix for the mortgage program you folks are promoting for him. I heard everything was resolved. Is that not correct?" he asked.

"Yeah. The regulatory issues are all resolved, but I was wondering if Liveenwel might have been the attorney Alberto Ferer used to create the legal structure related to those machinations around my mother."

"No. I remember working with one of the original partners of the firm, Stuart Brown. A very bright fellow. He died years ago," he said factually.

"So, Liveenwel was not at all involved with my mother's matters?" Suzanne pressed.

"Not that I'm aware. I never heard his name mentioned. Why do you ask?"

"The *notaire* I used for issues related to my mother's death, a Monsieur LaMontagne, told his son about an attorney in Toronto who was connected to Multima. Monsieur LaMontagne and his wife were brutally murdered a few weeks after he shared that information with his son. But there's more," she said as John George appeared ready to reply.

"His son, a priest, was the person who asked me to meet with him in Quebec. You'll remember the incident I had there on Labor Day? It was he who mentioned an attorney in Toronto that he believed was connected to Multima. You may also recall his fatal car accident occurred just hours after meeting with me," Suzanne said, closely watching John George's face for any reaction before she continued on.

"Now, I've discovered that Roger Liveenwel was murdered in Toronto, the same night as Alistair Fitzgerald died of a drug overdose. In a conversation I had with James Fitzgerald, he told me Liveenwel, Douglas Whitfield, and his son were all fraternity buddies. Apparently, they were all in Toronto that evening for some sort of reunion. Whitfield claims he left Toronto earlier than planned because his friends were either too stoned or wrapped up in pursuit of sex for his taste. He claims to know nothing of either death. But I think we may have a major problem developing."

Before John George could respond, Jasmine entered the room with a tray of Chinese food. Wordlessly, she arranged the steaming hot dishes in the center of the table and immediately retreated to the kitchen. They both remained silent as they loaded their plates with a sampling from each container. Suzanne made a point of waiting for John George to speak first.

"Are you suggesting that Douglas Whitfield might be involved in some way?" he asked.

"I'm suggesting that any number of people in our Multima hierarchy could be involved. I also wonder if my mother's death was really a heart attack," she replied, looking him directly in the eye.

"Wait for a second," John George quickly replied. "Are you suggesting there was something untoward about your mother's death?"

"I have reason to believe it may have been more than coincidental that her death occurred just a few days before the board of directors meeting where Howard Knight tried to unseat you as CEO," she replied without hesitation.

"I detect a dire implication as a subtext to that comment. And I'm shocked," he said, setting down his utensils and focusing his gaze directly into her eyes. "Let me be very clear and unambiguous. If you think – for a single moment – that I am involved in your mother's death in some way, let me clear that impression away right now. I know only what you told me in our telephone conversation and what Sally-Ann Bureau relayed from her call with Eileen. Like you, I was terribly saddened to learn of her death, and I, too, grieved her loss," he said with passion.

"I don't doubt your sense of loss at all," Suzanne countered. "But I have heard through the corporate grapevine that a fortuitous conversion of preferred shares you had granted to my mother allowed you to block Howard Knight's rebellion."

"That's true. I converted those shares in the numbered company to preferred shares in Multima, and that gave me enough votes to defeat any decision with which I didn't agree. But, it had absolutely nothing to do with your mother's death. I had the legal right to cancel her shares and convert to preferred Multima shares anytime. I waited until the last possible minute to do so, but when I was pressed to make the conversion, I did. It was purely a coincidence that share conversion took place only a day or two after your mother's passing," John George insisted with fierce determination in his eyes.

Suzanne paused to assess his response. "Okay. I believe you. But the young priest was insistent she was killed, that it wasn't a heart attack as we all thought. He wouldn't tell me where he got that information, but I suspect it was the lawyer he met in Toronto. Who could that be if it's not Liveenwel? Would Alberto be aware of anyone else who might have known about your schemes surrounding my mother?"

"Good question. Let's call him," John George replied as he pulled his cell phone from his pocket and dialed. He activated the speaker before Alberto picked up, then explained he was with Suzanne when his legal chief answered.

"John George has explained the background on the secret companies and special shares you concocted in relation to my mother. I think I understand all that now. Here's what I need to know. Who at Berister Law LLP might have known about your arrangement?" she demanded.

"Well, we did the deals with Stuart Brown," he said. "When Stuart died they moved the files over to Reginald Smith, another partner. But when I called to convert the shares from the numbered company to Multima preferred shares, Smith referred me to a newer partner. Apparently, they decided several months earlier to move the entire Multima relationship to him since he was already doing occasional work for Financial Services. I think his name was Liveenwel, Roger Liveenwel."

Suzanne gasped audibly when she heard the news and watched Mortimer pale as realization set in. Alberto Ferer couldn't see the body language, but he sensed trouble from the stillness. They spent several minutes bringing him up to date with Suzanne's suspicions. Then, he counseled patience.

"Let's not jump to any conclusions yet," he cautioned. "There may be a connection, but it feels a little too easy. Even if Liveenwel knew about our secret transactions, what motivation might he have to be involved in a potential murder? It's a big leap."

"You're right, of course," John George replied. "But let's bring Dan Ramirez into the conversation. It might be useful to get his perspective."

Alberto Ferer offered to locate the chief of security, then use Skype to get back with them. Suzanne provided her home Skype address so they could video conference using her wall-mounted television. In the ten minutes it took him to make all the arrangements, Suzanne and John George wolfed down their cooling Chinese food, and Jasmine cleared the dishes to leave them in privacy for the call.

The facts they took turns explaining to Ramirez were intriguing, he agreed. But he, too, found the confluence of events more coincidence than indicative of a crime. "We don't have a motive," he emphasized. "The priest's claim that some unknown party murdered Louise Marcotte, and who also claimed to have some connection to a lawyer who might have some connection to Multima, is fascinating, but it doesn't explain why any of those hypothetically connected people had a reason to murder her. Further, the hospital reported no signs of foul play. It was a heart attack."

They went around and around on the subject for more than a half hour. All seemed sympathetic to Suzanne's unease, but the session produced only one conclusion they could agree upon. James Fitzgerald might be able to help. Although they all knew he had been devastated by the death of his son, they respected his grounded logic and keen analytical skills. Alberto offered to reach him at home to see if he could participate in their Skype conversation. It was another ten minutes before he joined, so they rehashed possibilities while they waited.

"I agree there seems little motive for the notary public and his wife to be killed," James began when he linked in. "Their son, the priest, is even more perplexing. We don't even know if any of them ever met Roger Liveenwel. However, Alberto's revelation that he recently had access to the secret files related to Multima and Madame Marcotte does raise red flags. Of course, the police think Liveenwel was killed by an enraged lover of the girl with him that night," James said as his voice trailed off, suggesting he was deep in thought.

"I can't think of any possible connection to my son," James continued after only a moment to take a deep breath. "I can't imagine he knew anything about secret shares and payments. Even I didn't know about them until now. Besides me, the only connection I think my son had at Multima was Douglas Whitfield. I know my feelings towards that character have changed dramatically. I can't forgive him for leaving Alistair behind, especially if he was already stoned.

"The man should have had the decency to help my son get back to New Jersey alive instead of leaving him alone to die there on a street in Toronto," he said with his voice breaking. "But as angry as I am with his behavior, it doesn't prove he's involved in a conspiracy to commit murder."

It continued that way for a few minutes, until John George suggested they'd exhausted all possible scenarios at this stage. Maybe it would be better for everyone to sleep on the information they had discussed and see if anything else surfaced. He proposed Dan Ramirez should become the point person to collect any additional information any of them came across. His last suggestion was for the security chief to check with his police contacts in both Toronto and Quebec. Did they have any additional leads or theories they might share?

Once the Skype screen dimmed on the television, Suzanne felt discouraged. Over months, her frustration had grown. Her expectations for resolution of loose ends going into this evening's meeting were sky high. She now realized how unrealistically high they had been.

"It's like watching a TV crime show or a movie about organized crime," she complained as they looked at each other in disbelief. She could see John George was uncomfortable and assumed he didn't know where to go next with this summit she had demanded.

"There is one additional piece of information I should probably share with you. The others know bits and pieces about it, but I haven't shared any of it with you. And I really should," he added.

For almost an hour, Suzanne listened dumbfounded as he recounted Multima's history with Venture Capital Inc. He started at the beginning, with Howard Knight bringing to his attention the opportunity to buy Countrywide Stores, the Canadian supermarket chain Suzanne was managing. He explained how he paid VCI a finder's fee for bringing him the deal but declined the offered financing. He reminded her how he raised personal funds to purchase Countrywide and how that all fit in with her mother.

He told her about Knight bringing him the opportunity to buy Wendal Randall's tiny logistics company several years later and the deal they struck for VCI to provide funding with an ownership position in return. He candidly revealed the reservations he had at the time and the whispered rumors about VCI he'd heard over the past few years. He walked her through the steps Howard Knight took to try to replace him as CEO with Wendal Randall and reviewed the intricacies of the Canadian numbered company share conversions to defeat Knight.

She was aghast as he described the demand by Earnest Gottingham to become a director, John George's refusal of the request, and his suspicion that this was related to the threats towards Suzanne. Together, they made the link to the subsequent bombing of the Multima store in Kissimmee. When he mentioned that Dan Ramirez had now uncovered that The Organization completely controlled VCI, she noticed her hands trembling.

When he explained what they thought they knew about The Organization, she felt faint, with her mind blurred. It was too much to process, with too many implications. She was grateful when he suggested they ask Jasmine if she could round up some strong coffee.

When he finished some minutes later, Suzanne noticed that John George appeared near total exhaustion. His face lacked color. His eyelids drooped. And his usually steady hand quivered as he raised the cup to his mouth. She invited him to use a spare bedroom and fly back to Fort Myers early in the morning, but he refused. It was better to get back, he insisted.

As he prepared to leave, he again spread his arms wide and gave her an awkward embrace. This time, she returned the gesture, squeezing his neck tightly with her hands as she returned the hug and, to her own surprise, giving him a tender, lingering kiss on his right cheek.

Fifty-Two

Multima Financial Services, Hoffman Estates, Illinois.
Monday October 31, 2016

"I realize it's raining," Natalia Tenaz said to her boss. "But can we meet outside for a bit?"

Within a few minutes, James Fitzgerald extricated himself from the press of the day's activities and was walking along the path behind the office with an umbrella raised. He didn't mind the interruption. It gave him some time to catch up with the young woman who had recently become a superstar performer in his division. He was in awe of her accomplishments and was continually amazed at the volume of work she could process. And he was always keenly interested in the information she had to share.

That morning she required no prompting. As soon as they reached the magic distance about two hundred yards from the buildings, the range they considered 'safe' from potentially prying recording devices, she started.

"There's something very wrong going on over at Multima Solutions," she confided. "My friend in corporate security has been working overtime this week. Every night when she returns home, there's an alert on her special software. Sometimes, there are several."

"What's she learning?" James interjected a little anxiously.

"Douglas Whitfield is up to something, but she can't determine exactly what. It seems he has contacted someone in Russia every day over the last week. The conversations are long, but they're all in Russian. My friend can only pick-up the occasional English word, and she hasn't been able to find a translation app to incorporate into her software. But one word she hears every time sounds like 'motyga'."

"Which means?" James prompted with a little impatience in his tone.

"She thinks it means 'hack'. She thinks they're discussing hacking activities. Within an hour of each conversation, Whitfield also makes calls to a cell phone number in New York. She can't trace it to identify the caller because that person is using one of those cheap disposable cell phones."

"Wait a minute," James interrupted again. "If her special software only records conversations that use a specific word or phrase like you explained to me before, how can she record a Russian conversation?"

"She applied a very general code word to Whitfield's line – Multima. It's picking up every conversation he makes using the company name."

"No wonder she's getting a lot of hits," James scoffed. "A president of a business unit uses the name Multima in almost every conversation!"

"Exactly," she replied with a cheerful smile. "I asked her to find a way to capture as much as possible. I just don't trust the guy. Anyway, Whitfield and this person in New York apparently talk almost in code. It's as though they expect their conversations to be recorded. There are no complete sentences. They often refer to 'the boys' or 'our Russian friends'. However, my source thinks she has connected enough of the dots to understand they are trying to sell something to some Russians related to Multima but can't agree on a price. There's only one thing she's certain about. Whatever they are trying to sell involves billions of dollars. That amount is used over and over in their coded conversations."

"It's vague, Natalia," James said. "You usually bring me information with more meat on it. I'm not sure what this tells us."

"I know. I made the same comment to my friend. She said there was just one more thing she could glean. They frequently refer to a meeting taking place the fourth of November. Apparently, whatever they are planning will occur right after that meeting," she told him.

Once James determined that his usually reliable resource had no further intelligence to share, he quickly switched the subject to the home mortgage program launch with Supermarkets.

As they walked back towards the office building, his smile broadened with almost every step. Full-time employee participation in the program now surpassed seventy percent after only two months, and Natalia reported retail customers were already applying online at a rate of more than fifty per hour. They were exploring ways to speed up the website to avoid delays and backlogs. It was almost unbelievable!

Fifty-Three

Suzanne and her team had completed one store visit, her first in the US since the bombing in Kissimmee, and were just starting their descent into Savannah for a tour of the planned second location when her cell phone buzzed. She noted James Fitzgerald's name on the screen and excused herself from the roundtable discussion. She took a seat apart from the group and buckled in as she answered the call.

"I hear background noise, Suzanne," he started. "Is it convenient to talk?"

"I have some people with me, but listening is no problem," she responded with a lighthearted laugh.

"Good," he chuckled in return. "I won't take much of your time, but I've got some thoughts I'd like to share with you."

"Fire away," Suzanne replied with a glance at her watch.

"Our Skype conversation yesterday got me thinking about some things. I hope you won't find this out of line, but I'm becoming increasingly worried about Whitfield over at Solutions. You know I've been a big supporter of his in the past. Hell, I once even had my sights on him as my replacement if John George ever decided to let me retire," he harrumphed. "But something has changed in the last few months. I don't know if it's the hubris of power or some other factor, but his behavior worries me."

"That's troublesome, James," she commented. "I know you don't like gossip and have exceptionally grounded judgment. What do you see?"

"First, I'll repeat that I'm mystified by the way he just left Alistair to die there in Toronto. After all we've done for him over the years, I can't imagine him not ensuring my son was well and home again before he ran off. His story just doesn't compute for me, and I'll never forgive him for that. So, there's my bias right up front," James blurted out, waiting for just a second, perhaps to see if Suzanne would react. She didn't, so he continued.

"But I've also been perplexed about why whoever issued the threat against you chose Whitfield to carry the message. Why wasn't it someone from your team? Or someone in John George's office? To me, it's incongruous that someone delivering a threat to you would use a colleague completely separate from your business unit. I just have this awful feeling that Whitfield is more involved with The Organization than any of us suspected."

The plane was about to touch down, and Suzanne would soon need to break away from the call to deplane, so she carefully tried to guide him to a point if there was one. "I understand your concern, James. Are there any particular new developments since we all spoke yesterday?"

"Just one thing. I've learned something from a source who I can't divulge. I can tell you that I have almost one hundred percent confidence in the accuracy of this person's information. Her track record is impeccable.

"Apparently, Whitfield has been conducting negotiations with someone in Russia and another party in New York. My source says both discussions involve selling something from Multima related to hacking. The only sense I could make of that was a possibility they were referring to the new software your folks developed. The product John George subsequently shipped over to Solutions to refine and market. Can you think of any reason Whitfield might be interested in selling that software to a Russian? Or any reason someone from New York would be involved in a deal?"

"No. Nothing comes to mind," she replied vaguely. "It does all sound a little bizarre, though, doesn't it? Do you have any theories?"

"Only one. If Whitfield is more involved with The Organization than we realize, he might see some potential new use for that software, maybe even an illegal use, that benefits both The Organization and some Russian outfit. Maybe I'm completely off base. Maybe my judgment is clouded by the circumstances surrounding Alistair's death. But I hope you'll think about it. See if you can uncover anything more concrete. I've already relayed the info to Ramirez, and he also found it very curious."

They ended their call on that note, and Suzanne gathered her belongings to deplane. She hadn't told Fitzgerald, of course. But she had a very good idea why Whitfield might want to talk to Russian interests. They were notorious for their hacking capabilities. They might be the best in the world at it. If Whitfield didn't fix the backdoor flaw in the software, then sold the application in its current form, it would be like giving a key to the vault to anyone with harmful intentions. And it could be worth billions of dollars to the Russians or anyone else.

She made a mental note to check with Dieter Lehren to see if he'd talked with his counterpart at Solutions about getting that defect fixed.

Fifty-Four

Dan Ramirez was apparently thrilled with the information. Right after John George finished his morning-long meeting with Alberto Ferer and CFO Wilma Willingsworth, the chief of security bounded into his office almost breathless with enthusiasm. To show his full attention, John George set down the protein bar he planned for lunch, then looked up expectantly.

The head of security needed only a few moments to summarize the conversation he had with James Fitzgerald during which the Financial Services president had relayed information divulged by Natalia Tenaz, as well as the resulting action he took.

"I only had to twist his arm a little. It wasn't too hard to identify the woman's friend. It was the same young lady James himself had asked me to find a job for earlier this year," Ramirez continued as John George listened intently.

"I called her in for a chat and got her to confess to a whole range of illegal activities she's involved with in her spare time. I certainly didn't tell her, but I have more than a little admiration for her technology expertise. I've only heard of software that sophisticated at the CIA. Once she broke and told me everything, I put her in touch with one of my old contacts at the FBI who quickly located a Russian-speaking resource. They just got back to me with more information about Whitfield's conversations," Ramirez went on as John George listened without posing a question.

"That sonofabitch Whitfield is trying to exploit some defect in the new software program you asked him to introduce. It seems this Russian contact of his has worked out ways they can use the software vulnerability to surreptitiously install malware not only in the mainframe of every buyer of this software but also in the systems of every one of that customer's clients!"

"Let me be sure I've got that right, Dan," John George clarified. "Whitfield has actively been working to sabotage our software and hack the system of every customer who buys it? Then, hack the computers of every customer downstream from the original buyer?"

"That's right. It can capture far more data than the original hack. We're talking the potential to steal hundreds of billions – maybe trillions – of dollars. We've got to stop it, John George. And we've got to stop it fast. They're planning to start immediately after the board of directors meeting on Friday."

"Any ideas about how we might prevent it?" John George asked.

"I think we should call Suzanne. Her people initially wrote the code for the software. Maybe Dieter Lehren or one of his people can figure it out," Ramirez suggested.

Within moments, Sally-Ann Bureau had located Suzanne in a Multima supermarket in Savannah where she and her team were inspecting the store as part of her recently revived visitation schedule.

Dan Ramirez repeated his story for Suzanne, then asked if Supermarkets staff might be able to help. Within minutes, her director of technology joined the call and was briefed on the situation.

"It's doable, certainly," he said when he understood the scope of the problem and the request for a remedy. "But, it's not quick. We always intended to close that backdoor when we were using the software for our own purposes. We never got around to it because the fix is complicated, time-consuming, and expensive."

"Dieter," Suzanne interjected. "We don't have time. Dan Ramirez has information that some sort of attack may take place within the next week. What do we have to do to find a fix by Friday?"

"Friday?" Lehren shouted into the speaker. "To have a chance of completion by Friday, I'd need to take every analyst and engineer on our team and work them around the clock. It's almost impossible!"

"Well, Dieter, we'll have to ask them to do the impossible. We developed that software, and we're responsible for any potential damage it causes. This must become the priority of your entire team. Regardless of the costs we incur, there's no alternative. We simply must fix it by Friday," Suzanne said quietly but with a tone of voice that sounded like steel to her chief executive officer.

As they ended the impromptu conference call, Suzanne asked John George if he had time for a separate private conversation. They needed to talk about another matter.

Fifty-Five

I Gemelli Ristorante, South Hackensack, New Jersey.
Monday October 31, 2016

Neither had been to the restaurant before, but Giancarlo Mareno heard the food was good and it was only a few minutes' drive from Teterboro airport and just off the I-80. They met there at noon as agreed and had just finished their delicious meals. Mareno chose the veal *scallopine francese*, and Douglas ordered the chicken *saporito*.

While they ate, conversation was limited to the weather, families, recent sporting activities and planned vacations. Douglas knew well that Mareno never liked to mix dining with business. In the old Italian tradition, he maintained that meals should be relaxed, stress-free, and enjoyable for optimum digestion. Douglas wanted the important man's meal well-digested before he made his pitch.

First, he was relieved Mareno finally agreed to meet in person. This discussion had the potential to be life-altering and he needed the powerful man's undivided attention. As Douglas flew in on the company jet that morning under the pretext of a sales call in New York, he polished his presentation. He thought about every word he used in the slides and checked the math in each of the charts and graphs.

He started with a recap of the status of their current project. By Friday, Earnest Gottingham, the president of VCI, would become a new director on the board of Multima Corporation. Before the company's fiscal year end in June, Gottingham would nominate Douglas Whitfield to replace John George Mortimer as Chief Executive Officer. With news of Mortimer's cancer public by then and Gottingham's continuing influence over those directors who voted with Knight the last time even stronger, there was little doubt Douglas would become CEO.

They'd be able to launder phenomenal amounts of illicit money. With sales of more than six hundred and fifty million dollars *per week*, they'd be able to scour unbelievable amounts of revenue from other illegal operations through

Multima. The only downside was the trend for more customers to pay with debit and credit cards. Over time, it might become somewhat harder to camouflage their funds among the actual business revenues.

But they'd still have the opportunity to boost sales into Multima by those suppliers they already controlled. That would increase legitimate earnings considerably. They'd also have the possibility of creating a submissive employee union where they could siphon off a few million dollars from weekly employee contributions. There was also the promise of some currency manipulation through Multima Financial Services. That was more difficult though because of the continuous oversight of the Federal Reserve. Their project still had the potential to alter the landscape of The Organization's financial control and provide a foundation for exponential growth for a decade or more. It fit their needs perfectly.

However, Douglas Whitfield was there to recommend they change that carefully crafted plan, and he knew the course he was proposing would mean a radical shift in thinking. First, they'd need to cut off discussions with the Russians about selling the software. Then they'd need to raise a few hundred million, maybe a billion, dollars. But the potential payoff was almost beyond comprehension. They could earn trillions of dollars in a matter of months!

As Douglas subtly swung discussion towards his brilliant new idea, he was careful to make sure Giancarlo Mareno stayed with him.

"You remember our discussions about the backdoor flaw with that software package Mortimer gave me to sell at Solutions?" he asked and waited for Mareno's nod before continuing.

"When Mortimer first told me about the flaw a few months ago, I had some conversations with a Russian guy I met years ago at Pickering College. He's not with our guys over there, but he might be the best systems hacker in the world and we've kept in touch over the years. I gave him a copy of the software to play with, and he's now come up with some slick new malware. It not only sneaks in through this backdoor defect, but it also attaches to the banking information for all accounts connected to the host system," Douglas explained slowly, taking care the less computer-savvy Mareno didn't get lost on any of the buzzwords. With the man's nod of comprehension, Douglas carried on.

"Then, like a worm, it wiggles from one bank account to another. On command, the malware activates and scoops all the funds in every single account within seconds and cycles the proceeds through untraceable offshore bank accounts until instructed to divert elsewhere manually. With a customer like Bank of The Americas, in one swoop we could drain not only their corporate bank accounts but every bank account of every single one of their customers. We can make trillions in a day!" Douglas exclaimed.

Mareno appeared intrigued with the information but remained skeptical. "It sounds too easy. What can go wrong?"

"Nothing. He tested it already. Do you remember those widespread systems failures in the news last month? That was my friend. He emptied Bank of The America's accounts, transferred all the funds to a bank account in Cyprus and returned them all to Bank of The Americas accounts in less than a minute. The outages were just a diversion to distract systems engineers. He did it all in the seconds between a systems alert and the temporary shutdown of the computers. No one even noticed. Or, if they did, they probably assumed it was a glitch related to the outage. No money actually went missing."

As Mareno gradually became convinced of the technical capability, his questions became more direct. "So, you want to stop talking to our Russian friends. Is that to make sure they don't get this for themselves?"

"Exactly. You know they'd go ballistic if we freelanced on this after selling them a version," Douglas replied. "But we'll also need to move quickly after we move Mortimer out. We can't deploy it in the current Multima publicly traded corporate structure. There are way too many checks and balances. Plus, their business culture is far too open. It would never work.

"What I think we should do is spin off Multima Solutions as a separate company. We need to buy that new entity ourselves and keep it private. Maybe move it offshore too. Here's the rub. I'll need to get between five hundred million and a billion dollars for the company to justify a sale. Even with Gottingham controlling the directors we influence, we'll need to raise enough capital to avoid a Securities Exchange Commission inquiry."

"You need me to raise a billion dollars?" Mareno gasped incredulously.

"More or less. It'll only work if we carve it out of the Multima business, and I can't envision a scenario where the board would accept less than a half-billion".

There was a long pause. That was good. At least Mareno was giving it serious consideration. Douglas knew it was best to remain silent, so he just watched him think about it, amazed at how nonchalantly the powerful man could detach himself from a conversation for whatever time he felt necessary to process his decisions.

After several minutes of silence – Douglas guessed five or more – Mareno shifted in his chair and started to speak.

"We're not going to change anything with our plans to make you CEO. That goes ahead exactly as we designed it. I get your rationale for spinning off Solutions. It will be neater that way and much less likely to attract attention," he said as a smile slowly started to take form on his huge face.

"I'll see what might be possible to raise some capital, but I have nowhere near one billion that's liquid," Mareno continued. "Maybe I could do twenty percent of that. We can't talk to the Russians for obvious reasons, so I'll just wait for them to bring the subject up again. The Europeans are challenged financially. With the economic crisis over there, they lost banks in Greece, Spain, and Italy. The Latin Americans might be good for a couple hundred million, and the Asians in Singapore might be willing to put together the same. But I doubt we'll be able to enhance the Multima balance sheet by more than about seven hundred million. You'll need to start conditioning the board of directors to expect that valuation when you take over," he said with no further room for negotiation.

"Okay. I get the picture, and I should be able to work within that amount. I'll start to dampen expectations for the new venture at the next management meeting," Douglas said.

Looking at his watch, Giancarlo Mareno lifted his large frame from the wooden chair and stretched. "I need to be on my way," he said. "But I want to thank you, Douglas. I really appreciate you bringing this opportunity to my attention. When we do it, you'll get your full share."

After a firm handshake, he turned on his heel and left the restaurant. Mareno didn't even offer to pay the bill for their lunch, Douglas noted sardonically. Evidently, bringing him an opportunity to reap results in the trillions didn't warrant any special consideration or change of habit.

Fifty-Six

Outside a Multima Supermarket, Savannah, Georgia.
Monday October 31, 2016

Suzanne had no idea about wire-tapping, recording devices, or that sort of thing. But, intuitively, she sensed it was probably better to have this kind of conversation outside, away from thin walls and curious ears. She left her entourage enjoying a quick lunch at the store deli, went outdoors, and found a tree with some shade near one corner of the parking lot. With her two bodyguards watching from a respectful distance, she glanced around a little nervously as she hit the speed-dial for John George Mortimer's private line at his office.

"I know you've probably already thought of this," she said once the greetings were out of the way. "I didn't want to mention it in front of the others, but do you think it would be a good idea for Wilma Willingsworth to raise a red flag with her counterpart at Bank of The Americas? You know, alert them to our backdoor problem on the software they're testing?"

"Absolutely. I've got a call to their CEO on my 'to-do' list. I met him when I was doing a CBNN interview a few years ago. I plan to call him right after we hang up. How are your store visits going today?"

"I didn't sleep at all last night," she replied, determined to lead the conversation. "Your flood of revelations was almost more than my brain could comfortably process."

"I realize I shared a lot with you in a very short time. A lot is going on," he said patiently. "What in particular caused you unease?"

"As we were discussing with Dan and Alberto a few minutes ago, there certainly seems to be something amiss over in Solutions, and someone suspicious might wonder just what Douglas Whitfield's relationship to The Organization might be. It gives me goosebumps to think about the possibilities," she said as her body shivered.

"James Fitzgerald certainly thinks so," Mortimer said.

"I know you feel strongly about the future potential for Solutions to market the new software we developed. And I don't intend to second-guess your strategy, but I wonder just how crucial you think the Solutions division really is to our core business?" she probed.

"You've every right to second guess strategy. After all, I tried to make it quite clear last night that I hope one day soon to see you in charge of those strategies. What's your issue with Solutions?" he asked a little more brusquely than Suzanne expected.

"Even if we are overreacting. Even if everything Douglas is doing over there is legitimate and proper, I wonder if we aren't still courting danger. I don't think technology is our core competency. Solutions has done some great work to make us the great supermarket chain we are today. The people Solutions transferred over to support our business are outstanding and talented. But that is when they are working for us, doing things that we can oversee every day and modify swiftly when needed.

"I'm not sure that I'm as comfortable as you with the responsibility we bear when our software, and ultimately our people, get access to computer systems of other companies. I wonder if that doesn't create a liability we really don't need for a benefit yet to be proven," Suzanne said with a tinge of doubt in her voice to soften the message.

"Your thought process makes sense. There are clearly some implications I didn't think through completely during the flush of my victory fighting off Knight. I realize we need to introduce a different culture in a technology entity. I realized that with Wendal Randall and thought Douglas Whitfield had the right stuff to plant and grow that kind of culture. I was wrong. But I wonder. Is there a chance your judgment is also perhaps clouded by a suspicion he is in some way connected to The Organization?" he asked.

"The entire situation with this outfit you call The Organization is a problem for me. These people are criminals," she replied. "I think we should all be very concerned about the safety of our customers, employees and ourselves. If they control Venture Capital Inc. and VCI holds the second largest block of shares in Multima, we should find a way to get rid of them."

"Oh, I'd like to, Suzanne," he retorted smoothly. "Unfortunately, I don't have a billion or so sitting around that I can use to buy them out."

"Is that what it would take?"

"Well, they invested a billion ten years ago. They've earned dividends of two to three percent per year on their investment, but I expect they would want a few hundred million in profit to go away quietly. I just don't know where we could raise that kind of money," he stated.

"I have an idea," Suzanne said. "It will take a few minutes more, but let me bounce this off you."

It took quite some time as she stood in the oppressive heat and humidity of a Georgian autumn day, but she became oblivious to her surroundings as she confidently outlined her idea with John George posing questions of clarification every few sentences.

Part way through their discussion, John George Mortimer became impressed with her scheme. She could tell. First, his tone of voice became more confident as he queried her strategies. Then his speech pattern quickened. Finally, he asked her to hold on a minute while he asked Alberto to come over from his office next door.

Soon, Alberto also agreed it could work, and she could feel his enthusiasm grow, too, as their discussion about her idea evolved. He was making notes as they spoke and worked rapidly from a mental checklist to be sure they covered all the bases. They agreed. Her course of action was the best chance they had to resolve their simmering problems and growing fears.

Notably, John George proposed they Skype together again about eight o'clock that evening so they could bring Suzanne up to date on their progress.

Fifty-Seven

Multima Solutions headquarters, Miami, Florida.
Tuesday November 1, 2016

Douglas Whitfield almost dropped his telephone in surprise. Alberto Ferer just finished casually telling him that John George Mortimer was considering an initial public offering for Multima Solutions. It seemed inconceivable. An IPO meant the chief executive officer was seriously considering disposal of his division. What form that sale took was immaterial. The fact they were even thinking about selling off his business unit could ruin everything!

"You caught me a little off guard there, Alberto," Douglas responded after a long pause while he regained his composure. "A possible IPO comes as a real surprise. When did this idea hatch?"

"I don't know how long the idea has been germinating, but they just brought me into the discussion yesterday. I know John George has always been impressed with the potential for that software and he feels the current stock market fascination with technology stocks might make this a good time to divest. He thinks we might be able to get up to a couple billion dollars."

"Well, it's certainly good to hear he's thinking of selling for positive reasons," Douglas ventured.

"Yeah. But he thinks there may be only a small window of opportunity. That's why he wants to discuss it at the special meeting of the board of directors on Friday," Alberto explained.

"This coming Friday? You're talking about three days from now?" Douglas clarified with a mixture of surprise and horror.

"Yes. John George feels he needs the support of the board before he sets the wheels in motion. He's asked me to make it the first item on the agenda."

That was a problem, Douglas instantly realized. If discussion of an IPO for Solutions was to be the first thing they considered, that meant Mortimer was squeezing any decision to move forward onto the meeting agenda before Earnest Gottingham became a voting director. Was this one last poke at The Organization before Mortimer accepted defeat?

"I thought the special meeting on Friday was called expressly to reorganize the board," Douglas probed tentatively.

"Yeah, that was the original plan. But John George wants to give the outgoing board an opportunity to make a legacy decision. Something they can all be proud of in the future and help soften the blow of their dismissal from the board. You know how John George likes to make sure departing directors, management or employees leave with a positive feeling about the company," Ferer said with a tone suggesting he perhaps didn't feel the same.

"Well, I'm not sure I see why there's such haste in making such an important decision. I've only had about six months to get this ship sailing. By the way, Alberto. No offense, but why has John George asked you to carry the ball on this call? I'm a little surprised he didn't phone me himself," Douglas said, showing a tinge of anger.

"Apologies, Douglas. I should have told you that up front. John George has been in and out of the office quite a bit lately. Seems he's not yet fully recovered from that cancer. Today he's out of the office, but he wanted to give you a heads up that Wilma Willingsworth will start working with your financial controller immediately. She intends to get the financials and balance sheet cleaned up so they can discuss the current picture with the board.

"He also asked me to invite you to make a presentation at the meeting," Ferer continued. "You won't be able to stay for the vote because you're not a director, but he'd like you to make a thirty-minute presentation. You can present the pros and cons of a spin-off. He'll leave it entirely up to you. I just need a PowerPoint from you by tomorrow so I can get it out with the agenda."

Somewhat placated, Douglas tried to quickly assess the risks to his other plans and decided he needed a little more perspective. "Who else will present on the IPO?"

"Wilma will present the financials. She'll deal with your current profit projections, tax implications, impact on the corporate balance sheet, all the financial stuff. I'll cover regulatory issues, the mechanics of an IPO and stock exchange listing requirements," Ferer recited.

After they clarified a few more preparation details, Alberto sympathized with the unreasonably short window to prepare but said he knew Douglas would ace the presentation Friday – whatever direction he favored.

Resisting his first inclination to press the speed-dial for another call, Douglas paused. This was too important to rush. He'd do some more research and think through this latest wrinkle. Particularly, he'd really like to know what else Mortimer had up his sleeve.

Fifty-Eight

Multima Supermarkets headquarters, Atlanta, Georgia.
Tuesday November 1, 2016

Dieter Lehren finally connected with his counterpart, Ricky Technori, the technology leader for Multima Solutions. As he strode into her office suite, Suzanne assessed that he was not at all comfortable. His shoulders slumped, his forehead looked creased with worry lines, and his usually sparkling blue eyes were bloodshot.

"I'm reluctant to ask how it's going," she opened with a welcoming smile.

"And I'm hesitant to share the status with you," he replied with a half-hearted effort at a grin. "The situation couldn't be much bleaker. I finally connected with Technori. He was working from home. Apparently, he's been shunted to the sidelines. When he approached Whitfield about a fix for the backdoor problem on the software, he learned that Whitfield knew all about it. Didn't consider it a priority, he said. Then, rather than authorizing Technori to start working on a solution to fix the problem immediately, he sent him home. Told him to do some project planning to ascertain the total expense and time required."

"Disheartening," Suzanne said. "That leaves it all up to you."

"Yeah, we can't count on any help from Solutions at all. But it gets worse. Technori discovered one copy of the master software is missing. When he poked around in their system, he found the missing copy was sent to someone in Russia. Wait for it. Sent to this Russian by Whitfield. Despite some amateurish efforts to cover his tracks, he left a clear electronic trail."

"Oh, no!" Suzanne gasped as the implications set in.

"Yeah, Technori felt the same way. He was mortified anyone could do something like that. In the wrong hands, this software has the potential to cost the global economy trillions of dollars. Hell, it could even bring down the entire global banking system!" Dieter exclaimed.

"Where do we go from here?" Suzanne wondered.

"I discussed our dilemma with Technori. He's given it a lot of thought. Apparently, he knows an ex-navy guy in Maryland who worked in systems intelligence. They're the folks who wage cyber espionage and warfare for the Feds. Ricky thinks this guy could write some code to blow up the copy in Russia," Lehren told her.

"Tell me more," Suzanne said as she leaned forward with keen interest.

"According to Technori, this guy can write code that causes a copy of the master to implode and destroy the data file when the Russian downloads automatic updates to the software. It would wipe clear the entire database," he added.

"Any idea how long this might take?"

"Writing the code isn't very long, maybe fifty hours of programming. The complication we have here is a need to not just eliminate that copy in the hands of the Russian; we also have to detect if any additional copies were made and where they reside. That will take some work. Then we'll have to develop a worm to work its way to those sites in the nanosecond before the entire database blows up. The worm will infect the other copies and destroy them when someone tries to open the files," Dieter explained. "We'll probably need a week."

We don't have a week," Suzanne responded without hesitation as she watched him wince. "We've got until Thursday midnight. Let's send the jet to pick up this guy in Maryland. We need to get him here as quickly as possible, so I'll ask Eileen to coordinate everything with you. Let's bring in Technori too.

"Have a chat with him today. Let him know we have a place for him here. If he's working from home these days, Whitfield probably won't miss him. We have to get this done by Thursday midnight, and I'm counting on you to get us there, Dieter," she said as she rose from her chair to signal the end of their discussion.

As she called in Eileen to describe her mission, Suzanne felt a rush of adrenaline. There certainly was something decidedly stimulating about playing games with incredibly high stakes, she thought. A gal just might become comfortable operating at this altitude.

Fifty-Nine

Multima Solutions headquarters, Miami, Florida.
Thursday November 3, 2016

"I don't like the smell of it," Douglas Whitfield told Earnest Gottingham. As soon as he received his copy of the board of directors' information package, he noticed the subtle changes to the agenda. After pouring himself another cup of strong coffee at his desk, he had quickly assessed the dangers and dialed the president of Venture Capital Inc.

"It's a little different than we expected," Gottingham concurred. "What do you think they're trying to do?"

"They've moved the question of an IPO for Multima Solutions to the top of the agenda. That's good. The current board will decide, and you can influence four or five of them. It's the wording of the discussion item that waves a red flag for me.

"Look at what they say: 'Discuss all options for Multima Solutions – Initial Public Offering, Sale, Windup, or Status Quo'. Why would they suddenly add a suggestion to close us down completely?" Douglas asked with apprehension.

"Do you think Mortimer might be aware of the backdoor issue with the software?" Earnest Gottingham wondered.

"Oh, he knows about it already. I doubt he has the technical expertise to appreciate the implications, though. It was he who let me know it was there and needed to be fixed. He was very casual about it," Douglas explained.

"But I think there may be some significance to the order of presenters," Gottingham pointed out. "I see they lead off with your presentation, knowing you'll paint a glowing picture for an eventual IPO. The CFO, Willingsworth, follows you. She paints a picture of the financial pros and cons. Mortimer is last. If winding down the operation is one of the discussion points, wouldn't it be logical to expect him to make that case?" Earnest asked.

"I reached exactly the same conclusion. But I doubt he'll make a strong case. Remember, it was his idea to reorganize Solutions and charge me with marketing the new software package. I guess that he'll go through the motions but do it in a way that makes one of the other options appear more appealing – status quo or IPO."

"He invited the other two division presidents, too. What do you make of that?" Gottingham probed.

"Yeah, that's curious. None of us can vote on any of the proposals. Ferer already told me I wouldn't even be there for the vote on Solutions. It seems like he's bringing them all that way just to hear the discussion about Solutions and then meet the new director. But there's no cocktail reception after the meeting or any sort of meet and greet," Douglas mused.

"Here's my guess at his strategy. I think he's going to follow your recommendation. You plan to tell the board that an IPO in 2018 will probably generate the best return for Multima. Wilma Willingsworth will almost certainly reach the same conclusion from the data she included in her presentation. Mortimer's the only one who doesn't have any presentation materials. With his political skills, I expect he'll recommend the board support a recommendation that management begins preparation for a spin-off in 2018," Gottingham said.

"You're probably right. But what if he's already got an offer from somebody? Or an investment banker has convinced him that it's better to move right now? Has Mareno made any progress on funding a buyout right away if we need to act quickly?" Douglas worried aloud.

"Yeah. Good news on that front. He's got the folks in Singapore and Europe onside for a hundred million each. Plus, I managed to get a loan commitment from a German bank for five hundred million. With Mareno's two hundred, we're just one hundred short of a billion. That's the low end of Willingsworth's estimated valuation for the division. We should easily be able to raise the other hundred in the coming months, well before they're ready to move." Gottingham replied.

"When do you arrive?" Douglas asked.

"Ferer suggested I plan to be at the office about eleven o'clock. He thought the Multima Solutions issue would be done by then. They'll vote on the new board structure next. Then they make me a director right after."

"Okay. Keep your cell phone on in case I need to reach you. And make sure Mareno knows we need him reachable in case that wily old fox has a surprise card in his hand," Douglas said as they signed off.

That reminded him of his last phone conversation with Mareno. Douglas hadn't yet contacted that Weissel girl in Chicago to 'make nice'. Now would be a very good time to mend that relationship. Plus, a weekend with her in a bed in Martinique would be a fantastic way to celebrate this coming weekend.

Sixty

Multima Corporation headquarters, Fort Myers, Florida.
Friday November 4, 2016

It was almost like a little parade in the sky. Separate Multima jets carrying the three division presidents lined up among a half-dozen other planes all planning to land about eight-fifteen in the morning at Page Field in Fort Myers. They all shared the same purpose: arrive at Multima headquarters by eight-forty-five for a special meeting of the board of directors. As they touched down, separated by thirty-second intervals, one followed the other to the terminal dedicated exclusively to private aircraft. They parked in an orderly row beside each other within yards of the building. Sally-Ann Bureau was there to greet each arrival and point them to a waiting limousine.

There were three separate cars. John George had asked Sally-Ann to arrange that only one division president traveled in each car. That allowed every director the opportunity to chat with a division president during the fifteen-minute ride to headquarters in downtown Fort Myers. After elevators whisked the arriving executives and directors to the fourth floor, a receptionist guided them to the meeting room where John George was waiting to greet and welcome each guest to the meeting personally. Wearing his most charming smile and most expensive Armani suit, John George felt he presented the appropriate image of a vibrant and successful chief executive officer.

He certainly didn't feel that way, though. The side effects from the new treatments had flared up again during the night. For hours, he tossed and turned trying to find a way to get comfortable. His legs cramped uncomfortably for minutes at a time. Hydration didn't seem to help, and the cramping seemed to move around. From a sharp pain in one calf, it would suddenly spread to his feet or move higher to his thigh. It was confounding and left him drained and dispirited. But he was determined that no one at the meeting would detect his misery. The show must go on.

Douglas Whitfield was assigned to the last of the three cars. Mortimer knew this made sure he would be the last person to greet before the meeting began. Division presidents always deferentially followed directors as John George trained them they must, so he was prepared.

"Douglas, it's so good to see you again," John George enthused as he grasped the offered hand of his division president. Then with a practiced movement, he put his other arm around Douglas' shoulder and shifted their direction away from the group. Continuing to grip his hand, he guided him towards a vacant corner of the room, speaking as they moved.

"Sorry I have to do this at the last minute," he said, still with his arm around Whitfield's shoulder. "I want you to go ahead with your presentation as planned. And I'm sure you'll do a great job. But I want you to know that I'll be recommending we hold off on a decision.

"I have to let the board of directors know about the backdoor problem," John George continued. "I understand it hasn't been corrected after all these months. It's a great liability for the corporation. I know you can fix it, but I'll position it with the board that if we don't have it done by the end of the year, we need to consider closing your business unit. It's that serious," John George said softly, then watched for his division president's reaction.

Whitfield stiffened as he heard the news. John George could feel it with his arm still draped around his shoulder. Then, Douglas quickly shrugged off his arm and turned to face him directly. John George was taken aback by the fire in his eyes as his division president said, "If that's the way it's going to be, I need some time. I think I might have a buyer for the division. You're right, the issue is a serious one. But we can fix it. However, if you take that tact with the board, dozens of other companies will soon know we have an issue. Our market credibility could be destroyed. Let me see if the potential buyer might make an offer quickly," Whitfield said, barely concealing his anger.

Coolly, John George looked him directly in the eye and said, "Fifteen minutes. I'll tell them an emergency came up and delay discussion for fifteen minutes. Talk to your potential buyer and let me know if they're serious. We'll decide where to go with it from there."

After Whitfield scampered from the room to make his call, Mortimer took his seat at the head of the table as a signal for the others to do the same. A moment or two later, he explained the circumstances.

"Thank you all for attending this special meeting. I know several of you had to modify other plans, and I sincerely appreciate your accommodation on such short notice. Our initial subject is Multima Solutions, and Douglas Whitfield is our first presenter on the agenda. Unfortunately, he just let me know of an emergency he needs to address. I agreed to delay the start of our discussions about Solutions for fifteen minutes.

"Maybe I could ask Suzanne and James to each give us a brief informal overview about how things are going in their divisions this month. I know you're both unprepared and apologize for putting you on the spot like this. But please take just five minutes or so each to give us some highlights of what is going on in your business units. Suzanne, perhaps we can start with you."

Suzanne confidently moved to the front of the room and started. Even John George was a little surprised at how quickly she fully captured the attention of the board. With short precise sentences, expressive hand gestures and colorful descriptions, she condensed performance numbers and strategic objectives into a story of success from every perspective.

After precisely ten minutes, Suzanne returned to her place at the table as James Fitzgerald took his turn.

As usual, the Financial Services leader was equally well prepared. He needed only five or six minutes to reassure the board that his team too was humming on all cylinders as they matched projected revenues with existing products and were well ahead of schedule with the launch of their new home mortgage business.

With a sense of satisfaction, John George permitted himself a tiny smile as he wondered how well prepared his president of the Solutions division would be when he returned.

Sixty-One

"The bastard figured it out. He's giving us the squeeze," Douglas said into his cell phone as soon as he was a respectable distance from the building and close to the sounds of the river. Seeking privacy, he was unaware that he was standing in almost the exact spot Howard Knight stood to make his calls of desperation a few months earlier.

"He pulled me aside to give me a heads up that he was going to divulge the backdoor access issue with the software. He fucking well knows that he'll severely damage the goods if he tells the directors about it. But the bastard's ready to do it anyway. He's trying to force our hand," Douglas seethed.

"Clever," was all that Earnest Gottingham said immediately. After thinking about it for a few seconds, he fished for perspective. "Is it possible he's just trying to knock you off balance for the presentation? Scare you a little bit to get you off your ass and fix the issue?"

"No. He was clearly setting a trap for us. I see it now. The subtle changes to the agenda. The waiting cars at Page Field. The order his assistant selected for each limo to depart and arrive. Allowing me only fifteen minutes to come up with an offer. He's meticulously planned this to put us in a spot where we have to shit or get off the pot," Douglas replied, still angry.

"What do you think we should do?" Gottingham asked.

"We know the CFO has established a minimum value of a billion for the division. But, if I remember correctly, you told me this morning we only have access to nine hundred million. So that has to be our highest price, right?" Douglas clarified.

"Right. Of course, I'll have to talk with Mareno. But assuming he's for it, that's the most we have available. I think we can expect Mortimer's not willing to extend any favorable payment terms," Gottingham replied sarcastically.

"Well let's do this," Douglas proposed. "When I go back to the meeting, I'll tell him we've got an interested buyer prepared to offer a half billion. He'll never accept that offer, but it will show we're serious and buy me some time to negotiate with the bastard. Meanwhile, you can talk with Mareno and get his support up to a billion."

Back up on the fourth floor, Douglas tracked down Sally-Ann Bureau. She agreed immediately to fetch Mortimer from the meeting. She almost appeared to be expecting the request, he noted sardonically.

The conversation in the privacy of John George Mortimer's office was short.

"I'm really sorry you don't have confidence we'll fix the software defect, John George. I realize I should have treated it as a higher priority. But I'm not willing to see the product destroyed by this minor oversight. I know you won't be happy to hear this, but I went directly to VCI. Ernie Gottingham and I are old friends from college," he revealed and watched for a reaction before continuing.

"When you sent out the meeting materials this week, I suspected you might have something like this in mind. So, I felt him out about the possibility of VCI buying the division. He agreed to think about it. I just spoke to him, and he understands my dismay about your intention to reveal the temporary problem. Like me, he doesn't want to see the Solutions brand sullied by the divulgence of one temporary weakness," Douglas explained.

"That's an interesting approach," John George agreed. "What sort of price is VCI prepared to pay?" he queried in an even tone.

"Gottingham's willing to pay five hundred million and sign a purchase offer when he arrives later this morning, with a caveat that no information be divulged about our temporary weakness with the software, either publicly or privately," Douglas said.

"Not enough," Mortimer said as he rose from his chair. "You know very well that Wilma will be advising the board the value is somewhere between one and two billion dollars."

As he stepped around from behind his desk, he added, "I could be insulted by such a lowball offer, but I'll choose to ignore it instead."

"I realize it's on the low side, John George," Douglas replied as he rose as well. "But that's apparently Gottingham's limit without the approval of his board. I told him he'd need to come up a bit, but he has to talk with his people. He's doing that right now. Can we consider this? Will you agree to take a break after Wilma's and my presentations? That way, I can get back to him after he's had a chance to talk with some of his board members. He assured me he can bring the amount up, but he can't do it on his own."

"There will be a fifteen-minute break after Wilma's presentation. Use your time wisely," Mortimer said in response.

Sixty-Two

A meeting room, Multima Headquarters, Fort Myers, Florida.
Friday November 4, 2016

Mortimer's discreet adjustment to his tie as he entered the room behind Whitfield signaled to Suzanne Simpson that it was game on. The negotiations were about to get serious.

Despite the high stakes, the division president of Multima Solutions performed masterfully. She was intrigued. Whitfield showed no stress at all as he carefully chose the words that accompanied his PowerPoint slides. He used humor and self-deprecation to relax his audience and hold their attention. An impartial observer might see only a polished and articulate executive executing his role with aplomb.

But she detected the nuances. First, there was a casual insertion of the phrase 'absent any issues' when he covered the glowing sales forecasts for the coming five years. Later, with a shrug of his shoulders, he referred to 'software code tweaks' in the same sentence as 'routine updates' as possible risks to achieving the upward climb of profits pictured on his graphs.

Earlier in the presentation, she heard him highlight an endorsement from Bank of The Americas. She couldn't be sure. Was he not aware the CEO there had already shut down the project even before John George's courtesy alert? Or was he lying with conviction? Either way, it would be easy for the directors around the table to believe they were about to vote on a product that had the potential to earn billions of dollars for Multima's coffers over time.

After regaling the directors for precisely his allotted thirty minutes, Whitfield closed his pitch with a perfect balance.

"I hope you'll agree we have a strong story to tell the market. Suzanne's engineers over at Multima designed this software package brilliantly. Ours are tweaking it to make it even better. And the value it brings companies looking for proven cybersecurity is extraordinary. We can reasonably forecast five to ten years of growing sales and profits for Multima.

"But should the board decide to sell Multima Solutions for strategic reasons, we think the optimum time to do that would be in late 2018. At that point, we can command the highest market multiple on some very impressive operating profits. An earlier sale would probably fetch a much lower price. Later than 2018, prospective buyers might focus more on Solutions' pipeline of new software products to justify their purchase price. I don't know yet how much potential that pipeline will carry.

"As a proud Multima employee, I'll work diligently to execute whatever strategy you decide most appropriate," Douglas Whitfield concluded with an expression of humility and grace.

Meanwhile, Suzanne masked her contempt with a cough that allowed her to cover part of her face. She noticed her knees were trembling. Today's charade was her idea, and she recognized that her opponent was even more formidable than expected.

Her unease grew as Whitfield handled questions from the board. They were clearly impressed with both his message and delivery. More than one director complimented the division president for delivering such an informative presentation before asking his or her question. Even more disconcerting, they seemed to be buying into his message and recommendations. There were no challenges about either the forecasts or his recommended timing for an IPO.

As Wilma Willingsworth approached the head of the table to deliver her message, Suzanne took a long sip from the bottled water on the table. She knew how much it helped her manage stress.

Wilma's delivery matched Whitfield's in quality. There were many good reasons the CFO was considered among the fifty most influential business-women in America, Suzanne thought. It was nothing short of amazing to watch how she enthralled the directors with her command of the numbers and their implications.

And her political skills at least matched, and maybe surpassed, Whitfield's. She didn't overtly contradict his forecasts, but she skillfully raised doubts when she reminded the directors how fickle buyers of technology could be. Suzanne noted that more than one director nodded affirmation with her contention that it was unlikely the software giants would sit idly by while Solutions carved out a sizeable share of the market.

"Microsoft, SAP or Oracle have mammoth resources to build a competing product and already have inroads with corporations globally," she said. "We must be mindful that it will be necessary to revisit all forecasts as one or more of those giants develop a competing offering."

As expected, she estimated the current value of Multima Solutions and suggested a price range of one to two billion dollars would be realistic. On the question of timing, she was less precise than most directors hoped. Her comments implied that she might prefer to see a sale sooner than later, but she didn't make a specific timing recommendation as Whitfield had. Instead, she thought it most prudent for the board to authorize preparation for a sale or IPO now and for management to act when the circumstances seemed most opportune.

With such a rather mushy conclusion, directors' questions were much more challenging. Why could she not be more precise about timing? What financial impact would the entry of powerful competitors have on pricing, sales, and net profits? Could she establish a narrower range of value?

John George let the questions run longer than the allotted fifteen minutes. He was apparently comfortable with Wilma's skillful stickhandling and maintained his impassive facial expression as he listened intently to both the questions and Wilma's answers. Suzanne hoped she was masking her trepidation just as successfully.

Wilma handled the questions well and with poise. She used an ingenious technique of providing just enough additional detail to satisfy the questioner, but not enough to box her into a single position that might be difficult to modify later. In Suzanne's mind, Wilma was the clear winner of the first round.

After glancing at his watch, Mortimer noted they were running a bit behind schedule and apologized for not keeping the proceedings on track as efficiently as usual. But he thought the directors could all use a break. The meeting would resume in fifteen minutes, he said as he stood from his chair at the head of the table.

Suzanne watched as he left the room. Moments later, she saw Whitfield excuse himself from a conversation with a director and also step out. Round two was about to begin.

Sixty-Three

John George Mortimer's office, Fort Myers, Florida.
Friday November 4, 2016

"You did a very nice job with your presentation," John George opened. "Even I learned a bit more about your operations over there. But we're not here to talk about presentations, are we? Did you have a chance to connect with your people?"

"I spoke with Gottingham. He was just touching down and expects to arrive in about twenty-five minutes. He asked if we could wait until he gets here."

"No. I won't delay our directors further. Their time is valuable. I thought I made that clear when we spoke before the session started. This coffee break is the deadline," he said tersely, starting to rise from his seat.

"Just a minute, John George. I'm not wasting anyone's time. I'm confident Gottingham is serious. He just asked for a little more time. He'd like to present a revised offer to you himself," Douglas Whitfield protested.

"Fine. Let's get him on the line, and we'll talk," John George responded calmly as he passed over the handset from his desk. "Just activate the speaker, please."

It took only two rings after Whitfield keyed in the number before they heard the greeting, "This is Earnest Gottingham speaking."

"Earnest, this is Douglas Whitfield, and I'm here with John George Mortimer. We're on a speaker. I relayed your request, and he's reluctant to wait until you arrive. Do you mind if we chat while you travel?" Whitfield started politely.

"Hello, John George. How are things going?" Gottingham replied.

"Let's pass on the small talk, Earnest. I appreciate you taking our call, but I'm a little pressed. The current board of directors is waiting. If you are seriously considering an offer to buy Solutions, I'd like to hear an acceptable offer now. If you're not comfortable with that, let's just put it on the shelf for a later date, and we'll conclude this meeting so we can get to your appointment on the new board."

"Okay, John George. I get it. You'd like us to show you the money. I talked with the most important folks on my board after Douglas called this morning.

We're prepared to offer seven hundred and fifty, with the same conditions I explained to Douglas earlier."

"That's not enough, Earnest. And you know it. My CFO thinks we should accept no less than one-point-five billion. That's the amount she just confirmed to the directors, and it's the same amount she included in the briefing documents we shared with you as a courtesy. I can't consider your offer a serious one," John George insisted.

"Douglas, a question for you. Are you prepared to put your job on the line for those projections you shared with us?" Gottingham asked theatrically.

"Of course," he replied, winking to John George. "I'll be the first to suggest you fire my ass if Solutions doesn't meet and exceed those numbers."

"Well, John George. If Whitfield has that level of confidence, I think I can get the support of my people to get closer to the minimum number you were hoping for. But we can't quite get there. If you're prepared to respect the conditions and accept nine hundred million, I'm confident I can get the support of my people," Gottingham postured.

"It's not enough," John George replied. "Let's agree to disagree on this one. I need to get back to the meeting."

"This isn't a one-way negotiation, John George," Gottingham interjected, his voice rising slightly. "We, too, have some leverage. Suzanne Simpson. When exactly do you intend to share with your board of directors that your division president at Supermarkets is actually a daughter you abandoned for almost fifty years? How do you think those nice citizens from the Midwest might react when they hear that?

"And, do you ever wonder what CBNN might report if they learn about those frequent trips to Latin America? Or, perhaps the news that you're undergoing treatment for cancer again? We've been patient John George. Now, you're going to be patient. I'll make another call. I'll try to get a bit more from my board. In return, I need you to hold off on your presentation and any decision on a sale," Gottingham pressed.

"Okay. I'll wait for a half hour. That's all the time I'm willing to give you," John George replied firmly.

"Doug, can you call me back on a private phone? I may need to link you into another conversation I'm going to have. I might need your expertise to justify any increase they might be prepared to consider."

Sixty-Four

A meeting room at Multima, Fort Myers, Florida.
Friday November 4, 2016

"We'll need to modify the schedule today. I apologize for the inconvenience, but there has been a sudden and unexpected development with Multima Solutions," John George said as the meeting resumed. Pointing to the vacant chair, he added, "Douglas is on the line with our friends from Venture Capital Inc. Apparently, they are seriously interested in making an offer to buy Multima Solutions outright.

"They just made a verbal offer to me during the break. That's the reason I was a little late returning. However, the offer was too low. I won't waste your time discussing it because it was well below the valuations Wilma suggested might be reasonable. I've given them a half-hour to prepare a final offer for your consideration," Mortimer said as he looked around the room, reading the faces of participants. He took a gulp of water from his glass to give the directors time to absorb the news, then he continued.

"In the meantime, I'd like us to do three things. First, I'll need to leave the room to prepare for discussion of their revised offer, if there is one. I'd like Alberto, Wilma, Suzanne, and James to join me for that discussion. You know we like to make monumental decisions with the entire management team involved," he said with a grin. "I've asked Sally-Ann to get Edward Hadley, our vice president of corporate and public affairs, to come in.

"He's been working on a new video to use at major fundraisers and other events our businesses support locally. It takes about twenty minutes and we originally planned to show it to you at the end of the day. I hope you won't mind this slight adjustment as we deal with the Solutions issue," he said, looking around the room for acceptance.

It wouldn't be immediate, he wryly noted when a director from New York pointedly asked if there weren't more important subjects they should tackle in the meantime. It was the same director who so blindly defended Wendal Randall even as he sat in an FBI holding cell, he remembered. John George found her persistent, barely concealed jibes at inopportune times a little annoying, but knew every director would study his reaction intently. So, he paused, took a deep breath, and patiently said, "Of course, Elizabeth. I deeply respect the value of everyone's time. Is there a specific subject you would like to raise while the management team is out of the room?"

Embarrassed, the woman sputtered a reply that she had nothing specific in mind, while the remaining directors studiously rustled their papers in an apparent attempt to avoid adding to her discomfort.

John George reacted quickly to assure there was no damage to their working relationship. "I value you holding my toes to the coals for productive use of the board's time Elizabeth, and if there are any new issues we need to escalate to the agenda today, please let me know at the next break. I promise to add them. Do any other directors have concerns about our schedule for the next couple hours?" he asked with all the patience he could muster.

Apparently satisfied there were no further objections, he added one more comment before leaving the room. "Sally-Ann has also ordered lunch. They've agreed to deliver it a shade earlier than planned. Why don't you all enjoy lunch after the video? That should give us adequate time to deal with Solutions."

Along with the other direct reports, Suzanne proceeded down the hallway to John George Mortimer's office anxious to compare notes and plot any new steps in the unfolding saga. The adrenaline rush of a few days earlier had now evaporated, she noted after a glance at the other grim faces. It was apparent they all now had some doubts about the strategy.

Sixty-Five

Outside Multima Headquarters, Fort Myers, Florida.
Friday, November 4, 2016

"Nine hundred is all I can do," Mareno said after Gottingham shared the results of discussions so far. "We can't bring in the Russians. The Europeans are maxed out. The Asians are reluctant participants at even one hundred, and the guys in Mexico tell me they're looking for ways to get their money out of America, not invest more. If Mortimer won't accept that, let's move on."

There was a long pause as both Whitfield and Gottingham waited to see if the other would proceed first. Finally, Douglas decided to carry the ball.

"It may not be that easy," he started timidly. "I know Earnest will do his best to win approval for my appointment as CEO. But we should assume Mortimer has already told the board we've made an offer. If we don't move forward, they'll want to know why. Mortimer will tell them about our current defect, and they'll immediately agree to suspend all sales until we get it fixed.

"I'll lose Bank of The Americas, and it could be months before we're ready to start selling again. With Mortimer afflicted with cancer once again, the board will surely want to move sooner rather than later. When it comes time to vote on a successor to Mortimer, I'll be out of favor. There's little likelihood we'll get me elected to the CEO role," Douglas explained patiently.

"That's exactly right, Giancarlo," Gottingham piped in. "The composition of the new board will make it almost impossible to get him elected if we fail with Solutions. All the time, money, and sweat equity we've put into this over the past several years will be wasted. We'll be left with the quarterly dividends from Multima and not much else. If we can find a way to do the deal and buy Solutions right now, before word of the defect gets out, we can make untold billions."

"We know he's going to favor Suzanne Simpson for the CEO role. He's already subtly giving signals throughout the company," Douglas piled on. "We'll always be very limited in how much we can control Multima without the CEO's power. In a publicly traded company, any subordinate position limits us. I agree. We need to find a way to improve our offer. I know you don't easily change direction, but the real money in this deal is getting Solutions, not trying to control the entire corporation."

"Doesn't it strike you as odd that Mortimer's willing to sell out the rest of the business community for a billion or two?" Mareno asked pensively.

"I admit it's out of character," Douglas conceded. "But look at it this way. The guy has just found out he's dying. You saw that oncologist's report we received. He's probably got less than a year. Maybe he just doesn't care about the other guys. Let them fend for themselves, you know? Selling Solutions at this stage makes his succession planning a little cleaner. It puts money on the Multima balance sheet immediately. He goes out with a final hurrah."

"Maybe. I'm not so sure. I know you young bucks are excited about the potential to exploit this technology issue. I understand there are potentially billions for us, and I like the idea of outflanking the Ruskies after the way they've been treating us lately. But I'm not so sure this deal is doable. I'm surely not going back to any of the boys again," he said emphatically.

Conversation continued for a few more minutes, with Mareno pushing back on every suggestion either Gottingham or Whitfield proposed. They even tried to get his agreement just to give more security to the German bank and ask them to increase the loan. That didn't work either. Finally, in desperation, Douglas decided to throw out a football-style 'Hail Mary' play as a last gasp.

"There's one tool we could use, if you can agree," Douglas ventured. "There's the equity. If we buy Solutions, we don't need Multima, and we don't need an equity position in the corporation. What if we give up our equity?" he asked.

There was a long pause. Both Douglas and Gottingham knew the next person to speak had to be Mareno – no matter how long it might take. Clearly, he was having trouble making a decision. Douglas imagined that he was sorely tempted by the potential billions they could harvest from unsuspecting companies by exploiting the software vulnerability.

On the other hand, he knew that Mareno had craved *respectability* his entire life. It was he who convinced the rest of The Organization that their future demanded respectability. They needed to infiltrate and control well-regarded legitimate companies to survive and thrive in the long-term. Making a choice would be agonizing for him, Douglas knew.

Finally, after several minutes passed, Mareno said quietly, "Okay. If you have to. Use the equity – but only the equity. I won't use one cent of cash if we're giving up our share of ownership. And, Douglas, I'm only doing this for you. Don't disappoint me."

Once Mareno abruptly left the line, the conniving pair took the few remaining minutes to plot their final desperate strategy to confront their most daunting opponent.

Sixty-Six

John George Mortimer's office, Fort Myers, Florida.
Friday November 4, 2016

She was impressed most by his calm demeanor throughout. From the moment Suzanne first suggested her elaborate scheme to expunge Venture Capital Inc. and The Organization from Multima, Mortimer had shown little emotion. Alberto reported that he had just a flicker of amusement, or perhaps even admiration, in his eyes as she laid out the plan on their call.

Alberto Ferer also admitted that he felt perspiration at least one time as they worked through all the intricate legal details and Wilma Willingsworth fretted about every aspect of the idea each step of the way, worried about both her future and reputation. But John George always urged patience, and merely suggested they try different solutions each time they encountered an obstacle.

In those few short days, she learned more about the character of her colleagues, and her father, than she had ever imagined possible. And she liked what she saw. Equally disturbed as she about the infiltration of organized crime into their company, each of them was still concerned foremost about 'doing the right thing'.

For what they presumed to be the final act in their high stakes play, John George had dismissed all from his office but Suzanne. "I don't really care what they think when they find you here for their revised offer. I want you to do the deed," he said with a crooked grin.

As it turned out, neither showed any visible reaction to her sitting in a chair at the large circular table in John George's office. Nor did they waste any time with pleasantries.

"We're not able to improve the offer, John George," Gottingham said as soon as they were seated. "That's the highest my board will authorize us to go."

"Well, I guess this will be a short conversation, gentlemen," Mortimer responded without hesitation. "I made it very clear we need to be around the mid-point of Wilma's evaluation before I present anything to the board."

"We tried, John George. I even got Douglas to pledge his job and soul again," Gottingham said with a carefree grin. "Our people can't see the value over nine hundred. Despite the excellent selling features of the software, our people see too many risks. They think it'll take ten years or more to get back our investment, and ten years is just too long in the technology world.

"They're prepared to wire transfer nine hundred million to Multima's bank account today – even before we sign an agreement. We'll work on a handshake, and we can finalize the details later. You can still show your board a nine hundred-million-dollar boost to the balance sheet, and relieve any anxiety you have about its marketability. We think it's a good deal," Gottingham insisted.

"You're right," John George responded quietly. "I have some concerns about marketability at the moment, but Suzanne's technology people assure me we can ultimately fix the vulnerabilities. If we don't accept your offer, I think we can still realize acceptable returns on our investment over time. But it would certainly be nice to see those returns more quickly."

"We tried everything," Gottingham emphasized. "Douglas is a very persuasive guy. He gave it his best shot with the chairman of our board. The problem is not just some skepticism; we just don't have any additional sources of capital we can go to right now.

"We're tapped out at the bank, and none of our partners is prepared to inject new capital today. With the elections next week and an uncertain economy, we just couldn't raise one dollar more than the nine hundred million we offered," Gottingham repeated, shaking his head.

"Is the equity position sacred?" Suzanne asked.

"You mean our preferred shares in Multima?" Gottingham asked with a look of surprise.

"Yes. If you were prepared to redeem some of the preferred shares you hold, it wouldn't be such a stretch to get to the price we're looking for," Suzanne said. "It could offset your short-term capital shortage, and we could always talk about reissuing replacement preferred shares later."

Gottingham's body language suggested only mild interest at first, even though it appeared he might also be trying to stifle his enthusiasm. Gottingham and Suzanne parried back and forth for a few minutes longer, exploring different scenarios. Gradually, she concluded that he might only be going through the motions of stalling and prolonging the negotiations.

After a gentle nudge, he finally agreed to go back to his chairman one more time to see if it might be possible to make an offer using cash and redemption of shares. He'd need fifteen minutes or so, he suggested. Again, he asked Douglas to join him, just in case the chairman needed expert knowledge only he could provide. Suzanne stifled a smile as she realized their tactics were apparently meant to perpetuate the charade that Douglas was not actually a part of the repulsive outfit.

They returned from their conference outside the building after only ten minutes. Of course, Dan Ramirez had already called to report they were on their way up and the time Gottingham and Whitfield held cell phones to their ears was less than five minutes. He also noted that tracking devices indicated the entire time was spent talking to each other.

John George welcomed them back. Gottingham again acted as spokesman.

"We were able to get support for a little more. But it has some complexity as well," Gottingham started. "Our board is prepared to redeem three hundred million of the Multima preferred shares – about one-third of our total holding. To that, we'll add seven hundred million cash. The maximum amount we will pay is one billion.

"Now, we realize this is still short of Multima's asking price, but we're hopeful the board can accept a valued partner's best offer in good faith," he finished with an air of resignation.

John George refused the offer again. "We made it fairly clear. We're only interested in selling if we can get close to the mid-point of Wilma's evaluation. After all these gyrations, you've only come to the minimum valuation. I'm disappointed. Douglas, what do you think about such a low offer?"

Clearly caught off guard by the unexpected request for an opinion, Douglas at first squirmed in his chair, wrung his hands, then quickly regained his composure.

"Earnest is right," he started. "I heard him trying to persuade his chairman. He gave it all he had. I also shared all the value highlights again from my presentation to the board. But he wouldn't budge. He told Earnest that he thought one billion was too high, but he'd support his judgment if you were prepared to come down to that level in your expectations."

"But that wasn't my question," John George pressed. "I asked for your opinion of such a low offer."

"Right. VCI's offer is lower than any of us would like," Douglas began, adopting the posture of a Multima executive again. "But value is relative. If you go back into the meeting with the board of directors and divulge that we have some temporary unrepaired weaknesses with the software, the current value will plummet. We won't be able to make any sales in the short-term, and the brand will be damaged in the longer-term. It will take years to build the value to the mid-range you seek. The way I see it, Multima is better to accept the billion dollars on offer, or you decide to keep our temporary defect confidential and give us time to fix it. I'm comfortable either way. But those are the only two options I see."

"What do you think, Suzanne?" John George asked, continuing to look directly at Whitfield.

"I think Douglas may be right. Those appear to be the only options. I think Alberto Ferer is also right when he says we have a fiduciary responsibility to advise the board of the software's shortcomings and the potential liability. I know I'm very worried about my legal exposure right now. I think it would be straightforward for shareholders to sue us personally if we don't divulge the information. I think I would be inclined to accept a billion dollars," Suzanne said with a shrug of acceptance.

John George didn't respond for some time. Everyone around the table knew how important it was not to speak next. He masterfully projected the image of a conflicted man wrestling with a monumental decision. But, at the same time, he also projected calm and deliberation, unwilling to be pressured.

"Alright," he said finally. "I'll do it at one billion. But the deal is all equity, no cash. VCI redeems all preferred shares in the corporation in return for ownership of Multima Solutions and all its assets, liabilities, and employees." •

Portraying surprise, Gottingham responded after a few seconds. "Well, we didn't expect *that* negotiating posture! You're asking us to give up our sizeable ownership in Multima to buy Solutions. That's a big shift. I'll have to go back to our board to get their reaction."

"No. You'll make a decision right now, without further delay," John George calmly insisted. "You've had enough time to consult with your board. You must know precisely what their position is, and I've wasted enough of my board's valuable time. Are you ready to surrender equity in exchange for Solutions, or not?"

"We'll do it," Gottingham conceded.

"Fine," John George said as he stood from his chair and offered his hand for Gottingham to shake. "Alberto Ferer has drawn up some documents. He'll be here in just a few minutes to go over them with you. I'm going back to my board to get their approval on the sale. I'll break from the meeting to sign them whenever you, your legal team, and Alberto are satisfied. But I insist it be done today."

"You won't say anything to the board or anyone else about the software fault?" Douglas asked.

"My lips are sealed," John George replied as he stiffly shook Whitfield's hand and left the room with Suzanne.

Her knees still trembling and her adrenaline soaring off the charts, Suzanne followed him down the corridor. His pace was even quicker and his stride more determined than usual. A man on a mission, she thought.

Just before she reached the meeting room, she heard a text alert and glanced at the message. It was the one she was expecting from Dieter Lehren, and the message was cryptic.

Received confirmation of detonation in Russia this morning. Surgery in Miami completed five minutes ago.

Suzanne instantly felt a weight lift from her shoulders. Her adrenaline shot even higher. As she looked up from her telephone, she noticed that John George had already taken his seat at the head of the table. She flashed him a discreet 'thumbs up' and a billion-dollar smile.

Sixty-Seven

John George Immediately called the meeting to order, with a short, but heartfelt, apology for the delay and an announcement that he had accepted an offer from Venture Capital Inc. to buy Multima Solutions. He explained that Alberto Ferer would not be joining them because he was currently finalizing a memorandum of understanding. They'd sign that document if the board of directors authorized him to proceed.

Then, the CEO succinctly outlined the terms of the sale. He emphasized the strategic benefit of narrowing Multima's focus to its core businesses – supermarkets and financial services. He reminded the board of the original rationale for buying the business unit a decade earlier to support the growth and digitization of the supermarkets and the board's decision months earlier to relocate all the Solutions personnel focused on Supermarkets to Suzanne's division in Atlanta.

John George then touched on the uncertainties of technology businesses as Wilma Willingsworth had explained earlier, and avoided any derogatory comments towards either the Solutions division or Venture Capital Inc. His sole veiled reference was to 'avoiding drama and uncertainty' for shareholders as one reason for accepting a price at the low end of the spectrum.

There was no doubt. Every director could do the math. Should they deny him approval to move forward with the deal, John George had the right to put the matter before the preferred shareholders with greater voting rights. He owned almost two-thirds of those shares, so his will would ultimately prevail. However, he had too much respect for his board to play that card in either tone or implication. He took care to weigh every statement before he made it. And he maintained an air of dispassionate objectivity.

When he finished his comments, he invited questions. There were only a few procedural clarifications requested and no questions or comments that suggested opposition or uncertainty. After only a few minutes, he felt the time was right to move forward.

"If there are no further questions," he prefaced, "I'd like to make a motion to vote on the proposal Sally-Ann is now distributing to each of you."

After he saw the document, a board member from Chicago seconded the motion and added his hope that the outcome of the vote would be unanimous. When John George was satisfied everyone had received and read a copy, he asked all those in favor to so indicate. Every hand around the table raised almost in unison. Even those directors who consistently voted with Howard Knight a few months earlier did so without apparent hesitation.

John George acknowledged the positive outcome and advised the board that he would absent himself from the room to sign the documents as soon as Alberto Ferer was ready. In the meantime, he wanted to move forward with the next item on the agenda – reorganization of the board of directors. First, he needed to ask all current directors to resign.

Wilma Willingsworth took careful note of each verbal resignation as they worked their way around the table. She was the last to do so and advised the assembly that Alberto Ferer had already submitted his resignation, in writing, before the meeting started.

"We're going in a new direction," John George began. "We need more diversity, and I'm reducing the size of the board so we can make decisions more quickly. Both will better serve our stakeholders.

"We'll reduce the number of directors to ten. That means I won't be inviting several of you back to the board. I want to thank each of you for your service over the past years and emphasize that I value the contribution each of you has made. If I don't announce your name, I will not be inviting you to join the new board. You're welcome to stay for the remainder of the meeting, but won't be able to vote on the next steps forward. If you choose to leave, Sally-Ann will arrange transportation for you to Page Field or RSW," he offered, referring to both private and public airports in Fort Myers.

"Here are the names of the people I am inviting to join the newly composed board of Multima. There will be five independent directors. Chuck Jones and Cliff Williams, our current directors from the Midwest. Fernando Disputas from Tallahassee, Florida, who is the president of our supermarket employees' union. Warren Wrigletts, a world-renowned economist from New York. And finally, Abduhl Mahinder, the chief executive officer of Bank of The Americas in San Francisco. These will be the five independent directors.

"The following executives of Multima will join or return to the board. Alberto

Ferer, James Fitzgerald, Suzanne Simpson, Wilma Willingsworth, and myself," John George said in a matter-of-fact tone.

"Again, I thank all of you other directors for your valuable service, and invite any former directors who prefer to leave the room to do so now," he added, then noted that no one moved from his or her seat.

"Okay," he continued a moment later with a broad grin. "I see your curiosity overrules any animosity!"

When the burst of laughter stopped, John George continued with his narrative. First, he needed to share information about his current health condition with the board. It was hard to get out the words, and he was certain his emotions were more on display than he would like, but he let them know the prognosis. He was on his last lap around the track. He pointed out that he planned to remain actively engaged in every aspect of the business but realized it was time to choose a successor.

"I'd like to nominate my preferred candidate for the position of chief executive officer now," he said. "I'll entertain nominations from other members of the board of course, but my nominee is Suzanne Simpson, the current president of our Supermarkets division. Are there any other nominations?"

After pausing for a decent interval and glancing around the room to see there were no suggestions, he resumed. "With six directors here today, we have a quorum. Is there someone who will second my motion to appoint Suzanne Simpson our CEO effective January 1, 2017?"

All six hands rose again in unison. John George acknowledged the result and then told them he had something further to add. Pausing for several seconds as he collected his thoughts, he realized he was creating more suspense than desired.

"In addition to offering my congratulations and welcoming Suzanne to her new role, I want to thank all of you who supported my recommendation and agreed she is the person most suited to manage this corporation. I'm pleased to see there is a unanimous consensus that she has proven herself worthy of this position and demonstrated that she can handle the responsibility.

"I should also share with you some information that is more personal, news that I probably should have revealed more openly several years ago. Suzanne Simpson is not only your new CEO, she is also my daughter," he stated. A hush of surprise fell over the room for a moment. Then, John George smiled widely and said, "I can't tell you how happy and proud I am to be her father, and how delighted I am that she will lead this company to its next remarkable level of success."

Sixty-Eight

Guantanamo Bay, Cuba.
Friday November 11, 2016

The last few days had been entirely idle, and Howard Knight realized something was going on. It had been a week since he saw any sign of Wendal Randall. They'd never allowed contact between the two, but his minders had acknowledged openly that Randall was indeed helping them. Finally, one of the female guards who usually showed a little more empathy admitted that Randall, too, had gone. Howard was the last American prisoner in Guantanamo. Only a handful of suspected terrorists made up the remainder of the captive population.

Almost all the interrogation team left as well. Only the chief interrogator remained according to that same guard. Howard brooded throughout the day, confined to his reasonably comfortable cell. Like most Americans, he had spent much of the last few days glued to cable news networks trying to understand what had happened to their country in the presidential elections. He imagined that his own life was about to become more complicated.

That morning his fears were realized. Just before noon, a single guard came to fetch him for a meeting. When they entered the office of the chief interrogator, the man was visibly angry. His face was the color of a red apple. The large vein on the side of his neck was bulging and pulsating far faster than usual. His hair was disheveled, and his hands trembled as he raised a cup of coffee to his lips.

"It's over," he spat out as he slapped his hand hard on the desk. "They're not going to move forward. Those bastards at headquarters are terrified about what's going to happen."

Howard decided it was best just to sit quietly and see what direction this tirade would go. It took only a moment or two.

"The fucking director turned it down. He said there's no possibility of conviction now. The bastard says even he expects to be fired. All the time and money we spent on this. All the great information you provided. All the evil these people have done. They just don't fucking care!" he said with his eyes bulging and lips curled in scorn.

"They told me to honor the deal we made with you. We're to give you a new identity and secure protection just like we promised. But we'll have to sit on any action for a while. Then, when my cowardly superiors think we have a chance of convictions, we'll have to bring you in again, then hide you one more time. It's a royal fuckup," the exasperated interrogator complained vehemently.

"What's later?" Howard asked quietly.

"When's the next election? Or the one after that even?" he replied with scorn.

"I won't do it," Howard said quietly and paused to be sure he had the angry interrogator's attention. "I won't survive four to eight years. No matter where you try to hide me, they'll find out I've cooperated with you. Mareno will redouble his efforts to find me. They'll infiltrate the FBI if they need to, but they'll find me. So, I'm not going into your protection program."

"You just want to stay here in this hell-hole?" the interrogator asked.

"No. You're going to negotiate a new deal for me before your director gets fired," Howard replied calmly. "The new deal starts with an agreement that I don't testify. Ever. You videotaped the hours of interrogation. I saw the little red lights on the cameras lit up all the time we talked.

"You folks will have to find a way to get the videos admitted as evidence when you get around to charging the bad guys – if that ever happens. It's not my problem. It's yours," he stated, then paused to read the interrogator's body language. Satisfied he was still following him, Knight continued.

"I want a new identity just like we agreed. New ID. New passports. Everything new, just like we discussed before. But you're going to release me into the wild with a million dollars cash in small bills and a yacht. Specifically, a Carver yacht, model 34 Coupe.

"Don't grimace now," Howard said in response to the interrogator's reaction. "You're actually going to save the American taxpayers money. I figure you can get me a nice fully equipped Carver yacht for about a half-million. You'll need to spend a few dollars to remove all serial numbers and tracking details. You'll take out the standard GPS and related digital equipment. I'll replace it all with stuff I buy myself. You'll deliver the boat to a secluded harbor in Belize and anchor it offshore there."

"Any other wishful demands?" the interrogator asked sarcastically.

"You'll deliver me to Panama by chopper and provide me with another boat. Just a small one will be okay. But all identifiers will be removed, and there will be no tracking devices. I'll travel to Belize in the smaller craft and abandon it there when I'm done with it. I'll spend whatever time I have left before The Organization finds me sailing the seas," he finished.

As he expected, the chief interrogator calmed down. His signs of distress reduced as he mulled over the proposal he first thought of as absurd. The only sounds in the room were the sounds outside – birds, insects, and the gentle breeze blowing in from the Caribbean Sea.

Finally, he said, "Do I get this right? We get you a new identity, a boat, and a million bucks and you simply disappear somewhere around the equator? No more payments? No more protection?"

"Right. For about what it would cost you to provide me shelter in hiding with personal protection for just a couple years, I'll take my chances on my own. I'll consider us all even," Howard told him. "Why don't you run it up the flagpole?"

The interrogator thought about it some more, shook his head a few times, then stood up to finish their discussion. "No promises. I'll see what I can do, but it will probably take some time. They're up to their asses in alligators in that fucking Washington swamp."

Sixty-Nine

An estate home on Berkeley Lake near Atlanta, Georgia.
Sunday November 20, 2016

It was four days until Thanksgiving, and Suzanne sat on the artfully landscaped patio that spanned the entire rear of her ninety-five hundred square foot estate home. She loved nothing more than to sit there listening to the birds and sounds of a gentle breeze while watching a beautiful Georgia sunset. Here, twenty miles from the heart of Atlanta, she could relax, reflect, and recharge.

With a tinge of regret, she knew this would be the last time she could enjoy a repose for the rest of the year. The next morning, she would start the new drill. Determined to maintain a close connection to her Multima Supermarkets' employees as she transitioned into the role of CEO, she planned to visit every store in the United States and Canada before Christmas. She'd just finalized the exhaustive agenda with her team.

Every day except Thanksgiving, she'd travel to at least three stores during the day, reassuring them of her ongoing support even after she moved into the new role. At the end of each day, the company jet would drop her off at Page Field in Fort Myers. There, a limousine would meet and drive her to John George Mortimer's home where they would have dinner with a different executive from headquarters staff every evening.

John George had recommended this process to help her learn all aspects of his job before she took over on the first of January. They'd do that for two or three hours each evening, he said. After, they'd have some time to get to know each other better. Since they accepted the grim reality that he had only a few more months to live, she loved his idea and genuinely looked forward to finding out everything she could about this still mysterious man.

She had already decided she wasn't moving to Fort Myers permanently. John George might savor the sleepy small city with its winter snowbirds from across the continent. But it didn't have the action and vitality she loved in Atlanta, the business heart of America's Southeast. Headquarters would eventually move, but she saw no immediate reason to introduce the subject to either her father or the headquarters staff. She'd let a few months pass before making it a requirement for the small executive team to move north.

John George would gradually reduce his influence in the corporation as he transferred to the role of Chairman of the board in a non-executive capacity. She already knew she would treasure his guidance and advice for as long as he was around, but his weakening body and the ravages of cancer would probably limit such a relationship to only months. But that would give her enough time to prepare for the next stage.

Disposing of Multima Solutions was a good first move. They didn't need the volatility of the technology world sapping their focus. It might even be time to hive off Financial Services, she considered. James Fitzgerald reminded her in their first telephone conversation after the board of directors meeting that he was definitely retiring at the end of the next year.

He was even prepared to vacate the role earlier, he told Suzanne. She knew both he and his wife were desperate to reconstruct their lives since the tragic death of their only son. However, she had no concern at all about his dedication and knowledge. There was no one in the company – including John George – who knew more about the inner workings of Multima. She made a mental note to put together a plan to capture as much of that know-how from him as possible in the coming months.

Regardless of the details of their strategic direction, she had no doubt they would focus increasingly on growth in the supermarkets business. That was the area where the entire organization had its greatest expertise, and there was lots of space to expand. It was not unrealistic to dream of leading an organization that spanned the entire United States and Canada. In the years of her tenure at the helm of the corporation, there should be more than enough time to accomplish that.

John George had changed his mind about the disposition of his wealth in the past few days. But that was of surprisingly little concern to her. The block of preferred shares he had owned since the creation of the company would pass to Suzanne. However, he would donate the shares he converted from the numbered company related to her mother. Three charities, including the American Cancer Society, would benefit from his largesse. It made sense, and she would already be far wealthier than she ever dreamed with the promised inheritance. Where would she ever find the time to spend even a fraction of that amount, she wondered?

With a last sip of an excellent Pinot Noir, her thoughts darted back to John George and their coming weeks. It should be nice, she thought as the wine warmed her senses. Learning from him. Learning about him. And enjoying whatever time remained. They'd start with that break together at Christmas when they traveled to join Lana's family in El Salvador. She remembered the mischievous gleam in his eyes when he suggested they all go there together. Just what other fascinating surprises would she discover about this guy?

ACKNOWLEDGEMENTS

My novels are truly a collaborative effort. The process starts with an outstanding team of editors who provide input and suggestions. Their incisive feedback and comments are valued beyond words. Paula Hurwicz, Mariana Abeid-McDougall, Simon Ogden and Gabrielle Volke all helped me to polish the story with critical editing and proofreading that improved my work beyond measure. Any remaining shortcomings are entirely mine.

Next, I asked people whose expert opinions I trust to read early drafts and give me critical feedback on content and special industry knowledge. Cheryl Harrison, Heather and Dan Lightfoot, Cathy & Dalton McGugan, and Murray Pollard all read early versions. Their incisive feedback and comments were valued beyond words.

Tracy Kagan (our daughter), and Murray Pollard (a friend and former colleague) provided valuable insight about their personal experiences with breast cancer and inspired my goal to create more awareness about this insidious disease.

The team at Tellwell Talent performed admirably. Special thanks to Tara Price for her outstanding design work, Francesca Jackman for her extraordinary promotions expertise, and Jessica Palmer for seamlessly pulling it all together with unmatched professionalism and continuous good cheer!

As always, gratitude to my extended family and many friends around the globe for all providing a lifetime of support and encouragement. You're the ones who instilled my confidence that anything is possible with enough patience, determination, and perseverance.

I'm working on another new story. Please checkout and follow my Facebook page www.facebook.com/gary.d.mcgugan.books or visit my website www.garydmcguganbooks.com/ for more information.

Finally, it would be out of character for me not to 'ask for the order'. If you enjoyed *The Multima Scheme*, please help me achieve commercial success by telling your friends and writing reviews wherever you buy books.